'Roland Perry is a skilled storyteller with a great capacity for bringing the reader along with his book people and their exploits. His extensive knowledge of his subject manner is always evident as is his intellectual and emotional investment in the themes. His humour is also a constant . . . like real life, this fiction world is not all gloom and doom. *The Shaman* is a ripping suspense thriller.'

—Barbie Robinson, Living Arts Canberra

'Reviewing Roland Perry is a constant battle with superlatives . . . Among the strengths of his work lies the unbowing obedience to scholarship. His plots lead the reader from one valid point to the next . . . while *The Shaman* can be described as a thriller that has the complete recipe viz. murder, travel, a smidgen of sex, as well as plenty of intrigue.'

—Ian Lipke, Queensland Reviewers Collective

'Roland Perry is a prolific author who wanders over a vast spectrum of literature, fiction, non-fiction and documentary film writing, so when a book such as *The Shaman* is launched it titillates the curiosity to see where the storyline will travel. The book travels in every sense across the world, into the world of spiritual healing and expounds on cold-fusion technology, which harnesses atomic energy from water.'

—Ian Banks, Blue Wolf Review

'*The Shaman* is Roland Perry's latest novel about the personal and political repercussions when wealthy companies and self-interested states vie for control of the oil industry and the elusive key to controlling cold fusion.'

—Anna George, 3CR

'A gripping, thrilling read.'

—Sally-Anne Whitten, 2TM

Also by Roland Perry

Fiction
The Assassin on the Bangkok Express
The Honourable Assassin
The Shaman
Programme for a Puppet
Blood is a Stranger
Faces in the Rain

Non-fiction
Anzac Sniper
Céleste: Courtesan, Countess, Bestselling Author
The Queen, Her Lover and the Most Notorious Spy in History
Horrie the War Dog
Bill the Bastard
Red Lead: The Naval Cat with Nine Lives
The Fight for Australia (originally published as Pacific 360°)
The Changi Brownlow
The Australian Light Horse
Last of the Cold War Spies
The Fifth Man
Monash: The Outsider Who Won a War
Monash and Chauvel
The Programming of the President
The Exile: Wilfred Burchett, Reporter of Conflict
Mel Gibson, Actor, Director, Producer
Lethal Hero
Sailing to the Moon
Elections Sur Ordinateur
Tea and Scotch with Bradman
Bradman's Invincibles
Great Achievers and Characters in Australian Cricket
The Ashes
Miller's Luck: The Life and Loves of Keith Miller, Australia's Greatest All-Rounder
Bradman's Best
Bradman's Best Ashes Teams
Don Bradman (originally published as The Don)
Captain Australia: A History of the Celebrated Captains of Australian Test Cricket
Bold Warnie
Waugh's Way
Shane Warne, Master Spinner

Documentary films
The Programming of the President
The Raising of a Galleon's Ghost
Strike Swiftly
Ted Kennedy and the Pollsters
The Force

A VICTOR CAVALIER "ASSASSIN" THRILLER

THE SHAMAN

ROLAND PERRY

ROLAND PERRY PUBLISHING

Based on a true story.

First published in 2021 by Allen & Unwin
Second edition published in 2024 by Roland Perry Publishing

A catalogue record for this
book is available from the
National Library of Australia.

Roland Perry
Email: rolandjp2@gmail.com
Web: rolandperry.com.au

ISBN: 978-969-53-9256-0

To:

Al Haut and Malcolm Bendall,

the memory of Tim Fischer,

the memory of William Sam Conley

AL HAUT

Piscis Australis is a star constellation in the southern sky.

Al Haut, meaning 'the mouth of the great fish', is the brightest star in this constellation.

The ancient Greeks depicted Al Haut as swallowing the water (of all knowledge) poured by another star constellation, Aquarius, the water bearer.

One interpretation is that the Age of Aquarius, which began in 2018, will deliver comprehension of all things to the one known as Al Haut.

PART ONE

TASMANIAN DEVILS

1

THE INTERVENTION

Pon Cavalier drove the motorbike from a dirt track up to a main road. She stopped, looked left and right and then began the ride up a small gradient that would take her over the road. She didn't see the fast-moving motorbike coming from her left, which was obscured by an advertisement hoarding. They collided with a thud that sounded like a gunshot. Pon was thrown five metres in the air before landing against a fence. The middle-aged driver of the speeding bike was knocked out on impact.

The accident happened near the local Buddhist temple in the village of Wang Takhian, near Mae Sot on the Thai–Burma border. Six young, yellow-robed trainee monks, followed by as many dogs, rushed to the scene. The monks held up traffic. The speeding driver had head injuries. Pon was also out to it, with blood coming from her mouth and nose attracting two of the dogs, who sniffed around her head as fluid trickled to the road. A third dog, his back leg damaged from a previous accident, balanced and lifted his crippled limb to urinate on one of the bikes.

A chubby adult monk arrived, looked at Pon's eyes, put his ear to her chest, and ran fingers down her neck. He could hardly detect a pulse as police cars and ambulances arrived, sirens blaring.

'I think she's alive,' he said, 'but just.'

***

'I'm afraid, Mr Cavalier, your daughter has less than a fifty per cent chance of survival,' the Thai doctor in Mae Sot said over the phone, 'she is haemorrhaging from the head.'

Cavalier had gone to desperate lengths just six months earlier to save his 33-year-old daughter from a Mexican drug lord, who had captured and brutalised her for several years. Now she was in big trouble of   a different kind. In shock, Cavalier got on the phone at his Chiang Mai apartment and tried to book an immediate flight. There were none.

He decided to drive his Harley motorbike the six-hour trip south to Mae Sot. Just as he was throwing together a travelling bag, his phone rang. It was his good friend Tommy 'Wombat' Gregory in Australia.

'Have someone I'd like you to talk—'

'Not now, mate,' Cavalier said. 'Pon's been in a terrible crash. May not make it.' He told Wombat about the Mae Sot accident.

'You're on speaker,' Wombat said. 'There's someone here who thinks he can help. His name is Al Haut.'

Cavalier wanted to get off the phone.

'Not now, Wombat.'

'It's Al Haut,' a voice said. 'I'm a pastor. I'll pray into it.'

'What does that mean?' Cavalier asked impatiently.

'I'll pray for her.'

'Thank you.' Cavalier hung up.

He finished packing the bag and was just locking up the apartment when the phone rang again.

It was Al Haut.

'I've prayed into it,' he said. 'God is merciful.'

'What does that mean?'

'That's the message I received. Your daughter will be fine. The bleeding will stop. Her brain will be fine.'

Shaken, Cavalier asked,

'What about her body, her limbs?'

'There will be no damage. She'll be okay.'

'Thank you, Mr Haut,' a bewildered Cavalier said as he rushed to the condo's lift. The phone rang a third time. It was the Mae Sot doctor.

'Mr Cavalier? There has been a miracle! Your daughter has stopped haemorrhaging. We can't believe it. All her vital signs are good. She'll be in a coma for some time. That's the usual outcome after such an injury. But it is amazing!'

Cavalier was stunned. He thanked the doctor uncertainly and jumped on his Harley. He pushed the powerful machine harder than ever on the long drive. He easily outgunned the Thai 'cowboys' thrashing their motorbikes with threatening roars as they tried to overtake, even during a one-hour downpour that made the trip extremely dangerous.

Two hours into the trip, his former wife Pin called. Cavalier juggled the phone to answer it in the treacherous conditions. She was distressed, despite the doctor also informing her of her daughter's amazing recovery.

'What happens if she's paralysed, or has some severe limb damage?' Pin asked.

'She won't have any problems.'

'How do you know?'

Cavalier spoke of the strange call from Al Haut. Like most Thais, Pin was spiritual.

'Serena and I think you're right. Pon will be fine.'

Cavalier smiled. He had always disliked Pin's obsession with her scruffy, weird, lifelike doll. But this time, he would settle for the comfort Serena seemed to bring her.

'Tell me about this pastor,' she said.

'All I know is that he was with Wombat in Melbourne when he called me.'

'Must be some sort of faith healer.'

'I've no idea.'

'You know I lost my firstborn?'

'You told me very little. It was too painful to discuss.'

'I try to forget. She was the reason I married my first ex. Serena had a few complications at birth.'

'Serena?'

'Yes,' Pin said quietly. Cavalier didn't have to ask why her beloved doll had the same name as her lost child.

***

Cavalier sped the bike even through the tortuous mountain barrier that had to be negotiated after the city of Tak to reach the town of Mae Sot. He manoeuvred his way past trucks and other vehicles. Few drivers seemed to be paying respect to the woeful conditions that caused him to make sliding skids as he ducked in and out of the traffic.

He arrived at the town's main hospital at 1.30 a.m. and hurried through a maze of corridors reeking with antiseptic to a ward populated with road accident victims. Most of the patients were young; many had been in motor-bike crashes. It was the first day of the school holidays and teenagers had been celebrating, some with more gusto than they should have.

Pon was lying on her back, tubes attached to saline drips, her bed surrounded by relatives, including her grandmother, with whom she had been staying.

Cavalier kissed his daughter on the cheek. His eyes were moist, his emotions mixed. For a few moments he recalled seeing her for the first time in seven years in a terrible state on the Bangkok Express, where she had been drugged and beaten by her captor. Again, Cavalier was grateful that she was alive, but distressed to see her in this state. He had visited her at the Chiang Rai hospital where she had recovered slowly from a long ordeal. Pon had begged her parents to let her travel to Mae Sot to see her grandmother, whom she had not seen for so long. Pin had relented, much against Cavalier's wishes. Eager to resume a normal life, Pon had borrowed the bike which had led to the accident. Now she was motionless and helpless again. He squeezed her long-fingered hand. There was no response, just the steady beep of the machine monitoring her pulse.

Pin was there, fussing around her daughter, quizzing the doctor as if he were on her staff at her Chiang Rai hospital. They learnt that the driver of the other bike had recovered and was in another ward. He was expected to be released later that morning. Cavalier relieved the doctor from Pin's intense questioning by asking about the crash.

'Did the police do a blood test on the other rider?'

'You'd have to ask them about it. But from all accounts he was drunk.'

The doctor examined the vital signs monitor next to the bed.

'She was saved even though she was not wearing a helmet,' he said.

'You said her recovery was a miracle,' Cavalier prompted in Thai.

The doctor, a well-groomed, bespectacled man in his mid-forties, shook his head.

'I've seen a lot of inexplicable things in more than twenty years of medicine. This was mysterious.'

'The bleeding just stopped?'

'She was haemorrhaging from the mouth mainly, but also the nose and ears. It seemed like serious brain damage. Then it stopped. I am speaking about less than ten seconds. Never seen anything like that. Ever. It was as if . . .'

'What?'

'It was . . . I really don't know. It went against all my medical knowledge, and that of any other medico in this hospital, for that matter.'

'Had you given her any medication?'

'No. We were still assessing her when she recovered.'

'Could there still be brain damage?'

'She will be incoherent in speech, to start with, and may need therapy. But going on her current signs, I expect her to be back to normal in a few weeks.'

***

The doctor's analysis was accurate. Pon came out of a coma on day three. Her sentences were tangled yet she recovered well enough to be taken home five days after the accident. After ten days her speech and thoughts were coherent.

'Mummy,' Pon said from her bed early one morning, 'I saw Serena and grandpa.'

'What?' Pin said.

'What did you see, darling,' Cavalier asked, 'in your dreams, yes?'

'No, this was real,' Pon said, eyes wide. 'I was walking towards a house. Grandpa was at the big wooden doors to a beautiful home. So was Serena. They waved me away. They wouldn't let me come in.'

Pin and Cavalier glanced at each other.

'How old was Serena?' Pin asked, her voice shaky.

'She looked . . . I don't know; older than me. Mummy, she was really beautiful; long hair . . .'

Pin went white. She looked at her forearms where she felt a sensation.

'That's wonderful, darling,' Pin said, holding back tears. She left the room with Cavalier.

'Oh my God!' Pin said. 'She saw Serena! She would be mid-thirties, if she had lived.'

'And her grandpa; he died three years ago.'

***

Pin began asking questions about Al Haut again. Cavalier promised to find out more. The next day, they were surprised when Haut rang to find out how Pon was faring.

'I'm pleased that my radar is working,' Haut said. 'Not had a case like that for more than twenty years, during the Port Arthur massacre. I was the "go to" pastor.'

'Meaning?'

'I ministered to the dead in and outside the cafe where Martin Bryant murdered thirty-five people. One of the victims was in a coma for five days. The state governor wanted me to have a look at her. I sat with the woman in hospital for five hours. I persuaded her not to go to the light.'

'You mean, *die?*'

'She had terrible gunshot injuries. Her son had gone over. She wished to be with him. I talked her out of it.'

Cavalier was silent for a moment.

Haut added,

'I did that with your daughter. She was making her way to the spirits of relatives when I talked her back.'

Cavalier felt a chill up his spine. This was more or less the story Pon had told him about what had happened when she was in the coma. He didn't tell Haut of this, but asked further questions, learning that Haut was a Tasmanian geologist, and the leading pastor and director of a fundamentalist church with Pentecostal roots: Full Gospel Business Men's Fellowship International.

Wombat had told Cavalier that Al Haut had been anointed as a key spiritual adviser to the US president.

'Do you literally advise the American president?' he asked Haut now.

'I pray for him.

I'm a prophet of nature,' Haut said.

'Meaning?'

'I'm responsible for the planet's well-being.'

Cavalier didn't respond.

Haut added,

'I'm also a Shaman.'

'A Shaman deals with spirits, doesn't he?'

'Good and evil spirits, yes.'

***

Cavalier had scheduled a trip to Melbourne to discuss his work as a freelance correspondent in Southeast Asia with some newspaper and magazine editors. His payment for a recent project with CIA backing had made him more secure financially than ever before, yet he still wished to continue his journalism work. And, as usual, he wanted to be debriefed by Wombat, who had been recently appointed Head of Homeland Security in Australia, making him the nation's intelligence supremo.

Just before booking his flight, he received a call from Wombat.

'The Thais are beginning to introduce facial recognition at airports,' Wombat said, 'starting with an experiment in Bangkok.'

'So not wise to travel through there?'

'Not until we know that the DNA sleuth Topapan Makanathan has dropped the case of the Bangkok Express killing. If she began using the technology to compare passport photos from people on the train it could prove awkward. They could have two passport photos that may look remarkably like yours.'

'There is no reason to link me, is there?'

'No, but what if she snoops around your condo in Chiang Mai?'

Cavalier shrugged.

'I have Jacinta Cin Lai monitoring it.'

'I've got my Thai contacts on the job too. But remember, within a couple of years as soon as you pass through a major Thai passport control, they'll have your photo.'

'I'll use another way out of Thailand.'

'Which is?'

'There are border crossings into Burma where I can move undetected.'

2

WOMBAT ASSIGNMENT

'How's Pon going?' Wombat asked Cavalier as the two men strolled Melbourne's St Kilda beach. The sun was coming up on a warm late March day. Cargo ships could be seen on Port Phillip Bay's horizon, trailing into port. Two female joggers were chatting as they moved along the beach path. A sole bike rider paced along. A short, muscular man emerged from the water.

'Incredible. She's recovered. After what she went through for so long in captivity to that Mexican cartel, and now this accident, she has to take it easy, but she has shown no serious after effects. Pin is looking after her.'

'How's the relationship with your ex-wife? It's been, what, eight years since you split?'

'We rarely converse anymore,' Cavalier said with a rueful look. 'As you know, I'm being cautious about spending much time in Thailand, at least until I'm clear of the Bangkok Express episode.'

'You reconnected with her after Pon's accident, didn't you?'

'Pin was grateful that I saved Pon from the Mexicans, I'll admit. But she was suspicious when I avoided telling her how I managed to extricate Pon from the train.'

'Does she know?'

'She's very smart. She knows that my journalism work explains a certain amount of my travels but she's suspicious of my sudden absences. She's caught me cleaning my weapons in the past. That shook her. I lied, saying I sometimes went shooting abroad. Said I didn't wish to alarm her or the kids. She didn't buy it.'

'You never considered getting back with her?'

'No, Wombat, no. Why the interest in my long-ago marriage?'

'I may have an assignment for you in which it would be better if you had a partner, as a cover. But I'm not ready to discuss it just yet.'

Two more bike riders flashed by. Walkers, mainly pairs of women, were doing their morning constitutional. Melbourne was wide awake with the build-up of traffic on the nearby Beach Road. Helicopters roared overhead.

'Tell me about Al Haut.'

'You might recall him coming to national prominence a few years ago when he organised small Tasmanian tin miners to lobby against restrictive quotas, when they were being gobbled up big tin miners. MRT—Mineral Resources Tasmania—tried to shut him down, but the department's inspector examined Haut's tin products, including a pewter mug, and he then pulled out a craft licence. He had the right to make his own products, from digging it up to work on his kiln.'

'Crafty! In more ways than one.'

'He's the most brilliant character I've ever met.'

'How do you know him?'

'He was one of my best mates at school.

Was very much the nature boy as a kid. Says going into the forest alone teaches him more than any university. He prayed and fasted in the Tasmanian wilderness for forty days on end.'

'Forty days! That would lead to self-cannibalism. The body would turn on its own muscles for food, wouldn't it?'

Wombat patted his ample stomach.

'I don't want to find out,' he said. 'He's made some astounding claims about oil discoveries on Tasmania. Says he has found one of the world's biggest deposits, and has the evidence to prove it. Big Brother would like a report on him.'

'Why would the CIA be interested? Are they operating for the big oil groups?'

'The five sisters? No. Big Brother's activities are independent of the conglomerates. Not all are American owned. For instance, the biggest, Conquer, is based in Europe. It gobbles up leases anywhere it can like nobody's business. Big Brother works on tying up oil leases on the US's behalf, particularly for the navy, so it has permanent supply.'

'They want quick access?'

'Right. The Americans are looking at their main threat. They've identified it as China, both economically and militarily.'

'Okay. The Americans want access to oil in the Pacific.'

'Australia's as good a source as anywhere. Remember the Americans learnt about the geography of our sizeable island in World War II. They had one million personnel here, with bases everywhere. Even Albany in the south-west was a strategic base for subs.'

'They've always seen us as a floating aircraft carrier, now we may be an oil tanker as well.'

'They'll pay well for a report on Haut and his claims. So would ASIO.'

'Won't be necessary. I'll do a feature on him. I can do a separate report for you.'

'We can pay expenses for this assignment to see Haut.'

Cavalier shook his head.

'Suit yourself.' Wombat shrugged. He glanced at Cavalier. 'Make sure you take some hardware. Better go and see old Anthony Jones. He has a couple of items for you.'

'Oh, why?'

'Haut has plenty of enemies. Tasmania is like the Wild West. Corrupt politicians and bureaucrats, saboteurs, thieves and the odd killer. And that's only the nice ones.'

Cavalier smiled.

'I'll take the night ferry. Easier to hide a shooter in a car than a suitcase.'

'You're in for a real treat,' Wombat said with a mysterious grin.

'What do you mean?'

'Haut's unusual, to say the least. Highly spiritual, as you already realise. His church believes very much in literal Old Testament prophecy. We know Haut has done special study courses on it.'

'Anything else?'

'I'll let you find out for yourself. Just keep that very open mind open. I said he was "unusual". I could add "unique".'

'In what way?'

'I'll leave that to your inquisitive self. But I'm sure that you'll say you've never met anyone like him. One other thing about Haut. He's in a bit of bother at the moment. His business has struggled, mainly because corrupt politicians and mining bureaucrats have held him back. They are in the pocket of Conquer, who wish to crush him.'

'Not the best time to meet him?'

'Just be aware. He borrowed twenty-five million for his mining exploration, seismic surveys, drilling and so on. Crooks are wanting to take his leases.'

'Claim jumpers?'

'You'll see when you're down there. Anyway, he told me last night that the banks are asking for their twenty-five million. He said he was shitting himself over a meeting he has soon with his two main creditors.' Wombat chortled ruefully. 'He says he has been praying overtime for a solution.'

'What did his God say this time?'

'Tell jokes.'

'What?'

'God told him to tell jokes when he meets his bankers.'

They both laughed.

'I'm not kidding!' Wombat said. 'Haut has been gathering jokes in a booklet ever since.'

'Well at least it shows that his God or he, or both, have a sense of humour.'

'You are still the same old sceptical atheist you always were. Even after what happened with your daughter.'

'That shook my deep faith in atheism, as did a ghostly experience

I had in England in the 1970s.'

'Yeah, well,' Wombat said, 'atheism is fashionable.'

'I know you go to church every Sunday.'

'Not every Sunday.'

'You're not telling me you believe Haut? You think he has a chat with an unseen God? C'mon.'

'I didn't say he chats, as such. It's more about "communication".' He glanced at Cavalier. 'I can see you think he has a screw loose.'

'No. I'll make that call after I've chatted to him.'

'I've been a close mate of his ever since school days in Launceston and Hobart. But I've never understood him. Some of the things he says seem delusional.

'He was a brawler from an early age,' Wombat continued. 'Toughest kid right through until he left school at eighteen. He's womanised forever. Mind you, he loves the best lookers. He was captain of the rugby team and played all sports.'

'Then how did he slip into his religious ways?'

'He told me he'd had an epiphany; a real turning moment. He just happening to be flicking through a Gideons Bible, you know, the one that used to be in every hotel room. Al came across a passage that said—and I'm paraphrasing—that Jesus drifted up to heaven after being crucified to be at the right hand of God. That left the Holy Spirit hanging around on Earth.'

'Mate,' Cavalier said cynically, 'you should have been in the pulpit yourself, with that sort of ecclesiastical descriptive power!'

'Al collapsed one day after bashing his head accidentally. He woke up, to quote him, "filled with the Holy Spirit". After that he gave up the wine, ciggies and women.' Wombat laughed. 'The women bit didn't last long. But he tried.'

'So he joined a church?'

'Not exactly. We had a mate called Peter Mullens. He was a prophet in the Full Gospel Church.'

'The fundamentalists.'

'Yeah, well, you know how Tasmanians all know each other. This Mullens fella got to chatting about things and was dumbstruck by

Al's knowledge of the bible. In his moment of interaction with the Holy Spirit, Al was struck with . . .'

Wombat hesitated.

'An ugly stick?' Cavalier prompted. 'What?'

'It's hard to explain. But he collapsed for about five hours and claimed to know the bible inside out.'

'He speed-read it?'

'You'd better ask him.'

'When was this?'

'Let's see. We left school at the end of 1976. Al had his accident— the bash on the head—after we'd been surfing down at Bruny Island.' Wombat screwed up his face, squinted over his double lenses and added. 'Then he had his chat with Peter Mullens about Christmas time. Mullens was leaving the church or wanted recruits or something, and he asked Al to preach there. Al, imbued with the Holy Spirit, or whatever you want to call it, said he would have a crack every three weeks, which he did. But not in church. Al brought a hundred people home for a barbecue and did his sermons there.'

They paused and watched a group of people on the beach setting up to do yoga exercises.

'Just take Haut a gift when you meet,' Wombat said.

'What?'

'Tell him a couple of good jokes.'

3

DIVINE JOKER

Even if he had any funny stories up his sleeve, Cavalier would not have a chance to tell Haut. Haut was already meeting his bankers that morning in Melbourne's CBD.

Brown-haired Haut cut a business-like figure in a smart light-blue suit and dark blue tie when he arrived at the Stock Exchange on classy Collins Street, a mix of heritage-protected nineteenth-century buildings and modern skyscrapers that fought for domination of Melbourne's uncertain image.

Despite his natural smiling demeanour, Haut was nervous as he clutched his briefcase in one hand and a small notebook in another. He didn't even notice the four young women in the lift with him as he nudged the button for the tenth floor, keeping his eyes on the jokes in the book instead. The lift did not move. The girls chatted. Haut looked up.

'Morning,' he said to them, 'I've got to make a speech. Any of you have any good one-liners?'

The girls giggled and shook their heads. The lift door closed.

'C'mon,' he pleaded, 'you must have one!'

A chubby redhead with a cherubic face piped up,

'I've got one.'

The lift began to move.

'Okay. Let's have it!'

'What do you call a magic dog?'

'What?'

'A labracadabrador.'

Haut pulled a face and scribbled.

The girls were in a paroxysm of laugher as they bundled out of the lift at the fourth floor.

Haut scribbled this new joke in his book and alighted at the tenth floor. He was confronted by a phalanx of security guards, all ex-SAS and armed with sub-machine guns. Haut was frisked and his briefcase was checked. He was asked for ID and then ushered into a huge room. There were twenty more security guards, fifty suited people from fourteen banks and about a hundred customers who owed, or who were owed money.

There was one large, wide bench, which was four tables jammed together and covered by a green carpet-like fabric. Sitting on the 'Billion Dollar' table was more money than Haut had ever seen— a billion dollars in notes and a further two hundred and fifty million in bonds. The notes were stacked in lots of five million in one hundred dollar bills. There was a freshly minted look and smell about the cash. The Great War General John Monash's powerful military head on the one hundred dollar note had never had such prominent exposure. Haut, with his outstanding twenty-five million, was small fry in comparison to some of the big players of Australian finance and business who had been summoned to account, or to collect. By the close of business at 3 p.m. all transactions had to be made and debts settled.

There was electricity in the air. The bankers, some in suits, some with jackets off and sleeves rolled up, were ready for the grand game of settlement. There was no pirate glint in the eye though. These were the controllers with their ever-developing and greater Ponzi schemes to suck more money from everywhere and everyone.

In this speed money game, rather like speed dating, every debtor had to face his bankers. Haut shook hands with the chairman from the Bank Presse Internationale and the deputy chair from Continental East. Bank Presse's Sinclair Adams was forty-five, tall, definitely a former private school boy in his born-to-rule manner and clipped speech. He was leaning across the table looking over papers that instructed him how much he had to collect from whom, and the amount he had to give away and to whom. The deputy chair from Con East—auburn-haired Harriett Cullum—was in her mid-thirties and a recent recruit from the Royal Bank of Canada.

The doors were bolted shut with security men parked at each exit, arms crossed and a shoot-to-kill demeanour for anyone who might even wish to go outside for a pee, or even a biscuit. With so much cash on display, there was always the possibility that some foolhardy armed criminal gang might try for the biggest bank heist in history.

No one could leave until all transactions were completed or the final bell was sounded. Once the deal was done on that day, it was over. No correspondence would be entered into.

Haut had six dollars to his name, in his jacket pocket and not in his account. He didn't even know how he was going to reach Melbourne airport for the humiliating flight back to his Hobart home. Ms Cullum ('Please, call me Harry') seemed sweet, or so Haut thought, in a sea of suited male sharks.

Haut's first job was to sign about four hundred pages of documents on behalf of the fourteen companies he represented in his mining operations. He was nervous, but pretended he was cool and unperturbed as he sat down with Sinclair and Cullum; Haut in the middle, at a table close to the Monash pile. He felt many pairs of eyes on him, even Monash's, as he began signing pages.

He paused, looked up and said: 'Got a joke for you. What do you call a pony with a cough?' The on-lookers faces were blank. Haut added: 'a little horse.'

This elicited a few smirks from on-looking bankers and lawyers. They all relaxed. This bloke from Tasmania was either a bit thick or remarkably calm, they thought, considering his financial plight.

Eighty minutes on and Haut was yet to complete the documentation for his companies. Some of the on-lookers lost interest and began talking among themselves or moved off to scrutinise other settlements. Haut had still not signed over a commitment to pay back the twenty-five million dollars he owed.

Lanky Sinclair Adams looked over half-moon glasses as Haut explained how he had been caught in a mining industry downturn. He told how he had been 'claim-jumped'. Adams' eyebrows shot up, as if he were a little sympathetic. Otherwise, he was silent. Then he began to interject impatiently and wanted Haut to commit to pay up, with any asset he had, from any money he had in the bank, or even his car. When Callum was distracted, Haut said:

'Looking around at the dough and people here, I can't help thinking about the line: "To see what God thinks of money, just look at the people he gave it to."'

Adams winced a smile. He either didn't understand or like the remark. Haut tried again.

'I saw a sign on the way into the city which said "Watch for children". I thought that was a fair trade.'

Adams frowned and then smiled as if awoken from a stupor.

'I like it,' he said, animated. 'I'm thinking about re-marrying my ex-wife, but I'm pretty sure she'll figure out I'm just after her for the money!'

Haut chortled as Adams slapped his knees at his own marginally funny line.

'My psychiatrist told me I was crazy,' Haut grinned, 'but I said I wanted a second opinion. He replied, "Okay, you're ugly too."'

Adams laughed hard and went red. He grabbed a sheet of paper and began scribbling down the joke.

After twenty minutes of funny and counter funny, Adams was distracted by another banker. Haut referred to his little book of jokes and then turned to Cullum.

'Didn't know this settlement business could be so much fun,' he said.

Perplexed, she began to discuss his plight.

'Now, Al –' she said.

'Yes, Harry. You know I'm just wild about Harry. But at this point I don't think Harry is wild about me!'

Cullum laughed.

'So nice to hear someone not spout that song's line the right way,' she said smiling and revealing very white teeth that were too big even for her exceptionally large mouth. 'I hate clichés!'

'So do I,' Haut said.

'I always say "I plan to live forever." When people look sceptical, I add: "The plan has worked so far."'

Cullum laughed.

She was then tapped on the shoulder and soon engrossed in a conversation. There was now a frenzy of activity as the deadline approached. Big bundles of notes and bonds were being raked across the table as settlements were made before the deadline. The two bankers, who had both been distracted by bigger deals being done around them, looked at each other a half-hour later as a gong sounded.

It was close of play. Haut's ordeal was over.

Neither of the banks' representatives had sealed anything with him. As he left the building and was given a lift to the airport by one of the bankers who had not dealt with him, it dawned on him: *I will not have to find the 25 million dollars I owe the two banks.*

At the airport, he bumped into Adams and Cullum at a bar, waiting for a plane to Sydney. Adams looked alternatively angry and aggrieved. Cullum seemed nervous. They had both assumed that the other had settled the deal over the money Haut owed.

'You got out of there scot-free,' Adams snarled, and then added a guttural, 'Fuck!'

'I didn't know what was happening,' Haut said, opening his hands.

'Well, we have your property,' Adams said.

'Good for you. It's rented.'

Adams was furious.

'Well, Harriett has your mining assets,' he sneered, 'so fuck you!'

Cullum reached for a napkin and took out a pen.

'Bulldozers and drill rigs aren't much good to us,' she said with a shrug. 'We'd have a hassle selling such items. Been there done that.' Cullum turned to Haut. 'Have you got a dollar on you?'

'I have six,' Haut said.

'A dollar will do.'

Haut fished it out of his pocket and put it on the bar.

Cullum wrote on the napkin:

'I hereby accept, on the behalf of Con East, one dollar, paid in full, for all the mining and business equipment assets of one Al Haut and all his company operations.'

She signed it and handed it to Haut. He signed and dated it. Adams stood, grabbed his briefcase and stormed off. Cullum, all toothy grin, shook hands with Haut, who laughed and laughed, as much from relief as anything else.

Later, when on the plane to Hobart, he thanked his God for the advice and intervention.

4

KEEPING UP WITH THE JONES

The next morning Cavalier drove to the Melbourne suburb of Murrumbeena and entered a car mechanic's garage, thick with the smell of fuel and patrolled by twenty grease monkeys. He walked to the back, past cars on hoists, and pressed an intercom button. It was answered by Tony Jones, a corpulent man of seventy, his shirt half out of his trousers, and a cigarette behind an ear.

'Victor!' he said, shaking hands, 'so good to see you. I hear your escapade on the Bangkok Express was a success!'

'I'm still here.' Cavalier grinned as he opened his arms.

That elicited a belly laugh from Jones.

'Are you back in Melbourne for good?'

'I was in Chiang Mai for a while but was advised to take a break until the heat went out of certain investigations. What happened to your grandson, Anthony?'

'He's on leave. I fill in for him.'

'Wombat has some presents for me?' Cavalier asked.

'Yes, indeed.' He showed Cavalier to a desk with two small boxes and a manila envelope.

Christmas is early this year,' Jones said with another guffaw. 'It's a long way from the first equipment I gave you.'

'It was a brick-like analogue phone. Dumped it after a month.'

'Yes, but it was long before anyone else had one!'

Cavalier opened the first box. He unwrapped a new phone device.

'It's about a year ahead of the market and has too many apps to bother you with here. Its name says it all: "Genius 1".'

Cavalier skimmed through a small instruction manual and raised an eyebrow, registering he was impressed.

'I like playing Santa Claus!' Jones said with a laugh and then a prolonged cough. 'Now the other present is from Wombat.'

Cavalier opened the second box and removed a handgun.

'It's a Glock 19 Plus,' Jones said with reverence. 'I recall you have used a Glock from time to time. This one is undetectable, even with an airport scanner. It has a polymer frame as usual but includes an additive that avoids scanner detection.'

Cavalier juggled the gun.

'Lightest gun I've ever touched; useful for concealment,' he noted. 'Smaller too.'

'Exactly. You can draw it from a holster anywhere on your body.'

'Pity I can't practise with it here.'

'But you can. My offices are a padded cell. That makes everyone happy.' Jones bustled to the back of his workshop, pushed open a wide door and slid a mobile bullseye target in view. 'There are twenty bullets in the box.'

Cavalier loaded the weapon. He took up a crouched position and fired twice. The two men examined the shots. He was off centre with both.

'Not right on target,' Cavalier mumbled. 'Have you a screwdriver?'

Jones found one. Cavalier made a slight adjustment. He fired at the target again.

'Dead centre!' Jones observed in admiration. 'Still the best in the business.'

'Not drinking as much,' Cavalier said.

'Pity. I was going to open some Champagne.'

'I said "as much".'

Jones laughed and took a bottle from a fridge and poured them both a glass.

'Congratulations, Doctor Edwin Harris,' he said.

'What?'

'Wombat insisted I prepare you a new identity and passport. He sent me photographs. You're an English doctor. There are CV notes on your life so far, where you lived and graduated, until age fifty-eight.'

'Did he say why I needed a new passport?'

'I think he wants you on an assignment.'

'He mentioned something but without any details.'

'You're a doctor of Art and Literature from Cardiff University.'

'A lifelong ambition.'

'How's your comprehension of my home state, Van Diemen's Land? Have you been there?'

'I confess, I haven't.'

'Shame on you. Do you know anything about it?'

'Just that it's home to David Boon and Ricky Ponting.'

'Trust you to name bloody Test cricketers!'

'Okay. Max Walker, too. He was a Test cricketer and played football for my team, Melbourne. And Nick Riewoldt for St Kilda.'

'Anyone else?'

'Errol Flynn and Simon Baker.'

'Oh, yeah. Every male thinks of Errol!'

'A lot of females too, by all accounts.'

'Errol died sixty years ago. The state's had a few more prominent people since then. Anyone else?'

'Truganini.'

'The last Tasmanian Aboriginal person. She died in 1876. Very good.'

'*One* of the last.'

'True. Al Haut agrees with that. He says there are around fifteen thousand with at least claims to being Indigenous. His paternal grandmother was an Aboriginal woman. Tommy Gregory knew her when he was a kid. He reckons it's true.'

'That might explain Haut's spirituality; his claims to being a Shaman.'

'Maybe.'

'You haven't mentioned the two-headed monsters.'

'A rumour started by Tasmanians to keep tourists away.'

5

THE ISOLATED PROPHET

Cavalier took the overnight *Abel Tasman* ferry from Melbourne to Launceston in Tasmania's north, and drove his 2005 model Mercedes Sports Coupe west to the Alberton alluvial gold-mining area, near Mount Victoria. Using his phone tracker, he made a few wrong turns as darkness fell until he picked up the landmarks and signs to Al Haut's lease area. It was near midnight when he drove along a rough track, stopping at a water tank as directed. He alighted from the vehicle, its headlights on high beam. They picked up a tent about forty metres away.

He had walked a few paces when a bullet pinged into a tree. Cavalier fell flat, crawled back to his car, switched off the lights and fumbled in a pack for his handgun. He eased out of the vehicle again. Another shot was fired and whistled over his head.

'Hey!' Cavalier cried.

'Who goes there?'

'Cavalier!'

'Put those lights back on and walk straight along the beam.'

'Why?'

'Out here you can never be too careful.''Okay.'

'Chuck any weapon you have out in front of you.'

Cavalier did as directed.

'Are you alone?'

'Yes.'

Haut bustled forward, high-powered rifle over his shoulder. He bent down and picked up Cavalier's handgun, then strode forward and shook hands with him. Haut's face was expressive. The first impression for his visitor was of a jut-jawed tough bushman of average height. His forearms were big, like an axe-man's. Haut wore a bush hat, loose pullover, short pants to the knees, thick wool socks and boots. Minutes later, they were sipping beers from cans inside the tent, lights out. Haut lit a small fire and warmed his hands. Cavalier scrutinised his host. The visage was of regular features, with no distinguishing marks. His forehead was high, the fair hair unkempt. Cavalier could see evidence of Haut's Tasmanian Indigenous background.

Cavalier noticed Haut was staring into his eyes.

'Anything the matter?' Cavalier asked.

'No, all good,' Haut said, his face relaxing. 'You have eye movement.'

Haut held up two fingers and made an oscillating movement.

'Please explain?' Cavalier said.

'Those without the movement have dead souls,' Haut replied. 'It can mean they could be evil, Nephilim even. My radar works better without too much light. We need the warmth though. It falls below zero out here at night.'

'Radar?'

'My brain has five frontal lobe orbits. It's very sensitive. I sense things coming too close that may be a threat.'

Haut handed Cavalier the Glock.

'Why do you use one of those?'

'It's reliable.'

'For what?' Cavalier paused and smiled before he said, 'Shooting is a hobby. I had a Glock for practice in Thailand years ago. This is a new one. Wombat thought it might come in handy.'

Haut nodded, as if there might be kinship already between them.

'Was a hobby for me too,' he said. 'Now it's a matter of self-preservation.'

'Wombat told me. May I ask about the process behind your prayer? Is it some sort of mental telepathy you have with those on the brink of death?'

Haut shrugged.

'It's to do with God. I pray; he responds.'

'How?'

'The response fills my mind. It's sometimes from a flash of light.'

'You told me "God is merciful" when you intervened with Pon . . .'

'That was easy to grasp. It meant your daughter would be spared. Sometimes when I pray very hard, the answer can be more complicated. I have to write things down.'

'It doesn't stay in your mind?'

'The answers are not from my mind. I must record them.'

Cavalier took notes.

'Wombat and I thought it would be good if I wrote a report about you and your oil discoveries.'

'Can you read an assay report?'

'I had a stint as a financial reporter when I first began in journalism. But that was long ago.'

'I can bring you up to speed,' Haut said, bustling to a backpack and pulling out a folder. 'Have a look at this. This is a summary of our assay results for our oil drilling on all our wells on North Bruny Island in Variety Bay. The full report is locked in my Hobart office.'

Haut went through the superficial report, explaining much of it as Cavalier probed and used a tape recorder for the discussion. After an hour, Cavalier was impressed.'It seems you do have a mighty find there,' he said. 'I'd like to run it by a couple of experts.'

'There's a huge load under the island running into Bass Strait. I've had the biggest gush ever seen in these parts. Had to do a lot of work to seal the well.'

'How big is "big"?'

'Bigger than anything in the Persian Gulf.'

6

BIG MAC

An eighty-five kilogram bull-mastiff wandered into the tent, looking somewhat sheepish.

'Mac! Where have you been?' Haut asked. The dog stepped forward in supplication and licked his master, who stood to greet him. Mac got up on his hind legs and rested his paws on Haut's shoulders. Then he noticed Cavalier, and seemed uncertain about the stranger. Haut stood between Cavalier and the dog.

'Mac, this is Victor, he's a friend, right? Got that?'

'That head is as big as a lion's!' Cavalier marvelled.

The dog glanced at Cavalier, still unsure. He gave a slight growl. Cavalier stood and reached out the back of his hand. Mac sniffed it, glanced up with a begrudging look and wandered outside the tent again.

'He goes on my reaction,' Haut said. 'We've had so many issues with people trying to do damage to me and my equipment, Mac's always at the ready. He has a real instinct for those who would do me harm.'

Haut went to a portable fridge, pulled out two more cans of beer and handed one to Cavalier.'You out here alone, apart from Mac?'

'Once or twice a week. I have six men working for me. They have tonight off.'

'Why all the opposition to your discoveries?'

'Huh! Where do I start?'

'Wombat tells me you've had trouble with the state's mines department, MRT.'

'And the rest! I've got leases they want. Try the European Conquer Group, for starters. They don't want my wells drilled. They will wait and try to take up the leases themselves. In the meantime, they'll bribe anyone to kill my company's operations. Conquer has tens of billions to play with.'

'I know a little about them. I read Anthony Sampson's book *The Seven Sisters*.'

'There are five big conglomerates now. You've haven't worked for any of them, I hope?'

Cavalier shook his head. Haut stared for a moment. Cavalier returned the look without giving anything away. He guessed that Wombat may have hinted to Haut about Cavalier's second, secret profession. Mac lumbered back into the tent and lay at Haut's feet.

'Conquer would do anything to get those leases,' Haut said, fondling Mac's ears. 'They stole my assay reports. They know I'm sitting on the world's biggest find. It would lift their reserves worldwide by maybe twenty-five per cent. They've already bribed officials here to destroy my report.'

Cavalier glanced at his tape recorder.

'You can publish all that,' Haut said.

'It's a big story but no paper would risk a law suit.'

'Have a look at Conquer's record. Nothing stands between them and the sniff of a big oil find.'

'Still can't make unsubstantiated claims about your situation.'

'It's substantiated. Earlier this year

I was chatting with a guy called Gene McDoe. He agreed with my findings.'

'The significance?'

'He worked for MRT. He admitted he had seen my submitted reports but they'd been substituted with other reports. My core sample has been stolen.'

'Who stole it?'

'People in Conquer's pocket at MRT. You should look into that.'

'I'll do the appropriate research. But first, can we look at how you started in the mining business?'

They were interrupted when Mac sat up, growled and pushed his way out of the tent. Haut grabbed his rifle. Cavalier followed him. The dog went a few paces into the bush, growled again, lifted his leg on a tree and led the way back into the tent.

'He can pick things up a kilometre away,' Haut said, patting the dog and giving him a biscuit. 'Must check his reaction out though. He's a cool character.' Haut chortled in a halting way and added: 'Saved my life a few times. Once I was out working on the drill when a bloke came up behind me with a big knife. Mac came from nowhere and put his big jaws around the bloke's forearm. The man dropped the weapon and ran off before I could reach my rifle.' Haut grinned and scratched behind the dog's ears. 'He'd be easy to identify. He'll have deep teeth-mark scars for life.'

'He wanted to kill you?'

'Well, he wasn't going to use the knife to butter the bread!' Haut said, laughing.

'Have there been other attempts?'

Haut rolled his eyes back as if to say 'plenty.' He seemed unprepared to give further instances. Cavalier prompted him.

'I'll tell you one more, but I don't want you to publish it, okay?'

'Whatever you say.'

Haut paused for a moment, then said,

'I was tying things onto the back of my ute at one of the mines.' He stood to demonstrate how he was standing. 'I slipped, like this, and lowered my head. Just as I did, a bullet whizzed into my hat, splitting it in two. Had I not ducked at that moment, I would have been murdered.'

Cavalier was scribbling notes. He checked his tape. He wanted to ask 'what happened next?' but he waited.

The memory gave Haut a few seconds of emotional reflection.

'Various acts of God,' he said, dropping his voice.

'What?'

'There have been innumerable times when "coincidences" have occurred, sometimes in saving my life. Except they are not coincidences. They are acts of God.'

'Tell me about this one.'

'At that moment, an old mate, Sid Clarke, arrived in his car up on a rise at the road. He was walking, with his rifle over his forearm, always ready to shoot snakes, our Sid. Anyway, he spotted the would-be killer taking aim at me and firing. Sid wasn't the type to yell or ask questions. He just took aim at the bloke and fired. I saw Sid hurry into the bush. A few moments later, he sauntered out of the scrub and came over to me. I had grabbed my rifle. Sid told me not to worry about anything. He said: "Take your ute and piss off for an hour." Sid was an old bushie and well-respected. He had a no-nonsense reputation. At age sixteen he had knocked out Jack Dempsey, the world champion boxer, in a bout in Queensland. It happened a few seconds into the first round. Sid was still hard as nails later in life. He had a gnarled face, but was a kind old bugger.' Haut paused again, and seemed to be hiding his emotion and affection for a man who had saved his life. 'That day, he was just coming to see if I was okay. That was Sid. Good bloke. Passed on now.'

'What happened to the body of the attacker?'

'I never asked. Didn't want to know. Old Sid wasn't going to tell me. We just had a few beers that night.'

'But someone would find the body, wouldn't they?'

'Sid would have looked after that.'

Cavalier waited again.

'I'll give you an educated guess,' Haut said. 'There's a tailings dam nearby. He probably put the body in it. You know what's in a tailings dam?'

'Waste, chemicals, acids . . .'

Haut nodded.

'If he put it there, everything, including bones, would have been consumed long ago.'

'Nice story,' Cavalier said, 'pity I can't use it.'

7

THE VISION

Cavalier asked questions of Haut for another two hours, beginning with the much talked about, and often ridiculed, 'vision from God' that he had as a teenager.

'Can you tell me about the original vision? How old were you and where did it happen?'

'It was at a secluded beach at Variety Bay, Bruny Island,' Haut said. 'I was nineteen years old and surfing.'

'In 1977.'

'Yes.'

'Bruny Island? That's where Truganini lived, isn't it?'

'Her people were my people—the Nuenonne clan—on the Island. The traditional name was Lunawanna Alonnah, before the land was misappropriated by early Australian settlers.'

'So you were surfing there . . .' Cavalier prompted.

'It's the most beautiful country on God's Earth. You've still got teeming fauna—mutton birds migrate from Siberia every year and nest in the craggy rock outcrops. Penguins migrate from Antarctica. The sea is full of life: abalone, oysters, flounder, crayfish. You name it. It was easy to live off the land. Inland, the Nuenonne people used controlled burning to create a big area of grassland to support a strong wallaby population.' Cavalier was patient. Haut was passionate about the area and his people.

'Where were you when you had the vision?' he asked.

'I was wandering inland a short distance, at about fifty metres above sea level, when I saw one of my people placing a flintstone in a hole he had dug. I stood and watched him bury the stone. He knew I was there.'

'About how old was he?'

'About forty. It was five hundred years ago.'

Cavalier checked his tape and scribbled notes on a pad, as if there was nothing out of the ordinary about this revelation; just something very interesting.

'Wombat told me about you seeing things without a time dimension . . .' he prompted.

Haut nodded. 'The Nuenonne man came from an earlier era. He was a forefather of mine. A king.'

'Wombat told me you have Tasmanian Indigenous blood.'

'I am in the direct bloodline of this man. I have the same genetic make-up. I am King of Tasmania, in effect.'

Cavalier was well-practised at interviewing. He didn't react, or even blink at this utterance, having been forewarned by Wombat.

'Weren't the local Aboriginal people wiped out by settlers?' Cavalier asked.

'Some were. But the big genocide was by mainland Aboriginal people before that.'

Cavalier made a note to check this.

'The significance of this . . .' Haut began.

'Encounter?'

'You could call it that. He had buried the flintstone where the major oil deposit would be found. You see, we are talking about a singularity point.'

'What's that?'

'It is where there is no time, as such. It is "still".' He paused.

'Everything happens in the same moment. It is where God is.'

'I'd like to explore that with you later,' Cavalier said concealing any bafflement or disbelief. 'You started drilling at this point where the stone was?'

'Not immediately. I wanted to learn as much as I could about geology.'

'An epiphany?'

Haut nodded.

'I enrolled at Tasmania University, learnt all I needed to know about the subject in theory. My real comprehension came from being on drilling sites. I was very hands-on. Dr Harold Burnside, my lecturer, gave up his teaching job to work with me.'

'He accepted your vision?'

'No,' Haut said and after a spluttering laugh, added, 'Harold thinks it is irrelevant. But he does agree with the practical, the real: my analysis on huge oil discoveries on Tasmania.'

'You began mining?'

'In 1981. I was twenty-three. I worked for BHP Minerals as Head of Field Operations,' Haut said. 'We discovered oil and gas at Styx River Bridge. A road was cut but, for reasons unknown to me, BHP was deterred from further exploration.'

'So you began your own operation?'

'In 1984, I applied for a fifty-square kilometre oil and gas licence on Bruny Island. But guess what? MRT said they, quote, "would not give me a licence for exploration of something that wasn't there"!'

'Very Orwellian speak. After all, it was 1984.'

'Yeah, right. The next year I went over the heads of MRT and approached the Minister for Mines, Ray Groom.'

'Ray Groom? He captained the Melbourne Football Club.'

'He was Tasmanian Premier too. I sat in his office every day for three months...'

'Hope they had good back copies of *Women's Weekly*!'

'I had a few books to get through, and a bible.'

'How did Groom react?'

'He said "Gidday, Al" every day to me when he came in and when he left. One day he called me in and granted me the licence.'

'I'm not surprised. Groom was schooled under the disciplined but brilliant regime of Norm Smith, one of Aussie Rules' greatest coaches. He would admire your determination.'

'I borrowed from a bank to do the first onshore seismic survey at Bruny Island and offshore at Stormy Bay.'

They broke off while Haut made a fresh brew of coffee. Cavalier took the time to scribble down his thoughts.

> Haut speaks in the same pulse about the 'real' as he does the spiritual. To him the latter is the norm. I, a mere heathen, can't grasp his breath-taking commentary and certitude about his almost symbiotic connection to his God. I must explore the ecclesiastical route further . . .

'I told you before that I have an unusual brain,' Haut remarked handing him another coffee. 'Most brains have three orbits. Mine has five. Very different structure. That's why I have trouble keeping on one track in a discussion like this. You see things in a linear way.' Haut waved his arms in different directions. 'I contend with five different dimensions. When I look at topography for instance, I see all around, under and over it.'

Cavalier thought of challenging him on this claim but remembered Wombat's advice to keep an open mind.

'I think I read that Leonardo di Vinci and Pythagoras had something similar.'

'It's late,' Haut said. 'I have to give my orbits a rest after this grilling!' He handed Cavalier a sleeping bag. 'You'd better stay the night. It's three hours' drive to the nearest hotel. We can continue this in the morning.'

'Right,' Cavalier said. 'I have limited orbits. Just need my beauty sleep.'

8

THE SCARE

Their sleep was interrupted by the zip of a bullet piercing the tent fabric. Mac was about to dash outside but Haut restrained him, then doused the small fire. He scrambled for a coffin-like box and pulled out a Bentley pump-action rifle. He handed it to Cavalier and signalled for him to get down. A second bullet whistled through the tent. Mac struggled to leave. Haut held him.

'We can move out the back,' Haut said. A car engine revved and they could see a four-wheel-drive vehicle skidding into a tyre-screeching turn. Haut let Mac go and he bounded after the car.

A shot was fired at the dog.

Haut called Mac and the dog trotted back to them, wagging his tail, his back bristling.

'I'd better give chase,' Haut said, moving out of the tent. He ran to his ute. Cavalier followed. Mac jumped in the rear.

'What was that about?' Cavalier asked as he slid into the front passenger seat.

'Bastards! They've smashed vehicles and loaders, destroyed shafts. That's the first time they've pumped bullets into my tent!'

Haut flicked through gears until he reached top speed. His lights were on high beam and they flickered over the escaping vehicle. Another shot came from it, but it was well away from the pursuing ute.

The speed of the chase on the bumpy track meant it would be difficult to hit a target.

Haut's knowledge of the winding road meant he was gaining ground. He fumbled in a glove box and put a black hood in Cavalier's lap.

'Better put it on. They know who I am. They don't know you.'

Cavalier placed the hood on. They were now just fifty metres short of the vehicle.

'What do you want to do with them?' Cavalier asked.

'Scare the shit out of them.'

'How?'

'Threaten them with Mac. First we gotta bail up the bastards.'

They gained another ten metres.

'You left- or right-handed?'

'Both.'

'Good. Could you put a bullet into a back tyre? My rifle's loaded.'

Cavalier reached across to the rifle lying next to Mac. He barked his approval. Cavalier lowered the left-hand front passenger window.

'Put a bullet in the left rear tyre, if you can.'

Haut's vehicle was thirty metres away when Cavalier fired.

'Did you hit it?'

Cavalier said nothing. The vehicle careered on another fifty metres, listed to the left and ran off the road. It hit a tree and came to an abrupt halt. Haut pulled up behind and Mac jumped out. Haut restrained him as two men struggled to extricate themselves from the vehicle. They both groaned. One held his head; the other his shoulder. Their rifles were in the vehicle. Mac growled. Haut pretended to have trouble restraining him by the collar.

The men were both in their early twenties.

'You tried to kill me,' Haut said. 'You could have hit this bloke or my dog . . .' His words were menacing yet controlled. Both men spluttered denials. 'Who sent you?'

They looked at each other. Mac bared his teeth. Haut now had real trouble holding him.

'What do you think I should do?' Haut asked Cavalier, turning and winking at him.

'I wouldn't let the dog loose,' Cavalier said, shaking his head. 'He'd rip their throats out.'

'He would!'

'Shit!' the taller one of the two said. 'No, Reverend Haut! Please! We only meant to scare you!'

'I repeat,' Haut said, 'who sent you?'

'Fuckin' tell him!' the other young man, short and stout, said, his voice trembling as he stared at Mac. The dog's bull-neck strained against Haut's grip.

'We . . . it was . . .'

'C'mon,' Haut said. 'You're bleeding from the elbow. You know what that means to an outback dog. He smells it. He wants to have meat! That's you.'

'It was Neil Farquar.'

'Ah! It had to be!' Haut said, dragging Mac back to the ute and ordering him onto the tray, where he was held by a chain attached to his collar.

'What were you asked to do?'

'Fire into your tent. High, Reverend Haut, high,' the taller one said.

'Let me look at your injuries,' Haut said, moving close to the taller man.

He bent down, showing his scalp.

'Bit of glass from the windscreen. Just splinters,' Haut said after a cursory examination. He looked at the other man. 'Flex your arm.' Haut held the arm and manipulated it.

'Christ!' the man yelped.

'Not broken,' Haut, 'and don't take the Lord's name in vain.'

'Sorry, Reverend Haut.'

Haut and Cavalier examined the front of the Toyota. The bumper bar was dented and the engine hood damaged. The engine was intact.

'Change the tyre and see if you can drive it,' Haut ordered the men.

Haut and Cavalier watched as the taller man took five minutes to change the tyre. Mac filled the silence with the occasional growl and bark of frustration. Haut took the men's rifles, wandered off the road to a ravine about twenty metres away, and hurled them into it.

Cavalier examined the spent tyre. The bullet hole was low and to the left.

'Good shot,' Haut said, running his fingers over the hole, 'or a fluke? It meant a slow drift off the road.'

Cavalier did not reply.

'Wombat did say you were the best shot ever.'

Cavalier smiled. Haut turned to the two young miscreants.

'Drive to the nearest hospital,' he said, 'and get yourselves fixed up. If you come out this way again, you might not be so fortunate.' He moved up close to the taller man, bent down and scooped up some earth in his hand. 'The earth is soft here.' He stared at both men in turn. 'Very easy to bury a man. Understand?'

Both men nodded.

'Now make yourselves scarce.'

The men scrambled for the vehicle, much to Mac's fierce protest. After a nervous minute of attempting to start the car, they left in a hurry.

Cavalier removed his hood.

'Will they be back?' he asked.

'Nar, not them. Farquar and his thugs will choose men next time, not boys.'

'Farquar?'

'Yeah, Neil Farquar. He runs a security firm. That's where his killers come from. He's Estonian but has been in Tasmania for decades.'

They began the drive, slower this time, to the gold-mine site.

'Farquar wants me out of the way. He once worked for MRT and is one of Conquer's stooges in Tasmania, doing their bidding. I had him organise protection for me until I realised who his real masters were. This effort to scare me is proof he's back again.'

Haut swerved the car and jammed on the brakes. Mac barked. Haut took his rifle, alighted from the ute and pumped bullets into a two-metre long reptile.

'Black snake,' he said as he jumped back into the car. 'Deadliest of all. Never miss a chance to kill one.'

'Many out here?'

'Some. But don't worry. You won't see another while you're here.'

***

Next morning, Cavalier was outside the tent and lathered up for a shave with a safety razor. He used a small mirror hanging from a tree. He looked around to see Haut emerging from the tent.

'Uh-huh,' he heard Haut say in a hoarse whisper, 'don't move a muscle, I mean not even in your face.'

Haut crept up behind him with his rifle. He fired three times from three metres at another black snake that was poised ready to strike Cavalier from a branch a metre above his head. Pieces of the snake's head fell on him. He jumped back. Mac leapt around the snake's still wriggling body as it hit the ground. He barked and wagged his tail, enjoying the kill but not ready to bite the reptile's headless body, even in its death throes.

'Thought you said I wouldn't see another one!' Cavalier said, wiping slime from his shoulder.

'Sorry about that. It's rare you encounter two in a month let alone ten hours.' Haut chortled for several seconds and added: 'You have to say that was a close shave!'

Less amused, Cavalier said, 'Next time I'll bring an electric razor.'

9

BIKIE INVASION

Cavalier followed Haut's BMW roadster to Hobart, where Mac was left with Haut's parents. They then drove to Haut's office behind the Myer store on Liverpool Street. A biblical quote was tacked on the front door of his ground floor suite of rooms.

> Proverbs 11:3: The integrity of the upright will guide them. Integrity is the purity of thought motivation, intention, attitude, speech and action.

They spent four hours going through the detailed assay reports for Haut's various oil finds on and around North Bruny Island, and gold at Mt Victoria. At the end of the interview, half-eaten sandwiches, empty coffee cups and the crisp remains of a bucket of French fries were littered on the table in a small conference room of filing cabinets, a single bed and a TV set on a stand. A bookcase of oil brochures, technical books, bottled samples of oil and minerals covered one wall.

'That's twenty billion barrels of oil and twenty-four tons of gold,' Haut said, 'not bad, eh?'

'I see why Conquer wishes to stop you.'

'They want those reserves. Simple as that.'

At that moment, the office door flew open and four bikies, wearing telltale gear of leather jackets, fancy belts and studded wristbands, burst into the room brandishing rifles.

Cavalier dared not look at his valise sitting next to his chair. His handgun was in it.

The biggest of the four, hair sprouting from above a multi-coloured sweatband, stepped forward, aiming his gun at Haut.

'You Haut?' he grunted.

A second bikie, wiry and wide-eyed, moved between them.

'Hang on a tick!' he said. 'It's the Reverend Al! He gave that great service for Barry Price a few months ago. Well bugger me dead!' He scratched his speed-hump of a nose and shook hands with Haut.

'I'm Bert Renolds,' he said.

'Beers?' Haut said. The bikies nodded, put down their weapons and accepted cans that Haut passed around.

'We came to bump you off!' Renolds said, astonished by his own words. 'Would never have come if I'd known it was you. We were just told the target was a Mr Haut. Not the Reverend Al. We didn't put two and two together, until now.'

'It's comforting, you're not mathematicians then,' Haut said with a nervous chortle, before introducing the bikies to Cavalier as Dr Edwin Harris.

'Who sent you?' Haut asked. The four men glanced at each other.

'No, let me guess,' Haut said. 'It wouldn't have been someone protecting you and your drug business, would it?'

'Aw, mate!' Renolds replied. 'We can't let anyone know that.'

'But how will you explain it to that bastard Neil Farquar?'

'We'll just tell him the truth,' one of the gang blurted out. 'You weren't at home.'

'You went to my place?'

'We saw that there was no one at home and then came here.' He sniggered. 'And you weren't here either.'

Haut delivered his telltale gruff giggle and said, 'Saved a lot of wasted bullets.' The others laughed at his relaxed bravado. Cavalier remained on edge, however. He couldn't quite believe what he had just seen. Four thugs hell-bent on killing turned into respectful worshippers inside a couple of minutes.

'How much were you going to be paid?'

'Enough.'

'Enough for a very good night on the piss in Hobart with a bunch of sheilas!' the biggest bikie drawled. The others guffawed.

'No,' Haut said with a forced laugh, 'I guess you bastards are making enough from your bloody drug-manufacturing business not to worry about funds too much, eh?'

The bikies were stunned by the remark.

'C'mon, boys,' Haut said, 'everyone knows about your wee commercial enterprise and how the cops protect you and they're paid off by Farquar. That's why bumping me off would be swept under the carpet, eh?'

Tension filled the air again.

'Aw, c'mon, Rev, we don't want to talk about that,' Renolds said, his tone placatory.

Cavalier wondered if Haut's comment might see them revert to their original goal.

'One day, someone will have to burn that bloody factory down,' Haut said, his voice stern. 'The police won't take action, so I guess some vigilante will have to take the law into his own hands.' He looked at each man in turn. 'Someone with some real guts and authority on this godforsaken island.' He locked eyes with each of them in turn. 'Perhaps you should do what you came here to do, boys. Because that someone with authority might be me.' Haut's face was grim determination. 'Hear that? One day, I may well burn it down.' He paused for his words to sink in and added: 'And not you or the cops, or even the devil, will stop me!' He paused again. 'It will be God's will; his righteous anger. I will be just carrying out his wishes.'

There was a chill in the room. Cavalier edged his valise closer with his foot. He thought he might have to slide a left hand down under the table and pull out his gun.

Haut raised his can of beer.

'Let's not leave on a sour note,' he said, 'your mate and mine, Barry Price would not want that, eh? To Barry!'

Everyone raised their cans and repeated, 'To Barry!'

The chill factor fell away again.

'That was the best service I've ever heard,' a third bikie, an overweight man in his early twenties, said, 'and I've been to plenty. Guys killed on the road. Mates bumped off in gang wars on the mainland.'

'Well,' Haut said with a tilt of his head, 'we all gotta go sometime. It will be my pleasure to preside at your parting too.'

The bikie took it as a compliment. Cavalier thought Haut's comment was double-edged.

The bikies finished their beers, shook hands with Haut and Cavalier and were about to depart when Haut said,

'How about a small contribution?'

'For the church?' Renolds asked.

'For the door you just bashed in!' Haut said.

The bikies scraped together six hundred dollars and handed it to Haut.

'Now go and seduce those sheilas and have a good time,' Haut said.

'Can't,' Renolds said, 'you have all our bloody cash!'

'A good thing,' Haut said with a laugh.

When the visitors had disappeared, Cavalier remarked,

'That was a close-run thing! Must have been quite a sermon you gave at the funeral.'

'One of my best,' Haut said. 'I was the only minister of the cloth in Tasmania who would do it. The gang was most grateful. I had them all crying at the end of it.'

They began clearing the table.

'You see,' Haut said, 'many have done bad things, but they are still God-fearing men. They know that their business leads to short lives. They want to be sent off in style.'

'You handled the situation with style,' Cavalier said. 'It was a trace menacing at the end, but it was done with aplomb. You stayed calm.'

'Had to,' Haut said and then delivered a biblical quotation: '"Not by Might; nor by power; but by my Spirit, says the Lord." Those blokes sniff fear much like Mac does.' Haut then gave his trademark stuttering chortle. 'Besides, I was relying on you.'

'What?'

'I knew you had your gun inside that valise. I could see you edging it closer to your hand.'

'Don't know if I would have used it.'

Haut laughed again.

'C'mon, Vic! Your reputation precedes you.'

'I hope not. Won't last long if it ever does. I suppose Wombat said something?'

'Only obliquely. He just thought we should meet for security purposes.'

'Meaning?'

'With these mining discoveries, one day I'm going to need security services.'

'I'm not in that business.' Cavalier paused and, thinking of Haut's alleged part in his daughter's survival, added: 'Although I could make an exception, under certain circumstances.'

***

Cavalier had enough material on Haut for a freelance Saturday magazine article entitled,

'Survival in the Wild West of Tasmania.' He quoted Haut's claims with some caution, and tried to obtain comment from Conquer. They denied they had pressured Haut in any way and threatened to sue the magazine if a derogatory piece was published. Cavalier, as usual, had to fight the publication's lawyers over the story. They didn't like the references to Conquer's ruthless tactics to acquire oil leases over the decades. The piece was watered down to Haut's struggles as an independent geologist–miner trying to build a mining business. There was a brief comment about his odd association with a bikie gang, and the burial of its commander, but no mention of the office confrontation.

Cavalier's questions to Conquer, and the subsequent article, were sent to the company's HQ in Paris. The head of corporate relations marked the article as 'benign' but categorised the questions as 'potentially hostile to corporate activity'.

A file on Cavalier was begun.

10

THE OFFER

'The article on Haut was published last weekend,' Cavalier told Wombat when they met at the cricket bar of Melbourne's Windsor Hotel on upmarket Spring Street.

'I read it.'

'It was too soft for my liking. The lawyers held sway.'

'Might have been a good thing. You don't want Conquer treating you the way they have Al.'

They sat quietly for a few minutes and looked out at the grand state parliamentary building, designed in the mid nineteenth century.

'I cut out some of the more spiritual stuff,' Cavalier said. 'The rational, pragmatic material was fine, but even some of that was too fantastic for public consumption.'

'Big Brother is very happy with your deeper report,' Wombat replied. 'It wants to pay you for it.'

'Not necessary. The magazine has paid for the feature.'

'They're insistent.'

'How much?'

'Fifteen thousand.'

'Tell them to send a cheque to the Bradman Foundation. Earmark the money for development of young Indigenous cricketers in remote areas.'

'You serious?'

'You bet. Bradman signed his name, the greatest in Australian sport, over to the museum thirty years ago to raise funds for such purposes.'

'Your report to Big Brother was optimistic about Haut's oil reserves. You believe he has something?'

'I had the full assay reports assessed. Most experts agree there is a more than ninety-five per cent chance he has a considerable find.'

'This has really pricked the CIA's interest. The US Navy is extremely interested in Haut's discoveries. They know he has had trouble with Conquer.'

'He says he is reluctant to sell to any of the five sisters, after the way he has been treated.'

'Right. So he has to sell his crude somewhere.'

'The US Navy would be a good outlet for him.'

'Well, they are both aware of each other now. Your report will be digested, filed and perhaps acted on even before Haut is in production.'

Wombat sipped his beer.

'Have an assignment you may be interested in,' he said, glancing around the lounge area of the bar. It was 4 p.m. Two other drinkers, looking like interstate tourists with their luggage next to them, were sitting in a far corner, well out of earshot.

'An ASIS operative disappeared while checking some big illegal drug-dealing out of the Golden Triangle.'

'Who?'

'I was coming to that.' Wombat paused before adding, 'Geoff Deere.'

'Geoff!'

'You worked with him on the Guam story.'

'Is he . . .?'

'He was monitoring a group of drug smugglers. Then something happened.'

'Geoff was a good bloke; a fine operative too. I'm very sorry to hear this. What do we think occurred?'

'Big Brother think Deere was caught and liquidated. Now fish-bait in the Mekong.'

'What did you have in mind?'

'We'd only want an intelligence report. Big Brother believes the smugglers may have the cover of a tour operation up the Mekong into Laos. Perfect for shipping through borders. No one checks luggage. Visas and passports aren't needed at a few points. They run a few converted fishing boats for tourists, mainly for Americans, Brits, Australians and New Zealanders. The local Thais and Laotians are easy to pay off if needs be. The tourists have no idea of the illegal operation. They are shown a few schools being built for the local mountain and river people. They stay in the villages overnight.'

'Why me, though? You have official operatives in the area.'

Wombat paused and then said, 'Given your base in Chiang Mai, I thought it might be an opportunity for you, especially as the investigation into the murder on the Bangkok Express is over. I have it on the highest authority that you can come and go from Thailand when you want.'

'Good news, but I'm surprised that Makanathan has given up.'

'She has been ordered to stop the investigation. Both the Thai and Malaysian governments did not want anything about what happened on the train to be public, especially the terrorist attack.'

Cavalier was reflective before he said,

'I don't mind doing a report on the smugglers, but nothing else.'

'Your cover would be an article for one of the weekend colour magazines—you know, a feature on the tour. Best to take your ex-wife.'

'What?'

'You said you were on better terms with her . . .'

'Not that well!'

'I'm aware, Victor. But in this case, it will avoid suspicion. The tourists, we are informed, are mainly couples.'

'She'd never take time off from Chiang Rai hospital.'

'Have you another partner to take? Someone you could trust.'

Cavalier was contemplative.

'You'd only have to note the gang's movements and so on,' Wombat added. 'Where they load the stuff on, where they get it off. Detail. Once we have that, we'll send in operatives to do the rest.'

They sat in silence for a few moments. Cavalier weighed up the offer.

'There is another local connection,' Wombat said. 'A Tasmanian is financing the Mekong drug operation. He works also for Conquer on a freelance basis. His name is Neil Farquar. Have you heard of him?'

PART TWO

SPY

11

ASSIGNMENT LAOS

Cavalier was surprised that Pin was enthusiastic about going on the Mekong River Cruise. She had never taken a vacation in more than twenty years but after the recent traumas over Pon, she believed she might have a breakdown if she did not take time off from her stressful hospital regimen.

'For once, your timing is right, Victor,' Pin told him.

They agreed it would be on a platonic basis and that Cavalier would pay for the trip.

Cavalier and Pin were picked up by a minibus at his riverside condo and joined several other tourists. The tour was 'Mekong Adventures', run by an ex-pat New Zealander, Colin Geoffreys. He was a good-looking and personable 45-year-old who had spent twenty years in advertising before a sea change saw him running boat tours on the Mekong. Wombat's intelligence was that Geoffreys was not aware that Farquar and his team of five were drug-runners. And if he were aware, he turned a blind eye. His salary was more than he had earned as a senior advertising executive, and this might explain his 'hear no evil, see no evil' attitude.

Two buses collected all the tourists. Cavalier was soon on alert when he realised that the gang he would be spying on were in the second vehicle.

***

The convoy stopped at a plantation area fifty kilometres short of Chiang Rai. Farquar and the other five moved off to talk to farmers, while the rest of the group was shown a black rice crop.

'It's not all black rice, is it?' Cavalier asked Geoffreys, waving his arm at fields several hundred metres away.

'There may be other crops out there,' Geoffreys replied. 'Bananas, I think. But the main export produce is black rice.'

Cavalier wandered towards the outer crops, but was waved away by farmers and a security guard. As he moved back to the main group, he noticed two trucks pulling up along the road at another entrance to the plantation. A gate was opened and the two heavy vehicles trundled along a path in the fields to a distant warehouse.

Cavalier was about to ask Geoffreys more questions but thought better of it when he saw he was in a heated discussion with the muscular Farquar, who was tall and covered in gaudy tattoos. Cavalier moved within a few paces and gathered that Geoffreys was far from happy with the behaviour of Farquar and his group in the second minibus.

***

The two vehicles reached Chiang Rai an hour later and the tourists alighted to look at the White Temple, and have lunch. Pin was perplexed Cavalier wanted to join the tour too.

'You've seen the temple and Chiang Rai so many times,' she said.

'I always like to walk through it,' he said, taking a photograph with a small camera, 'it's spiritual.'

'You've never said that before.'

Other tourists turned to look as their chat turned acrimonious. Cavalier led Pin out of the temple and across the road to a restaurant. In the cafe next door Farquar and the gang of five were sitting drinking beer. Cavalier changed direction and entered another restaurant.

They were joined by Geoffreys, who sat with them.

'That bloody cabal,' he said, dropping his voice and nodding in the gang's direction, 'they've been drunk all the way from Chiang Mai.'

'Who are they?' Pin asked.

'Neil Farquar, the goatee-bearded wonder, owns the tour business. He and his mates join the trip once a year. The other tourists have all objected to their boorish behaviour. They wanted to join the bus you are on. The guys are all arseholes! They have beer for breakfast and three of them work out in the gym for two hours every day. They only seem to eat protein drinks and beer at lunch and dinner.'

'They all look like brutes,' Pin observed, 'even the woman.'

'Farquar will sometimes drink twelve vodkas and then work out.'

'How old is he?' Pin asked.

'Thirty-six.'

'He'll have a stroke before he's fifty-six,' Pin predicted. 'Imbibing alcohol like that lowers the blood pressure. If the physical exertion is so much, the heart can't pump blood to the brain. Hence the stroke.'

They all glanced over at Farquar, who was saying goodbye to his squad. He looked back at them.

'Where is he from?' Cavalier asked.

'Estonia. Brought up in Tasmania.'

'What's he like?' Cavalier asked, as casually as he could.

Geoffreys shrugged.

'In the mood he's in now,' he said, 'I think of four letter words.' Geoffreys glanced at Pin and added, 'He's a real "See you next Tuesday."'

'What's that?' Pin asked.

'Darling,' Cavalier said, 'it's Kiwi code for not a nice person.'

'Oh.'

Geoffreys went on,

'Farquar changes personality somewhat when he's with those other five. They're a nefarious bunch. Don't know what they get up to, but I doubt it would be any good. He swoops in, gives orders and pisses off. Washes his hands of whatever they do.'

'What do you mean by nefarious?' Pin asked, unwittingly doing Cavalier's work. 'They're crims or something?'

'I don't know.' Geoffreys shrugged. 'But I don't like or trust any of them.'

'Why work with them?'

'I'm paid very well, and only have to deal with them for a week once a year. It's worth it for me. Besides, I love the work on the Mekong. You'll see why.'

12

PINPRICKS

The small cavalcade drove on another two hours to the border town between Thailand, Laos and Burma: The Golden Triangle.

'Why are we going there?' Pin demanded.

'The tourists want to see it,' Geoffreys said.

'Don't you remember,' Cavalier said, a touch feebly, 'it was the first trip we made together...'

Pin gave him a withering look.

'I've spoken to some of them,' she said. 'No one wants to go. The trip is supposed to be on the Mekong, is it not?'

'It's an option for the tour.'

'But it adds four hours to the road trip!'

'I'm afraid my boss wants the detour,' Geoffreys said with an apologetic hand gesture.

'I'll speak to him,' Pin said.

Cavalier became nervous.

'It's his tour company, darling,' he said, touching her hand.

'All that time on the road, pfff!'

Pin became obstreperous and abused Cavalier for asking her on the trip. He knew these sudden mood swings far too well. Her depression, self-diagnosed about the time they met, meant she became irrational and threatening. He had to stand between her and their

57

children from a young age to shield them from their mother's tirades.

Now, Cavalier's memories of Pin's tirades, buried for more than eight years, resurfaced.

He was treading cautiously but Pin's face was a giveaway. She looked darkly at him as the bus took them on to the Golden Triangle. An attractive Korean–American woman of about fifty sat next to Cavalier and struck up a conversation. Pin folded her arms and looked out the window. Cavalier tried to bring her into the conversation. Pin became hostile. When the bus arrived at the Triangle, Pin said she wanted to go back to Chiang Mai, putting on a show in front of the tourists from both buses. The last thing Cavalier wanted was to become the centre of attention so he tried to placate her. They wandered away from the group. Cavalier noticed Farquar and his men speeding off in a truck.

'You wouldn't buy a house,' Pin said, reviving a long-buried dispute. 'We had a rented apartment that was not big enough for five. The girls and Serena should have had their own room.'

'A room for the doll?'

Cavalier could see her ire rising fast.

'I told you many times,' he said in a conciliatory tone, 'I didn't have the money. I paid for the kids' private school. We agreed that this took precedence over buying land.' He paused. 'It's all so long ago, Pin. Can't we be friends? Let the past stay there.'

Pin's tirade continued. Many of the tour group rubber-necked. Other passers-by stopped to watch the rant. Cavalier sat on a bench in silence. Finally he said,

'You can leave the tour if you wish.'

Geoffreys walked past in deep conversation with Farquar, who had returned from his truck ride. Cavalier looked around at the truck, parked next to the buses. He noticed that it was now laden with an unknown cargo.

'You can't berate me in front of my men like that,' Farquar said, waving a finger at the New Zealander. 'I have to leave tomorrow. But if I hear you have mishandled my team, I'll fire you.'

Geoffreys stood his ground.

'Just remember I run the boat,' he said.

'No, I do.'

'But you're pissing off, as usual.'

'Hollos is my deputy and you'll do what he wants.'

They walked on in heated discussion. There were two dramas on the sidewalk now. Pin tried to retrieve her bags from the van but couldn't find the driver. She had calmed down half an hour later and was silent on the drive to the immigration border town of Chiang Khong and the Riverside Hotel. Pin seemed intent on leaving but changed her mind at the very last moment when the minibus drivers were about to return to Chiang Mai.

The hotel room she and Cavalier were in overlooked the river and mountains and may even have been romantic on most occasions but not this one. The warring couple sat on balcony chairs contemplating the lights of the town opposite and on the mountain. They both had books. Cavalier couldn't concentrate. He mulled over how to watch Farquar's gang, while attempting to appease Pin. After his initial fears about being noticed, Cavalier now thought that he would be seen as the hapless husband, which would help him avoid suspicion.

Pin was still in a volatile mood the next morning over breakfast. The low, black cloud, the mist floating over the mountains before it evaporated, the muddy brown Mekong and the heavy rain, all seemed to conspire in a pall of gloom. The break from this grey environment was the wonderful, phosphorescent green mountain foliage.

Using his mobile, Cavalier managed to take photos of Farquar's gang, who again drank beer for breakfast or helped themselves to protein booster drinks.

Cavalier was intrigued most by the sole woman of the group. She had a lithe walk and leap—from boat to shore—of a cross between an athletic female shot-putter and a 100-metre sprinter.

Pin was irritated by Cavalier positioning her to allow the gang in the frame. His fussy directorial arrangement annoyed her, although he was thankful for the small mercy of her conversing with him.

His remark of, 'Verbal intercourse is better than no intercourse at all,' brought a reproachful look.

He saw the gang leave in the truck before the tour buses, and would like to have followed them rather than engage in a pointless, lopsided disagreement with his ex-wife.

13

UNEASILY UP THE MEKONG

There was the usual disorganised, scramble and delay passing through customs and immigration into Laos. Cavalier had his false British passport, which he concealed from Pin, telling her he had dual British and Australian nationality, which was not a lie. Yet it was a deception. His real passports were in a safe in Chiang Mai.

Cavalier knew how to slip out of Thailand into Burma and had done so recently to avoid passport controls. Here he made a mental note of where to do it on the Mekong into Laos and China. He had always been challenged by avoiding borders security, even around Australia. Cavalier once hired a light plane in Jakarta, which was flown by an Australian ex-Qantas pilot he met in a bar. It took him to West Irian, Ambon and then south over the Arafura Sea to Australia's Northern Territory. Cavalier landed on an old military airstrip 70 kilometres from Darwin and this way entered his own country illegally.

'The trick,' he wrote in his diary in 1980, 'was to land on a weekend when the coastal patrol did not leave its radar on.'

***

The tour group boarded a wooden, narrow Thai-style riverboat, number 092, which was 45 metres long by 2.8 metres wide. The middle section had sixty-six seats, set up in cubicles of four. There was a bar area aft. The twenty tourists took seats. The gang, now without their boss Farquar, plonked themselves in cubicles. They nibbled at a meagre breakfast, disgruntled that the bar would not open for an hour. This was Cavalier's chance. He ordered a coffee and placed a small recorder, about the size of those used in telephone receivers, behind some ornamental carving about a foot above where the gang would be sitting at the bar. Cavalier casually asked Geoffreys for the register of guests.

'I'm fascinated to know where they've all come from,' he said.

Geoffreys opened a red book and ran his finger down the guests' names, and that of Farquar's team. Cavalier memorised the gang's names: Hollos, Castro, Leni, Amaz—the girl—and the lone wolf of the group, Dubois.

On cue at 9 a.m. the gang, except for Dubois, proceeded to drink beer and talk, with Leni chain-smoking cigars. The aroma wafted through the boat throughout the rest of the day, depending on the breeze.

The boat was due to stop at eight villages, some of which were reached by tractor a few kilometres into the jungle interior. Unlike Thailand, the Laos government had bought some of the land to limit or avoid deforestation.

Cavalier and Pin read and dozed for most of the long first leg that took them 140 kilometres along the river over six hours. The weather was cool. The rain of the morning continued well into the afternoon. The brown water was high. Staff on the boat lowered plastic flaps to protect the tour group from rain sweeping in. It was hard to see anything through the mist, and even when the sun appeared here and there, it turned the river into a blinding flash of tinfoil.

Cavalier paused every now and then to take a photograph from the helm. The green jungle in the centre of nowhere was captivating, even mesmerising at times for its rustic beauty on mountains and hills. It was so luxuriant and fecund that the trees seemed reluctant to stop at the water's edge. Their wet, twisted roots held the banks together and it seemed as if the trees either side were destined one day to transcend the river and join up.

Cavalier saw few humans on the banks. Some were discernible at steps down to boats and at the outcroppings of villages near the water's edge. When the boat drifted close to either bank, the squawk of an unseen bird could be heard. Otherwise there were few signs of life.

Not even mosquitoes, which the passengers were warned could be an issue if they did not use repellent, were evident. The wind and rain were keeping them inactive, for the moment.

During the Vietnam War, which had finished almost half a century ago, the North Vietnamese used the Ho Chi Minh Trail through Laos to avoid the Americans in their quest to take back South Vietnam.

'When it was discovered as a covert route,' Geoffreys told Cavalier, 'the Americans bombed it for years, just as the French did before them. But the communists persisted.'

Oblivious of the unfolding monochrome of natural grace, the gang, minus the loner Dubois, went on devouring bottle after bottle. Their consumption at the boat's bar led to rowdy antics. Yet Cavalier noticed that every now and again they moved closer to each other and spoke softly. Those were the conversations he wanted the recorder to pick up.

The main boat, 092, was followed by a second, identical boat, 0092. A heavy tarpaulin covered white sacks. There were no tourists onboard. One traveller asked Geoffreys what the 'produce' was.

'They produce wealthy Farang,' he replied with a grin. 'Not sure but I think it's coconuts and maybe some bananas. But, I kid you not, they don't trust me enough to let me know!'

The six-hour first leg ended at Pak Beng. The wind had dropped and the rain had abated but the earlier torrents that had preceded the boat had caused the jetty to be almost consumed at the high-water mark, twenty metres above normal. The stone steps were submerged. The tourists had to slip and slide up the muddy area above the staircase, backpacks swaying.

'Pak Beng is a shithole,' Geoffreys told the assembled group at the hotel. 'You'll never come back. We're staying at the only habitable hotel. It's run by Indians who have a good restaurant across the road.'

The curries and condiments wafted and enticed the guests before they entered the dining room. Pin insisted on sitting at a table away from the others. She detested small talk unless it was with other medicos. She also wished to distance herself from the raucous drinking party, who parked themselves at one end of a long table. At 9 p.m. she announced she was tired and wished to go to bed. Cavalier said he wanted to walk down to the village before retiring.

'What for?' Pin asked. 'You heard what Geoffreys said.'

'I need the air.'

'More likely you want to avoid me.'

Cavalier wanted to say, 'That too,' but held his tongue.

He stepped out, wearing a light jacket to protect against the inclement weather. It also concealed his handgun.

14

DETECTIVE UNDERCOVER

It was raining again when Cavalier wandered the two hundred metres down to the water's edge where a whiff of dead fish lingered. A security guard was on each boat. Cavalier signalled for the gangplank to be placed on the shore and the guard obliged.

'Left my glasses at the bar,' Cavalier said in Thai. The guard grinned and let him walk to the bar area. Cavalier was quick to slide his hand under the carved woodwork. He removed the tiny recorder, pocketed it and made his way forward again. He showed the guard his glasses and stepped down the gangplank. He had gone twenty metres up the slippery bank to the road when he saw four silhouettes with torchlights coming from the hotel restaurant. Despite the downpour, he could make out Hollos and three of the others in the group. For once, they were silent.

Cavalier sidled away to the village shops and hid under an awning, which stopped him receiving a complete drenching. Hollos and his team were soon animated. Orders were shouted. They boarded the cargo boat. Locals appeared and were directed. Minutes later, a stream of about twenty men, loaded with white sacks on their shoulders, were filing down a gangplank from the boat, and then along a track, where they disappeared into the rain mist like a colony of ants.

Cavalier cursed himself for not bringing his phone or camera. He had visual knowledge of the unloading, but not where the sacks were being put. He wondered if they were being transported overland.

There was a commotion onboard the cargo boat. Cavalier could see Castro gesticulating in his direction. Cavalier hurried up the track towards the hotel, a couple of the group in pursuit. He slid along the embankment back towards the water and scrambled into the bush below the hotel.

He could hear shouting as the gang searched for the possible interloper. Cavalier crept up to the hotel. Other tourists came from the dining area and hotel rooms to see what had caused the disturbance. In the commotion, Cavalier crouched low, climbed the stairs and knocked at the door to his room. Pin let him in.

'What have you been up to?' she asked, with a teapot stance as she pointed at his muddy shoes and trouser cuffs.

'I just wanted time to think,' he said, slipping off his shoes and removing his trousers. He hurried to the bathroom with a small brush and proceeded to clean his shoes.

'I want to leave the tour,' she called as she climbed back into bed.

'Why? Because I have dirty footwear?'

'I saw that second passport in your things, *Doctor Edwin Harris*! I don't know what it's about . . .'

'I can explain.'

'I don't want to hear it.'

'I'll tell you in the morning.'

'I won't be here.'

He used toilet paper to wipe his shoes. Then he brushed the dirt from his cuffs, cleaned up the sink, placed his trousers on a hanger and set his shoes down near his suitcase in an alcove next to the bathroom. He hid the tape recorder in his case, removed his jacket and other clothes, and showered. He had just dried off when they heard loud raps on doors to other rooms. The gang members were asking other tourists if they had been down by the boats, or they had seen anyone suspicious in the hotel.

'What is going on?' Pin demanded.

'I said I'll explain in the morning,' Cavalier said, when there was a knock at the door. Cavalier slipped on a white dressing-gown and answered it. Two of the gang stood there, dripping wet and frowning. Hollos was wearing a vest which seemed to have been painted on, so tight and bulging was his torso. Amaz wore a smart rainproof red and blue jacket, and tight jeans. She was barefoot. Her hair was awry and wet. A strong waft of perfume, which Cavalier recognised as Chanel No. 5, emanated from her but could not counteract Hollos' body odour.

'Have you been outside in the last hour?' Hollos asked, his bicep muscles flexing as he spoke.

'In the dining room, and then back here,' Cavalier said. 'What's wrong?'

'Nothing,' the man said, peering in. He could see Cavalier's shoes in the alcove. 'We'd like to have a look around.'

'Not on,' Cavalier said with a firm shake of the head. 'My wife is in bed and I'm about to go to sleep myself, after this interruption.'

Hollos and Amaz looked as if they might insist but Cavalier's square-on stance saw them hesitate. Cavalier thought Hollos had the look of the bully-boy about him; insecure and bursting to show how tough he was. His face was gnarled—from too many cage fights, Cavalier guessed. The nose was off centre. The cleft chin looked more like a scar than a natural indentation. His dark, sunken eyes were steady but with a squint that hinted at nerves.

Whenever he faced someone dangerous, Cavalier looked for a physical weakness he could exploit. Hollos' jaw was strong; he had a broad chest and six-pack abdomen. Cavalier decided that a square-handed knuckle thrust to the throat was the one sure way to disable him, apart from the time-honoured knee to the testicles.

'We haven't met,' Cavalier said with a disarming grin as he introduced himself to both of them with his well-trained bruising handshake. 'What's this all about?' He kept his eyes on Hollos but with a relaxed smile of easy trust.

'Aw, nuthin',' Amaz said, tapping Hollos on the arm. Cavalier considered her light green eyes and decided that she had an odd sort of sex appeal. Her face's regular features, cute nose and fine jaw, were not quite beautiful. Yet there was an androgynous aura about her. Amaz sometimes batted her eyelids as if she were given to flirtation, a mannerism that did not fit with her body language. Cavalier stroked his chin as if in thought while glancing down at her hands. The knuckles were flattened, a bit like his from his schoolboy days playing Australian Rules football. The hands hung low at her thighs. Yet her walk and movements were more balletic than baboon-like.

'Can't be nothing, mate,' Cavalier said, folding his arms and keeping a smile. 'You were wanting to search our hotel room . . .'

Pin appeared in a matching white dressing-gown. She looked fierce.

Hollos and Amaz moved off.

'What is going on?' she asked Cavalier again as he closed the door.

'You heard the woman—"nuthin'". I think they were searching for somebody.'

Cavalier followed her to bed, where she was soon asleep after a mumbled barrage about his stupidity and the rudeness of the couple at the door. Cavalier eased out of bed, retrieved the tape recorder, put in earpieces and moved into the bathroom to listen to what had been picked up in the gang's drunken conversation.

***

It took him just on two and a half hours to listen to the recording. He skipped over the asides and the cryptic, insulting remarks about almost all onboard; and abuse about Geoffreys. They spoke in bursts about 'the product' and where they were going to market it. Cavalier learned they would unload a third of it at this first stop. 'The product' would then be trucked to an airfield and flown to Chiang Mai, where it would be distributed. The bulk of the shipment would be boated up the river to Luang Prabang, Laos' second biggest city, where it would be flown also to Chiang Mai.

Patches of conversation indicated they feared there might be another American or Australian agent on board. They listed him as one of four men on the boat who could be an agent. It chilled him to hear them debate their suspicions about him.

Hollos remarked,

'He is English and his wife is Thai. They are doctors. . .'

'He is about fifty-five, right?' Amaz said. 'He is bull fit, I reckon. He always has dark glasses on as if he is hiding somethin'.'

'That's crazy!' Castro said. 'We all wear 'em too!'

'Kinda makes my point!' Amaz said.

'Just keep an eye on the doctors,' Leni said. 'We can handle anyone we think may be agents.'

'What if they all are?' Amaz asked.

'Geoffreys doesn't suspect anyone,' Hollos said. 'I doubt the ten single women on the boat could be armed spies!'

'Geoffreys doesn't have a clue,' Leni said. 'Doesn't even know we got rid of the last one. He doesn't want any trouble on the boat.'

Cavalier noted that Amaz volunteered to kill him if there were any clues that he was spying on them. The others chided her on her bloodlust and bravado. She was not only the sole woman in the group; she was also the least experienced.

'You should let us men do this dirty work,' Hollos said.

Amaz was annoyed. The men had a good laugh.

'Where's Dubois going tonight?' Castro asked. 'He says he won't be with us.'

'He'll be fucking some teenager in the village, for sure,' Amaz said. 'He always does.'

'Do you trust him?' Castro asked Hollos.

'No, but he is good at what we want him to do. Very good in fact. Remember who tracked that Australian agent in the bush. None of you wanted to do it.'

'A serious psychopath, if you ask me,' Leni commented.

'Nobody asked you,' Hollos snapped, 'did they? So what if he is a psycho? He's our psycho. That's what counts. He shoots and—'

'Asks questions later,' Leni said with a cynical expression.

'Wrong,' Amaz said. 'He never asks question. He just does.'

Cavalier now knew the identity of Deere's killer. When he wrapped up his review of the tape, he was in a quandary about what to do. His first instinct was to isolate Dubois and assassinate him. But that would be difficult. And his priority was to protect Pin.

Cavalier look at his watch. It was 4 a.m. He had to come up with something by dawn. In the meantime, he spent an hour handwriting a report on the gang of six for Wombat:

Their 'leader', Neil Farquar, in his mid-thirties, is well over six feet with the physique of a bodybuilder. He covers a weak chin with a goatee beard. He has links to Conquer and Tasmania. There are few laughs in a stern face, made more serious in expression by close-set eyes. He left the trip at the Golden Triangle before the boats began the river voyage.

The second of the 'team' is Emmanuel Hollos, who claims a Mexican background. He stands just over six feet, and is as heavy as Farquar at about one hundred kilograms. Hollos' head is shaved yet he is hairy in all the wrong places. From some angles he seems not to have a neck. The just discernible partition between head and shoulders makes him appear more bull-like than the biggest of Rugby League footballers. Hollos has a pock-marked face, and a granite jaw. This fellow, too, is a gym freak. He is so muscular that he wears a multi-coloured sleeveless vest, probably because he wouldn't fit into any shirt with sleeves.

The third in the group, known as 'Leni', is shorter and lean. In the tape enclosed there is no record of his background, although he speaks English and carries an American passport. He has close, fierce eyes and a stub for a nose. His thick black hair is pushed back from a low forehead, with greasy product. Leni is the smoker of the five and favours pungent Cuban cigars.

Number four is a forty-year-old Cuban-American, Ferdinand Castro, with the biggest nose I have ever seen. Whenever he speaks it bends forward. He is shorter than the others, but fit-looking. There were hints on the tape that he had spent about a decade in a Peruvian jail for armed robbery. Castro claims a marriage to a Venezuelan beauty queen, who he blames for most of his six children and all his woes. Gets laughs telling everyone he has to do three jobs to keep them all happy. Castro boasts he was an actor in his twenties and was cast as an Arab sheik, whenever they wanted a nasty one! He makes a joke that it was either his nose or big cock that secured him parts. Whatever the truth, he ended up circumcised, in the celluloid sense, and on the cutting room floor.

The fifth character is 38-year-old Frenchman Gerard Jean Dubois, or at least that is his nominated nationality and name on a passport, according to the tour organiser, Colin Geoffreys. Dubois claims to be a former member of the French Foreign Legion, which, despite its name, did take in a minority of Frenchmen. But he is fluent also in English and German. Narrow of shoulder and wide of hip, this laconic individual is about 180 centimetres tall and a fit eighty kilograms, without being a weights fanatic. His hair is longish, as if clinging on to the 1970s, when he was first incarcerated in the UK. He has distinguishing eyebrows which almost have no break between, and need trimming. The nose has a serious bump on it. He has long arms and walks with a strange ape-like gait.

On closer examination, his brown eyes are the main feature. They are cruel and soul-less with a tendency to stare or hold another's gaze for longer than necessary, perhaps in an attempt at intimidation. The face is pinched and that of someone who has sampled some of the illegal drugs in which he tells the rest of the group he has dealt with over twenty years. Dubois' mouth is thin-lipped and ever-ready to utter a cynical or vicious remark, if he speaks at all. He has had a life of crime, which has seen him jailed in several countries for drug dealing, and never for his most outstanding skill, which is assassination, as you'll deduce from the tape conversation. Dubois is one of just two Westerners to ever escape from

Thailand's notorious 'Bangkok Hilton'—Klong Prem prison.

He is a loner, who does not always drink with the others. You can smell him when he's ten metres away. He showers in cheap aftershave. It's repugnant, and seems to match his personality, if he has one. Geoffreys says he is 'a bloody predator for all the girls from twelve to sixteen in the villages.' Geoffreys spoke to Farquar and Hollos about it. They just laughed. I suspect they are too scared to warn Dubois off. He murdered Deere.

Number six, known as 'Amaz', is a woman, so well-built that I find it hard to judge her age, which seems to be about twenty-eight. She has short-cropped hair, which accentuates chiselled features of cheekbones and jaw. A former Laotian kick-boxer with an American father, Amaz has been based in Thailand for the last decade. She plays up to Farquar and Hollos, enough to suggest she is sleeping with both of them.

Cavalier sent photos of the gang by phone to Wombat and put his notes in an envelope. He marked it for sending to Wombat and slipped it into Pin's handbag.

15

THE PLOT

Cavalier managed less than an hour's sleep and woke at 6 a.m. to the sound of discordant music in the village with a drum prominent. He sat up to see his ex-wife packing her case.

'Good morning,' he said, hopefully.

'Maybe for you,' she grumbled.

'Relax. The boat doesn't leave until 8 a.m.'

'I'm not going. I can take an earlier one back to Thailand. I checked with Geoffreys last night.'

Cavalier protested. Yet he knew her mood fluctuations and expressions so well that he believed she was serious.

'I don't like the tour; the drunkenness of those people. The fact that they tried to invade our room last night! Not to mention your secret life.'

'Darling—'

'Don't darling me. I always suspected you of having a double life. All those las-minute trips for your paper!'

'They were legit!'

'Rubbish.'

The tension was high. Pin finished packing.

'You could try it for another day,' Cavalier suggested.

'I don't like the heat.'

'I want to carry on.'

'You can do what you want.' Pin zipped her case.

'I beg one favour of you,' Cavalier said. 'There is an envelope in your handbag. Could you please send it on to Wombat? The address is on it.'

Pin fumed.

'So you are on some spying mission! Do you understand why I couldn't live with you anymore?'

'Just do this one last thing,' Cavalier said. 'Please.'

***

Pin found a boat that left a half-hour before the tour group. Cavalier was relieved although he was now more exposed as a lone traveller. He knew the rudiments of the presumed smuggling operation. Staying on tour meant he could learn more, although he imagined he was now top, or near the top, of the gang's suspect list.

Cavalier, wearing the rain jacket that hid his gun in a zip pocket, saw Pin off. He then boarded 092 with his backpack. Making sure he wasn't seen, he replaced the recorder with a fresh tape in the same position near the bar. He wandered back up to the village, bought some fruit and sat down at a bench to eat it.

Cavalier took pictures of the vista off the mountains across the river where a light mist was already being devoured by the sun. The early morning rain had stopped. The day promised to be good for the tourists who would not have to squint through the rain with their cameras and phones. Cavalier watched the tour group straggle down the hill from the hotel.

He returned to the boat and had to endure various questions about his wife departing the tour. Cavalier was embarrassed and had to smile through the quizzing. He was alert to the gang coming onboard, minus Dubois, who was already on the cargo boat.

Leni, Hollos, Castro and Amaz carried cartons of beer and began their daily consumption ritual. They were all wearing the same blue jeans they'd had on the day before. It seemed to Cavalier like some sort of uniform. The more they drank, the more Cavalier relaxed. He reasoned they would not be in a state to confront him, or even kill him, if they were inebriated by lunchtime. Yet he was alert. Amaz was fidgety. She consumed less than the other three. He noticed that she glanced his way at least twice.

There was also Dubois, out of sight on the cargo boat. Cavalier worried about him more than the others. Dubois would be the one who killed without compunction, but no doubt for good money. On the rare occasion Cavalier had been close or looked into Dubois' face, he noted something he recognised well. Dubois wasn't as big as Hollos, but his look had an indestructability about it. It was prison-hard. He was a survivor from the worst incarceration places in the world, which said much about him.

Cavalier looked in the mirror and recognised some of Dubois in his own visage. Not so much the toughness, but the survivor in him. They were both lone wolf operatives. Dubois seemed out of place with the other four, and uncomfortable.

***

Cavalier read a book as they boat chugged along the river. It stopped at a village where he joined Geoffreys and the other tourists as they walked inland to inspect a school building. They left Dubois and the alcoholics, except Amaz, onboard the two boats.

Geoffreys was raising funds to help build schools in these remote areas. This altruistic enterprise was his life, after his long 'servitude', as he called it, in advertising in Singapore. He wanted to help educate the children of these isolated areas; to give them some chance in life.

'It is my salvation,' this stepson of an Anglican minister told Cavalier. 'Instead of preaching our existence, I do something about it.'

Cavalier joined a ceremony conducted by Geoffreys and then a photo session with happy village children, who received gifts from the tourists.

Amaz strolled along at the rear of the tourist pack with about twenty laughing children aged eight to ten. Cavalier fell back beside her.

'Did you find your woman last night?' he asked with a smile.

'What? Oh, no, we didn't. What makes you think it was a woman?'

'Oh, nothing. Except half the people onboard are women.' He smiled. 'Why is it that men are blamed for things? I assume there has been a misdemeanour, a theft—an attack even?'

He locked eyes on her and, for a fraction of a second, Amaz seemed startled.

Cavalier moved away and began talking to an attractive New Zealand woman of about fifty. He could see his remark had befuddled Amaz. If he were going to do her harm, would he forewarn her like that?

'We were sorry to see your wife leave,' the woman, introducing herself as Vivien, commented.

'Ex-wife,' Cavalier corrected, giving nothing away. 'I am sorry that our little tiff and the bad behaviour of the drinking cabal has put a dampener on the tour, although it's still fun.'

'Colin confronted them.'

'Brave man.'

***

When the group returned to the boat, Leni, Amaz, Castro and Hollos had joined Dubois on the cargo boat 0092 and were drinking and in discussion. Dubois stayed put while Hollos, Leni, Castro and Amaz moved back on the tourist craft. Both boats were soon heading further north up the river.

Hollos was necking another beer bottle within minutes. Amaz did not join him this time. She seemed displaced and refused to sit and drink with her companions. Instead she fixed herself a coffee and sat alone at a cubicle for four. She was about three metres from the next occupied cubicle. She still had on her jeans jacket. Cavalier caught her eye. She looked away.

The boat trundled on, stopping at villages for more gift-giving and pledges to raise funds for building schoolrooms. The destination village this time provided rooms for the tourists, who were fed and entertained with a Shaman ceremony, where all their wrists were wrapped with white string. The tourists crowded into a meeting room where a local Shaman, a withered 65-year-old with a massive boil on his forehead, conducted the show. He prayed to the Buddha and made incantations before the village's headman sang a repetitive, unmelodic number.

Cavalier kept an eye on Amaz, who sat cross-legged and pretended to be attentive to the performances. She was distracted by the appearance of Hollos and Leni. Amaz bustled outside and embraced them. Cavalier felt that the hugging and kissing of Hollos now, and Farquar earlier on, was confirmation of them being more intimate.

The Shaman and headman did the rounds with the local Saki-like whisky. Then the Shaman moved outside to the group of five. They accepted his offer of small cups of the harsh drink, each throwing down four shots in a row.

Rooms were allocated for the tourists. Cavalier slipped away on the excuse that he wanted to see the temple at the top of a hill. Instead of returning to the village he walked to the boat and retrieved his tape recorder. With no one on board, he decided to go through the tape there. He took notes. The group discussed his demise, having come to the conclusion that he was the 'spy'. Amaz was forced into agreeing to her first murder. Her earlier brave talk had collapsed. The conversation chilled him.

'You have to do it,' Hollos told her. 'Otherwise we must get rid of you.'

'Get rid of me! What does that mean?'

'Whatever you want it to.'

There was a long pause before Hollos added,

'You know too much.'

'You are either with us in everything, or out,' Leni chipped in.

'You've been with us in a lot of things,' Hollos said. 'This will be easy. Isolate him in the Pacou Caves. He has put his name down for the tour to climb to the top. It's over three hundred steps with lots of twists.'

'But other tourists will be with him,' Amaz protested.

'Only three are listed to go. The other two are Vivien, the Maori woman, and William, the American.'

'You can't be sure the doctor is the agent,' Amaz said.

'We've spoken to Geoffreys,' Hollos said. 'He has known William, the American, for two decades. He runs a family business in Tokyo and he is married to a Japanese. He's what he says he is. Geoffreys knows the Maori woman. They're both Kiwis who go back thirty years, and are former lovers, at a guess.'

'That leaves the good doctor,' Hollos said, 'who gave himself away by his comment to you at the village.'

There was another pause, longer this time. Cavalier checked the tape, thinking it may have finished. Then Amaz asked,

'How do we know he has been spying on us? There is no evidence.'

'We have an informant in the CIA,' Hollos replied. 'The information was that there would be another Australian agent on the tour this month.'

'You said he had an English passport.'

'English, Australian; what's the difference?'

'About twenty thousand kilometres!'

'He would have a false passport,' Leni said.

'Shouldn't we interrogate him first?' she asked.

'That would draw attention to us,' Hollos said. 'We need a quick, untraceable elimination. You can get him in one of the top caves.'

Amaz began to splutter a protest but Hollos stopped her and added, 'That's only if you are alone. There must be no witnesses. Use your silencer. Drag his body well into a cave. There are small wells or holes in them. Leni will follow and help you.'

A shuffling movement could be heard on the tape.

'What's wrong with you?' Hollos asked. 'Come back here!'

'Fuck you!' Amaz hissed as she moved away.

Cavalier switched off the tape and settled down in a cubicle in an attempt to sleep. He awoke at dawn, walked to the village and sat down at an outside table where breakfasts of fried egg and bread where provided. The tourists straggled out and joined him. Cavalier found time to use a bathroom and wash. He was just leaving it when he bumped into Amaz.

'Good morning,' he said.

Amaz did not respond as she slammed the bathroom door shut.

'Yes and good morning to you,' Cavalier said in a mocking voice, loud enough for her to hear. He moved outside and accepted a coffee from one of the smiling villagers. Hollos and Leni were slumped on chairs, beers in hand and looking the worse for wear. Again mystery-man Dubois was not around.

Cavalier sat the other side of the table from them and next to an Englishman with a Thai wife. Cavalier had avoided them until now, fearing they would ask too many questions. He feigned a hang-over and sipped his coffee in silence. Amaz joined the table and sat at the other end from her gang and Cavalier.

'Where to next?' someone asked Geoffreys.

'The Pacou Caves,' he replied, loud enough for the benefit of everyone at the table. 'They are about twenty-five kilometres out from our final destination, Luang Prabang.'

Cavalier glanced along the table and caught Amaz's eye. She looked away too quickly, he thought.

16

NOWHERE TO HIDE

The Pacou Caves, on the west of the Mekong, offered a useful place for a kill where the victim would never be found. There were caves near the top, which the faint-hearted should not attempt to climb to, and the lower caves, which had more crevices, nooks and crannies. Knowing there could be an attempt to kill him, Cavalier had the choice to stay on the boat and avoid any confrontation. Yet if the plans he'd heard had been changed and the men had decided to take part in his demise, he would be just as vulnerable onboard. Most of the tourists stepped off the boat to wander around the lower cave area. He decided to call Amaz's bluff and take the walk up the stone steps. He went to the toilet, checked his handgun and began the ascent.

It was raining. Overhanging branches provided shade, which made the testing climb easier. Cavalier began moving up. He looked back to see Amaz rushing to stride over the gangplank to the shore followed by Leni. Cavalier waited until he was out of sight and then began to move fast, leaping up the steps. Halfway up he looked back. Amaz and Leni were not in sight. At the two hundredth step, Cavalier jumped off the stone fence and slid into a narrow crevasse. A few minutes later, he heard Amaz and Leni hurrying past. An out-of-breath Leni said,

'He'll be at the top cave . . . it runs fifty metres into the mountain . . . have you a torch . . . ?'

Amaz didn't reply. She was struggling. Like all weightlifters who did little aerobic work, such a climb was hard work. It was even worse for Leni, whose main exercise appeared to be lifting a glass or cigar to his lips. Even now, Cavalier could see Leni held a cigar, but when they stopped for a few minutes, he didn't have the energy to puff it.

When they continued the climb and had curved up out of sight, Cavalier jumped back to the steps and made his way down, slower this time. The steps were wet and slippery. He boarded 092 and joined a group drinking beer. He received glares from Hollos, who could not hide his concern. When Amaz and Leni had not returned after half an hour, Geoffreys was keen to continue on.

'They can take the cargo boat with Dubois,' he said when Hollos protested. Moments later, the two late-comers came onboard, looking distressed and furtive. Leni was holding his shoulder. He explained he had slipped on the way down and had hurt his collarbone.

'Could you have a look at him?' Geoffreys said to Cavalier.

'No,' Cavalier said bluntly. He paused and locked eyes with Hollos. He smiled and added, 'I am a doctor of literature. My wife is the doctor of medicine.'

Geoffreys and two of the women onboard helped strap Leni's shoulder. Hollos and Amaz then took him to the cargo boat where a heated discussion took place. Amaz rushed from the cargo boat, looking angry and nervous, and returned to the tourist boat.

The cargo boat started up and moved on. The tourist boat followed. After a half-hour, Cavalier moved over to where Amaz sat alone.

'Mind if I join you?' he said.

Amaz glared but said nothing.

'Your mates have taken off without you,' he observed. 'Will you be going on to Luang Prabang?'

Amaz stirred her coffee and looked around as if she would protest. Geoffreys was up the other end of the boat.

'Are you trying to intimidate me?' she asked, her stare steady.

'Are you planning to kill me?' Cavalier replied, his expression now cold.

'What?'

'I know you have a gun under that jacket. What is it? A small berretta?'

Amaz was stunned.

'No, I guess that would be a bit pussy for a big gal like you, eh? It might be something more brutal. A revolver that would put a big hole in someone, rather than a small one.'

He looked around. No one was paying attention.

'Maybe it looks a bit like mine,' he whispered, opening his jacket and giving her a glimpse of his handgun. 'So you'd better be a very accurate shot. Otherwise it will be your last.'

'You don't know what you are dealing with,' Amaz said in a hoarse whisper.

'Oh, yes I do,' he said. 'I know you killed an Australian on this trip four months ago. I don't know how you did it though.' He paused. 'Perhaps you'd like to tell me?'

Amaz's eyes widened. Fear had seeped into her expression. Mingled with her aggressive manner, it was unpredictable. Cavalier drew the gun from his jacket but kept it hidden.

'Don't move,' he said, his voice steady and quiet. 'I have every right to kill you. Right here. You followed me up the mountain with a view to kill me.' He paused and then added, 'Put your weapon on the table, very slowly.'

Amaz eased out her gun and placed it on the table between them. He picked it up with his left hand. In a deft movement, he tossed it into the river.

'Tell me how you killed that Australian agent,' he demanded. 'You should know that he worked for the CIA too.'

'You're mad! You're a racist to hold me like this.'

Cavalier looked surprised.

'Where did that come from? Mad, yes; racist, no. I always see people who label others, such as screaming "racist", as limited. Labelling is the first refuge of an idiot.'

Amaz looked at the cargo boat, which was a hundred metres away.

'They own you, don't they?' Cavalier said. 'They use you when they want you. You play along because the money is good. But you want out.'

He leaned back in the cubicle. Amaz was distressed, but her manner was less aggressive.

'They will pin the deaths of the agent on you,' he said, and waited to let his words seep in. Then he added,

'I guess it was fun taking drugs, drinking champagne, travelling everywhere, having sex. Then the murder happened.'

Amaz turned away.

'You can walk away from this,' Cavalier said. 'I'll make sure you get immunity if you inform on these . . .' He nodded in the direction of the distant cargo boat. '. . . criminals.' He grimaced as if a bright idea had come to him. 'No, I'll make it easier on you. You only have to tell us about Dubois and what he did. I know he murdered the Australian agent. I want to know what he did with the body.'

The boat chugged on. They both looked out in silence at the sheer cliff-faces either side of the river, broken in places with deep inlets, which opened to wooded valleys.

People came to the bar for coffee and soft drinks. They glanced at Amaz, who was looking sullen, and Cavalier who had put on sunglasses. The awkward silence was broken by Geoffreys who stood close and pointed to a manmade tunnel entrance that ended near the top of a cliff.

'See that?' he said to both of them. 'That's just the beginning of a through-the-mountain tunnel to bring Chinese to the Mekong by very fast rail.'

'Tourists?' Cavalier asked.

'Yes, but useful if they wanted to bring troops,' Geoffreys said with a chuckle. 'Just like everywhere else on the planet they are building silk roads and train tracks and creating protected sea lanes in the region.' He moved on to another cubicle.

'You'll get a minimum of thirty years jail in Australia,' Cavalier said to Amaz under his breath, 'maybe even the chair in the US. You don't kill CIA agents with impunity.'

After a few moments, she seethed under her breath,

'I didn't kill anyone!'

'It's irrelevant. You're an accomplice. There will be police and US agents in Luang Prabang. You will be apprehended.'

Tears welled in Amaz's eyes.

'I didn't kill anyone,' she repeated, choking back tears.

'I happen to believe you. Dubois is the real assassin. But I am the only person who will back up your story.' He paused and smiled. 'Better to keep me alive.'

Amaz sipped her coffee. It had gone cold. Cavalier slipped his gun into his jacket and made them both another cup.

'Where is he taking the cargo?' he asked.

Amaz seemed in two minds. She looked around.

'I'll support you,' he said. 'But you must give me the right information.'

'Chiang Mai,' she whispered.

'From Luang Prabang?'

Amaz nodded.

'There is a cleared area not far from the big waterfall about forty-five minutes' drive from the city. Light planes can land there. It's dangerous taking off with a load.'

'How much will the cargo weigh?'

'Maybe a ton. They may change the plans now that Leni is injured. He's the only one who can fly the plane.'

'What make?'

'Cessna. Twin engine.'

'It would not be big enough for the load.'

'It has been modified to take a big haul.'

'But not all of it. That was why you unloaded some of it earlier, right?'

'Yes. Leni always clips trees on the way out. The others are so drunk, they don't care. I'm sober. I wet myself.'

'So five of you—adding up to more than four hundred kilograms.'

'What are you saying?'

'Only a pilot should be onboard.'

Amaz shrugged but said nothing.

'Where's the airstrip?'

'It's hard to find.'

'Tell me.'

Amaz looked around.

'Draw me a map,' Cavalier said, pushing a pen and a sheet of paper from his notepad in front of her. She bit her lip.

'There is a village, Tao Boa, near the waterfall,' she whispered. 'You must find a track due west of it.'

'How far?'

'Half a kilometre, maybe.'

'Any signposts?'

'A water tank. It's a few hundred metres from the strip. There is a track due west. If you take the other track, you'll end up at the waterfall.'

'And the plane's destination is the main Chiang Mai airport?'

'No. There is a small airstrip about four hundred metres from it.'

'I know it. I've flown there myself. When will the plane be loaded?'

'Tonight. Well, maybe not, because Leni is injured. But they must have the shipment there by noon tomorrow.'

'I think you should escape.'

'How? They'll track me down and—'

'I have contacts who can help. Farquar and the others are marked men.'

Amaz's eyes welled again. Her bottom lip quivered, but she remained silent.

'Your choice,' Cavalier said, scribbling a number on his notepad and handing the page to her. 'That's my mobile number. If you change your mind, ring that.'

17

DRUG THIEF

Cavalier was first off the boat at Luang Prabang. He found a taxi. As he was placing his backpack in the trunk, he looked down to the shore and noticed a line of locals carrying unmarked white sacks on their backs from the cargo boat to a waiting truck. Hollos was organising things as Amaz walked up to him. They spoke for a moment. Then Hollos backhanded her across the face. She fell to the ground. When Amaz got back to her feet, Hollos grabbed her by the arm. Cavalier stood at the edge of a cliff feeling helpless. He took out his phone and slipped down the cliff to a rock outcropping. Half-hidden, he took several pictures of the truck being loaded.

Minutes later he tried to ring Wombat but the call failed. He sent a text instead.

> Plane load of product will land between 5 a.m. and noon tomorrow at
> Chiang Mai airport no. 2. Send Ian Gillman. Evidence they killed Deere.

Cavalier checked into the hotel at the town's waterfront on the Mekong and was pleased when his passport was not checked. There would be no record of him staying, just a booking, which he'd made under another false name. He did not want to be seen by Hollos and co. Cavalier rang the hotel at which Geoffreys and the tour group would be staying. The manager found Geoffreys in his room and took him down to a house phone.

'Is your cute gang of thugs staying with you?' Cavalier asked.

'No, at the Dortman. It's an upmarket hotel. Where are you?'

'In a non-descript place I've stayed in before.'

'Doctor, what's happening with that Amaz woman? She seemed upset about something.'

'It's the company she keeps.'

'I may try to buy Farquar out.

His thugs have been disgusting on this trip.'

'Good idea. Have you an idea of the contents of those bags?'

'It's black rice. You saw it at his plantation.'

'But he picked up a shipment of bags at the Thai–Lao border.'

'Farquar told me he had a load of produce there; probably bananas and coconuts. It's his side business. You've seen 0092 following us.'

'Are you sure it's just black rice and bananas?'

'I can't be certain. Maybe not all of it.' Geoffreys paused and asked,

'Are you joining the tour dinner tonight? We'll be dropping in on some of the key spots in this heart of Laotian culture.'

'I've seen it all. One of the region's most beautiful spots. Will the thugs be with you?'

'I doubt it. They're not culturally inclined beyond drinking and more drinking.'

'Then I may be there.'

***

At 11 p.m. Cavalier put on his rain jacket, placed his gun inside its zip pocket, hoisted on his backpack and left the hotel. There was almost a full moon above as he hailed a cab at the waterfront and directed the Lao driver to take him to the small village of Tao Boa about a kilometre short of the huge waterfall, one of Luang Prabang's biggest tourist attractions. Even though the driver understood Cavalier's Lanna Thai, he could not believe his passenger wished to be left out in the area. It was bushland, where the driver claimed there were wild animals.

'It's okay,' Cavalier said. 'I have plenty of water and food.'

The driver drove off shaking his head.

Helped by the strong moonlight, Cavalier took the track due west and passed the water tank as Amaz had indicated. He was near it when he heard the roar of a truck. He eased behind the tank until the truck was well past. Then he continued on in its wake as it growled its way towards the crude airstrip. He ducked behind trees. The truck's lights stayed on to reveal the Cessna and a short runway hemmed in by scrub and jungle. He noticed a hard structure a few metres from him. He eased to it and realised it was the shell of a plane's fuselage. Broken wings, still tangled in the trees and undergrowth, indicated it was the result of a failed attempt to land.

Cavalier watched until three men, rifles slung over their shoulders, and Amaz loaded the plane with about thirty sacks. Its back windows were opened to accommodate more of the load. Then the truck with two of the armed men bumped its way back to the track and was soon out of earshot. Amaz rolled out a sleeping bag on the ground. The remaining man lit a cigarette, rested his rifle on the ground and slumped against a plane wheel.

Amaz looked at her watch. It was 1.30 a.m.

'You have anything up to four hours before the others come,' Amaz said to the man. 'They won't take off in the dark. Too dangerous.'

'*Mao, Mao!*' the guard said.

'What? Oh, yes, they'll be very drunk, except for the pilot.'

The guard laughed.

'*Sa Mao!*' the guard said, and then produced some Laotian whisky. He offered the bottle to Amaz, who refused it. He took a hefty swing and offered it again.

'No, thank you,' Amaz said.

It seemed the Lao guard was intent on finishing the bottle.

'Don't fall asleep!' Amaz said and made a sleeping action with her hands and head.

The guard laughed and then fell over as he tried to stand. When he was on his feet, he stumbled behind the plane to urinate.

Cavalier broke out of the bush and took the rifle.

'Keys,' he demanded of Amaz.

'Don't try to fly it in the dark,' she warned. 'There's a crashed plane back there ...'

'Saw it.'

The guard returned. He put his hands up when he saw Cavalier brandishing a handgun at him.

'Tie him up,' Cavalier ordered Amaz.

'What are you going to do?' she asked. 'The others will be here—'

'Before dawn,' he said, indicating that the guard lie on his front. Cavalier supervised the tying.

'You have a choice,' Cavalier said as slung his backpack into the cockpit. 'Come with me or stay with the gang.'

'You won't fly this thing out of here!' Amaz insisted.

Cavalier seemed oblivious of the warning. He hauled out a sack and, using a pocketknife, slit it open. Black rice sprayed on the ground. He burrowed his hands deep into the sack and pulled out small white bags. Cavalier slit open one. He put the white powder to his lips. He glanced around at Amaz.

'Heroin,' he said.

Cavalier circled the plane.

'Too heavy,' he mumbled. 'If you come, I'll throw out three more bags.'

'I'm not going in that thing at night. Are you a pilot?'

Cavalier ignored her.

'There is a steep cliff after those trees. Even if you clear them, you won't have the power—'

'Suit yourself,' he said. 'But I'll say it once more. Leave that pack of hyenas for good. You'll only end up in big trouble if you don't.'

Cavalier dragged the guard well clear of the plane and ordered Amaz to walk with him the length of the runway to the clump of trees. They pushed through the undergrowth.

'See that!' she said pointing to a rocky valley below, discernible in the moonlight. 'It's a drop of maybe seventy metres.'

Cavalier stroked his chin as he led her back to the plane.

'It's a good night for flying,' he said, shaking her hand. Amaz stood well back from the plane, too much in shock to say anything. He climbed into the cockpit. There were maps in a glove box. The route to Chiang Mai was marked. He checked the tank's fuel tank. It was full.

He started the engine and put his foot on the accelerator. The plane did not move at first but churned up dirt and mud beneath it. Cavalier put his foot down hard, the over-burdened machine jumped then rumbled forward. Cavalier built speed on the short strip. He began to ease the joystick. The plane lifted about a metre, then slumped back to the rough ground. Cavalier built more speed, urging the plane to lift. It would not respond. Seventy metres short of the tree, he jammed on the brake causing the plane to shudder, slide, tilt and almost tip over. It stalled.

Cavalier tried to start it again several times. The engine was flooded. He waited and looked back at the other two. The guard was still prone on the ground. Amaz was standing, waving. Cavalier jumped back in, started the plane and backed it up to her. He alighted again and asked her to help clear debris in the jungle so that he could have another ten metres of runway.

Cavalier did some quick calculations about the weight he thought the plane could manage. He reckoned he needed to dump eight bags, leaving 21 on the plane. He tossed out the surplus. With Amaz's help he pushed the plane as far back as he dared, checked it was not jammed in the undergrowth, and climbed back in.

'There will be room next to me,' Cavalier said above the engine's roar. Amaz hesitated. She began to cry but couldn't bring herself to respond. He turned off the engine and beckoned her to the cockpit window.

'I'll say you helped me escape,' he said. 'You'd have to give evidence against the others.'

'No,' she blubbered. 'They'd track and kill me. I know them. Killing is their business.'

Cavalier jumped from the cockpit and tried to calm her down.

'It's okay. I am an experienced flyer.'

She hesitated, and then began walking to the plane.

Just then a truck rolled up. Cavalier could see Dubois behind the wheel and Castro, Leni and Hollos singing in the cab. Dubois was first to see what was happening and took out a revolver and ran towards the plane. He shot Amaz in the head. She fell back to the ground, motionless. Cavalier dashed for the cockpit. Dubois fired again, catching him in the side as he slid into the seat. Cavalier pulled out his gun and fired, causing Dubois to run for shelter behind a tree. Cavalier started the engine with his right hand and fired again with his left, forcing Dubois to remain behind cover.

Cavalier manoeuvred the machine. He heard shots being fired and the bullets pinging against the fuselage. He waited until the plane seemed to have momentum before he began the lift, which had to be much sharper than any pilot would like. The plane swerved, bounced and was airborne. Cavalier struggled with the joystick.

'Lift, you darling! Lift, you bloody beast!' he yelled. The plane obeyed but not before the wheels clipped the treetops. The Cessna wobbled clear, as if uncertain whether to crash into the ravine or continue straight. It dipped a stomach-churning twenty metres into the ravine, then lifted and held its line so that it was clear of the opposite cliff-face one hundred metres away. Yet it was still listing to starboard close to the magnificent waterfall.

Cavalier was forced to fly too low over it. He was in no mood to take in the cascading natural beauty which sparkled in the strong moonlight. He kept struggling with the controls until he steadied the reluctant machine.

Cavalier's adrenaline subsided. He noticed that blood was seeping into his clothes. He became more conscious of the pain of the bullet six inches below his heart but to the side of his torso. He pulled out some towels from his bag and wrapped them around the area he had been hit. With the plane on auto-pilot, he scrambled for the first-aid kit that he always carried and bandaged the wound.

He sent another text to Wombat.

Wombat. Am travelling with a ton of stuff to Chiang Mai. Have been shot in the side. Losing blood. Have ambulance ready at Chiang Mai airport.

18

A HOSTILE RECEPTION

The 351-kilometre flight to Chiang Mai took three hours and thirty-one minutes in the Cessna, which performed well in the, at times, rough weather. Cavalier's main worry was the bullet wound. He had been able to limit the bleeding yet some dribbled down his stomach and legs and into his sneakers. He had to fight not falling asleep but managed to keep alert by flying off the instruments when he reached a heavy bank of cloud over Chiang Rai.

Once through that, it was plain sailing over mountains leading down to Chiang Mai. He flew in low, took note of the airstrip, circled and flew higher to make the landing. The Cessna glided in with a mild crosswind causing a wobble as it bounced along the grass runway. Cavalier drove the plane to a corner of the small airfield, switched it off and sat in silence for a moment. There were the sounds of cars in the distance. The main airport was closed with one light covering a small part of the field. Planes sat like large toys in the distance.

Cavalier looked around. There were three small planes parked nearby, one of them half in a hangar. He tried to ring Wombat in Melbourne. This time he got through. The line was bad.

'I've landed in CM with a load. It's heroin.'

'Jesus! How did you do that?'

'Long story. Is Ian Gillman coming? Has he got an ambulance?'

'I emailed him. Couldn't reach him on the phone. I did organise an ambulance.'

'I can't see one. It's not yet 6 a.m. here. I need to be at a hospital. Tell him to do what he wants with the plane and load. There's about a ton of the drug. Sorry to wake you.'

Cavalier rang off, put the phone in his backpack and eased out of the plane. The pain was worse than ever. Every extra movement caused blood to seep. He began to limp away when a jeep, lights on high beam, began speeding towards him. Cavalier stopped. A bullet whistled past. He ducked for cover behind the plane when a second bullet brought up dust near him. A third hit Cavalier on the side of the head. He was slammed against the plane and knocked out.

Three CIA operatives, led by 40-year-old veteran agent Ian Gillman, approached in the jeep, unsure if their quarry was hit or foxing. They rolled forward until they were fifty metres from the plane. The three agents jumped from the vehicle and crept to the plane from different angles.

'He's down,' Gillman said, as he holstered his revolver. The three men examined their victim.

'Jesus H Christ!' Gillman said, 'It's the guy we're supposed to help!'

They tried to prop up Cavalier. 'Lift him into the jeep and take him to the hospital on Changklan Road. Fast!'

'Shit!' one of the agents said, opening Cavalier's jacket. 'He's lost a lot of blood.'

***

At 8 a.m. Wombat was in phone contact with Gillman.

'Your email said something about a drug haul and the guys that murdered our guy,' Gillman said, confused.

'Do you know how to scroll an email?'

'Yeah.'

'I sent you the entire exchange! I said at the top that our wounded man was onboard but you just went in all guns blazing!' Wombat was fuming. 'If our man dies, you're in big trouble.'

At about the same time in Chiang Rai, Pin was told that her ex-husband was in a critical condition with 'bullet wounds to the head and side'. She jumped in her car and motored to Chiang Mai, arriving two hours later at the Central Chiang Mai Memorial Hospital on the Changklan Road, a mustard-coloured, colonial-style hotel.

Pin burst into the operating theatre to see Cavalier lying unconscious on an operating table. A saline drip and blood transfusion tube were attached to him.

She composed herself and asked for a report from the medico in charge.

'The head wound is minor and we've already stitched it up; and he was concussed,' the young Thai doctor said. 'The other bullet wound in the abdomen is the issue. We need your permission to operate. He may have internal injuries. Can't tell unless we open him up. Are you next of kin?'

'No. I'm his ex-wife.'

'We need permission.'

Pin took a deep breath.

'Cut into him,' she said, the pragmatic, professional side taking charge over her emotions. For the moment, her former partner, the father of her children, was just another human on a slab to be saved, if possible.

'What are his chances?' Pin asked.

'Fifty-fifty.'

Pin looked despondent. Seeing Cavalier lying there, helpless and his life slipping from him, she was touched. She admitted to herself that he had been a devoted, if an often absent, father and a good husband. Her trust in him had slipped since she became suspicious of his activity on missions, which he alleged were journalistic. But he had been evasive rather than lie to her. On everything else apart from his secret work, he had been trustworthy.

Pin stayed at the Chiang Mai hospital until after the operation, in which bullet fragments were removed from several points in Cavalier's lower abdomen. The doctors had removed his spleen and saved his pancreas.

At midday, the chief medico took her aside.

'Are you a religious person, Doctor?' he asked.

'Spiritual. I am a practising Buddhist.'

'Then it may be best to pray to the Buddha.'

Later at night, when alone, she prayed to her spiritual doll Serena. At midnight Pin drove from her hotel on the river to the hospital for the second time to check on Cavalier. He was in a coma, his condition still precarious. The next morning she rang the hospital. His condition had slipped during the early hours.

In desperation, Pin contacted an acquaintance, a 33-year-old Burmese deaf near-mute named Swe Win, who lived outside Yangon City. The disabled psychic was nicknamed ET, because she looked like the extra-terrestrial in the movie. She was a respected soothsayer whom many prominent people—from generals and film stars to prime ministers and presidents—went to see for guidance. Pin didn't want guidance, just comprehension of whether the future would be with or without her ex-husband.

Pin rang ET and spoke to her sister who always asked the questions of the client, and took the sign-language responses from her famous sister.

'We must be brief,' the sister said, 'she is not well herself. In fact, very sick. But she will answer what she can. She regards you as a friend.'

'I am very sorry to hear she is ill,' Pin said. 'Is there anything I can do?'

'No, she has not long.'

The sister consulted ET.

'She does not see death for him,' ET's sister said, 'but she does see death all around him.'

Pin was shocked.

'What does that mean?' she asked, losing her composure.

There was a longer than normal 'chat' with ET before her sister said,

'You have consulted my sister before, decades ago, about Victor. She told you that he is a good man. That is constant. You can trust him. But his life and work deals with death.'

'As a journalist?' Pin asked, perplexed and concerned.

'Whatever his work is, death lurks with him.'

'Could you expound, ET?'

The comment came back to Pin,

'She sees an avenging angel.'

Pin was stunned. ET refused to elaborate.

Pin was both comforted and discomforted by ET's words. The remarks were definitive yet mystifying.

Pin took a taxi to the hospital. Cavalier was conscious. His speech was incoherent. He did not recognise his former wife.

'It does not mean a good or bad recovery,' the doctor handling Cavalier remarked. 'The loss of blood and the severe concussion means his brain is scrambled.'

'Could it be permanent?'

'I can't say.'

'I've seen such cases. Most recover but some never do.'

'One thing in his favour is his physical shape. I've never seen a man of his age like him. Very strong heart. Exceptional lung capacity.'

'I did medical research on his body at thirty,' Pin said. 'His heart is an abnormal size, more like a horse's. And the lung volume is off the charts.'

'It's more than just excellent genes, though, isn't it? I've never seen a more muscular abdomen wall than his. It's like a brick, even though the bullet fragments pierced it.'

'He did gym workouts and ran daily.'

'One thing,' the doctor said, 'he has a scar not far north of this bullet entry. How did he get that?'

'Don't know. We haven't been together for eight years.'

The doctor tugged his ear, frowning.

'What?' Pin inquired.

'There is scar tissue in the abdomen wall. I don't think it's more than a few years old.'

Pin frowned, embarrassed that this was another secret Cavalier had kept from her.

Over the next three days, Cavalier's speech returned. He had no memory of the flight from Luang Prabang or the shooting incident.

He had trouble even recalling the Mekong River trip.

'Probably a good thing,' Pin mumbled to him as she thought of the blow-up between them. She always regretted her behaviour but because Cavalier rolled with the abuse and anger, she didn't feel the need to apologise.

Cavalier did not recognise their daughter Pon when she made a tearful visit to the hospital. She was so emotional that Pin and the other doctors were not sure that she should make further visits. But Pon insisted on staying with friends in Chiang Mai so that she could be with her father every day.

***

Pin rang Cavalier's good friend Wombat. She had never quite understood the relationship between this man and her husband, but she knew there was a strong bond between them.

'That Shaman who saved my daughter,' she said to Wombat, 'can I contact him? I want him to help Victor.'

'Al Haut? He already knows about him. He "prayed into it".'

'And?'

'He knows Victor is out of a coma and on the mend. He told me he had not seen him in the spiritual. He said Victor had not "crossed over" and won't. God, he claims, made that decision some time ago.'

After a week of daily visits by Pon, Cavalier recognised his daughter. They embraced and both were moved to tears. During the second week, his step-daughter Far, now thirty-seven, flew in from New York to be by his side. Far, much to Cavalier's pleasure, had become a doctor and married an American heart specialist. His two daughters' presence brought him great comfort.

After a fortnight there was an improvement.

'I think he is going to make a fair recovery,' the main doctor in the Chiang Mai medical team told the family.

19

THE RECOVERY

Cavalier concentrated on his rehab. The wound on the side of his head left him with a scar which was mainly covered by hair. The abdominal injury was more problematic but even by the end of the hospital stay he started walking a few kilometres with Pon, who had stayed in Chiang Mai to help in any way she could. Three weeks after leaving the recovery ward, they both did a three-kilometre jog along the River Ping. His gut hurt with every stride.

Pon thought of telling him he should take it easy and wait a few months before commencing any strenuous exercise. But aware of his determination, she joined him for every session, which was therapy for her too.

Within weeks they were jogging four kilometres. After six weeks they were up to a slow jog over his usual ten K, and swimming every day at the pool in his condo. He began adding a forty-minute exercise route for all body muscles, with a cautious start of sit-ups and press-ups. At this point Pon decided to return to Chiang Rai to be with her mother.

'I can't thank you enough,' Cavalier told her at the bus station. 'You have helped save me!'

'Least I could do after what you did for me,' Pon said. 'I've been piecing it together, as much as my enfeebled but improving mind will allow me. Mother has told me how you never stopped searching for me. That you took a risky trip to Mexico; that you must have had something to do with my rescue from the Bangkok Express.'

Pon paused and looked into her father's eyes. He avoided saying anything by hugging her.

'You are not going to tell me, are you?' she said.

'The main thing is that we are both recovering well,' Cavalier said. 'One day I may talk about it. At the moment, it is better that you don't know.'

'And Far, you helped her too, didn't you?'

'That was a long time ago, darling.'

'She and I have discussed it often. Someone killed her father, who had brutalised her, mother and our grandmother. Forgive me, but we wondered if—'

'Not worth discussing,' Cavalier said, cutting her off gently. 'I read the coroner's report. So did your mother. Murder was ruled out. "Death by misadventure was the verdict."'

'Just like that of Mendez on the train?'

Cavalier said nothing as the bus prepared to leave.

'I still don't know what happened to him but I am so, so very glad he is dead,' Pon said.

Cavalier waved as she boarded the bus and took a seat. She was crying but smiled when he blew her a kiss.

***

Cavalier's next move was to practise his firing skills with both handgun and a rifle. His first session at a local range was tougher than he imagined and had him wincing with every rifle shot. For the first time since he began used a gun at eleven years of age while duck-shooting with his father in the Australian bush, he was well off target. Even his actions with a handgun caused pain in his injured side. It crossed his mind that his clandestine profession could be untenable. His accuracy from all ranges and angles was his greatest asset. Killing was a business of centimetre-perfect precision. Cavalier's confidence was down but his plan was to build up his fitness, concentrating on his core strength.

***

When well enough to fly, he returned to Australia and met with Wombat at the lounge in the Lindrum Hotel on Melbourne's Flinders Street. Wombat was spending so much time away from his home in Mandurah, Western Australia, that he was considering buying an apartment in Melbourne. In the meantime, he based himself as usual at the Lindrum.

During a billiards game, Cavalier said, 'The paper that commissioned my article is still waiting for the story on the Mekong River trip.' He paused to line up a ball. Without looking up at Wombat, he pocketed three shots and added, 'The editor wants to know if the piece should appear in the travel section or something else.'

They both smiled wryly.

'Best in the travel section,' Wombat said.

'The editor thinks there must be a link to me being "sick" and the trip.'

'What did you tell her?'

'I said it was a stomach virus, a serious one.'

'She bought that?'

'I was laid up in Thailand, remember, not here.'

'She didn't notice your head scar?'

'My hair covers it.'

They finished their billiards game and sat on leather chairs well away from others and ordered whiskies on the rocks.

'What happened to the heroin?' Cavalier asked.

'Big Brother confiscated the plane and the haul. Claimed that it was all in connection with the death of our agent Deere, who worked for it too, and the US's DEA efforts to tackle the illegal drug trade. The Thai government didn't agree at first, but some incentives were given to the right officials. The Americans impounded the plane in Chiang Mai. I don't know what happened to the heroin.'

Wombat paused to take a shot, then said,

'Our job in this case is to deal with Deere's killers.'

'Has Big Brother done anything towards that yet?'

'No. After you were incapacitated and we couldn't extract any sense from you for a month—' Wombat began with a laugh.

'I was half-dead!'

'Nine-tenths, more like it. Hollos, Castro, Leni and Dubois disappeared. Farquar has an alibi. He was in Hobart when Deere was dealt with. We think Hollos, Castro and Leni are on Conquer oil rigs in Nigeria now. When they're not drug smuggling or assassinating, they love their work as riggers.'

'You can't arrest them?'

'Easier said than done. First, they are difficult to find. Second, your taped evidence is helpful, but it only *implicates* Dubois. We'd need more evidence to extradite him from wherever he is and charge him.'

'And Amaz? Dubois shot her when I was taking off in the plane. I think she was dead.'

'Not pretty. Big Brother has forensic people there now looking at a torso found in the waterfall. No head, no arms, no legs. No ID.' Wombat noticed Cavalier's sad look. 'She was their whore, wasn't she?'

'She was trapped into that and working for them.'

'You said you gave her the option to fly out of Laos with you.'

'She feared they would kill her.'

'I'm sure Big Brother would pay a fair whack on top of the reward if you were to track Dubois. Apparently, our man Deere was doing special work for your friend and mine, the delightful Melody Smith.'

'I take it "track" is a euphemism for something else. I've already tracked them.'

'True, true. I mention it because well . . .' Wombat hesitated.

'C'mon, Wombat, spill it.'

'You've always knocked back so many opportunities. Don't you think it's time you put aside your, with respect, high-minded principles to cash in on your exceptional skills? You did on the Bangkok Express assignment.'

'I was not actually a hired gun. I was on that project regardless of help.'

'But you did take the money.'

'I did. But I don't intend to make it a habit. Then the work has no meaning.'

'Big Brother would love you to help find Dubois, who they want for several murders, including three more of their agents. They think he is lying low in Myanmar, Thailand or Cambodia.'

'Forget it.'

'You know Melody is about to be appointed deputy CIA director. Apparently Potus loves her. She is in the new breed that have been moved in while the old deep staters are moved out.'

'She is a very good choice. But I prefer to work alone.'

'I'm sure she would pay big-time again.'

'That makes me a hired gun. Not on.'

'So you're not interested in me talking to Big Brother about you helping deal with Hollos, Leni, Castro and Dubois?'

'No.'

'Sweet Melody wants to team up with ASIS to square off for Deere's death,' Wombat said. 'I think you could ask for a million a hit, plus the reward.' He paused to stare at his companion. Cavalier did not react. 'That'd be five or six million US.'

'I've already said I'm not interested.'

'Christ, Victor! You'd be a serious multi-millionaire!'

'Without a soul!'

'Yes, an *arse*-soul, for sure. But a very rich one!' Wombat paused to swirl the ice in his glass. 'You don't even wish to avenge the death of our man Deere? And the girl Amaz?'

'Tracing the killers would take years. That means I'd be drawn into dealing with the agencies. I won't do it. I didn't really need Melody on the Bangkok Express. I wouldn't want to be dependent on her or anyone else.'

'Is that because those agents shot you at Chiang Mai airport?'

'No. But it does illustrate the problem of reliance on others, who let you down, even if accidentally.'

They paused again to watch the game near them.

'If I had your skills,' Wombat mumbled, 'I'd do it myself, for that money.'

'As Al Haut says often: "Get thee behind me, Satan."'

***

They had a second game of billiards before sitting down to chat more over coffee.

'I see your eye is still "in",' Wombat remarked obliquely.

'If you're asking me about my other sporting "capacities",' Cavalier said, 'they're fine.'

'So you've not given up on the other, entirely?'

'Never say, never.'

'I'm sorry the Laos assignment ended the way it did.'

'My fault, not yours. Once I had the information you needed, and I wanted for an article, I could have walked away. Depriving that nasty little gang of returns from their drug running was too tempting, especially as they were using a plane I could fly.'

'Risk-taking is in your blood, Vic.'

'And I lost a lot of it.'

Wombat took an envelope from a jacket pocket.

'We have something else you may be interested in, journalism-wise,' he said. 'You recall Ivan "the Terrible" Serov?'

'You mean the ex-KGB and later GRU Chief?'

'You wrote a bit about him in the early 1990s when you interviewed KGB master spy Yuri Modin.'

'Serov was Modin's boss. Modin hated him.'

'Well, gorgeous Ivan's diaries have been found.'

'Oh?'

'Apparently when the Russian intelligence services dumped him, he cemented the diaries into the wall of the garage at his Moscow dacha way back in 1971.'

'As you do.'

'His granddaughter discovered them when she was having the

garage demolished. Some of the diaries were published in Russian in an obscure military museum. The Russian government has since stopped the publication, but not before our friends at MI6 obtained a copy. It has a complete translation. They'd make interesting reading, don't you think?'

'Very.'

'We can get you access, if you wish to see them.'

'Of course I would. Remember, I'm freelance now. Have to grab the big stories where I can. Do you know of anything juicy in the diaries?'

'We believe he has said that the French third Baron Bleulance was a KGB agent.'

'Bleulance? His son is the fourth baron who has a controlling interest in Conquer, which is Al Haut's nemesis.' Cavalier paused and added, 'I can feel a trip to London coming on.'

PART THREE

VISION FOES

20

THE FOUR BARON BLEULANCE

Cavalier flew to London, booked into a serviced apartment close to Notting Hill Gate and a day later took public transport to MI6's headquarters on the Thames. He had access because of his long links to a senior MI6 operative and the added recommendation of ASIS. Yet he still underwent a thorough search and was ushered through a metal detector. His phone and notebook computer were removed.

Cavalier had a quick debriefing from archivists who quizzed him about his intentions. He was joined by his best British Intelligence contact, Liam Hunter, a lean fifty-year-old former London squash champion. He had been born and educated in Sydney but had moved into British Intelligence after graduating with an Arts Honours degree in languages: Russian, Mandarin and Arabic. Hunter was a dapper dresser, which was his rebellious act within the staid intelligence world, which abhorred any form of showiness, it was said, because people in their employ should stay grey, unmemorable and anonymous. Hunter's manner seemed introverted and secretive, befitting his position. But his youthful background as an extroverted Australian with a love of surfing had never left him. It was always refreshing for him to chat with Cavalier with whom he opened up.

Hunter disappeared after introducing Cavalier to a tall, black librarian calling herself Emma. He learnt in their brief conversation that she had a double degree from Cambridge in languages.

Emma told him of the rules,

'You must not photograph anything,' she said, 'but you may make notes, only with pencil and paper we supply.'

She brought him a file marked 'Strictly confidential' and reminded him that the information must not be used for any media or publishing purposes. He was asked to sign a declaration to that effect. Emma then led him to a reading room. He noted cameras.

Cavalier spent the best part of the next three days reading Serov's translated diaries and taking notes. On ten occasions he asked Emma for clarification of the original Russian, which was also given to him in a folder.

The entries were clear about the third Baron Bleulance. He had worked extensively for the French Underground and British Intelligence during the war, when he had also sent valuable information to the KGB via his good, French-speaking Francophile English friend, Sir Anthony Blunt, the 'Fourth Man' in the Russian-controlled Cambridge University spy ring.

The third baron had died thirty years ago, but his son, the fourth Baron (Jacques) Bleulance was alive and well, and living part of the time in his chateau at Berry, two hundred kilometres due south of Paris. Some cursory research in London discovered that Jacques hated his father, which meant he just might open up a little about him.

A *Sunday Times* business journalist told Cavalier:

'The third baron in the mid-1970s eased into Bleulance Credit Internationale, pushed his son, the fourth baron, out, and replaced him with his son's French cousin. This riled the fourth baron. He set up his own Paris-based merchant banking operation, which has been a monumental success. In the last decade he has gobbled up as much of the world's energy operations as possible, especially oil.'

Cavalier, trying a long shot, found the fourth baron's phone number. Using his guise as Dr Edwin Harris, Cavalier rang him on the pretence that he wished to write a feature on his art acquisitions for the British magazine *Food, Art, and Antiquity*.

It helped that Cavalier spoke fluent French and had more than a passing interest in many forms of art from paintings to porcelain. Bleulance agreed to the interview. Cavalier then contacted the magazine, which was only too happy to accept his freelance piece on someone, the editor claimed, he had been trying to meet for twenty years.

'You do realise that the fourth baron has a twenty-five per cent stake in us?' the editor asked.

'Of course,' Cavalier said, although he'd had no idea.

'Just be kind to him, please,' the editor said.

***

Cavalier flew to Paris and hired a Harley, similar to his motorbike in Chiang Mai, and made the 200-kilometre ride to the Bleulance's property near the town of Chateauroux. Despite the chilling February weather, which made the roads slippery, it took him just under ninety minutes and earned him a speeding ticket en route. From a distance of five kilometres he could see the tops of the chateau, a stunning 300-year-old building, and glimpses of snow-covered high ground behind it.

He sped round a tight bend in the road. There in front of him was, if not Versailles, then a zany, brilliant version of it in the form of a fantasy chateau, all turrets, curlicues and grey pointy spires. It was bit of a French castle here, a touch of Byzantine Istanbul mosque there, and a delicious, large wedding cake overall.

Cavalier had done his usual meticulous preparation, noting that this castle-like structure with the imaginative name of Napoleon V, had been given to the French National Trust post World War II (after the Nazis had pillaged the property), in a slick buyback arrangement, in which the Bleulances ran it for the trust as a foundation.

Cavalier looked up at the blue sky, interspersed with threatening white cloud, as he alighted from his bike. He decided he should put a weather-proof cover on it. There had been a snow before dawn and he had an unhealthy suspicion of French weather from his many visits to the country. Just as he was fastening the cover, a butler in pinstripes, waistcoat and tails bounced down the front steps of the chateau, and thrust out his hand.

'I'm James,' he said in French, 'the baron is waiting for you in the dining room.'

Cavalier was ushered into a vast pavilion-style room, festooned with works of art from statuettes to busts; from paintings to pastels. Long coffee tables were piled with books on art, food, antiques and a smattering of war history. Several copies of *Food, Art and Antiquity* were conspicuous. Exquisite flower arrangements gave the room a delicate freshness.

Tall, thin Jacques Bleulance uncurled himself from a soft beige sofa, dropped reading glasses to his chest, and placed some papers on a small table. His movements were languid, no rush to ingratiate. In tweed jacket, dark green turtleneck jumper, brown corduroy trousers and black shoes, the baron took a pace forward. His attire made him look like a French country squire who had never farmed in his life. His handshake was wet-fish, perfunctory and brief. His long oval face ended in disappearing thin folds rather than a chin. Yet the face was anything but weak. His high forehead would have still looked intelligent if he had a full head of hair. The eyes were eagle-like under hooded arches.

Bleulance's family were part of France's nouveau riche who had cashed in after the French Revolution with trade and land deals. They aped their ancient predecessors of the French elite in habitation and dress, but underneath a gentrified façade they were the modern thrusters, the accumulators of massive wealth, never flaunted with flash cars in public, yet instead on show in the form of 'tasteful' art: Rodins, Matisses; or exquisite, rare porcelain, each piece worth much more than any Lamborghini.

The diverting look was deceptive. When Bleulance did lock eyes it was with force. It registered 'You would never be here to mess with me, would you?' while still maintaining a hint of charm, albeit a keep-your-distance non-embrace.

Cavalier turned and moved close to a portrait of Bleulance.

'A very good likeness,' Cavalier said, folding his arms and stroking his chin.

'I thought I looked awful and old when I first saw it,' Bleulance said. 'But I'm told that as I grow into the look with age, I might well appreciate it.'

Cavalier nodded and smiled.

'Of course, it's a Freud,' Bleulance said.

'Lucien or Sigmund?' Cavalier asked, poker-faced.

Bleulance was about to respond, but checked himself when he noticed Cavalier's expression change to a grin.

James announced that lunch was served, swivelled around and disappeared. Bleulance led Cavalier to a four-metre diameter circular table covered with a white, embroidered cloth. It was weighed down with silverware, candles, odd assortments of cigar and cigarette boxes, and a staggered book pile. Cavalier examined the spines of a couple, all French editions. He picked up one titled *Celeste*.

'Ah, the biography of Celeste Venard,' Cavalier said, opening the book and flicking through pages. 'She married a count from this region, I recall.'

'The Count de Chabrillan,' a surprised Bleulance said. 'Have you read it?'

'Excellent book,' Cavalier replied with a nod. 'She out-sold her mentor and lover Alexander Dumas Sr with a number-one seller, in about 1858: *Voleur D'or*.'

Bleulance's eyebrows went up as if impressed. He noticed Cavalier glancing up at a massive white chandelier.

'That's a Giacometti,' Bleulance noted, unable to rid himself of patronising his 'English' guest. It was his way of stamping his superior knowledge of all expensive artefacts.

Cavalier balanced on tiptoe for a better look.

'Not Alberto, must be Diego,' he said.

Bleulance was surprised again.

'Yes, it's Diego. You like his work?'

'No,' Cavalier said, with a frown, 'too ornate for my tastes. Besides, I'd worry it might fall on the table. So heavy!'

'All the chandeliers in my house are by him,' Bleulance said, a tad miffed by Cavalier's remark.

'I prefer Alberto,' Cavalier said, turning and nodding to a reclining dog statuette. 'More integrity.'

'Oh, yes,' Bleulance said, a short spasm of enthusiasm seizing him, 'I just adore Alberto's work. A genius!'

Help-yourself serving dishes were spread on an antique sideboard. Entrées of salmon, fennel, avocado and orange were in one bowl; pork belly, miso, red cabbage, sesame and grapes in another. The variety of food had an enticing aroma and had Cavalier salivating. He took the salmon; Bleulance, the pork belly.

They sat opposite each other. James appeared and poured them both a crimson Bordeaux. Bleulance made great play of sniffing, swirling and swallowing some of the seductive liquid.

'I hope you like it,' Cavalier said, deadpan. 'Embarrassing if you send it back.'

Bleulance pretended to ignore the flippant remark. James smirked and said,

'We have twenty-five thousand bottles of all vintages and labels in the cellar, sir.' This drew a frown of disapproval from his master.

'You must have fun down there, then,' Cavalier said. James stifled a smile. 'I meant counting them. Or playing spin the bottle, perhaps?'

James made himself scarce, while Cavalier took a sip and gave it the thumbs up.

'Tell me, Dr Harris,' Bleulance said, 'what are you intending to write about me?'

'The truth, Baron,' Cavalier said.

'Always a noble cause. Always.'

'I confess I would like to discuss your father as well. Just to make the piece topical.'

'Oh?'

'Are you agreeable?'

'It depends.'

'There is now evidence that he spied for the KGB during World War II when in exile in England, and afterwards.'

Bleulance looked away, pulled a slight face, and asked,

'You mean the Serov diaries?'

'You've heard about them?'

'There was speculation in a French paper.'

'I've read the translated diaries.'

'Translated by whom? The Russians or the British?'

'The British had access to the original diaries.'

'Hmm,' Bleulance said, swirling the wine so it glistened under the chandelier umbrella. He seemed unperturbed. 'I trust neither of them.'

'I believe they are authentic. I was wondering what you thought, Baron.'

'Oh, good heavens! I know little about the espionage world. I have not a jot of interest in it.'

'You had no inkling that your father may have been a double agent?'

'We were not close. My mother left him for a Spanish painter and I regarded him as my father figure.'

'You were never aware of your father's proximity to Sir Anthony Blunt, the art curator and buyer for King George VI and Queen Elizabeth?'

'Blunt came to our home on occasions,' Bleulance said. 'He never related to me at all. I did go to a lecture of his at London's Courtauld Institute. Never spoke to him.' Bleulance brightened a fraction. 'I am now a benefactor there.'

There was a longish pause before Bleulance asked if the food were to Cavalier's liking. He smiled and nodded.

'I was more thinking about your instincts about your father,' Cavalier said. 'Sons are pretty good at observing their fathers' behaviour and foibles over time.'

'And your father, Dr Harris? What was his profession?'

'He was a master surgeon. Cut his teeth, so to speak, and plenty of POW limbs on the Thai–Burma railway in the war.'

Bleulance nodded and raised his eyebrows enough to show vague interest.

'Did you trust your father?' Cavalier asked.

Bleulance took a deep breath. He stared at an antique French clock on the table.

'You know the rules?' he asked, glancing back. 'First you must forgive me for thinking you might be here under false pretences. . .'

'I seek impressions. No quotes from you, I assure you.'

Bleulance blinked, picked at his food and said,

'You asked about trust. My father was a brilliant man, a polymath with interests in so many fields. But part of his life was in the shadows.'

'In intelligence?'

'For some time, yes.'

'He worked for the French Intelligence, the DGSE.'

'You must understand that I was with my mother when my parents separated. As I said, I had a stepfather, an artistic man who painted and wrote music. He had more influence over me.'

'And the trust?'

'My father was difficult to become close to. I never knew where he was; what he was thinking. For that reason I could not trust him. I did, however, admire him for what he did against the Nazis.'

'He double-crossed you and chose your cousin to run the Bleulance Bank, did he not?'

'I don't want to discuss that. I left the bank to run my own race.'

Bleulance broke off to help himself to a main course. He chose duck breast and beetroot; Cavalier took a potato gnocchi, with pumpkin and spinach. James hovered, filling wineglasses.

'For the purposes of your magazine article, please note that all the food is from the estate,' Bleulance said, 'wonderful produce.'

Cavalier nodded. When they sat down again, he took notes and then tried another tack.

'Many people have broken away from a parent to show them what they could do,' Cavalier began. 'Were you doing that with the third baron?'

'Let's just say that I considered my chances better by striking out on my own.'

'And that has worked so well,' Cavalier said, opening his hands and looking around at the salubrious pavilion and its artefacts. 'My research suggests that you are one of the richest men on the planet. Is that true?'

'Oh, come, come, Doctor. Don't believe all you read in the papers.'

'I don't rely on the papers or any of the media,' Cavalier said, staring. 'But I am reliably informed you are worth many hundreds of billions.'

'All speculation. I don't even know myself.'

'I discovered your investment companies have bought into at least twenty of the world's top twenty-five corporations.'

Bleulance smiled. Underneath the cool French stonewall of an impression, Cavalier detected a vacillation, somewhere between pride and caution.

'You have a big slice of Conquer, a large share of Shell and pieces of the other three oil sisters.'

'I have to tell you,' Bleulance said, 'I have people who work all these things out.'

'But you sign off on them?'

'No, not often.' He paused to wave a hand at his paintings. 'This is what I love doing best.'

Cavalier leant forward to devour some of his food.

'Best gnocchi I have ever tasted!' he said.

'I shall tell the chef, thank you. I trust you will write accordingly regarding your nourishment today.'

Cavalier smiled but did not respond. He leant back in his chair and savoured the wine. He examined the bottle's label, and smiled before he said, 'You have an obsession with oil, or should I say, energy.'

Bleulance was now uncomfortable. Cavalier went on.

'You have, by my calculations, more control over the world's oil and gas reserves than any other individual. Would you agree?'

Bleulance sipped his wine but did not meet Cavalier's inquisitive gaze.

'That's way off the mark,' he eventually said, with a dismissive wave of the hand.

'Really?'

'You have strayed away from my food interests and art acquisitions, don't you think?' Bleulance said, with a stern schoolmasterly look.

'You are right.' Cavalier nodded with an apologetic smile. 'I must say I am fascinated, like all people who have little, in the rich and powerful.'

'Rupert owns your magazine, doesn't he?'

'You mean Murdoch? I'm not sure.'

'Do you write for other magazines?' Bleulance asked, deflecting the conversation.

'*The Sunday Times* occasionally; on art, and cricket.'

Bleulance grunted cynically.

'That stupid game! You know the French created it.'

'Not sure about that. I don't think the French have ever beaten the English at it, have they?'

Bleulance gave a dismissive Gallic pout and wave.

'Do you know Rupert?' he asked.

'Not personally, no.'

'Have you done business with him?'

'Not quite. I suggested a documentary series on the art world to him in the 1980s. He had acolytes in England give me a good hearing. In the end, he didn't go for it.'

Bleulance winced a smile.

'I have shares in Rupert's company.'

'How fortunate.'

'I also have quite a few shares in the magazine you're writing this article for.'

Bleulance met his eyes again with the steel that Cavalier had heard about but not before experienced. He was pleased he had drawn out Bleulance's manipulative and threatening side in a couple of responses. The oil *baron* baron had wanted to imply that he could kill his journalistic outlets, if he wished.

Bleulance reached for a phone diary and wrote out five phone numbers.

'Get in touch with these people,' he said, 'they have a far greater comprehension of my father.' He ripped off the page and handed it to Cavalier. 'Now, what would you like to know about my art?'

'You paint too?' Cavalier asked in mock surprise.

'My art *acquisitions*,' Bleulance said, grinding his teeth.

***

Cavalier followed up on the phone numbers, all French contacts. Two were family that gave him nothing. The others were anti the third baron, which surprised Cavalier. They supported his belief that the third Baron Bleulance had been a spy for the KGB from his recruitment in 1934 until his death in 1991. But unlike other French double agents, he did not take a pension from the KGB. He didn't need one. Nor did he ever, from Cavalier's research, pass information direct to the KGB. Instead, when in exile in the UK for four years during World War II, he passed it to Blunt, who then passed it to their controls, such as KGB masterspy Yuri Modin. This way there was no direct trace to the third baron, except if one of the Cambridge Ring were exposed.

In the end, Cavalier was surprised that Bleulance would lead him to evidence that his father was a double agent, although he denied he knew anything. Cavalier concluded that the son, indeed, must have hated his father.

***

The moment Cavalier roared away on his motorbike, Bleulance rang the head of his personal security team, a muscular South African, Mawnie Schwartz.

'I want you to check on the background of Dr Edwin Harris,' he said. 'As long as he is investigating the third baron, that's fine. If he strays into asking questions about me, apart from my art, well, that's different. You understand, Mawnie?'

'Roger, sir.'

21

THE UPDATE

'Time for an update on Al Haut,' Wombat told Cavalier when they met at Melbourne's National Gallery after a concert in the Great Hall. They sat in a gallery cafe away from other concert-goers.

'How is Al?' Cavalier asked. 'I haven't seen him for eight months.'

'Seems in good spirits,' Wombat said, 'if that's the right term for him. His businesses are going well. He has managed to fund his exploration through mum and dad small investors from his Full Gospel Church, and other sources. Haut has set up an unlisted public company, Al Haut Minerals Limited, and another called Bass Resources Limited. He's in the process of setting up a US corporation.'

'I had an email from him in China—Hunan.'

Wombat smiled wryly.

'Yeah, well that's another story. He won't be going back there in a hurry.'

'Why?'

'He was doing top secret work on cold fusion with China's top scientific brains.'

'What?'

'We warned him. He was looked after royally while he was nutting things out with Zhang Wanxin, the so-called "Golden Brain of China".

They wanted Haut to work on special military projects. He and Zhang used to walk the beach of Hunan and discuss the science behind these projects. They would use the beach to avoid being spied on with electronic eavesdropping et cetera. On one occasion, he advised Al to get out of China fast, or they—the government—would never let him go. He would be a prisoner doing the government's bidding. That's where Al opted out. The Chinese have been gunning for him ever since.'

'How'd he become mixed up with the Chinese?'

Wombat took a deep breath.

'He can be naïve, even gullible at times. A Chinese "trade envoy"— Dr Richard Ni—went to one of his speeches in the US and approached him afterwards. Al was invited to China.'

'Let me guess. Ni was an espionage agent?'

'You guess well. The man was head of China's spy operations in the US. He organised the stealing of NASA technology, from reverse engineering to the formula for heat tiles.'

Cavalier waited, prompting Wombat to disclose more.

'We believe the Chinese put up five million dollars to develop Haut's oil project in Tasmania. The quid quo pro was that Haut worked on the cold fusion with the Golden Brain. The Chinese used a Hong Kong front company to put the money into the Tassie oil development. But then Al scarpered from China. The Hong Kong company is suing him over the issue. But we believe this is just a chess move to isolate him in a certain jurisdiction and eliminate him.'

'A jurisdiction?'

'You know, say Melbourne, where if they sued and forced him into the courts and making an affidavit, they would know where he was and act accordingly.'

'Al really knows how to excite wonderful enemies.'

'How much of this cold fusion development did Al get out of China?'

'Good question. He told me that individually he and Zhang Wanxin hadn't quite grasped a real breakthrough. But together, they had succeeded in nailing it.'

'No wonder the Chinese were interested in snaring him, like the Americans did with German rocket scientist Wernher Van Braun after World War II.'

'That's a fair analogy. The Americans were acutely aware that Al had been working on cold fusion in China. He was challenged by the Americans about it. Al answered that cutely, and correctly, by saying that without Zhang Wanxin's assistance, he might not have worked out how to harness the science. The Americans had to accept that. If they used Al's developments, they'd have to turn a blind eye to how the science was created.'

'The Americans would understand the situation pretty quickly. All the big nations spy on other nations and steal stuff all the time.'

'True. But the Chinese are less forgiving in Al's case. He has the cold fusion tech and will market it where he wishes. They realise they may miss out because Zhang is dead and his comprehension died with him. That leaves Al . . .'

Wombat took a folder from a suitcase and handed it to Cavalier.

'That's the file we have on Al at the moment. It's expanded somewhat since you last chatted with him. He is CEO of all the companies he sets up. He had a list of private set-ups as long as your arm. He's exploring for just about everything down there, from molybdenum and magnesium to gold, oil and gas. He has a finger in every possible mineral pie in or under the island and into Bass Strait. No one knows the structure of the island better than him.'

'Who wants the update on him?'

'We do. And Big Brother too. As I told you, he is of interest if he can produce oil in the quantities he claims are there.'

***

Cavalier flew to Hobart and met Haut at his office, and was surprised to be introduced to a tall, bespectacled fifty-year-old Texan, William B Donnelly the Third.

'William is considering support for me when he sells up his oil business in about a year.'

'"Considering" is not the word,' Donnelly drawled, 'I'm buying in as soon as I sell my company.'

'Can I say what?' Haut asked.

'Sure,' Donnelly said with a careless wave. 'I'm the supplier of jet fuel to the American and Chinese militaries. I'm in Australia on business. Thought I would drop in on my good buddy here, Al, to see how he is progressin''. Donnelly paused and then added, 'Perhaps we can tell you somethin' else in confidence. I'm here to learn Al's amazing methods since Potus has decreed he wants America to be a net oil producer by the first half of his presidency.' He nodded to Haut.

'I use special seismic techniques,' Haut said, 'to see through dolerite layers hiding oil reservoirs. That's how I found the huge deposits in Tasmania. The structure is the same as in Texas. When we use it there, we'll uncover a vast new source of oil for the US.'

'So you advise the US government?' Cavalier prompted Donnelly. 'How did you and Al meet?'

'Wombat introduced us,' Donnelly said.

'Oh, Okay. You're connected to the CIA?' Cavalier said, guessing. Donnelly nodded.

'Mind if I sit on the interview?' he asked.

'Be my guest,' Cavalier said, taking out a small tape recorder, phone and notepad.

'How do you juggle time in the mines with running the business here in Hobart?' Cavalier asked Haut.

'I still head up the drilling; do the heavy lifting, don't worry about that,' Haut replied. 'I am the most hands-on oil man in Australia. But the businessmen I deal with now are more impressed by the office than the holes in the dirt.'

Cavalier looked at Donnelly, who laughed and said,

'Hey, don't put me in that category! I'm an oil man from way back. So was my daddy, God rest his soul. I love it that Al is a real driller. Gets his hands dirty.'

'An industry magazine wants me to do a piece on your burgeoning mine operations,' Cavalier said to Haut, who chuckled.

'A nice colour piece about the lunatic with visions, who is making good?'

'No, I'm like the top scientists and geologists you have working with you. I will write about the pragmatic real areas, not the spiritual.'

They chatted for twenty minutes about the business, Cavalier as usual running a tape and taking notes. Then he said, 'Could you speak about your cold fusion inventions?'

'It will save the planet from extinction,' Donnelly chipped in.

'You're talking, what? War, the environment?' Cavalier asked, glancing at both of them.

'Many holocausts. I am going to develop technology that uses water as energy.'

Cavalier checked his tape. *Never a dull moment with the Shaman*, he thought.

'I recall Einstein said something about that.'

'He did,' Haut said, his enthusiasm building with Cavalier's interest. 'So did Nikola Tesla. More recently it has been Martin Fleischmann and Stanley Pons.'

Cavalier looked blank.

'You don't know them?' Haut asked.

'Expound, please.'

'Fleischmann was an electrochemist at Southampton University. Pons chaired the University of Utah's chemistry department. They developed cold fusion where they merged two or more nuclei at near room temperature. Fusion before this had happened at high temperatures, say in the intense heat and pressure found in a cold star. The press dubbed the new method a "star in a jar". Those two believed their discovery would solve the world's energy problems.'

'I do recall them now. They went public and were ridiculed.'

'It's been the same for more than three decades. I met Fleischmann at his home near Stonehenge in England a few months before he died. We chatted and I told him my aims and said I would succeed. He left this mortal coil content knowing that his dream of replicating the furnace of the sun at room temperature in a jar of water was going to happen.'

'Some scientists say it can't be done,' Cavalier said. 'Others say it can, but that it's maybe a decade away.'

'Al aims to do it in far less time than that,' Donnelly said.

Cavalier frowned as he scribbled notes. He looked up.

'But isn't there a contradiction here? You are all but killing yourself to develop what you believe is a huge untapped oil and gas resource. Then you want to create new technology that will do away with the need for oil and gas!'

'No contradiction at all. I see it as a means to an end. It's in the vision I had. I am on a mission from God. I can't deviate from it. It is his will.'

'Let me say something here, if I may,' Donnelly said, 'there is no contradiction and I am the living proof. I have invested in oil for decades. Now I'm ready to move on. Al's work is the best bet for the generation of new energy after fossil fuels.'

'What attracted you to cold fusion?' Cavalier asked Haut. 'Did Fleischmann and Pons inspire you?'

'Not directly. I was working on a hydrogen car a long time before their work emerged in public.'

'A car driven by hydrogen?'

'I was working on that from 1972 to 1974.'

'Hold on. You were just fourteen then.'

'At home in the garage.'

'Some kids played more sport, or collected stamps. You built a car?'

'I played a lot of sport too. But this car, shaped like a teardrop, was a passion.'

'You say you were using hydrogen to run this vehicle?'

'Correct. The problem was that I was using more energy to get it to work than the energy developed to run it. But it has been known for a long time that you can generate energy from the hydrogen in water. Water can be used to run everything, once you harness the energy from it. Big oil companies have prevented it. Times are changing. I must build on the shoulders of Fleischmann and Pons.'

'How?'

'In a nutshell, I'm going to harness the energy of thunderstorms.

Very hot air meets very cold air and creates lightning. I aim to capture that in my technology. The collision creates what I call "plasmoids". They are tiny atomic results of that collision. The plasmoids will be harnessed to create energy, which will fuel all engines. There will be no need for fossil fuel energy.'

'Once you have created these "plasmoids", what then?'

'They are passed through a thunderstorm electron generator. The plasmoids become loaded up with electrons and protons, and therefore bigger and negatively charged. The fatter plasmoids are then hit with a burst of plasma from spark plugs.'

'You'll have to explain "plasma".'

'It's one of the four natural states of matter. The other three—solid, liquid and gas—exist freely on the Earth's surface. Plasma is artificially generated by heating or subjecting a neutral gas to a strong electromagnetic field. This all happens in a combustion chamber.'

'Okay, so the plasma hits the plasmoids. Then what?'

'The plasma injection causes the plasmoids to separate the water vapour into its elements.'

'Two parts hydrogen and one part oxygen.'

'Correct. This then burns and creates H_2O—water—again.'

Cavalier paused and looked at his notes. He frowned.

'Are you saying that energy in the water is recycled?'

'Right. It never dissipates. Imagine what that means for everything from cars to space travel!'

Cavalier stroked his chin.

'What about advanced weaponry?'

Haut glanced at Donnelly, who smiled.

'Something we shouldn't discuss,' Haut said enigmatically.

Donnelly added,

'I think it's fair to say that any industry that uses "engines" as we have known them, will need this breakthrough high tech.'

'I take it you've already done a lot of work on this?'

Haut nodded. He seemed reluctant to add more.

'I should imagine that many countries would be interested in what you are doing.'

Haut nodded again, glanced at Donnelly, and remarked,

'I have already done some collaborative work with the Chinese.'

'Wombat told me about you and the Golden Brain. It didn't end well?'

'I realised that they were using me, and I got out.'

'I'd like to pursue that later. But let's continue on the technology. Did you work with any other nations apart from China?'

'Best not to discuss this now.'

'I guess it means that if you get this technology developed, pollution will reduce?'

'Vehicle pollution will be almost all eradicated. Today's engine efficiency is less than forty-five per cent. I will make it ninety per cent.'

'Your lovely mates at Conquer won't be too thrilled with you for this.'

Haut pulled a cunning look without answering. But Donnelly proffered,

'They are the most dangerous operators on Earth. I want to see Al screw 'em good and proper.'

'What is your ultimate aim with this?' Cavalier asked Haut.

'To save the living planet from extinction. It lives and breathes. I communicate with it. I know when it is troubled.'

Cavalier was reflective for several seconds.

'I don't think I can touch on all this in an oil and gas magazine,' he said. 'Needs a bigger feature. Can we take a step back? Where did the inspiration for all this come from?'

'My bible studies at first. Then I started researching the sacred geometry of the ancient Sanskrit text, the philosophical language of Hinduism. It has advanced science—long forgotten—intrinsically embedded in it. Tesla used it. So did Oppenheimer.'

Donnelly butted in. 'Oppenheimer said, "Now I become death, the destroyer of worlds," after he had seen the first nuclear bomb detonated at Los Alamos.'

'Oppenheimer had studied the Sanskrit text,' Haut added. 'He even hinted in interviews that atomic weapons had been used in ancient times. And there's a logic here. The water-as-fuel technology

I am developing uses information in that text.'

'What about his justification for being involved in the Manhattan Project to develop the bomb? He believed it was for the greater good.'

'That attitude is put in allegorical, philosophical terms in the Sanskrit. I agree with it. Don't forget the Nazis were very, very close to having their own bomb. Imagine what Hitler would have done, at the very least in desperation as he realised he could lose the war.'

'I know of your spiritual drive. What's the main aim here?'

'The search for truth.'

'That's a bit vague. Truth of what?'

'The universe. How it is a grand design. Finding the real source of energy leads to God.'

Cavalier was silent. He looked at Donnelly who was nodding approvingly.

Haut added, 'I figured out the link between all the elements was to do with their frequencies. Once that was established, I could build a unification model. This is it.' He showed Cavalier the model, which sat on his desk like a foot-long trophy in the shape of a doughnut. 'This allows me to link up all the elements, colour, sound, para-magnetism, biomagnetism, positive and negative charges, crystal formations and so on.'

Haut pointed to the tags on the 'leaves' representing the elements.

'This shape is that of the plasmoid itself,' he said. 'The model allows me to calculate everything to do with time and space.' Haut paused. 'In essence, I am trying to find a common denominator.'

'So that common denominator gives you the universe's grand design?' Cavalier proffered uncertainly. He would rely on going over the tape before he could claim comprehension of what Haut was on about.

'Yes. But understand that it has all been done before. The technology is not just building on Tesla, Oppenheimer and co. You can go back to Pythagoras and further to civilisations that inhabited the Earth tens, hundreds of thousands of years earlier.'

'So you are saying, as the cliché goes, there is nothing new under the sun?'

'It's true.'

Cavalier wrote in his notes here:

'*Not sure about this. Better get him back near the tangible.*'

But as he was writing, Haut said,

'You recall you asked me about a capacity to see things without regard for time? The visions, the downloads, are both back and forward in time. In the 1977 original vision I saw my Indigenous forefather place that flintstone in the ground about five hundred years before. The rest of the vision was into the future.'

'These "downloads" are from where?'

'From God.'

Cavalier nodded as if Haut had just told him nothing more than an interesting fact about the weather. This was in response to Haut's matter-of-fact enunciation of such unbelievable concepts; first the visions themselves, and second that they'd come from a higher being, his God. Cavalier frowned, while wrestling with the claim Haut could see backwards and forwards in time.

'So, you are talking here about a situation where there is no time dimension as we know it?' Cavalier mulled. 'Like a time-machine?'

'I'll have the technology for that,' Haut said. 'I can already conceptualise and build it. But there is the water-as-fuel technology I'd prefer to create first.'

Cavalier looked to Donnelly for a reaction.

'Better not to mention the "Beam me up, Scotty" stuff just yet,' Donnelly said, with a grin. 'But you can use your imagination on where Al and I are headed.'

22

THE BURNING

Cavalier questioned Haut for two more hours and then returned to his down-town Hobart hotel, The Woolstore, for a swim and gym workout, before dining with him. Haut explained that Donnelly had returned to Melbourne where he had other business.

'William has vowed to put a billion into my operations,' Haut said.

After the meal, Haut drove to his parents' house and picked up Mac, who squeezed into the back of the roadster and wagged his tail when Cavalier patted him.

'I'm pleased he remembers me,' Cavalier said.

'Oh, he recalls everything. He knows your character.'

'Where are we going?'

'You remember I said I would burn down the bikies' drug factory?'

Cavalier was not sure if Haut was joking or not. Haut threw him the black hood with eye slits that he had asked him to wear when they were in pursuit of the men who had fired into Haut's tent.

'Best you put that on when we get there,' Haut said. 'We don't want the mild-manner reporter from The Daily Planet being spotted as an accomplice in an act of arson.'

'This is not a smart move, Al. Think it through.'

'I have, for years. Now is the time to act. I want you as a witness and to consider writing something. It will be a story you won't forget or regret.'

Cavalier was uneasy.

'You mean you want me there as protection,' he said.

Haut chuckled but did not answer.

They drove for three hours to the north-east of the state, not far from Beaumaris Beach and the town of St Helens. En route, Haut explained his motives.

'There have been murders of young female backpackers near where we are going,' Haut said. 'I believe—no, I know that some of the drug-making bikies and at least one of their mules are behind them. That's why I want to do something.'

'Wouldn't it be better to let the police handle it?'

'They're providing protection for the drug-makers.'

'What? The entire Tasmanian force?'

'No, just a handful. But the business is widespread. The bikies have mules run the drugs to the mainland and even overseas. They are protected by the cops here and in Victoria. You remember that some cops were fired and charged in Victoria a decade ago?'

'I read about it.'

'That's what I'm talking about. The drugs are still being made and transported out of the state, with police protection.'

Cavalier grunted in surprise.

'You okay with this now? It'll be a great story,' Haut said. Cavalier didn't respond. He was on edge. 'I can drop you at a pub for an hour, if you feel uncomfortable . . .'

Cavalier still said nothing.

'What do you think?'

'I think it's dumb to attack a bunch of bikies who live by violence.'

The drove on in silence for a moment.

'You want to be dropped somewhere?' Haut asked again, glancing at Cavalier.

Cavalier pulled his handgun from a shoulder-holster and checked it.

'You came prepared,' Haut observed.

Cavalier didn't reply.

***

The moonlight was weak and this afforded some cover as they reached a hill at St Helens not far from Beaumaris Beach where the female backpackers had been killed. Haut drove the car to a gate in the wire fence that surrounded a ten-acre property.

'Best if you wait here,' Haut said, putting on his own black hood.

'If there are any surprises, such as bikies arriving, blast the horn.'

Cavalier, more uneasy than ever, nodded. Haut took a red sports bag from the back. It contained a shotgun, bolt cutters, a knife and petrol. Two rottweilers bounded to the gate, snarling and barking. Haut removed the bolt cutters from the bag and snapped the chain lock around the gate. He pushed it open. Mac rushed in and took on the rottweilers. He went straight for the throat of one and choked it within seconds. The second rottweiler circled as Mac turned to face him, his jaws dripping blood from the first encounter. Mac charged, again going for the jugular and dragging the second dog down. Within seconds, it too was dead.

'Goodonya, mate,' Haut said to Mac as he patted him.

The massive animal's hair was up on his back but this praise had him wagging his tail. Mac sniffed his two victims as Haut leashed him. A light went on in the factory. A bulky, bandy-legged bikie, wearing a black, studded jacket and ragged underpants, was silhouetted in the light at the door. He was rubbing his eyes.

'What the fuck are you doin'?' he roared.

Haut lifted his gun and fired above the bikie's head.

'Jesus!' the bikie cried. Haut strode towards him, holding back an angry Mac. Haut was twenty-five metres from the door when the bikie reappeared with an AR-15 rifle.

Cavalier jumped from the car and drew his handgun. The bikie aimed the rifle and fired at Haut who went to ground, still gripping the lead which restrained Mac. Cavalier propped at the gate, aimed and fired, knocking the weapon from the hands of the bikie, who yelped as if struck. Haut scrambled to his feet and held on to Mac, who was barking fiercely. They approached the bikie, who was on his knees.

Cavalier walked towards them, his movements alert to anyone else in the compound.

'You're going to vamoose,' Haut said to the bikie, 'or I'll let my dog rip your throat out too!'

'Okay, okay,' the bikie said, trembling and looking at Cavalier, 'you can have any stuff you want . . .'

'Fuck off!' Haut growled. 'Don't bring your mates back, understand?'

The bikie reached for his pants and boots, which were in a pile of clothes next to a mattress on the floor.

'Leave them. Got a bike?'

'Yeah.'

'Take the keys. You have ten seconds.'

The bikie scrambled for keys in his pants pocket. Mac lunged at him, snarling and snapping. The bikie took out the keys and bustled out the door. Haut followed him into the yard and fired one more shot above the bikie's head. He stumbled, fell, got to his feet and jumped on his motorbike. He rode to the gate and drove off down the hill at high speed.

Haut walked inside and went to the rear where all the drug-making equipment was. There were boxes stacked to the five-metre high ceiling. Haut slashed open two boxes, and put white powder to his lips.

'Have a look at this,' Haut said to Cavalier, who stood at the door. Cavalier holstered the Glock, took out his phone and snapped pictures.

Mac sniffed the powder and backed off.

'Smart dog,' Haut said. 'Not good for you!'

Haut then poured petrol over the equipment and wooden benches. Using a cigarette lighter, he set it on fire. Cavalier left the building, which was soon in flames, and Haut pushed Mac out the door and back to the car. They all jumped in. Haut drove a few hundred metres, stopped the car and turned it around to see the factory engulfed in flames. Muffled explosions suggested that a cache of ammunition was about to be obliterated as well as everything else in the factory.

Haut turned to Mac, who was slobbering and wagging his tail. His hot breath stank of his victims' flesh as he poked his outsized head between them. Mac made little grunts of satisfaction as if he approved of his master's act of arson.

'That was good, wasn't it, mate?' Haut said, as he kissed the dog on the snout and headed off on the drive back to Hobart.

After several minutes silence, Cavalier asked,

'You feel better now?'

'Oh, yeah, I do. I really do!'

Haut half-turned to Cavalier and said,

'You saved my life back there.'

'He had the drop on you when you went down. Lucky you or Mac were not hit.'

'Yeah, I confess I wanted you there as back-up. Wombat has told me about you.'

'Al, there will be repercussions.'

'Oh, there will be.' Haut chuckled. 'I'm going to the mattresses in Hobart.'

'You had a hood on. Would they recognise your voice? Mac?'

'Not sure but it will be the Melbourne bikies who come after me. I had a download saying "Flee".'

'Download?'

'From God.'

'Why Melbourne bikies?'

'They're distributing the drugs.'

'Why wouldn't the Tasmanian bikies go after you? You've burnt down their factory.'

'The same reason they backed off when you were here five months ago. Since then I have given another two more of them superb send-offs. They all want to have me bury them, not the other way around.'

'But you ruined their drug business!'

'The Tasmanian bikies will smooth it over. There will be a break in production. They'll build another facility and keep the supply going to Melbourne.'

'Then why did you bother destroying the St Helens place?'

'I was very angry after the backpacker murders on Beaumaris Beach. I felt compelled to make a statement.'

Cavalier was silent for a moment before saying,

'Al, I won't be there to protect you.'

'That's okay. God and Mac will do it.'

'Mac is your main protection.'

'Oh yeah! He's staying with my parents. As soon as I settle into my new home, I'll bring him with me.'

'Your new home?'

'I'll show you.'

***

They drove back to Hobart, arriving at Sandy Bay at just after 3 a.m. Haut wound his way up Nicholas Drive. Near the top there was a three-level house topped by a squat tower that had sweeping views of the bay by day and the heavens by night. A cross was just visible at the highest point.

Haut parked the car in front of the building.

'It's empty,' he said, looking up. They alighted from the ute. Haut let Mac loose to root around in the garden and the grass verge.

'I'll move in on the weekend,' Haut said.

'You bought it?'

'I was driving up for no real reason and noticed the cross. I got in touch with the architect. He knew who I was.' Haut chuckled. '"You're that spiritual geologist bloke," he said. He told me he built the place with a spiritual intent with the tower opening to the heavens. He wanted it to go to a man of God. It was perfect for me. He's letting me rent it while I get a bank loan to buy it.'

'You'll be safe here?'

'No one knows I'm moving in. I'll lay low with Mac.'

***

Cavalier wrote an innocuous report on Haut for *Minerals, Oil and Gas Magazine*, leaving out some of his more grandiose aims and claims. He decided not to do a bigger, more in-depth piece for fear of exposing too much about Haut, and Cavalier's connection to him. Then he produced a more incisive review for Wombat, which would be passed on to ASIO and the CIA.

There was an almost immediate response from Langley, CIA HQ, who wanted Wombat to monitor Haut even more closely.

Wombat rang Cavalier to inform him.

'Big Brother and the US Navy now have even more reason to keep up with his activities,' he said. 'First, because of the oil reserves he controls, and second, because of this cold fusion nuclear technology he wants to develop. The latter will have all sorts of ramifications for energy from vehicles and spacecraft to weaponry.'

'You want me to keep checking on him?'

'Any information you can glean would be useful.'

'I'll keep in touch. But I'll let him know of your interest. I'm not going to spy on him.'

23

FOLLOWING THE VISION

'God wants me to move more into developing cold fusion,' Haut informed Cavalier in a phone call three months after their encounter at St Helens. 'I'm resigning from my companies to work on it full-time. I own most of the shares so I can return when I wish.'

'Who'll run your oil business while you're away?'

'Sir Harry Askew. I thought it would be worth gaining some gravitas by hiring an ex-head of Conquer's exploration in Australia. I met him at the races. Askew had hinted he would like to work with my operation.'

'Ex-Conquer?'

'Don't worry. They had a big falling out. He's an affable, well-connected bloke.'

'I remember him from my very early days reporting finance. Big drinker. My advice would be to keep the liquor cabinet full and him away from the female staff. At least, I would have said that two decades ago. Perhaps he has matured, or become worse.'

'He seems an okay guy. But I'll keep an eye on him.'

'So you're going to develop that car-run-on-water technology you spoke about?'

'It's God's will.'

'Won't you become a bigger problem for Conquer? Your oil

development is a pain in its arse. In the end though, you just represent more competition. But that water-as-fuel-for-everything technology is a direct threat. It will wipe Conquer out. In fact, all the oil sisters will be stuffed. I mean, a multi-trillion dollar industry will go down the toilet.'

'It will. But I have plans for that.'

Cavalier waited for an explanation.

'What plans?'

'I'll tell you when my cold fusion technology is developed.'

'You are aware that there is a long history of guys like you being bumped off or forced out of business? That American Stanley Meyer who was murdered, for instance.'

'He was poisoned, right in front of his brother.'

'By two Belgium guys posing as businessmen. They put something in his cranberry juice.'

'Never drink it myself.'

There was a long pause.

'I admire your courage, as much as anyone I've ever met,' Cavalier said. 'But it will be a tough time for you if you go on with the cold fusion development.'

'It was in my original vision. I must go on with it. Besides they already tried to bribe and kill me. What more can they do than that?'

'There is a twisted logic in there, I guess.'

Haut chortled and said,

'Today I was speaking to an engineer in Melbourne who may work with me. He told me about an old bloke in the house next door to him who worked hard in his yard on a system of batteries running a car using a primitive form of water energy. Ford heard about him. They offered him a million in 1977—the year I had my vision—to stop his invention. They threatened him. The old bloke took the money, and Ford took away his invention—car, batteries and everything.'

'I sense you'd never capitulate.'

'Never!'

24

ORANGEY SQUEEZE

Haut's time away developing his cold fusion technology coincided with the rise of Ingrid Orangey, a political star who had her professional roots in the union movement. She was becoming a senior figure in Tasmanian politics. In a phone call to Cavalier, Haut pointed out his concern about this 'rather masculine' woman, already with a big reputation for former corrupt activity on the docks.

'She wasn't a bad sort at university when I was there, although I never fancied her,' Haut said. 'She was always boisterous and insecure. She had a heavy, busty figure and threw her weight around. You know, on university student councils and things. What she lacked in intelligence, she made up for in vigour. Since then she has become, let's say, "corpulent". Ingrid was known on the wharves where she worked as "Fat Bastard"—after the gross character in Austin Powers' comedy movie *The Spy Who Shagged Me*. She tossed around her extra weight on the docks. She could out-box any of the blokes. I'm fair dinkum. If she didn't get what she wanted by confrontation, she fornicated her way to it.' Haut paused and chuckled. 'As the one women's rep of note in the Painters and Dockers Union, Ingrid had little competition.'

'Is she going to give you trouble?'

'Oh, yes,' Haut said with a sigh. 'Conquer will bribe her, for sure.'

Despite this new concern, and another substantial figure lined up against him, Haut had completed several months' work on the cold fusion technology, spending a million borrowed dollars on building a reactor.

'I did take my eye off the ball with my companies,' Haut admitted. 'They have declined because of the busy inactivity of Sir Harry Askew.'

'He always seemed big on bonhomie and even bigger on industrial inertia.'

'There's more to it. Sir Harry's charm turned out to be a clever cover for his dirty work. We had break-ins, threats to murder staff, and sabotage, such as equipment being destroyed, *again*. I wouldn't mind betting that Conquer and Fat Bastard Orangey combined to destroy the company.'

'I'm sorry to hear that, but I'm not that surprised about Askew,' Cavalier remarked. 'He reminds me of a Barry Humphries character, the mythical cultural attaché, Sir Les Patterson. Always pissed at functions with finger food sliding down his tie over a pot belly.'

'That's him.'

'So that guy was a front in more ways than one.'

'I must add a tendency to flatulence in his maturity.'

'Sir Les Patterson, step aside!'

'He never got anything done! He filibustered, upset staff and groped half of the female staff.'

'I did warn you about that.'

'I fired him before it was too late. But even after he left, research and production operations were interfered with. More bureaucrats and politicians have been bought off. Even some of my workers have been bribed.'

'There are rumours Conquer wants to take over Shelf Energy.'

'Funny, isn't it? Shelf Energy is Australia's biggest energy provider. They have a massive reserve off Australia's north-west.'

'Conquer has a forty per cent stake in it.'

'They want to lift it to sixty per cent and take control. Then they can count Shelf Energy's reserves as theirs.'

'Will they go after it?'

'Could. But the federal government could be persuaded to stop a takeover. The treasurer is not keen on too much foreign investments, which has ballooned out in the last years with China trying to take over the country by economic stealth. The public doesn't like it. There are votes in stopping it.'

'Government action would be useful, wouldn't it? I mean for you.'

'Not sure about that. If Conquer can't grab Shelf Energy then they'll go in harder against me.'

'Why?'

'It's all about reserves, in actuality and on their balance sheets. If their reserves are high, the share price rises, Conquer's investors, such as Jacques Bleulance, are happy, and so are pension funds. Most funds worldwide have chunks of Conquer in their portfolios. Its executives feed themselves nice big bonuses. Oil companies like to present fat reserves figures. This indicates, on paper at least, they will always supply fuel for energy that the world is devouring at an alarming rate.'

'So you think you'll be a greater target if it can't snare Shelf Energy?'

'I'll still be a target, no matter what happens with Shelf Energy. I don't know why, but Conquer seems in a big rush right now.'

25

EXPOSE

A month later, Cavalier had used contacts at Conquer's oil company rivals to uncover a scandal. He emailed Haut and they had a phone conversation.

'Any smoking gun?' Haut asked.

'Not in the way you want, but it's something. Conquer has apparently sent big money to the state of North West Africa—NWA— as part of a three billion dollar deal to develop oil reserves there. The money should have gone into government coffers. It ended up in the oil minister's secret bank account.'

'Nice story! How did you uncover it?'

'Not as hard as I thought it would be. I once investigated the activities of Russia's Nafta Oil Company in the UK. It disappeared in about 1990, when Communism began collapsing. But from 1959 for forty years it was used to spy on the entire US, UK and NATO defence systems in the UK and Europe. Nafta's British and American opposition oil groups were happy to feed me information.'

'I think I read about that in *Future Energy Global Intelligence Report.*'

'Those old contacts in the UK oil industry are proving more than useful now. So all that effort in the 1970s and 1990s is paying off. I know where to go to collect insider detail on Conquer. As usual, opposition companies are only too willing to see their big rival exposed. The industry is reptilian in the way corporations attempt to devour each other.'

'What will you do with the information?'

'I'll either use some mates in the UK media to make it public, or I'll write it myself, under a pseudonym.'

'Use the mates. You don't need Conquer coming after you, I can tell you.'

'I hear you.'

'What angle will you use?'

'The article will infer that Conquer knew they were sending the money to the oil minister's personal account.'

'A very fat bribe.'

'That will put Conquer on the back foot. Then someone has to lobby the Australian federal treasurer about Conquer not being allowed to take over big Australian oil fields, both actual, and potential, like yours. The government will have two arguments. First, that a big foreign outfit should not be allowed to take control of Australia's major energy operations and reserves. And second—'

'That Conquer is unfit to take over Australian companies like Shelf Energy and my group?'

'Right.'

***

Three weeks later, an article appeared in London's *Financial Times* newspaper speculating about Conquer's bribing of the NWA oil minister. The company's share price took a dive. Its public relations people went into overdrive defending their business practices saying that, 'Conquer would never knowingly bribe a minister of a foreign government.'

Soon afterwards NWA's oil minister resigned. Conquer fired its African Operations manager without explaining why. The industry saw it as 'minor' mismanagement. Conquer's share price rose again.

Haut read the *Financial Times* report and rang Cavalier.

'That should put pressure on them,' Haut said, elated that

someone was pushing back against his enemies. 'I have been under attack for more than two decades. This is encouraging, thank you.'

'Not enough, though. As I said a month ago, the federal treasurer should be lobbied, after a fashion.'

'How?'

'I'm going to interview him for an article.'

***

Jacques Bleulance tossed an email of the *Financial Times* articles on the glass coffee table on the balcony of his villa on the Greek Island of Spetses. He phoned his top security man, Schwartz, in London.

'Have you read those pieces, Mawnie?' Bleulance asked.

'I have, Baron.'

'I have a big share in that damned company. I want to know who wrote the pieces. Heads will roll at that paper, if they don't tell me.'

'Right, sir.'

'And I want you to put a little scare into Haut . . .'

***

Cavalier secured an interview with the Australian federal treasurer, a tall man with a penchant for droll humour, in his plush Melbourne offices overlooking the city's Treasury Gardens, a refreshing sea of green next to the New York style grid of a city. Over coffee and biscuits, the two sat on a dark red leather sofa and discussed the un-official story that Conquer would try to take control of Shelf Energy.

'Yes, I've heard that tale,' the treasurer said, brushing crumbs from his black and red tie, the sole colour in an otherwise bland look of grey suit, socks and black shoes. 'It's a bit of a Grimms' fairy tale, isn't it? We've had no submission from the company or any of its reps.'

'But if you do, how will you react?'

'That's a hypothetical. Can't answer it.'

'Well, let me ask a real hypothetical. If a major energy com-pany wanted to buy a controlling chunk of a big Australian energy operation, would you block it?'

'That depends,' the treasurer said, stroking his upper lip as if deep in thought.

'On what?'

'Oh, on a variety of issues.'

'How would you expect the electorate to react? The media in general and the great unwashed have not responded well to foreign takeovers of household names. You know, Bigger Cheese for instance.'

'Well, in the case of a cheese or big wine company I would step in, of course,' the treasurer said with a look of mock concern.

'There would be revolution otherwise.'

'Oh, yes, there would.'

'On the far lesser important matter of oil and energy?'

'We'd have to look at it. We'd have to consider the fine print.'

'Such as?'

'Can't tell you until I see the fine print.'

'Well, such as your being able to take control in a crisis, in the case of a massive energy shortfall in the nation, or in a war situation?'

'Those things would have to be clear in clause agreements, otherwise, no deal.'

An attractive auburn-haired secretary swivelled into the office and asked if they wanted more coffee. The treasurer, a fraction uncomfortable but still in good humour, said no. Cavalier said yes. He wanted as much time as he could get. The treasurer had already glanced at his watch twice.

'Another hypothetical,' Cavalier said with a smile. 'Say, for example, the mythical predator wishing to control a big Australian energy provider had a record of bad practices. Would that impact on your decision?'

'It would depend on the bad practices.'

'I can think of a few, hypothetical of course.' Cavalier held the treasurer's gaze and asked, 'How about major bribery in dealings with other countries?'

'Hmm,' the treasurer mused, stroking his lip again. 'Now they would cause a few problems.'

'So, you would not allow a takeover?'

'Not if the predator was in the habit of bribing.'

'The European Conquer Group has been accused of bribery in NWA.'

'Yeah, I read that. Not good.'

'So you wouldn't allow Conquer to control an Australian company?'

'I didn't say that.' He leant forward. 'Now, Mr Cavalier . . .'

'Call me Victor.'

'This is all speculation until someone makes a bid, isn't it?'

***

Cavalier wrote the article under a pseudonym, entitled: *Treasurer would block takeover of Shelf Energy*.

It began: 'The federal treasurer would not allow Shelf Energy or any other big Australian energy company to be taken over by a foreign group, if the predator had a history of bribery or corruption . . .'

The article was a page one story a few days after the interview. It caused a stir and was republished in several countries. The treasurer put out a press release saying that 'the discussion with the journalist concerned was speculative and hypothetical'. The statement denied that he had mentioned any foreign corporation or any issue.

Haut rang Cavalier to say how much he liked the article.

'That should set the bastards back on their bums!' he said.

'I have another piece,' Cavalier said, 'that will make even your local Tasmanian government shy off dealing with Conquer.'

'What have you found?'

'Your delicate opposition has involved itself in assassination.'

***

The lean intruder, wearing a black hood, climbed the back fence of Haut's home. He had just landed on his feet when Mac came charging from his kennel at the rear of the yard. The man scrambled for the fence again. Mac tore at him and lacerated the intruder's forearm.

The intruder escaped and drove straight to a Sandy Bay doctor. His forearm would need plenty of stitches and was bandaged. He was given a tetanus injection. Next, he visited a butcher where he bought a kilogram of kangaroo meat and big bones. Then he went to a pharmacist and purchased arsenic and rat poison. The injured man mixed the meat and the poisons, and returned to Haut's home.

Carrying a big wrench, he climbed onto the fence, exciting Mac, who leapt at him. The intruder stayed out of reach of the animal's snapping jaws. The intruder then tossed the meat from a plastic bag and watched the huge dog sniff the meat for several seconds before chomping into it. Mac was soon vomiting. He lay down and moaned. The intruder climbed over the fence, ready to leave quickly if Mac attacked. But Mac was in no state to defend his territory. The intruder then bashed the dog's skull with the wrench until it was dead.

Calmly and coldly he then removed a phone and began to take shots of the home and all its entrances.

***

Haut drove home at dusk. Mac always made a loud fuss at his master's return but this evening there was no bustle at the side gate or bark from the yard. Worried, Haut went outside and found the dead dog. He began crying. After a few minutes of uncontrollable grief, he knelt on one knee and said a prayer, which ended with:

'Oh Lord, I cannot judge the perpetrator of his cruel deed. I shall leave that to you.'

Then, with a heavy heart, he wrapped the big animal in a canvas bag and buried him deep in the back garden.

Later, he rang Cavalier to tell him the depressing news.

'It's a warning,' Haut said. 'They may believe I'm behind the newspaper attacks.'

'Did you get CCTV footage?'

'No. I'm just installing it.'

'Do you want me to back off with the writing?'

'No,' Haut said, 'I want you to go as hard as you can!'

26

SINGAPORE ABORTED

Haut realised he would need capital from outside Australia to back his oil project. With that aim, he flew to Singapore. It was his first visit and he was struck by the clammy heat, which he abhorred. He blamed his discomfort on his Tasmanian Indigenous background. He also claimed the heat slowed the responses of his five-orbit brain. Only sleep in good air-conditioning could restore it to full force.

He was greeted by CK Pan, a billionaire Singaporean business-man, and chauffeured to the Marriott Hotel on Orchard Road. Pan—a jolly, corpulent 55-year-old—spoke impeccable English and was an Oxford University graduate with a wide range of contacts in the oil industry.

After registering and checking the hotel's security, Haut met with Pan in his salubrious hotel suit on the sixth floor. They sat on a long sofa. Pan's beefy bodyguard and chauffeur stood outside the suite's door.

'You have permanent protection?' Haut asked.

'When you have success in business,' Pan chuckled, 'you make worthy enemies.'

'Tell me about it,' Haut said with a grimace.

Pan ignored the remark and pulled out a folder on the table.

'We have done our research,' he said, 'and we believe your

Tasmanian project is a good investment risk.'

'Risk? You read my report?'

'Of course. I had experts judge it. They all were in favour.'

'There is no risk.'

'Risk and oil, Mr Haut, are soulmates,' Pan said with a laugh. 'I will obtain a two hundred million dollar loan to invest in your Tasmanian operation by staking as collateral the deeds to a property of mine in Jakarta.'

'Sounds good to me,' Haut said with a grin.

'Perhaps you can assist with another matter. The Singapore Petroleum Company could not obtain the contract from the United Nations to supply Basra Light oil for the company's refinery. As you know, since the war in Iraq ended, the UN has controlled most operations in that shattered state.'

'Let me guess,' Haut interrupted, 'the refinery is designed by Conquer to only take Basra Light. If the Singapore Petroleum Company can't supply the right oil, it is penalised by Conquer.'

'Correct! You know how Conquer operates.'

'Underhandedly, usually.'

Haut excused himself to make calls to contacts in Australia. After ten minutes, he returned to the meeting with Pan.

'Let me try to obtain the contract for Basra Light and supply it,' Haut said. 'This way the Singapore company avoids the penalty.'

'Can you do this? Singapore Petroleum would be most pleased.'

'It will pay the UN for the cost of the oil. This will then trigger a UN "oil for aid" deal. The UN will then supply the poorest people in both the north and south of Iraq with food aid. I will help by obtaining Australian planes designed for easy delivery of the food. Millions of lives are at stake, mainly those of children.'

'That will all sound very good to Singapore Petroleum!'

'Which bank are you using for our deal?'

'The Royal Bank of the Netherlands. They have the deeds to my Jakarta property. They are ready to supply the two hundred million.'

***

Jacques Bleulance hit the ball with grace and timing and watched it sail down the fairway of his private golf course at his French estate.

'Superb shot, Jacques!' the broad-shouldered Belgium, Robert de Cobb, CEO of Conquer, said, with an attempted smile. His nickname in business was 'the reptile'. His large, fleshy features, manner, and a record in defeating corporate opposition by any means, explained why.

They strolled the perfectly manicured course while half-a-dozen security guards prowled in the background.

'We have an issue with that pest Al Haut,' Bleulance said, his expression turning sour.

'I'm aware,' de Cobb said, grinding his teeth. 'He's doing some deal to supply Basra Light to Singapore, right?'

'We must prevent it. He has set up an oil for food arrangement. The dirty little do-gooder wants to feed the starving millions in Iraq.'

'What do you suggest?'

'Make sure the contract for the oil supply goes to someone else.'

'Who?'

'The UN Director General's son.'

'Can we do that?'

'They'd both be amenable to such arrangements.'

They strode on in silence. De Cobb played a fine shot onto the green. Bleulance lined up his ball, and when he slid it into a bunker, de Cobb said quickly, to avoid commenting on his poor stroke,

'I hear he's getting two hundred million for his damned Tasmanian oil project.'

'He won't get a cent.'

'Oh?'

'I own twenty-eight per cent of the bank he's using. One call will kill that.'

De Cobb sank his three-metre putt.

'We must deter him further,' Bleulance remarked as he took time to punch his ball out of the bunker. The ball lobbed two feet from the hole.

'Great shot, Jacques!'

'I want you to have a chat to Mawnie Schwartz about "influencing" that opportunist CK Pan.'

'Will do.'

Bleulance took too long lining up his shot at the hole. He missed. His face clouded and his chin receded into his neck. He said, just audibly,

'I want Pan to never, ever again countenance doing any business with Al Haut.'

***

Haut took a plane to Dubai to facilitate the deal for Basra Light and booked in at the most glamorous, stylish and expensive hotel, the Burj Khalifa. Singapore Petroleum picked up the tab for the ten-thousand-dollar-a-night suite. A facilitator supplied by the Singapore company met him and introduced him to several middle-men agents. But within a couple of days, Haut had trouble making headway with securing the Basra oil deal. He was unsure about Dubai's byzantine ways of doing business and, as meetings were delayed or put off, his instincts told him something was amiss. Pan and Singapore Petroleum reassured him in phone calls, but he could not get near securing the deal he was after.

After two weeks, Haut gave up. His dream of saving the lives of millions of starving Iraqis with desperately needed food drops was in jeopardy.

***

Ten days after doing the deal with Haut, CK Pan received a phone call.

'Who is this please?' Pan asked.

'Not important. Do you value the life of your beautiful daughter?'

'What? Who is this?'

'If you want your daughter to live, do not invest in Mr Al Haut's Tasmanian oil project.'

Pan was stunned and unable to respond.

'Do you hear me, Mr Pan? Your funds have been frozen in your Holland account. You can't access them.'

'You can't . . .'

'We have. Just remember, your daughter will come to serious harm if you deal with Haut.'

'Who are you?'

'Again, not important. Arrange a meeting at your office with Haut.'

'He's not in Singapore!'

'I'm sure you can persuade him to return.'

After the call, Pan scrambled to access his Holland account. After several hours of frantic calls, he realised his account had indeed been blocked. He had his personal assistant phone Haut in the hope of influencing him to fly back to Singapore.

***

A few hours later, Pan's thirteen-year-old daughter, Penny, was walking home from school when a car pulled up close. There were three men in suits. The back door flew open.

'Hey, Penny,' a gruff voice said, 'your father asked us to drive you home.'

The girl glanced at them and kept walking. The car eased along, keeping pace with her.

'He's worried about you,' the man called. 'C'mon. It's for your own safety.'

Penny broke into a run, then a sprint down the street. The car roared off after her but she had soon disappeared in a maze of city back alleys.

***

The next morning, Haut phoned Cavalier in Chiang Mai.

'My radar is on full alert,' Haut said. 'Pan has asked me to visit Singapore post haste. He has called for a meeting in forty-eight hours. There is some issue over the funds he has for my project.'

'What do you think it's about?'

'Bleulance. Jacques Bleulance.'

'The fourth Baron? Why?'

'He has a big slice of the Netherlands Bank. He could have Pan's Holland account frozen. They have a big investment in Conquer too.'

'Bloody Bleulance!'

After the call, Cavalier phoned Wombat.

'What do you know about Bleulance?' he asked. 'Have you got anything at all?'

'Oh, yeah, it's well known in the intelligence community that he pays a protection agency one hundred and fifty million US dollars a year to look after him. The agency, named ironically the Gentle Company, has top former operatives of European spy and police outfits—German, French, British, Israeli, you name it.'

'Christ! I'd better let Haut know.'

Cavalier rang Haut but his phone was off. It was already noon in Singapore. He sent a message:

Avoid meeting at all costs. Leave Singapore asap. Urgent. VC.

27

THE NAKED DISCIPLE

Haut walked into CK Pan's oak-panelled office on Singapore's Beach Road at precisely noon. Pan and three lean, suited, European-looking men aged between thirty-five and forty-five were seated at a round conference table. They did not leave their seats or proffer their hands when Haut entered. He knew instinctively that they were trouble.

Pan's demeanour had changed completely from their first meeting. He was awkward and very nervous when he tried to explain that their deal was off.

'The Dutch Bank won't release the funds,' he said finally. 'I've already taken steps to have deeds on my Jakarta property annulled. My Indonesian government contacts say they will give me another set of deeds.'

All the time the three men kept their eyes on Haut. Coffee and chocolate biscuits were served. The three men declined both. Pan took coffee, but could not hold the cup steady. His hands were shaking. Haut stayed as calm as possible. He sipped the coffee, ate a biscuit and began a second one.

'Any reason for the Dutch bank doing that?' Haut asked innocently, as if it were not a major problem.

'Not sure. I'm trying to find out. The time difference,' Pan said, wincing a smile, 'makes it hard sometimes to reach the right executive. But I won't raise capital with them again. Can't trust them.'

Haut feigned illness, asked where the toilet was, and left the room holding his stomach. He decided he would have to make an exit. Just as he returned to the conference room, one of the strangers was coming in his direction.

'Something wrong?' he asked, guiding Haut to his seat.

'Could be an ulcer,' Haut said, 'caffeine sometimes triggers it. I'll be okay, though.'

Haut asked for water, which was duly brought to him by Pan's assistant. He sipped it and asked,

'Your money was secured against land you have in Indonesia, correct?'

'That's . . . yes . . . yes.' Pan replied, his eyes glancing at the three men, who looked agitated. Haut doubled up.

'It must . . . be . . . oh shit!' He struggled to his feet. 'Excuse me again, sorry.'

He moved off towards the toilet, but instead of going in, he darted to a fire escape and hurried downstairs and into the street. Haut jumped in a taxi.

'Airport,' he said, 'as fast as you can!'

Haut arrived at Singapore airport. He saw Cavalier's message and then rang his assistant, Primrose.

'I have to vamoose, fast. I need a plane out of here.'

'What's wrong?'

'I'll tell you later. I want you to pack up all my stuff in the apartment and ship it off to my New York address. My computers, my clothes everything. There are even my plans for a tunnel in Israel up on whiteboards. I have my passport, wallet, phone and plane ticket. That's all.'

'I'll do it straight away. But please tell me what's wrong.'

'Sorry, not now.'

Haut went to a bar and asked for a beer. He kept watching the long concourse in case the three men from the meeting showed up. After a half-hour he began to relax. Even if they guessed he was at the airport, they would not be able to get through customs and passport control quickly enough to stop him. Haut had a call from Primrose, just as it was announced that passengers could board the plane.

'I got to the apartment block to see three men carrying boxes down the elevator from your floor,' Primrose informed him.

'Shit!'

'Your apartment is empty. They took everything. Even your leather suit that you love so much. Everything! Do you want me to call the police?'

Haut thought long and hard.

'No,' he said despondently, 'just be careful yourself and take the next flight you can out of Singapore.'

Haut took his seat on the plane and spent an intense three minutes praying. His thought was broken by a call from Cavalier. Haut related what had just happened.

'They'd be Bleulance's thugs for sure,' Cavalier said. 'Very adroit of you to do a runner.'

'They took everything.' Haut paused and chortled softly. 'I prayed to God and you know what his answer was?'

'Go on.'

'"Now you have nothing. That is how I want you. No possessions, no worldly goods."'

'Al, are you saying you heard voices this time?'

'No. Just a flash of light. A download of information.'

Keeping his tone free of scepticism, Cavalier asked,

'Did you ask why you are required in this state of "nudity"?'

'Yes. His reply was "Now I can give you everything."'

As ever, Haut's declaration, delivered with apparent sincerity, gave Cavalier pause. He took note every time Haut claimed a divine intervention. Cavalier accepted in his own mind that he should suspend belief and not query him at these moments.

Instead, he gave him advice.

'When you return to Hobart, change your address,' he said, 'talk to Wombat about a disguise.'

'Oh, sure.'

'Also, change your identity. Cut your hair short, buy a wig and wear dark sunglasses. If a wig doesn't work for you, dye your hair, preferably black.'

'You serious?'

'I am.'

'I forgot,' Haut said, with a trace of cynicism, 'you are the world's expert on this.'

'Change your suits too. You have to lie low. Also wear those floral Hawaiian shirts.'

'I hate them! Why?'

'They distract people from looking at your face. It's only a momentary thing, but it could save your life.'

28

THE BLOCK

Cavalier again used a long-time newspaper colleague, this time at *The Guardian* in London, to report on Conquer's brutal dealings in NWA. The piece was headed: 'Conquer to be accused of Human Rights Abuses.'

It began:

A leading United Nations Human Rights lawyer is set to file a suit against oil giant European Conquer Group (ECG) for allegedly collaborating in the execution of African writer Wol Waewying and several others in a NWA tribe. Waewying had led the accusation against Conquer of razing villages to install pipelines, flaring billions of dollars of natural gas, polluting rivers and lakes. The lawsuit will claim that Conquer conspired with the military government to capture and hang the writer along with ten other men and women. Conquer will also be accused of other human rights violations, including working with the NWA Army to kill and torture protesters . . .

'Great piece!' Haut said, in an email to Cavalier, who wrote back: 'It may well make our federal government think twice about letting such a monster take control of the biggest energy source.'

'The timing is perfect,' Haut said, 'my contacts tell me Conquer has made a takeover bid for Shelf Energy.'

***

Two weeks later *The New York Times* reported:

> The Australian government today rejected the European Conquer Group's proposed takeover of Shelf Energy Petroleum Ltd. The Australian finance minister (known as 'the treasurer') said that foreign ownership of Shelf Energy would be contrary to the national interest. Sources say that claims of Conquer's 'disturbing' activity in African countries, including NWA, may have played a part in this surprise decision . . .

Haut phoned Cavalier and said,
'Well, you've really put me in it now!'
Cavalier was thoughtful before he said:
'If that turns out to be the case, they must be desperate to build up their reserves. I'll have to examine their claims; their balance sheets.'

***

Bleulance leant back in his chair at his Champs-Élysées Paris office and put down a report he had been reading on the Thai-style dark teak desk. Opposite him sat three senior executives from Conquer, in which he had a thirty-eight per cent share.

'So you failed to acquire control of Shelf Energy,' he said with a patronising wince. 'You still have a thirty per cent shortfall in reserves compared to what's on the books.'

'There is still Tasmania,' de Cobb said.

'You've tried to acquire that for years.'

'The lease owner, Al Haut—'

'I know who he is,' Bleulance said, his cool façade broken for a split second. 'He is unable to be persuaded by normal means.

157

Correct?'

'That's right. He was offered twenty-five million dollars to hand over the leases years ago,' De Cobb said with a look of bewilderment. He turned to the other two executives for support. 'You know what his response to the offer was?'

Bleulance stared, unprepared to waste his breath on saying 'What?'. De Cobb quoted Haut saying,

'I'll accept the money if you can tell me how I explain to God why I am giving up on the mission he has set me to fulfil on Earth.'

'He is a serious nutter,' Conquer's British head of marketing—balding, super-fit forty-year-old Neil Joslin—said. 'He believes that God is his oil-diviner.'

The Conquer executives all shook their heads and smiled in derisive agreement over Haut and his beliefs. Bleulance remained expressionless. His forehead pitched forward and his chin joined his neck. His face clouded.

'You are telling me that one *minor* miner from the outback of Australia stands in the way?'

'Baron, we have tried everything,' de Cobb said. 'The appropriate Tasmanian politicians and bureaucrats have been given inducement, as has the Minister for Mines. Haut's equipment has met unfortunate breakdowns. We've had informers on his staff. We've had the press write negative articles. But he is unstoppable.'

'No one is unstoppable,' Bleulance said in almost a whisper.

'Baron, sir,' Joslin said, 'you see, Haut was a pastor of one of those American fundamentalist groups that take the bible literally. I mean *literally*. I know people who have worked for him. He is messianic in his zeal. No one can divert him from a vision he alleged he had at nineteen.'

'I had one of those at nineteen,' Bleulance said, deadpan. 'She was eighteen at The Sorbonne and won the university beauty pageant.'

The others laughed for far longer than the quip merited.

'What was this vision?' Bleulance asked.

'He claimed an old Aboriginal man directed him to a place to drill.'

'So God is an Australian native,' Bleulance commented.

The others overdid their appreciation of his remark once more.

'Can't you find a way to overcome someone as deranged as that?'

'He's weird,' Patricia Daniels, a handsome, auburn-haired 45-year-old French woman and Conquer's chief geologist, said. 'I saw him speak at a conference in Hobart. He's a real charmer. He is short, muscular and, while very Australian, somehow refined. The women flocked to him.'

'Australian and refined? That's an oxymoron,' Joslin quipped.

'Weird in what way?' Bleulance asked.

'He calls himself a Prophet of Nature,' Daniels said.

'Haut has profited from nature,' Joslin chipped in.

'How is he a prophet?' Bleulance asked.

'Oh, he says God directs his every move.'

Bleulance leant back in his chair again and motioned to de Cobb.

'I think we should adjourn until after lunch,' he said. Joslin and Daniels left the office. De Cobb stayed.

'If you could push Haut out of the way,' Bleulance said, 'could you gain control of the Tasmanian leases?'

'There's a good chance we could.'

'Then deal with Haut.'

'Not easy. He's a slippery customer.'

Bleulance stared at the bigger man in a manner that chilled him.

'Do whatever it costs,' he said, 'whatever it takes. If this over-statement of reserves ever gets out . . .' Bleulance paused and shook his head. 'You need to take control of those Tasmanian reserves for more reason than one.'

'I understand,' de Cobb said, 'and I agree with you. Tens of billions are at stake right now.'

'Don't let one god-bothering nobody stand in your way. Step up attacks on him. There is a knighted ex-Conquer executive in Hobart—'

'Haut sacked him.'

'You must have others you can influence in that Tasmanian government.'

'He's started a capital raising. He's using two well-known sportsmen in TV ads telling Tasmanians to put their money into his company shares.'

Bleulance thought for a moment.

'Didn't we put that repulsive female on our payroll?'

'Ingrid Orangey, yes.'

'She's Mines Minister or something, isn't she?'

'They reckon she'll be the next premier; the first female Premier of Tasmania.'

'Tell her to make a statement saying Haut's operation is not going to produce oil and gas. That will put a dent in his capital raising.'

De Cobb nodded. Bleulance eased his chair around so that he was looking out of the window at the vibrant Champs-Élysées.

'If that fails . . .' Bleulance began and trailed off. 'Even when you've succeeded in curtailing his capital raising, we must think about hiring others to help.'

29

FIRE, IRE AND MIRE

Ingrid Orangey, her flaming hair coiffured for the occasion, called a press conference at her government office and read a statement to the assembled media.

'Our professionals at Mineral Resources Tasmania tell me that Al Haut Minerals has *not* discovered oil and gas on Bruny Island or anywhere else in our state,' the 45-year-old said. 'So, as a government, we cannot, in all conscience, support this venture. Therefore the lease arrangement, which ends in a year, will be terminated.'

Orangey's top lip began to break out in perspiration, which highlighted a dark shade that looked like a moustache, despite attempts to cover it with make-up. After the statement, she lifted her bulky frame from behind the desk and was about to totter off, like 'a hippopotamus on high heels,' as one cheeky cartoon depicted. Orangey was stopped in her lumbering tracks by the media pack shifting in front of her and firing questions. Cavalier was at the rear, wearing a suit and tie.

'This will break the company,' he commented. He was attending the conference as a freelancer. 'Is it right for a state government to interfere in the free market like this?'

Orangey glared and took a big breath to control her apparent indignation. Her red face flared and suggested early on-set high-blood pressure, big drinking, or both. Her look was comical below her fire-engine hair and not quite matching off-pink dress, and maroon shoes. But her manner had no one laughing.

'Let me say this,' she said, in a time-honoured politician's way of stalling to think of something nebulous to say, 'we cannot, as a responsible government, countenance such a speculative venture.'

'Al Haut says he has found oil and gas,' Cavalier persisted.

'He hasn't.'

'I disagree. I've seen his assay reports.'

'So have I.'

'MRT said you have not bothered—'

'Are you calling me a liar?'

'If you've read them, what is your assessment?'

'I leave that to my experts,' Orangey thundered.

'That's not an answer. That's pollie doublespeak.'

One of her staff signalled that the conference was over. Reporters began to file out. TV camera operators started packing up equipment. Orangey waddled from the anteroom to her private office. Cavalier hovered near the door, pressing her with probes.

'Don't you fuckin' dare step through that doorway!' Orangey said. 'If you do, I'll fuckin' throw you through the window!'

Cavalier stayed where he was.

'What's your name, mate?' Orangey said.

'Cavalier, Victor Cavalier, minister.'

'Weren't you fired from one of the mainland papers a few years back?'

'I resigned. I'm freelance.'

'Why don't you fuck off!'

A staff member nodded to Cavalier with a rueful look and ushered him to an elevator.

***

Haut was devastated by the government's intervention, which he called 'political sabotage'. It left him well short of the funds required to get on with his drilling program. And now the leases would be terminated if the current government remained in power. In a phone conversation with Cavalier, Haut said,

'It would have been a directive from Bleulance and Conquer. They knew that Fat Bastard would do anything, I mean *anything* for a quid.'

'You can't speak of your beautiful minister in such terms!' Cavalier said in mock indignation. He wanted to placate Haut, who was angry. 'What are you going to do?'

'I'm hatching a plan with the Greens. I've been friends with them since the Franklin River dam fiasco. I helped them make the case that the dam would be a disaster.' Haut gave his stuttering laugh as he added, 'We even had the Greens fight the police while Greens leader Bob Brown and I sneaked down to the river to take samples that would prove the rock formations would not hold a dam. I was once arrested with Bob. We're mates.'

'How can the Greens help?'

'You'll see. Just keep watching and reading the news.'

***

A few days later, a Greens Party member rose in parliament to ask a question about Orangey's handling of Haut's company.

'Is the minister aware that many experts agree that the Al Haut Minerals company has indeed discovered oil, vast quantities of it, and that the report and core samples were lodged with the MRT?'

Orangey stood but seemed reluctant to approach the dispatch box to reply. She was confused by the fact that a *Greens* member had asked such a question. Weren't they against all mining?

'I have made comment on what I have been advised,' she replied and was howled down.

The speaker called for another question. It came from another Greens member.

'Is the minister aware that her false comment, and obfuscation as seen here, has ruined an environmentally sound mining operation that could bring great wealth and benefit to the state?'

Orangey noticed Al Haut in the public gallery behind the House members.

'Al . . . bloody . . . Haut,' she mumbled. She tried to catch the eye of the speaker to help her out by shutting down further questions. But he was distracted by a note passed to him, and was oblivious for the moment of the minister's embarrassing predicament.

A third Greens politician stood and asked,

'Have you an answer to the disparity of what MRT says and your suspect behaviour in making such damaging, untrue claims about the company?'

Orangey, puce, clung onto the side of the dispatch box, her white knuckles making a noticeable contrast with her face and hair. The speaker became aware of the minister's glares, indicating a need for help. The speaker called for a Liberal, QC Malcolm Hodges, to ask a question.

'Mr Speaker, when is the right honourable lady going to answer the question?'

A roar of 'Here! Here!' went up from the assembly.

'The minister has the floor,' the speaker said, knowing that he would receive a fearful blast from the fiery Orangey when the parliament was in recess.

'Mr Speaker,' Orangey said, shaken, 'I shall ask for a full explanation from the relevant department.'

This brought derisive howls of protest from the floor.

***

The incident left Haut with a personal right of reply in the parliament that he could exercise at any time. But Orangey instigated a change in legislation that prevented this happening.

'I know you are in the pay of your big oil masters,' Haut told Orangey in a phone call. 'Well, a day of reckoning will come, I assure you.'

'What are you talking about?' Orangey replied, 'Are you threatening a Minister of the Crown? This call is monitored, you know.'

'Good. I hope it is. Go and see the Austin Powers' movie *The Spy Who Shagged Me* to see how people view you.'

Haut had no choice but to bide his time and wait for a future government that would give him his day in parliament.

30

CONQUER'S CONQUEROR

Not long after Orangey's rebuke of Haut's oil operations, the Tasmanian Mines Registrar, Denis Guy, invited him to his Hobart office for a meeting. Haut was surprised to see 45-year-old Harry Jonas, the 200-centimetre beanpole former newspaper editor there as well. Jonas, an experienced reporter, who had attacked Haut in articles over the years, was a 'big drinking', bespectacled character on a retainer doing public relations for a gambling company. He shook hands with Haut as if they were acquaintances. They had only ever spoken over the phone when Jonas had tried to interview him.

Guy—fifty-three years old, short and rotund—removed his jacket, rolled up his sleeves and looked at his watch.

'Nearly five,' he said, 'yard-arm time. Beers?'

The others nodded. Guy took three bottles of beer from a small office fridge, kicked it shut and handed them around. He indicated seats, while he sat down at his desk, put his feet up, and took a swig of his drink.

'I brought you two together for a good reason,' Guy said. 'Al, Harry here has been at you for a decade, right?'

Haut nodded, trying to work out where this meeting was going.

'Well, he's set to go in harder, more often, if you don't stop your claims about oil and gas finds.' Guy sat up straight, and leaned forward on his elbows, the beer in his left hand. He pointed at Haut

166

with his right hand.

'You know they're solid,' Haut said, staying calm. 'We've got what we claim. There is a lot in it for this state.'

'I don't think so. The minister doesn't think so.'

'You've upset a lot of people, Al,' Jonas said, 'a lot of big people.'

'And little fellas too,' Guy said, 'with your comments about finds bigger than this-and-that raghead oil state. We worry about your future. We worry that some time, some day, someone may be tempted to take action.'

'That sounds like a threat,' Haut said with a slow smile.

'On the contrary, mate,' Guy said, his expression more serious. 'You've defrauded so many people with share issues in a company that have been given no returns.'

'No, I have not! If they still have their shares that will change when I go into production.'

'We don't think so, mate.'

Haut waited. He didn't touch his drink. Guy and Jonas guzzled theirs.

'I want to look into a crystal ball,' Guy said. 'You know, like you do with your visions.' He glanced at Jonas, who covered his mouth with his hand and smirked. 'Here's what I see will happen. Harry will step up his coverage of you, and it won't be pretty. Politicians in parliament who feel the same way as us will hop into you often.' Guy leaned back in his chair again and loosened his tie. 'Third, the SEC and ASIC . . .' He paused, opened his arms and added, 'maybe even the taxation department, will take a very close look at you and your operations. That's my vision.'

'I'm not stopping,' Haut said, his expression tightening.

'We know,' Jonas said cynically, 'it's in your vision.'

'I guess it's our vision against yours,' Guy said. 'To avoid anything nasty happening we reckon you should stop your mining activity. All of it. For your own good.'

'You could preach full-time,' Jonas said, as if making a viable suggestion.

'Or pursue your vision overseas,' Guy added.

Haut stood and marched to the door.

'You will be judged for this,' he said, opening it.

'What?' Guy said, standing. 'By you?'

'I don't judge, God does.'

***

'I have been interviewing some knowledgeable Europeans in the oil industry,' Cavalier told Haut on the phone a little while later. 'There are more than strong rumours that Conquer has overstated its reserves.'

'That's why they went so hard after Shelf Energy.'

'And why they have you in their sights.'

'Not a good analogy!' Haut said.

'If you publish something indicating Conquer's accounting tactics, it might keep them off me.' He paused and added, 'On the other hand, they may become nastier.'

'I'd like to pursue the story.'

'You should. In the meantime, I've had to employ security.'

'More problems?'

'Yes,' Haut said with a cynical chortle. 'I've had some very direct threats from the current Tasmanian Mines Registrar, Denis Guy. That bastard secretly sent my core samples overseas to Conquer, which was illegal. That began their "interest" in buying me off, then destroying my operations.'

Haut outlined his meeting with Guy and Jonas.

'Brazen!' Cavalier commented.

'The aim would be to put me in jail and then have me killed there. On top of that, I've had death threats; phone calls suggesting I depart the state, before quote, "You are carried out in a coffin". I've employed Pinkerton security, after your recommendation.'

***

While Pinkerton was guarding Haut with round-the-clock protection at his Sandy Bay home, a gang of fourteen burglars broke into his

Hobart office and went through all his filing cabinets, desk and computers. They were searching for one thing: a one-page document that was empty except with Haut's signature.

This became the basis for a fraudulent letter that passed all Haut's companies to another company. He learned of the fraud on a Thursday afternoon when a contact at the stock exchange notified him of the letter. Haut rang Cavalier and explained the situation.

'If this change of ownership is announced on Monday morning at the stock exchange and in the press, it could collapse my company's price and ruin not just my oil and gas business but all my operations.'

'Can you get me the original letter by special delivery overnight courier? I can try to have friends in forensics go over it for you.'

'I can get the letter. But it must be done by Sunday night!'

'It's doable.'

***

'Piece of cake,' Anthony Jones said, cigarette hanging from the corner of his mouth as he examined the letter. Cavalier had couriered it to Jones in his Murrumbeena offices.

'Go and have a coffee down the road next to the pharmacy, and come back in an hour.'

Cavalier did as instructed. Jones was a tech genius and whenever he said, 'No worries!', 'Piece of cake' or 'Piss easy' Cavalier knew he meant it. Jones had a bank of equipment, which covered everything from weapons modifications to spectroscopy, and from chemical to physical analysis.

'It's a dead-set fake,' Jones told Cavalier an hour later, handing him a two-page report for his analysis. 'Not amateursville, but not brilliant either. The page with the signature is at least a year older than the two other pages. The stock of paper is different and discernible. The computer font is the same but the ink is from two different types of toners.' He paused to draw on his cigarette. 'Forgers think they are smart by wearing gloves, but we can detect the make of gloves they wear. For what it's worth, there are also different fingerprints on the first two pages when compared to the page with the signature.'

The stock exchange and the police were notified of the attempted fraud. The police were slow to act, but when Cavalier investigated, he discovered that the company making the acquisition was registered at a false address in Hobart. It was a phantom set-up created to destroy Haut's entire operation. Mindful of this, and the apparent desperate, fraudulent action it represented, Cavalier stepped up his probes into Conquer's general operations.

31

A TARGET TOO DANGEROUS

Cavalier put together a well-researched, part speculative article on Conquer's probable troubles over reserves. He placed it again in the UK's *Financial Times* and it was by-lined 'Special oil industry correspondent Hugh Howsie-Montegue'.

'Who is that journalist?' Haut asked over the phone when he read the piece.

'Me. The editor is a very old friend who owes me. He accepted all my commentary after I sent him support documents such as balance sheets and so on. We both know that Conquer will huff and puff. If they were dumb enough to take it to court, the paper would extract more mileage out of the issue.'

Conquer reacted to the article, releasing a strong denial. The corporation delivered the newspaper a writ. The editor ignored it and sent Cavalier an email that he was going to keep following the story with a team of reporters.

'Go for it!' Cavalier emailed back.

'Thank you so much, oh, and check your bank account,' the editor replied. 'You should have an extra ten thousand pounds in it for your troubles.'

***

That day, Bleulance called for another meeting of Conquer executives at his Champs-Élysées office.

'Your lawyers sent the *Financial Times* a writ,' he said to de Cobb. 'Has that stopped them writing about Conquer?'

'So far. But I don't trust them.'

Bleulance turned to Joslin.

'No one seems to be able to tell me who the journalists are behind the attacks on Conquer. Always anonymous or a pseudonym. *The Financial Times* refused to release the real name. The editor was threatened with his position, but he still would not supply it. *The Guardian* editor also refuses to divulge a name.'

'We must be somewhat circumspect,' Daniels warned. 'If we push too hard, it may backfire on Conquer.'

'That's true. Perhaps you should organise a private investigation to uncover the clear cabal against Conquer.'

***

Two days later Haut was surprised to have the American head of Pinkerton in Australia, Michael Atheron, fly from Sydney to meet him at his Hobart home. Atherton, about forty, was a lean and fit man. He wore a smart three-piece suit. He was nervous as he played with black, square-rimmed glasses, while delivering Haut some disconcerting news. Atheron refused an offer of tea or coffee. He was on a mission that he did not fancy. Nor did he wish to stay long in Haut's presence.

'We've done a lot of homework over your case,' he said in a smooth Bostonian accent and with a sympathetic smile, He then delivered the bad news: 'I'm afraid we can't work with you anymore. The risk is too high.'

'Meaning?'

'Our contacts believe you are in serious danger of an assassination attempt.'

'How do you assess that?' Haut asked, shaken and taken aback at this stark categorisation.

'Mr Haut, we are the biggest protection agency in the world. We guard two hundred thousand clients. We have our sources in intelligence, industry, the underworld. We do our research. You have upset some big players, some very big in your industry. They have infinite resources to commission what they want. We can't cover that.'

'So you're telling me, as big as you are, you can't protect me?'

'That's correct. Conquer has a history—'

'Of murder?'

'I would prefer to say in achieving what they wish.'

'If it's a matter of money . . .'

'No,' Atheron said with a mirthless smile. 'They are just too big to take on, for us, anyway, while you live in Australia.' He paused and added, 'We have learnt that there is a thirty million dollar contract out on you. We have been told that the participants have been paid in advance.'

'Why in advance?'

'It's harder to trace when a deal is done *before* a hit.'

Haut remained calm but the information was frightening. He thought of Cavalier. He needed more information for him.

'Do you have any idea of who these sweet visitors might be?'

'All we know is that they are coming from outside of Australia.'

'Any idea how many? Thirty million sounds like enough for a small army!'

'Our sources say there is a capo who will organise it. There will be three or four people sent.'

Haut took a deep breath and digested the shock.

'You don't know when they will come?'

'Mr Haut—'

'Call me Al.'

'Sir, I've flown here to warn you. This could happen any time from now.'

'So that's it?'

'All I can say is, if you come to the US, we can look after you again.'

PART FOUR

STRIKE THREE

32

PASSPORTS TO SHOWDOWN

Cavalier had resumed part of his life in Chiang Mai and had quietly instructed a lawyer to purchase the property at Riverside Condo on the Ping River, which he had previously rented. It had excellent security and Cavalier had enhanced it with cameras and alarms. Besides that, people were not nosey or inquisitive, and he knew the area well.

In a typically Thai manner, locals were pleased to see the return of the quiet Frenchman, Laurent Blanc. Even his Harley had been muffler-modified so that it made as little noise as possible. His only regret was the lack of a partner, and he thought often of the beautiful, sensual Bangkok physiotherapist, Waew Ing. He had her number, but was concerned that if he made contact, she might turn him into the police. She had already been interrogated by the police over the murder of Leonardo Mendez, a Mexican drug bigshot, who Cavalier had been under suspicion for killing.

Cavalier fantasised over going into Waew Ing's rooms on his next trip to Bangkok and reliving their one-night stand. But when the time came, he was preoccupied in keeping a low profile.

***

Haut rang Cavalier to tell him of the Pinkerton rejection and the warning.

'You'd better arm yourself,' Cavalier said.

'I have my Bentley.'

'A pump-action weapon is not enough.'

'What do you suggest?'

'An Uzi.'

'A sub-machine gun?'

'You must become a one-man army.'

'You're kidding!'

'Conquer has taken on ragtag armies and rebels in Africa. Pinkerton is right. They won't send a lone assassin for you. They'll send a team.'

Haut took an audible breath.

'An Uzi, eh?'

'It will give you a chance to survive against several attackers. Your Bentley won't.'

'I've seen an Uzi in documentaries. Have you used one?'

Cavalier ignored the question and said, 'You could defend yourself against ten attackers. It will take a man's head off at ten paces.'

'Charming!'

'Pinkerton know what they are doing. You'll need something.'

'Where'll I obtain an Uzi?'

'I'll have Wombat send one, special delivery. The package will say, "Musical Equipment, handle with care." You'll receive it in a few days.'

'You serious?'

'It will be a doddle to operate for someone with your skills, after a bit of instruction.'

A few hours later, Cavalier rang Haut again.

'I've arranged for Wombat to do some research for me. I'll meet him in Bangkok in forty-eight hours. Then I'm coming to Hobart.'

'Why?'

'To show you how to use an Uzi.'

***

It took Cavalier nine minutes to reach Chiang Mai airport from his condo, which he considered one of the joys of living in this mountain-basin city, apart from the near perfect weather for half the year, which averaged three degrees less than that of hot, humid, polluted Bangkok, where he was headed.

A drawback was heavy traffic in Chiang Mai at peak hours. In the two decades he had spent half his time based there, he had noticed the inexorable increase of car and motorbike numbers as the population of this former capital of the Lanna Kingdom grew to more than a million. But in this respect it was no different from most cities in Asia and the rest of the world.

He landed at Don Mueang airport, Bangkok, at dusk and faced the drudgery of an hour-long ride to a rented apartment in a condo on Soi 22 off Suhkumvit, which he had used occasionally, partly because the managers never asked for a passport or credit card. Every transaction was in cash.

On arrival, Cavalier took keys from the elderly Thai woman who had run this condo ever since he'd first come a decade ago. She greeted him with a beaming smile, remembering his respectful manners and healthy tips. He dumped his bag in the fourth-floor room and left for his meeting with Wombat, who stayed at the city's tallest building, the 88-storey, 300-metre-high Baiyoke Tower II.

'My, you like doing it in style!' Cavalier said as they greeted each other mid- afternoon at the revolving roof deck on the eighty-fourth floor. It gave them a 360-degree view of burgeoning Bangkok. 'Always good to see you, Wombat, even in the worst polluted big city on the planet. It has four per cent less oxygen than anywhere else.'

'Yes, but forty per cent more fun!' Wombat pointed out over the skyline. 'I love this hotel.' Then he nodded to his briefcase. 'I have the things we discussed.'

They walked to the rooftop bar and music lounge, found a discreet table but still with fine views. Wombat pulled out a large manila envelope and handed him a passport.

'Jones is making you an Englishman again,' he said. 'This time called Roy Benjamin Malcolm.'

'Hmm,' Cavalier muttered, 'you've never given me a middle name before. Must be an important fellow.'

'You have your own medical supplies company. You'll be coming from London via Bangkok then to Melbourne. You'll make your own arrangements into Hobart. This time we've added some more background business and, of course, a solid profile.'

'Don't like my photo much.'

'Sorry about that.'

Cavalier held the passport photo closer.

'I look younger. Much younger.'

'Mr Malcolm is. We have you down as forty-eight.'

'Charming! And my hair! Strange haircut. You've chopped it away.'

'You can have that done here. You comb it forward.'

'No, won't be doing that. I might crop it short.' Cavalier examined the photo. 'And the colour. What happened to my pepper and salt?'

'Thought we could do away with your natural condiments. You dye it dark.'

'Glasses too.'

'There is a pair in the envelope. They partly hide your eyes. But please use them. They have a capacity to see in the dark; variation on infra-red vision. We don't want people remarking how much you look like Michael Caine. People remember such things.'

'I'll wear them on one condition. You tell Caine to stop imitating Roy Benjamin Malcolm.'

'That's another thing. We think you can risk the Cockney accent.'

'And not a lot of, uh, people know dat,' Cavalier said, copying Caine's accent.

Wombat laughed.

They both ordered double malt whiskies on the rocks. Wombat eased his chair closer to Cavalier, pulled out four photos and said,

'We—the Five Eyes—tracked hundreds of suspects for a whole range of projected crimes, especially those making unusual purchases over the last three years. That didn't get us far.' Wombat chuckled. 'We noted a guy trying to buy an island in the Pacific. Another took a controlling share in an online Paris brothel. But we did see patterns. Smaller buys coalescing around a certain time. That worked better.'

'And the dark-web?'

Wombat nodded and smiled.

'We—Australia—came across eighty-eight instances of people of interest trying to get rid of enemies: politicians, wives, husbands, even sports rivals. Half of them were scammed by fraudsters. But the main clues came from coded communications.'

'How many were genuine suspects?'

'Five hundred and four worldwide with all sorts of possible killing projects, some with photos, some not. Then Haut told us what Pinkerton said to him. That was the breakthrough.'

'Follow the money?'

'We did. A nice round figure of ten million came up three times within a week. We examined which of the suspects could have received such a lovely amount!'

'Moved through several front companies, no doubt?'

'Right. Apart from bank commissions and so on, the money was passed to destinations in accounts in the Bahamas. That got us down to thirty-eight possibles.'

Wombat picked up a folder and took out three photos.

'We then cross-referenced information and photos, including your snaps from the Mekong trip. Finally, we searched airline bookings over the last few weeks.'

'Thirty million to eliminate Al!'

'That's not much in the scheme of things if Conquer gains control of the billions worth of Tasmanian oil.'

'Once we had three guys, we coordinated surveillance on them—their emails, computers, phones and so on. Patterns emerged. Destinations for planes trips were noted. Then bingo! The names "Hobart" and "Haut" came up. Twice, mind you, but it was enough.'

'I take it they've bought plane tickets for Australia?'

'Again, patterns. It was unusual for a group to be arriving at about the same time. They are all travelling under false names.'

'If you didn't know their names, how. . . ?'

'We were supplied photos with most of the names and profiles. It was then over to old Anthony Jones to examine the photos and put real names to faces.'

'When are they coming?' Cavalier asked.

'We know Neil Farquar is already in Hobart. He is odds-on to be the capo, the organiser. We are trying to work out if he has been given an oil property in San Antonio, Texas. Maybe it becomes his once the kill happens. We don't know. Each of the other three has cancelled and re-booked three times. But they are all heading to Australia still. We think in about ten days, if they stick to their last schedule.'

Cavalier scrutinised the faces. His forehead stretched.

'You recognise them?' Wombat asked.

'Leni, Castro and Hollos, my "acquaintances" from the Mekong.'

'Correct.'

'Pity,' Cavalier mumbled.

'Why?'

'Gerard Jean Dubois is not on the list.'

'You'd like him to be?'

Cavalier didn't answer.

'We believe that this Leni character made a fleeting visit to Hobart not too long ago.'

'I wonder why? Reconnoitring perhaps.'

'Probably. They'd want to see Haut's home. See if it were suitable for a hit; how they would get into it and so forth. That reminds me. Our Big Brother mates, especially the lovely Melody Smith, keep asking us if the killers coming after Haut are linked to the death of our agent Deere. They'd like to arrest them, but I haven't confirmed it.'

'Let's keep it that way.'

'Just asking in case you wanted support from them or us.'

'No. You've done more than enough with this information. It's all I need.'

'I know you like to work alone. But three assassins? Can you handle it?'

'I think so,' Cavalier said.

'Aren't you a bit, you know . . .'

'Concerned? Not yet.' Cavalier grinned. 'But I will be as the job comes closer. I always overcome it beforehand by preparation. Besides, these three are very worthy. They fit my criteria for doing what I do.'

'And you want to look after Haut because of your daughter?'

'Not just that. He is doing work I believe in. I think he is important for the planet as a "prophet of nature", as he calls himself. Even if he doesn't make his goals, they are worth striving for; eliminating major forms of pollution being just one of several aims.'

'You have at least one thing in common.'

'What's that?'

'I've known you both for a long time. Neither of you has a price. You can't be bought.' He chuckled with a look that betrayed his joy at having one over his long-time close friend. 'Except on one occasion . . .'

Cavalier shrugged.

'It means one can't be suborned, which is useful over time in my field,' he said. 'Vital, I would have thought, in Haut's case.'

'Why?'

'He is answerable to a very unique boss.'

'So you have moved from agnostic to something else?'

'As you advised when I first spoke of Haut, I "keep a very open mind".'

Cavalier raised his glass to a waiter, indicating it needed a refill. 'Let's celebrate, for old times' sake.'

33

THE SHADOW

Cavalier arrived in Melbourne with his usual meticulous planning well in place. But, as with all such assignments, he had learned to expect the unexpected. He was still in the plane's aisle waiting to disembark when his phone rang. It was Haut telling him his offices had been broken into again two nights earlier.

'They did the same thing to my associate, the day before that,' Haut said, his voice calm but concern still evident.

'What did they take?'

'Computers, tape recorders, books. Even some kids' books that happened to be in the bookshelves were scooped up.'

'What did the police say?'

'Ask a silly question . . .'

'But you called them?'

'Oh, yeah. Had a former copper mate liaise for me. He reckons that there must have been about a dozen people involved in the break-ins. The places were done over thoroughly.'

'I'm in Melbourne, I'm going to wait for our visitors. Will track them if I can.'

Cavalier walked down the corridors, through the perfume and alcohol counters and used an automatic passport machine. He passed through but was then beckoned to a passport desk by a uniformed woman of about sixty with short blonde hair. She examined his photo and looked him up and down. He smiled, trying to appear relaxed. He submerged an urge to ask why he had been singled out when he had already gone through the automatic control.

'Mr Malcolm,' she said, her face expressive, 'did anyone ever tell you that you look like that British actor?'

A male officer leaned across and intervened, saying,

'Michael Caine.'

'No, I've not been told that before.'

'Yes, that's the one,' the woman said. 'He wore those thick-framed glasses in. . .'

'I saw it on TV a week ago.'

'*The Ipcress File,*' the male officer said, 'from fifty years ago.'

'I read the book it was based on,' Cavalier said, keeping the conversation pleasant and chatty 'a Len Deighton novel.'

'You even sound like him,' the female officer said.

'Yes, well I believe we are bowf Cockneys, aren't we? But I am many decades younger! Ease a very old geezer now, in'e?'

With smiles all round, Cavalier was handed back his passport. All that effort *not* to look like Caine and both he and Wombat had forgotten about the way the actor looked in *The Ipcress File*. It explained why he had been asked to the desk for questioning, not because he was in anyway suspect, but as a result of looking like someone famous. He cursed inwardly but was always relieved when passing successfully through any border, even into his own country.

That easy mix of authority and friendliness that characterised his fellow countrymen and women meant that he would not be grilled in any way by the officers. They had joked about his likeness to Caine, which was the Australian way of delivering a compliment, even if it may have been backhanded. Instead of probing about his business, his background and why he had been in Bangkok, they allowed him through without him having to lie and assume too much of his new persona as the English businessman.

He collected his luggage and had the strange experience of taking a small guesthouse room in semi-Bohemian, bayside St Kilda and not venturing to his Australian home in the next suburb of increasingly gentrified Elwood. He couldn't even drive his own car, which was sitting unloved under cover at the rear of his property.

Cavalier kept thinking about the weapon he didn't have with him. He could not recall more than a couple of assignments where he had not sent on a weapon, or when he did not have one handy. It was tempting to sneak into his own home and take the car and a handgun hidden there, but he decided against it. Cavalier was always looking ahead to the possible day when someone would be tracking his movements. No trace of him was a better option. This pre-condition also precluded him from visiting the offices of any newspaper or magazine to see editors, which was annoying yet essential when he was on a mission that had nothing to do with journalism.

After sleeping off jetlag, he checked email messages. One from Wombat said:

Team Roger, Skinny, Cuba 8.30 pm Fri. Q

Roger was the nickname Wombat had given Hollos in honour of former British MI6 chief Roger Hollis. Skinny was for Leni. Cuba was Castro. The time of arrival on a Qantas flight was 8.30 p.m. that day.

Cavalier noted again that the one fellow he wanted, Dubois, was not in the squad. He mulled over why, and came to the conclusion that he was such a loner, the others would not want him with them.

Cavalier hired a Mazda, arrived at Melbourne airport at 8.30 p.m. and waited in the cafe opposite the sliding doors for arrivals on a Qantas flight from Singapore. Cavalier, glasses on and sports cap jammed on his head, ordered a coffee and joined the throng of people watching the arrivals wheeling out luggage-laden trollies. There were two doors, and at first Cavalier found it tricky to watch both doors even with a video screen monitoring both. He decided he would track whichever assassin arrived first.

Big Hollos was easy to pick. He was wearing a sleeveless, multi-coloured vest and had one piece of brown hand-luggage. Cavalier put down his coffee, hustled to his car, drove out of the car park, and then circled until he was positioned behind the taxis meandering in to pick up passengers. Again, Cavalier did not have to use binoculars to pick out Hollos, who stood out in the line of people waiting for taxis.

The line moved slowly. An airport official tapped Cavalier's driver door window and indicated he should move on. Hollos got into a taxi. Cavalier drove off, keeping a few cars between him and the taxi, which seemed in a hurry to reach the Novotel Hotel on St Kilda Boulevard, familiar territory for Cavalier. He waited across a park and used his binoculars to watch Hollos stop just inside the glass door entrance. He was on the phone. Then a second taxi pulled up. Out stepped Leni and Castro. They headed to the reception and checked in.

Cavalier used his mobile to ring hotel reception. A woman answered.

'Oh, hi,' Cavalier said in a cheery voice. 'I've just dropped off two people from overseas and they asked me to pick them up. I can't remember if they wanted me back tomorrow or the next day.'

'Must be tomorrow, sir,' the receptionist said. 'They check out at 9 a.m.'

'For an 11 a.m. flight?'

'They didn't say.'

'Thank you very much.'

Cavalier rang Haut.

'Get a good night's sleep tonight,' he said. 'Your overseas mates will be in Hobart tomorrow about noon.'

Cavalier explained how he had tracked them.

'Do we have an idea of where they'll stay in Hobart?'

'Wrest Point Casino is my bet. They love drinking and gambling. On the Mekong, I heard them discussing the casinos they'd been to around the world. They boasted how they dropped this amount and that; how they won it all back. Usual gamblers' self-delusion.'

'What are you going to do?'

'I'll be in Hobart before them.'

'Where'll you stay?'

'With you.'

34

TOWER OF FATE

It was grey and raining when Cavalier took a taxi from Hobart airport to Sandy Bay. The chatty Indian driver described the sights on the way in an attempt to draw him into conversation. Cavalier nodded, smiled, grunted replies and otherwise remained quiet.

'You visiting?' the driver asked, looking in the rear-vision mirror.

Cavalier nodded.

'Staying with a friend?'

Cavalier smiled.

'Must be a wealthy friend to live up there at the top,' the driver said as they left Sandy Beach Road and drove into Churchill Avenue past Alexandra Park. 'Some of the houses up there are amazing with best views of the water and across the bay.'

Cavalier didn't react. He was making a mental note of every road turn and location points. They turned into Nicholas Drive, which wound up higher and higher. The driver began having trouble keeping traction on the slippery road. Cavalier looked up and could see the dome of Haut's home. It projected over treetops, and seemed to hover beyond the mountain like a Swiss chalet.

Cavalier told the driver to stop. He alighted in the rain and used his binoculars to zero in on the tower.

He stepped back to the edge of the road, thinking an assassin could get a shot into the tower. Distance was not a problem. Accuracy was. He eased back in the car. The driver was now concerned.

'What were you doing?'

'I may buy the place,' Cavalier said, as if this would explain everything. The driver raised his eyebrows and nodded. They stopped opposite number thirty-seven, Haut's home. Cavalier directed the driver on up beyond it. He was not happy having to reverse in the wet to turn around. Cavalier used his binoculars again. The driver taxied down to the house. Cavalier paid the fare. The driver scowled and took off.

Cavalier stood for a second, taking in the marvellous mid-morning views across the bay. It was peaceful. He walked down a few steps, hesitated at the front entrance and then moved left to other steps that ran down to a door leading to a laundry. Cavalier returned to the front door and knocked. Haut did not answer. Cavalier knocked louder. Haut, holding a rifle, opened the door. They shook hands.

Without indulging in the usual pleasantries, Cavalier said,

'They'll come in the door at the side leading to the laundry.'

'You think so?'

'I've checked it. Easy to jemmy it open.'

Cavalier asked for a tour of the property. He examined all the fences. He noticed a small cross over a dirt patch in the garden where a couple of roses were already growing.

'Mac?' Cavalier asked.

'Yeah,' Haut said with an anguished look. 'Wish he were here now.'

'I do too. What a beautiful brute he was!' Cavalier said. 'But it may be better he isn't here. Mac might've frightened them off.'

Haut frowned.

'We want them to come to us,' Cavalier said.

They moved back inside the house.

'Did you ever get a clue to who might have killed Mac?' Cavalier asked.

'Not really. There were traces of blood on his teeth and gums, so it's possible that he got a piece of the intruder. I rang around the local vets. One said he treated a guy for lacerations about the time of the killing. But this vet said all he could remember was that the bloke was thin and reeked of cigar smoke. The vet said he had an accent he couldn't detect.'

Cavalier thought of Leni, knowing he had been to Hobart a few months about the time of Mac's demise. He pointed to the glass panel beside the front door entrance, and said, 'This is too easy to defend from inside. You'd get in a shot or two before they could do their job.'

'Any idea when they'll come?'

'Put money on tonight.'

'Why?'

'They were given ten million each. That's a lot to play with. They'd enjoy living it up in luxury as soon as the job's done.'

'They wouldn't leave town fast?'

'No. Airport passenger lists would be scanned after the murder was discovered. They'd wait and have a good time at the casino, and later depart separately.'

Haut gave him a tour of the modern three-level home. He showed Cavalier a bedroom on the ground floor and then upstairs to the tower bedroom. The roof was a skylight.

'I lie here and look at the stars,' Haut said. 'I feel closer to God.'

Cavalier examined the winding staircase that separated from the wall and left a small alcove at the top of the stairs. The steps up were covered in a light plastic that squeaked when trodden on.

'I put it there so I could hear anyone coming up,' Haut said.

'Smart move.'

There was a view from the bedroom down the staircase.

'What do you think?' Haut asked.

'They'll come up the stairs,' Cavalier replied, positioning himself in the tiny alcove.

'Do you think we should defend from here?' Haut said, sitting on his bed and pointing down the stairs.

'No. It'll be dark.' Cavalier pointed to the alcove. 'That's the best spot. Where's the Uzi?'

'In that cupboard behind you.'

Cavalier leant down and retrieved it.

'It's loaded,' he said, fingering the clip, 'good.'

Cavalier tried to swing the weapon in an arc.

'Perhaps you have more freedom from here,' Haut said.

Cavalier shook his head.

'When they come up, this position allows me to be above and to the side of them.'

'What will I do?'

'It'd better if you left for the night.'

'No, no,' Haut said, 'I want to be here, in case. . .'

'What?'

'You need help.'

Cavalier stared for a moment and then smiled.

'You're a gusty bastard, aren't you?'

'What happens if they wound you . . . or . . . ?'

'Okay, but you must let me do my thing, okay? You must stay as calm as you can. It will be dark. I don't want you jumping in trying to be a hero. I was caught in some friendly fire once. I don't want to be laid up in hospital for six months again, or worse. Can you stay cool, no matter what?'

'I think so. Where do you want me to be?'

'Hidden beside the bed, looking at the stars, and praying.'

Haut managed a nervous smile, and nodded.

'Use your Bentley,' Cavalier said. 'If it all goes pear-shaped.' He grinned and added, 'But it won't.'

'How can you be so sure?'

'God's on my side,' Cavalier said with a grin, 'I think.'

'I have prayed into this very hard.'

'I knew you would.'

'I had a little play with the Uzi. It was manufactured forty years ago.' He stared at Cavalier. 'The Israelis use them. Or used to. How'd you come by one?'

Cavalier examined the weapon.

'Fell off the back of a survey ship in a container en route to Fiji in 1987.'

'1987? That's when there was a disturbance. A military coup. Were you . . .'

'No, I wasn't. But mates of Wombat were. One brought him back a souvenir.'

Haut showed Cavalier the alarm system set up in his bedroom. The front of the house, front room and laundry had hidden sensors that triggered lights in the tower bedroom wall, which would alert them.

'They'll be touching down in Hobart about now,' he said, looking at his watch. 'We have about five or six hours before dark. I believe they'll strike after midnight, when the street is at its quietest.'

'You're very sure.'

'I observed them up close in Laos. They are predictable to a point. But we must be alert from the next hour. Having said that, I want to rest.'

He picked up the Uzi. Haut led him down to a bedroom next to the front room and opposite the laundry.

'Don't know how you can sleep,' Haut said.

'Easy,' Cavalier said, patting the Uzi. 'I have my sweet friend here for protection.'

'I'll get water up in the bedroom and make sandwiches.'

'Good. It might be a long wait.'

Cavalier slept for four hours, then read and watched TV until it was dark. At 7 p.m. he and Haut then retired to the tower.

'Leave the lights at the entrance and front room,' Cavalier said. 'We want them to believe you are at home and that everything is normal.'

Haut nodded. He was tense.

'There is nothing worse than waiting for something like this,' Cavalier said. 'But we are ready.'

Cavalier proceeded to relax with an hour-long yoga and calisthenics session.

At 9 p.m. Haut's mobile phone rang.

'Answer it,' Cavalier said, 'just as you would normally.'

Haut did as instructed.

'Yes,' he said, 'Al Haut here.'

There was no response.

Haut hung up.

'That'll be them,' Cavalier said, 'just checking you're in. When do you usually switch off lights?'

'About 11 p.m.'

'Okay, then do it as usual.'

35

STRIKE THREE

At just after 1 a.m. Haut was lying beside his bed, his rifle next to him. The moonlight was minimal in a black sky, yet there was enough illumination from the skylight to see shapes in the room. Cavalier was on the floor at the top of the stair with a pillow for a headrest and his new night-glasses, courtesy of Anthony Jones, resting on his forehead.

They were alerted by a yellow light flashing on the wall.

Haut sat up.

'Vic,' he whispered.

Cavalier indicated he'd seen it. He got to his feet, tossed the pillow into the bedroom, slipped on gloves and picked up the Uzi.

'The laundry,' Haut whispered.

Cavalier positioned himself at the top of the stairs in the small alcove. He pulled the night-glasses over his eyes. Haut slipped a bike helmet onto the pillow on his bed. He then put on another helmet and lay flat on the floor gripping his rifle.

A blue light went on, indicating movement in the front room. They heard light, careful tread and squeaks on the plastic cover on the stairs. Cavalier had the Uzi's safety catch off. He gripped the weapon. He could feel his heart thumping.

Three shapes eased up the staircase, stair by stair, two men in front with the third behind them.

The size of the first shape indicated it was Hollos. He had his arm raised. Each intruder had a handgun. The stairwell curled round so that the three men were soon nearly level with Cavalier. He thought they would hear his heart. They hesitated for several seconds. Then they moved up another stair. What they saw was a shape on the bed. A head? Hollos was next to Castro with the lean figure of Leni one stair behind them. They lifted their guns to fire. Cavalier moved right so that he was a metre in front and above them. He pulled the Uzi trigger. He felt the jolt up and to the right. He kept his finger down hard, causing an ear-splitting *boom, boom, boom*. Hollos and Castro slumped, and the three figures thumped and tumbled down the stairs on top of each other. Apart from the crash and bang as the bodies fell, not a sound came from the three men.

'Vic!' Haut called, 'you okay?'

'Put on the light,' Cavalier said, lifting his glasses. His Uzi was pointed at the shapes. There was no movement from the tangled heap. He eased down the stairs and examined the bodies, pressing hard where a pulse would be on the necks of Leni and Castro. There was none. He did not have to check Hollos, whose skull had been shifted sideways like a slipped crown. Blood was trickling from a dozen wounds and landing on the plastic, creating little crimson pools. A bullet had gone right through Hollos to Leni.

Cavalier glanced at Castro. His formerly huge nose was no more. A bullet had destroyed it and passed through the centre of his skull.

'They're finished,' Cavalier said. 'Turn the light off and stay there. I want to check if they have a driver.'

Cavalier put on the night-glasses and moved to the broken laundry door. He bounded up the stair at the side of the house and into the street. He could see a Holden Commodore car parked fifty metres down the road. He eased to it. No one was in it. Cavalier hurried back to the house. Once inside, he raised the glasses to his forehead again and called,

'All clear. Switch on the light.'

Haut took a few steps down towards the bodies.

'Shit!' he mumbled.

'Cover your nose and mouth,' Cavalier said, 'don't take in the smell. There is nothing worse. Sweet and sickly.'

'You know it well?'

Cavalier didn't reply. He examined each victim.

'Funny that,' he said. 'This bloke at the bottom took just one bullet, right in the heart. Blood everywhere but not on his suit.'

'We need to dispose of the bodies,' Haut said.

'Do you have a mate, one you can trust? One who has a van?'

'Yes,' Haut said, stepping past the bodies.

'Tell him to bring rubbish bags,' Cavalier said, 'big ones and plenty of them.'

Haut made a call.

'You can really trust him?' Cavalier asked when Haut got off the phone.

'He's like a brother. Ex-SAS.'

'Name?'

'Ken Pringle.'

'Pringle, Pringle . . . I know that name. He competed for a place in the SAS when I did, decades ago.' He paused. 'When you introduce us, remember I'm Mr Malcolm.'

Cavalier moved to the bodies and took all items from their clothes, including wallets, cards, pens and hire-car keys. He placed everything in a plastic bag, except the keys, which he pocketed. He picked up two of the guns. Castro still gripped his. Cavalier loosened his fingers and released the weapon.

'Three bright shiny new Glocks,' he said. 'Very nice shooters, just like mine.'

Haut helped Cavalier ease Leni's body from under the others.

'Notice something?' Cavalier asked. 'They're all wearing the same suits.'

'What's that about?'

'I'd guess some sort of killing club; an insignia for assassins. They wore the same jeans suits every day in Laos, except Hollos. He couldn't fit into it.'

Cavalier struggled to remove the light-brown suit from Leni.

'What are you doing?' Haut said.

'Quality suit, this,' Cavalier said. 'Silk-lined. Look, no bullet holes; no blood.'

He handed the jacket and pants to Haut.

'I reckon you should wear it,' Cavalier said, 'it's about your size.'

'Why?'

'I don't know. A warning perhaps to any other would-be killers.'

Haut smiled nervously as he accepted the suit.

Cavalier looked down at Leni's arm. He carefully peeled back the shirt. It revealed several deep scars on the forearm and the back of the hand.

'That's Mac's killer,' Cavalier said.

Haut's hand went to his mouth.

'Dear God,' Haut whispered, his eyes welling. 'I think you're right.'

'Leni must have been checking out the place. Remember the vet said he patched up a skinny guy who stank of cigars?'

'I prayed for God to judge Mac's murderer,' Haut said softly, 'and he has.'

36

BURIAL PARTY

They were distracted by a van backing into the garage carport in front of the house.

'It's Ken,' Haut said.

Cavalier put on his black-rimmed glasses and casual jacket. Haut introduced them. Sixty-year-old Pringle had the wiry build of an ex-SAS man, who kept in good condition, as much as he could after suffering in Iraq when he was blown up and had many bones broken. His long black ponytail was a concession to another life outside the disciplines of Special Services. Opioids, including Kratom, the natural pain-relieving drug found in Thailand, had gone some way to ease the pain of a body and life disrupted.

Pringle didn't recognise Cavalier. He was distracted by the sight of the bloodied bodies.

'Jesus!' Pringle exclaimed, 'What happened here?'

'Just a wee party, where these three became dead drunk,' Cavalier said lightly.

'The shits came to kill me,' Haut said, with emotion.

'Deadshits,' Cavalier corrected.

Pringle returned to the van and brought in ten large garbage bags and tape. The three men slid two of the bags over each body, one bag from each end. They rolled up the plastic on the staircase, making a careful attempt to avoid smearing some of the blood on the wood-work underneath. They slipped it into the bags. Cavalier noticed blood spots on the stairs and said,

'Must get rid of that.'

'I'll do that later,' Haut said.

'No, better now.'

Haut hurried to the kitchen, filled a bucket with hot water, and threw in detergent and a scrubbing brush.

Cavalier took them, cleaned the floor and tipped the water down the kitchen sink.

'That bloody smell,' Haut said.

'Breathe through your nose,' Cavalier said. 'I can tell you, you'll never forget it.'

'That's right,' Pringle agreed as they wrapped the bodies, 'horrible!'

Cavalier walked up the staircase and examined some bullet indentations.

'You'll have to remove all the fragments,' he said, in his Cockney accent, while pushing his finger under splintered wood on the bannister.

'Ken and I will do that later.'

'Polyfilla and paint will do it. But make sure it's a thorough job.'

Haut taped the bags together. Cavalier guarded the street while Pringle and Haut loaded the three bodies into the van. Haut disappeared down the side of the house and returned with two spades. He tossed them in the back of the van and then jumped in front with Cavalier.

'You don't have to come,' Haut said. 'We'll bury them.'

'I'll come,' Cavalier said. 'Want to make sure this is done right. My responsibility.'

Pringle reversed the van and drove off down Nicholas Drive.

'We'll need a burial place wid soft sand,' Cavalier said in his best Cockney. 'We want them deep, untraceable.' He paused. 'Must burn dare wallets and everything in them.' He paused again and added, 'And du guns. Day are very nice shooters.' He tapped his jacket pocket. 'I'll keep one wiv me for the time being, if you don't mind.'

'Good idea,' Haut said. 'But when we're ready we'll hide the guns, including the Uzi and my Bentley. Best to leave them at my home for now.'

'I have a hiding place behind panels in the van,' Pringle said. 'They can go in there.' He glanced at Cavalier. 'Do I know you from somewhere?'

'Don't know,' Cavalier said, as they turned into Churchill Avenue. Pringle kept glancing at Cavalier.

'Did anyone ever tell you look remarkable like a guy named Cavalier, Victor Cavalier? Mind you, I haven't seen him for a very long time.'

'No,' Cavalier said, pretending to watch the side mirror, 'no day haven't. Most people think I look like a certain film star.' He paused and asked, 'Where do you plan to make this burial party?'

'I know a vacant allotment,' Pringle said. 'It's close to a beach. Very soft sand.'

'I've known a few assassins like dat,' Cavalier said.

'What?' Haut asked.

'Vacant allotments.'

The three men laughed. It broke the tension. Haut held his jaw. It ached from the strain.

Pringle drove for another ten minutes close to the beach. He turned into a side street and onto a piece of land covered in scrub. Trees hid the place from neighbours on both sides.

'This is perfect,' Haut commented, jumping out of the van.

'Dat's if no one ever builds on it,' Cavalier said.

'They will,' Pringle said.

'What?' Haut asked.

'I own it,' Pringle said. 'I'm putting down the foundations myself.'

Haut removed the two spades from the van's rear. Cavalier removed the bag containing the three dead men's personal effects. He went through the wallets item by item, examining bits of paper, credit cards, club memberships and passports.

Pringle and Haut began digging, piling up the sand in quick time.

'What an idiot,' Cavalier said under his breath.

'What?' Haut said, pausing to wipe his brow,

'Hollos has one credit card in his real name.'

He handed Haut a piece of paper marked 'Farquar' with a phone number scrawled on it.

Cavalier used some paper in the van to start a small fire. He tossed the items on the fire and watched them burn. He held a bundle of money, hundreds and fifties of Australian currency in his hands. Cavalier walked over to Pringle and motioned that he take the money.

'I want you to have it,' Cavalier said. 'You've gone beyond the call of dooty tonight.'

Pringle eyed the money, looked at Haut and waved it away.

'Nar,' Pringle said, 'I think you should take it. You've earned it.'

'No, mate, dares about four thousand dare,' Cavalier said and with a cool smile added, 'Gwave diggers are very hard to find deese days. It's a dying art.'

The others chuckled. Pringle pocketed the money.

They dug to about six feet. It took just short of an hour, with Cavalier relieving each man every ten minutes.

'Dat's deep enough,' Cavalier said, shovelling the charred remains of the personal effects into the hole. The three men took the bodies and the plastic matting from the van, laid them in the grave and then shovelled the sand back on top of them.

Haut bent to one knee and said a silent prayer.

'What did you pray?' Pringle asked as they returned to the van.

'I commended the bastards to God, for him to judge.'

'Did you fro in something for me, good Reverend?' Cavalier asked, as they drove off.

'Of course,' Haut said. 'I thanked the Lord for sending me a *guardian* angel.'

The other two looked at Haut, expecting a smile. But his expression was serious.

In the slow drive back to Haut's home, Pringle said,

'Funny you talk about a guardian angel. That bloke Cavalier I mentioned saved my life. One hundred candidates were competing for a few spots in an SAS intake at Albany, Western Australia. He was well ahead of the pack after a run and a swim. I was coming second but cramped in the water. A helicopter turned a spotlight on me. My pack was weighing me down and I couldn't remove it. Cavalier spotted me, swam to me and hauled me out of the drink. I was unconscious but was told later how he performed CPR and revived me.'

'When was this?' Haut asked.

'Back in the 1970s,' Price said. 'The irony is, I was selected in the SAS in a second trial a year later. Cavalier was by far the smartest candidate in that first trial, and the fittest. He won every single fitness and intelligence test. But he didn't make the cut.'

'Why?' Haut asked.

'He had a ruptured Achilles.'

'What happened to him?'

'He went into journalism. He's written some books.'

'Poor fellow,' Cavalier mumbled.

'You've got a double,' Pringle said to Cavalier. 'But of course that was so long ago. Cavalier had a six-pack abdomen. He'd be around sixty now. You look in very good shape. But you're younger, right?'

'Thank you,' Cavalier said. 'Philately will get you a nice stamp album.'

The van struggled up towards Haut's house. The three men spent the best part of two hours prying, cutting and digging bullet fragments from the walls and staircase. Then, after a beer, Pringle shook hands with Cavalier and Haut. He stared at Cavalier and said,

'It was a pleasure to help out,' and then drove off in his van.

'Ken doesn't say much,' Haut said, 'but he was clearly in awe of you for what happened.'

'Of me?'

'He knows I couldn't kill a fly. Not a human one, anyway! Notice he didn't ask for any details.'

'He's been there, done that, I'd say,' Cavalier said.

They sat in the lounge in silence. A cock crowed nearby, heralding the pre-dawn.

'You handled everything with a certain aplomb,' Haut observed. 'Almost as if you enjoyed it.'

'Not as much as writing a crisp article,' Cavalier said.

'I can't believe that. You've written stuff for forty years. Surely it can't give you the same adrenaline rush?'

'It's not really the moment for introspection,' Cavalier said. After a second, he added, 'But you're right. The sensation at the depths is unmatched.'

Haut wanted to ask more, but checked himself.

'How do you think your God will judge me?' Cavalier asked.

'He's your God too.'

'Okay, but what do you think?'

'In this case, he wanted you to act. I have a chance to fulfil his mission now.'

Cavalier ruminated for a minute and said,

'I've contravened a commandment.' He paused and added, 'Many times.'

'Is that a confession?'

'No, a fact.'

'His judgement would depend on the motivation; integrity . . .'

'Of a kill?'

'Yes. As long as you remain Dr Jekyll as well as Mr Hyde I believe you will be judged well. But that is up to God.'

'What if I'm Mr Hyde without Dr Jekyll?'

'Are you?'

'Just say I was.'

'Then God would not judge you well.'

Cavalier sipped his drink, and said,

'Perhaps it's safer to remain agnostic.'

37

WREST POINT OF CONTENTION

Cavalier awoke with a start and reached for the Uzi beside his bed and sprang to his feet. He heard a heavy scratching and bumping in the roof above him in the spare room and his first thought was that someone was trying to enter the building. The sound continued. Cavalier, his heart beating hard, stood stock still. The bumping was followed by scampering feet. Cavalier sat on the bed and put down the Uzi. It must have been a possum, he thought with a sigh.

He settled himself and looked at his watch: it was 7 a.m. and a winter dawn was breaking. Cavalier was sweating from a heater turned up too high. He'd had four hours sleep and the events of the night rushed into his consciousness. He wandered into the main room and looked at the staircase, which in the half-light filtering from the bedroom skylight, looked eerie. It seemed funereal, a bit like a modern morgue.

Cavalier could smell coffee wafting from the kitchen. Haut was up after managing just two hours sleep following a long period of prayer, in which he was thankful he had been spared. He began to face the fact he would have to escape Australia. Because of the oil business at stake, he felt there would be further attempts to kill him. It was better to go into hiding until a more propitious, safe time to return to Tasmania. The thought of leaving hurt him. His family, friends and business were in the state. Despite all the corruption and hurdles put in front of him, this was home. It offended him to have to run.

'I'm going to be around for a few days,' Cavalier told him over breakfast in the kitchen, 'just in case there are any more cowboys about.'

'You are welcome to use the house . . .'

'Thank you,' Cavalier said, 'but I'll check into a hotel. I thought about Wrest Point but Farquar may be there. He'll wait for a confirmation of a kill from his three amigos. When they don't appear, he'll become twitchy.'

'He'll come after me again?'

'You have to consider that possibility. Otherwise, he might not receive his property in Texas and, it's now thought, ten million in cash due to him.'

***

Cavalier booked into Rydges in North Hobart, a quiet hotel nestled next to a cricket oval. He drove the would-be killers' hire car to a wood near the city's Royal Botanical Gardens, left the keys in the car and rang the hire firm from a public phone booth to say where the car was.

The morning was cold and damp. He pulled his coat collar up, put on a scarf and made the five hundred metre walk through the gardens and scrub, over the Brooker Highway and down back lanes to the hotel.

He checked in with Haut twice a day. After two days, Haut rang him.

'Farquar wants to have a meeting.'

'Did he say why?'

'Wants to settle differences between us.'

'What differences?'

'Years ago we went on a business trip to look at possible oil investments in Burma, Laos and Thailand,' Haut said. 'This was long before I realised he was working for Conquer. He was spying on me. He claimed after the trip that he should be paid an hourly rate and gave me a bill for several hundred thousand dollars. It was extortion, pure and simple. He sends me a bigger bill every year. Now it's over a million.'

'That's an excuse to smoke you out. He realises now that his boys have failed in their mission.'

'The prick was trying to sound conciliatory on the phone.'

'What are you going to do?'

'What do you think?'

'Hmm. You could meet him. But you choose the location. Make it very public. Wrest Point would be good.'

'Will you be at the meeting?'

'Farquar knows me from Laos. He may or may not see through my disguise.' Cavalier was a silent for a moment. 'I won't be far away.'

'Will you, you know, bring protection?'

'I'll tell you something,' Cavalier said, reverting to his Cockney voice, 'I won't bring a condom, or du Uzi.'

'What about one of the Glocks?'

'Might bring that.'

'You won't be checked. Security is slack.'

'Do you know where I could pick up a shoulder holster?' Cavalier asked, reverting to his own voice.

***

Haut obliged and borrowed a holster from Ken Pringle. A meeting with Farquar was arranged for the next night, a Friday, at 8 p.m. for the revolving restaurant on the Casino's top floor. Cavalier, wearing a suit, took a taxi to the car park under the casino. The Glock fitted under the jacket, with the holster tucked against his rib cage, and to the back. It gave him an irritating itch that always left a welt but it never really bothered him. The weapon was his security.

He avoided the front entrance, where he noticed a gaggle of journalists with TV cameras. He walked around to the back of the building, past the gym and towards the large kitchen. A man walked out through the sliding door. Cavalier slipped in and found a service elevator. He pushed the button. A cook approached Cavalier as he stepped inside the elevator.

'Hey, what are you—' the man began, stopping the door from closing.

'Food inspector,' Cavalier said with a calm expression, pulling out his wallet and opening it as if there were a card of authority in it. 'I'll be back soon.' The cook backed off. The elevator took Cavalier to the revolving restaurant on the eighteenth floor. He noticed Haut in intense conversation with Farquar at a table for two. Haut was wearing Leni's light brown suit.

Cavalier stopped short of them and sat at the bar, facing a mirror and their reflection. An attractive brunette, wearing a red skirt split to the hip, parked herself two seats away. Cavalier noticed her perfume. It was pleasant, even alluring.

'Could I buy you a drink?' he asked.

The woman eyed him without saying anything for a moment.

'Do I know you from somewhere?' she said, her voice sultry.

'I would like to think so,' Cavalier said, dreading a comparison with Caine again.

'I'm Jane McBride, a friend of Al Haut's.' She lowered her voice. 'He has "business" with Neil Farquar. He said you would be here as his protection.'

'He wanted you here too?' Cavalier asked, watching Haut in the mirror as some finger pointing began between him and Farquar.

'I came here early to meet my mother for a drink and bumped into Al. He wanted me to keep you company before my friends arrive.'

Cavalier ordered drinks: Scotch on the rocks for him; sauvignon blanc for Jane. They chatted.

'You look neat in those glasses,' she said. 'They are so 1960s.'

'You're too young. . .'

'They're coming back. They hide your azure eyes.'

Cavalier chuckled.

'Never had an azure compliment before.'

Cavalier kept glancing in the mirror. Farquar was tapping the low table at which their drinks sat. He was making a forceful comment. Haut looked tense.

After five minutes, Jane turned and waved.

'Oh, my friends have arrived,' she said. She put her hand on Cavalier's forearm and asked,

'Why don't you join us? They are fabulous people. There's—'

'I had better stay here.'

'You can watch Al just as well from the table, using the mirror.'

He glanced over at the party of four that was sitting down at a table for eight. Waiters fussed around them.

Cavalier prevaricated.

'Who shall I introduce you as?' Jane asked.

'Roy Malcolm.'

'Okay, Mr Malcolm,' Jane said alighting from her bar stool, and reaching for his hand. She placed him with his back to the window and in a position to view Haut and Farquar. Cavalier hardly registered Jane's four companions when they were introduced.

***

Three tables away, the argument was becoming heated.

'You owe me a million,' Farquar said pushing his forefinger at Haut.

'I owe you nothing,' Haut replied.

Farquar held up his hand in the shape of a gun, directing it at Haut's head.

'I'm coming with three more guys,' Farquar said with vehemence, 'and this time we'll do the job.'

'Make sure you bring body bags,' Haut said.

'Fuck you!' Farquar said, stunned.

'I'm not wasting my garbage on Conquer rubbish.'

Farquar stared, his expression waxing between murderous intent and fear.

'Nice suit,' Haut said, opening the jacket, 'don't you think?'

Farquar's jaw dropped, realising that it was the suit worn by all his would-be killers.

'Tell Conquer I like wearing their assassins' suits,' Haut said. 'So next time keep up the dress standard.'

Farquar stood and stormed off.

'Don't worry,' Haut called after him, 'I'll pay for the drinks.'

38

ESCAPE

Cavalier was aware of Farquar's abrupt departure a minute after he was introduced to Jane's friend Mary and her Swedish husband Frederik, and two other Swedes, Henry and Robert. When Farquar left, Haut joined Jane's table.

'Thanks for looking after Roy,' Haut said to Jane, while sitting next to Cavalier. A few minutes later, when the rest of the table was chatting away in Swedish, Haut leaned close to Cavalier and told him of Farquar's threats.

'Unless you want some sort of business gang war,' Cavalier said, 'it might be time for you to disappear.'

'I think you're right.'

'If he brings three more killers that will make seven coming at you in a very short time. Money is no object in the attempt to destroy you.'

'It's too much for you?'

'It would get tricky and out of control. And I like control. Pack tonight and stay at my hotel.'

They made their excuses to the Swedish party and Jane, and headed for the elevator.

Cavalier steered Haut to a service elevator.

'Best to depart via the tradesman's exit,' Cavalier said. 'They may have a greeting party waiting for you.'

'Do you know who you were sitting with?'

'The Swedes? No, but their faces were familiar.'

'They were Frederik, Prince of Denmark, and his Tasmanian wife Princess Mary.'

'No!' Cavalier said. 'I did notice the other two were packing heat.'

'Their bodyguards. The party arrived last night. They're staying here.'

'That explains the media posse at the front of the hotel.'

'It will be all over the TV and papers tomorrow morning. Jane let me know they'd be there. The guards meant we'd have some extra protection on the outside chance Farquar did something stupid— I mean turn up with other thugs.'

They made their way out through the kitchen and down steps to the car park. Cavalier led Haut to a pillar. He scrutinised the area. About twelve media people had congregated near the hotel entrance.

'See that car parked forty metres from the entrance?' Cavalier said. 'That'll be Farquar.'

'You've got very good eyesight.'

'Yeah,' Cavalier said and adjusted his glasses, 'X-ray vision, almost literally.'

They walked to Haut's BMW roadster. He drove. Cavalier sat on the passenger seat. He pressed a button. The window wound down.

'You'll have to drive close to it once you leave the park,' Cavalier said, taking out the Glock. He attached a silencer and released the safety catch.

'You're not going to . . . ?'

'No, don't worry. Just slow them up a bit. Give them a little scare, like you did with that bikie at the drug factory. Drive at about forty. Once I've had my shots, take off.'

The roadster pulled up close to the Ford sedan with Farquar at the wheel. There was one other man in the front seat. Both were watching the entrance and the media throng. Cavalier aimed at the back right tyre and fired off two shots.

'Go!' he said. Haut put his foot down and sped off. Looking back,

Cavalier could see the two men getting out of the car, gesticulating and examining the punctured tyre.

***

Haut took a room at Rydges for the night and at dawn the next morning he and Cavalier checked out of the hotel. They drove to Haut's home, where the sickly odour of the triple killing still lingered at the staircase. Haut packed two suitcases while Cavalier sat in the roadster, alert to every vehicle coming up the road, or from the street behind him and further up the top of the mountain. Haut took a stressful hour. He had his phone to his ear all the time, talking to his parents, friends and business acquaintances. He told them he was going away and would not be back for some time. He kept on phoning over the next fifteen minutes as he drove them both to the airport. It was 6 a.m. when they arrived. Cavalier slipped off the shoulder holster and Glock and placed it under the seat.

'Better not get caught with that,' he said.

'I'm having my accountant pick up the car,' Haut said. 'I'll tell her to take it, the Uzi, the Bentley and the Glocks to Ken Pringle. He can look after the car and hide the weapons in the van.'

'Not that it matters,' Cavalier said, alighting from the car, 'I don't see Farquar complaining to the police that there are three missing murderers whom he sent to kill you.'

'I'm going to leave the keys under the seat,' Haut said. 'My accountant doesn't have a set for the car or the house.'

'They should be okay in sleepy Hobart airport.'

The airport was quiet. About a hundred passengers were waiting for the first flight out.

There was one seat left on a flight to Melbourne that was scheduled to board in five minutes. Cavalier insisted Haut take it.

'No one spoke to me, except your friend Jane and the Danish crowd. I've been like a ghost in Hobart.'

'Did Farquar recognise you at the casino?'

'Doubt it. I had my back to him at the bar and then when I sat with the Danes there was that stylish opaque partition between us.' Cavalier smiled and added, 'Last night he ducked when I blew the tyre out.'

'Yeah, I saw that too,' Haut said with a nervous chortle before checking in. He had two pieces of hand luggage, one stuffed with business papers.

Cavalier walked with him to the plane lounge on one side of the small airport. Passengers were boarding.

'After what happened at my home,' Haut said emotionally, 'I don't think I could ever return there.'

Cavalier put a consoling hand on Haut's shoulder.

'I understand, but never say never.'

They shook hands.

'Thanks for everything,' Haut said. 'You're my avenging angel.'

Cavalier smiled and said,

'Sounds more dynamic than being a *guardian* angel.' Then he added more sombrely, 'Thanks again for saving my daughter.'

Cavalier checked the next available flight to Melbourne, which was at 10 a.m. It would give him time to have a decent breakfast and coffee in Hobart.

Haut joined the line to board the flight. Cavalier began to leave the airport, fedora pulled down and dark glasses on. He saw a car speeding into the parking area. Four men, including a red-faced Farquar were in it. They alighted and rushed towards the entrance, side-stepping Cavalier, who was still coming out. He watched them approach the boarding gate, where they were blocked by staff. Cavalier could see much gesticulating as Farquar tried to get Haut off the plane. The staff called security.

Cavalier strode to Haut's roadster. It was unlocked. He got in and retrieved the gun and holster, then watched the airport lounge. Haut's plane took off. Moments later, Farquar and his henchmen walked out of the airport. They moved briskly to their car, which was parked uncomfortably close to Cavalier and the roadster.

Cavalier took a breath—they might recognise Haut's vehicle.

Farquar was still waving his arms wildly. The men climbed into his car, distracted by his tirade. Cavalier gripped the gun and rolled out of sight in the front seats. The sedan sped past the roadster.

Cavalier sat upright and breathed a huge sigh of relief. He decided that airport food and coffee would be a lesser but better option before he flew out.

PART FIVE

PROPHET IN EXILE

39

WOMBAT DE-BRIEFING

Haut's accountant, Rebecca Green, stepped up to the front door of Haut's tower home at 6 p.m. that night. It was dark and she was trembling. Haut had asked her to pick up some papers he had missed. She was also instructed to take his Bentley rifle, the two Glocks and the Uzi, and to leave them with Ken Pringle, who had already picked up the roadster and taken it to his home.

Forty-year-old Green had just collected the papers and had found the guns in the alcove cupboard at the top of the stairs when she heard a car pull up close to the house. She left the weapons hidden and stuffed the papers in a satchel. She wondered what to do: hide, or make a run for it? Haut hadn't told her about the killings, or Farquar's warning he would come back. But he had told her the place could be robbed for the papers, which pertained to his inventions.

With her heart in her mouth, she walked out the front door, looking back once to see a Ford sedan with people in it. She hurried to her Volkswagen car, thinking she might be attacked or even shot at any moment. The Ford's lights went on high beam and blinded her as she started her car.

Farquar and his men, carrying rifles, jumped from the sedan and surrounded Green's car. They motioned for her to get out.

'Is Haut in there?' Farquar said, pointing his gun at the tower house. Green was shaking. She tried to speak but the words wouldn't come out. She shook her head.

'Where is he?' he asked.

'Don't know. Over . . . overseas, some . . . somewhere. He flew out the other day.'

'What have you got in the bag?' one of the men, with a squeaky voice, asked.

'Just tax pa-papers. I'm . . . I'm his accountant.'

The man went to grab the bag but Farquar stopped him.

'We didn't come for that,' he said, 'only for him.'

***

On a cold Saturday in mid-July, Cavalier and Wombat had brunch at the stylish European Cafe, opposite parliament on Melbourne's Spring Street.

'I had a call from Haut in Los Angeles,' Cavalier said, as coffees were served. He related the story of the accountant's visit. 'She went back the next day and bravely took the weapons to Ken Pringle, who hid them behind a panel in his van.'

Wombat sipped his coffee and adjusted his glasses as two attractive young women wearing Melbourne red and blue colours walked by, on their way to a big game at the MCG.

'Are you going to talk about what happened in Sandy Bay?' Wombat asked.

'I'd rather not.' Cavalier looked up and added, 'One day in the not too distant future when we are both pissed on the best scotch money can buy, I'll tell you about it. For now, I'd rather forget.' He paused. 'The mind is a wonderful thing. It manages to block out the bad things.'

'You mean suppress them. They have to pop up somewhere.'

'Only when someone reminds you of them.'

'You don't have nightmares?'

'No. Never about missions. About other things, yes.'

'Such as?'

'How I made a bright four in a school cricket match when I had my mind on a century. It was against my school's greatest rival.'

'You're kidding!'

'No, don't laugh. Even Don Bradman said his biggest regret was not winning for Australia in his first Test in England in 1930. He was eighty-eight years old when he told his biographer that. That was sixty-seven years after the event. He had nightmares about it from then on.'

Wombat sat back in his chair and played with his bifocals.

'Haut's still kicking. There's no trace of the three assassins. Mission accomplished?'

Cavalier smiled.

'I have always admired your logical commonsense approach to analysis, Wombat.'

'So your disguise worked?'

'I wanted to talk to you and Jones about that. Those glasses made me look like Michael Caine in *The Ipcress File*. I know the movie was made a long time ago but re-runs on TV remind people. Drew attention to me.'

'Sorry about that.'

'Missed it myself.' Cavalier stirred his coffee. 'One other thing. I'm going back to that Conquer story. I expect to be able to break something big in a few months.'

'To do with what?'

'Their reserves. They've overstated them in what could be one of the biggest frauds in corporate history.'

'You're going to break that yourself?'

'No. If I do that, Conquer will draw a link between me and Haut.'

'You'll plant it?'

'With *The Wall Street Journal*. I might let the BBC have it as well. Nothing like a visual piece with Old Auntie to rattle the cage.'

'Will you be paid?'

'Nicely, I can assure you, but without attribution.'

40

ENTER MR X

In August, when half of Europe and the US were enjoying vacations, *The Wall Street Journal* and BBC TV broke a story that shook the financial world and beyond. There was no by-line on the newspaper article. It was titled: 'Conquer in History's Biggest Fraud?'

It began:

Oil industry insiders have been shocked by the rumors that the European Conquer Group, the number one oil giant, has overstated its reserves by 30 per cent. If so, it may prove to be the biggest fraud in financial history. There is a huge flow-on effect from the public comprehension of stated reserves. Conquer's share price has been kept buoyant for decades because of its capacity to gobble up new discoveries worldwide. This influenced insurance companies and pension funds to park their money in Conquer. It was regarded by them as the safest bet in the world. Millions of ordinary people with small savings, pension plans and insurance policies have long adhered to the corporate slogan: 'Conquer all with Conquer'.

Top Conquer executives are said to be in a panic with the alleged internal discovery of the cover-up. One executive, who would not be named, said: 'The oil slush will hit the fan soon.'

Another said: 'We are shocked and angered by this story.' When asked if it were true, one commented: 'I am not at liberty to say.' Further unsubstantiated claims were that Conquer's rush to take over Shelf Energy with its massive reserves on Australia's north-west shelf, and other potential finds in Tasmania, were part of the scramble to make up the shortfall on the books. Both efforts failed, leaving Conquer with no capacity to make up the 30 per cent.

***

Bleulance called a meeting at his Champs-Élysées Paris office with de Cobb, Joslin and Daniels.

'I don't have to tell you how bad this is for Conquer,' he said as they sat at a boardroom table. He lifted his spectacles and read a private intelligence report, which was set out on light blue A4 paper. 'There will be fines. You'll lose your triple A rating. The share price ...' Bleulance put down the paper and picked up the *Financial Times*. 'The shares have dropped twenty-five per cent in one day.'

He looked up again and stared at a large painting by Picasso on the wall as if more predictions were somehow etched there.

'You'll have to set aside a lot for class actions.' He returned his gaze to the others, and winced as he added: 'A *lot*.'

The others knew what all this meant for their own shares in Conquer, but nothing like that of Bleulance himself. A quick estimate would be that his investment company would have seen about twenty billion pounds wiped from its portfolio.

He seemed unperturbed. But they also knew that his hidden passion, his true love, was for energy. The blow to Conquer was personal. He looked up over his glasses at the three silent executives.

'The entire board will have to retire,' he said. 'Conquer will have a clean-out.' He put on his glasses again and returned his gaze to the private blue paper. 'You'll all have to leave also, I'm afraid. Have your offices cleared and be out of the building—' Bleulance glanced at his silver Bulgari watch, '—by 3 o'clock this afternoon.'

***

Haut had flown to Los Angeles where Pinkerton took him up as a client again

'You're still our biggest risk,' the security boss told him, 'but for some reason your adversaries have gone very quiet for the moment. We're not clear why. However, the upshot is we can take you on again while you are in the US.'

They moved Haut from safe house to safe house in Los Angeles, starting in Pasadena, until it was decided he'd be better monitored in New York. Haut took temporary residence at Manhattan's Theodore Hotel on East 55th Street. At first glance, Haut was happy with his new, luxury home, however temporary it might be. His suite was as big as an average apartment. The hotel had impressive eateries, which suited Haut's need for plenty of 'brain food' to keep his five orbits whirring efficiently. The most famous was the Theodore Grill, which served American food and was open all day for meals. There was also the Nixon Club Lounge, which featured a twelve-metre mahogany bar, two fire-places and stained glass windows that gave it an ethereal feel; not quite a church, yet unworldly.

***

Three days after Conquer's crisis became public news, Haut had a call from a man William Donnelly had contacted calling himself Mr X. They met over lunch at the Theodore. Mr X was a solid six-footer with a swathe of silver hair. He was well-dressed in an expensive navy blue suit, light blue tie and white shirt with starched cuffs showing monogrammed silver links. Mr X was no-nonsense and authoritative. He was there to quiz Haut about the Conquer encounters, his mining claims and his assessments of the size of the potential oil field under Tasmania, as well as talk about his cold fusion concept. Haut, forewarned and forearmed, had a briefcase full of supporting documents.

Mr X's opening was to lay down rules of engagement.

'If we are to assist you, Mr Haut, you must not leave the Theodore at any time unless accompanied by me or Mr Norman Timms, who will meet you soon. We can protect you inside the hotel. Outside the hotel you are more than vulnerable at this moment.'

'Understood,' Haut said, retrieving files from his briefcase.

Two days later, there was a message from the front desk.

'There's a Mr Norman Timms to see you.'

Timms was wiry and bird-like with hunched shoulders and an aquiline nose. He wore a grey suit and tie loosened at the neck and was more relaxed and less pristine in appearance than Mr X. He appreciated Haut's humour and had a light side himself. Neither Mr X nor Timms said what their role was, but over the ensuing weeks they formed a tag team, meeting Haut in his confinement at the Theodore, but never together. Timms acted like a journalist. He took notes and asked questions the way reporters did. Mr X was more interested in the ongoing battle with Conquer.

At the end of January, Haut phoned Cavalier in Chiang Mai and told him of the tag team.

'William Donnelly lined this all up,' he said, 'but I'm intrigued about where these guys come from. They are almost as efficient and thorough as you.'

'I hope more so.'

Haut described Mr X.

'Must be CIA,' Cavalier said. 'They're usually Ivy League, although that may have changed in the last decade.' He was thinking of Melody Smith and the new breed of American operatives coming in under the current presidential regime.

'And this Timms fellow?'

'He is the "reporter" of the two.

He mentioned he would write something for *Future Energy Global Intelligence Report.*'

'That's run by the CIA. They spend a lot of money and time on spotting and managing current and future American energy sources and reserves. You're being assessed right now by Mr X to see what you can offer, say the American Navy, in terms of future oil reserves.

And, of course, you've come recommended by Donnelly.'

'Why wouldn't the navy buy their oil from the US?'

'They do, but this is about, as real estate agents say, location, location, location. For instance, just say there was a confrontation between China and the US over China's attempt to control trade routes in the Pacific. The Americans would want big supplies close by. Hobart would provide the closest big supply. You will be the supplier, Al.'

'Your context explains the interrogation I've been under, and the angle of the questions.'

'If they like what you say, and the cut of your jib—that is, if you are trustworthy—they will support and protect you.'

'And Timms's report?'

'If he mentioned FEBIR then that will be his outlet.'

41

THE CIA STEPS IN

In the last week of August, Timms sent Haut an email saying: 'Have a look at the story for the September publication of *Future Energy Global Intelligence Report*. You're in it.'

Haut looked up the story on the net. It began:

Few oilmen have the unshakeable faith of Al Haut, a director of Full Gospel Business Men's Association International operations, a powerful body of business people worldwide with 8.6 million members and no particular denomination. But then again, none have had the vision from God that showed Haut, at age 19, there are billions of barrels of oil under the little drilled Australian island state of Tasmania. Or that its port of Hobart will one day be a key refueling point for the US Navy.

Timms's piece was hard-hitting and pro-Haut. It even quoted his former Tasmanian University professor, Harold Burnside, who once declared there was no oil in Tasmania.

But when he went to Oman, he noted the similarity of rocks there to the Permian Basin, West Texas and Tasmania. Burnside, a staunch atheist, who pushed Haut's spiritualism to one side, changed his mind on Haut's finds and deferred to the conviction of his former pupil. He was made a director of Al Haut Minerals.

'I still avoid Al's ethereal commentary,' Burnside told FEGIR. 'I am certain now that his claims are correct. But that certitude has cost me a lot of credibility. I have also had my home burgled and computer stolen. This is the work of Conquer's agents working overtime to stop Al. But it won't stop him. He has already defeated them once.'

'That is an amazing piece of writing from your point of view,' Cavalier said when Haut rang him. 'It would be considered actionable if it were not true. It means Big Brother is one hundred per cent behind you. Conquer will back off. They won't take on the might of the American government and its most influential and lethal arm, apart from its navy.'

'You think it's defamatory?'

'For sure, if it were not true. But Conquer won't do anything. For one thing it's the truth. For another, Conquer is weak from the reserve fraud being made public. It would not win anything in court with this pall of criminality hanging over its head.'

'I can't believe that a little bloke from Tasmania has brought down one of the five sisters!'

'In this case, the ugly sister.' Cavalier looked at the article again.

'What's your next move?'

'I want to fund a full-blown drilling campaign. I'm also working on a reverse merger of Al Haut Minerals into a US company that will be called American Empire Minerals. The Securities and Exchange Commission has approved it after a two-year review.'

'What will it do?'

'I expect it to create about two hundred million dollars market value. I can then pay bills with stock.'

'You'll base it in the States?'

'Not sure,' he chuckled. 'I'm Al the nomad at the moment.'

42

THE RUSSIANS MAKE THEIR PLAY

Less than a week after the CIA-backed FEGIR report, Haut received a strange call from someone purporting to be from the office of Russian President Vladimir Putin. Haut realised the call was genuine when Putin came on the line.

'I wish to put a proposition to you,' Putin said.

'Oh, what might that be?'

'I would prefer to do it face-to-face.'

'In Moscow?'

'Yes.'

'Sorry, I can't go into Russia just now. I'm dealing with the US government.'

There was a pause before Putin said,

'I understand. Would it be possible for you to fly to Hamburg to meet with my very good friend and adviser, Mr Anatoly Kisley? Do you know him, sir?'

'I'm aware he is a Russian ambassador.'

'That is the one.'

'I haven't met him.'

'We shall pay your first class airfares and hotel expenses. Could you see your way clear to make the trip?'

'If I come, I shall pay my own way, thank you.'

Putin had been polite but yet to the point and Haut found himself drawn to say he would make the trip. But he diverted from a positive response. He thought it best to run it past Cavalier first.

***

Haut had spent three months cooped up in the Theodore, which he saw now as a prison. He was keen to go anywhere.

'I'm stir crazy,' he told Cavalier in a phone call in which he divulged Putin's approach. 'Can't go out after 8 p.m. Can't go to a bar and chat up one of the endless charming women of New York.' He chuckled. 'Just for practice, you understand.'

'You need more than practice, by the sound of it.'

'You must know what I mean . . .'

'I have no idea what you're talking about.'

There was a pause, then they both laughed.

'Have you run it past Mr X?' Cavalier asked.

'Had to. He is against it. Says I can go if I wish but he can't protect me.'

'But you want to go?'

'Yes.'

'Curiosity killed the cat. You can't go to Hamburg without someone to guard you.'

'What about you?'

'I'm on an assignment. Can't break from it.' Cavalier paused. 'I'll see if I can persuade someone else to assist.'

'Where from?'

'Thailand.'

'Wombat said you had good contacts in Russia.'

'Not so much now. My main contact is Putin's mentor and hero, Ivan Modinsky. A gentleman spy if ever there was one. I liked him more than most. We got on well. I always enjoyed his company.'

'Honour among thieves?'

'Something like that.'

'Honour among assassins, perhaps?'

'Al, remember, this call could be monitored.'

'Sorry, listeners. I was joking. Neither Cavalier nor Modinsky is an assassin.'

'Nor are they thieves!'

Haut chuckled.

'Modinsky, Modinsky . . .' he reflected. 'He ran British spies, didn't he?'

'Ivan ran at least twenty British double agents from Cambridge, Oxford and the London School of Economics. He was the doyen of KGB spies. He was well retired when I knew him. A good time to talk to old spies.'

'Why?'

'They open up. I first met him in 1993, a few years after the Communist walls went down. The bottom had dropped out of the rouble in the massive sea change from the dissolving of the Soviet Union to the formation of the Russian state. Retired agents saw their pensions diminished. They were suddenly very poor. One US dollar bought you a thousand roubles. I offered Modinsky a thousand dollars US in cash for a TV documentary interview; that is, one million roubles. It would keep you going for a long time buying goods on the Russian black market.'

'I think I saw that documentary,' Haut said. 'Did Modinsky have a white beard?'

'That's the one. He looked like Colonel Sanders in the Kentucky Fried Chicken franchise.'

Haut took a deep breath.

'I don't know what to do about Hamburg,' he said. 'I'll pray into it.'

'Good idea and I'll give Modinsky a ring if you like. Run it past him.' Cavalier paused and added: 'Then you'll have two valuable opinions.'

'That would be most helpful,' Haut said with enthusiasm. 'You sure you wouldn't want to make the trip to Hamburg?'

'Love the place! So much sea-port atmosphere, and infested with espionage agents from several countries. But no. As I said, commitments.'

'Newspaper or—'

'I promised not to tell.'

'I'll pay for the airfare and hotel expenses. You can even bring a girlfriend.'

'Don't have one at the moment. But as I said, I'll see what I can do. I have a most reliable friend who is in need of a job.'

***

Cavalier parked his Harley in a grubby side street off Chiang Mai's notorious Loi Kroh, a road of cafes, bars and massage parlours, most of them staffed by prostitutes. He entered the Entertainment Complex, a place he had avoided for a year or so since one of his few friends in the city, an English bar owner and web designer, had split with his Thai partner and moved to Pattaya.

Cavalier walked out of the early morning heat and into the roofed complex, a hundred and fifty metre lane with bars either side. From nightfall it was glittering, and filled with cacophonous music sounds from opposing bars as the women competed for the wallets of tourists. Now, at 8 a.m., it was empty of people but for a few cleaners.

At the end of the lane was the Muay boxing ring. Cavalier stood for a minute watching as two fit young Thai men exchanged blows watched by Jacinta Cin Lai, wearing a green and yellow tracksuit and MAGA hat, which said, 'Make Australia Great Again'.

He watched as Jacinta stepped in and demonstrated a high kick. A rush of blood caused one of her boxing pupils to throw a punch. It collected Jacinta on the upper arm. In two flashes she had given him a half-punch and kick in return. The strikes were pulled but still the exuberant young boxer went down on his back.

Jacinta helped him up and admonished him. Then she noted Cavalier standing beside the ring. At first, she seemed to melt in indecision then, showing her exceptional suppleness, she did a backflip over the ring's ropes and landed on her feet two metres from Cavalier. They embraced. Jacinta stepped back, embarrassed that her sweat had left marks on his shirt.

'I'm sorry for not being in touch,' she said, blushing, 'but I know that I am still being watched and reported on.'

'For what happened on the Bangkok Express?'

She nodded.

'Very wise. I think we must avoid each other in Thailand for another year,' Cavalier said, taking her by the arm and walking her a few metres away.

'What are you doing here?' he asked.

'I have an Australian boyfriend.'

'Hence the hat and the tracksuit.'

Jacinta blushed.

'I think of you when I wear them,' she said.

'Bargwan!' He smiled. 'Are you living with him?'

'No. He sends me money each month, but not enough! I act as an instructor here and in a gym.'

'Would you be open to an assignment?' he asked.

Jacinta stared, searching his face.

'Not that kind of assignment,' he said with a serious expression, 'this would be one of protection.'

Jacinta sat down and watched her two pupils slug it out in the ring.

'It would be in Hamburg. All your expenses would be paid. Your fee for a week would be ten thousand American dollars.'

She eyeballed him.

'Would you be with me?'

Cavalier nodded.

'Then I'll do it.'

43

THE KISLEY CONNECTION

Cavalier rang Modinsky in Moscow.

'Caval-e-a!' the Russian said, pronouncing the name the French way rather than the English 'Caval-ear'. 'How are you?'

They exchanged pleasantries before Cavalier asked about Putin's proposition for Haut to meet Kisley in Hamburg.

'I know nothing about this,' Modinsky said, in his sing-song voice, which sounded more Swedish than Russian. 'If you call back this evening, I may have information for you, although I cannot promise anything.'

Cavalier rang back seven hours later.

'My advice is that he should go to meet Kisley, yes,' Modinsky reported.

'Can you say why, Ivan?'

'It will be very good for Mr Haut, I can tell you that.'

'May I ask how you know that?'

'I spoke to Vladimir.'

'Vladimir?'

'Why, Putin, of course.'

'I'm impressed, Ivan.'

'Why?' Modinsky said with a gruff laugh. 'Vladimir is only a colonel in the security services reserve. I am a general!'

***

Anatoly Kisley was not what Haut expected. Big-boned, and oozing bonhomie, he was warm. He kept sweeping back his grey hair and, but for his heavy jowls, was still a handsome man for his sixty years. Kisley's English was good, despite his Russian accent. They met at a bar in the middle of a Hamburg square not far from Haut's hotel, which the Russians had wished to pay for. Haut decided against that too. He was wary of being seen to have been 'bought' in any way.

Kisley was accompanied by two bodyguards, and a very tall, shapely blonde woman of about thirty years. They filtered away to another part of the bar.

'She can't be one of your bodyguards,' Haut said, smiling at her.

'Catherine the Great, we call her,' Kisley said. 'She is an assistant. Rather like Marilyn Monroe, don't you think?'

Haut was eager to learn what Putin's proposition might be. But at first Kisley did everything to avoid any business talk.

'The smoke in here is choking me,' Haut said with a grimace as he looked up at roof fans that were fighting a losing battle in dispersing the detritus of a hundred cigarettes and cigars.

Kisley then asked questions about Haut's life, and after an innocuous interrogation came the telling remark.

'You know that Putin is a devout Christian?'

'No,' Haut replied.

'Oh, yes, he is. But of course he keeps it quiet. Vladimir is a most private man. Most private.'

'Because Christianity is not the image you want in a communist country?'

'Not so,' Kisley said with a tilt of the head. 'We are not a communist state anymore.'

'But your history since Lenin. . .'

Kisley pulled a face.

'You would be surprised to see how religious our people are. They were suppressed for a very long time. But we Russians are a spiritual lot.'

'And you?'

'I am a Christian too. We are aware of your own spirituality.'

'Oh?'

'We have our spies in Australia,' Kisley said with a grin.

'And I have mine everywhere,' Haut said. 'I understand you have instigated the building of Russian Orthodox churches in communist countries.'

Kisley's eyebrows went up.

'I cannot comment on this. We have to move carefully.'

'I think Cuban and North Korean churches are under consideration, yes?'

Kisley smiled.

'I think your spies are as good as mine!' he said. Kisley turned to ask a barman to give them a bottle of gold-filtered Russian vodka. 'This is the finest vodka in the world. Will you join me?'

They began to drink the smooth liquor. 'You will not have a hangover with this,' Kisley said. 'The gold filters out impurities.'

After a third glass each, Kisley started asking questions about Conquer and what Haut thought about the giant oil producer.

'Huh!' Haut said with his faltering laugh, 'They have tried to kill me.'

Kisley ignored this until they were on their fifth drink and had all but demolished the bottle.

'Did they really try to murder you?' he asked, his expression serious for the first time.

'Oh, yeah. They sent three gentlemen and paid them thirty million dollars to do it.'

'Hmm,' Kisley said, 'I would have thought that figure was a gross under-evaluation of you.'

Haut laughed. Kisley's expression did not change. He called for another bottle of vodka. Pouring their sixth glass, he asked,

'How did you manage to survive? You had bodyguards?'

Haut explained how Pinkerton had dropped their security for him.

'Then how did you avoid being eliminated?'

'God sent me a guardian angel.'

Kisley was taken aback at first, then he laughed.

'And now you have American protection, again?'

Yes, well, Pinkerton returned to support me . . .'

'And the CIA?'

'I don't know officially. But I assume it is them.'

Kisley scrutinised him with an amused expression. It prompted Haut to add, 'The people who have been in the Theodore Hotel with me are from the US government. That is what I know. They have my interests at heart.'

'You mean *their* interests,' Kisley remarked without malice.

'Both our interests.'

On the second bottle of vodka, Kisley spoke more quietly.

'Vladimir wants to remove Conquer from Russia.'

'Kick them out?'

Kisley nodded.

'They control a huge field in Siberia,' Haut said, surprised. 'What is the problem?'

'*Problems*, plural.'

'Such as?'

'They want to narrow down payments for the lease. They want a greater share of oil and gas production proceeds. Far greater than the original arrangement.' Kisley sipped his drink. 'Vladimir is not happy.'

'Hmm. I know how he feels.'

Kisley threw back the glass's contents and poured them both more.

'Magnificent, isn't it?' he said, indicating the vodka.

'Yes.' Haut chuckled.

'We know you Aussies like a drink,' Kisley said with a slap of Haut's back. 'Even the smaller ones!'

This elicited much mirth from him. Then, in a flash, his expression changed.

'Vladimir wants to offer you a job.'

Haut waited.

'Yes, a very big job,' Kisley said, with a pulled face as if to emphasise the size. 'The president wants you to take over the Conquer operation.'

Haut's eyebrows went up.

'The whole operation, everything,' Kisley added. 'You see, we have done our homework on your outstanding work as an oil man, a geologist. Vladimir is in great admiration of how you took on and defeated Conquer.'

Haut took a deep breath. His shoulders slumped a bit.

'You can name your price for this work,' Kisley said.

Haut shook his head and moved his forefinger left and right, saying,

'Money is never the issue with me.'

'We are talking one hundred million dollars a year.'

'No. It's not the issue,' Haut repeated.

'Then what is the issue?'

'I am dealing with the US government. I can't double deal.'

Kisley frowned for the first time. He downed another glass, and filled Haut's again.

'Is that why you could not work with the Chinese?'

Haut was taken aback.

'Part of the reason,' he said, cautiously. 'They wanted me to work on certain applications I don't wish to discuss.'

'To do with oil exploration?'

'No, although I was showing them how to find it in the Pacific.'

'What then?' Kisley asked, topping up Haut's glass.

'I can't talk about it.'

'Your cold fusion work to use water to replace fossil fuels in combustion engines?'

Haut was surprised again.

'You don't miss much, do you?' he said. 'But it wasn't that exactly. I was told in secret by a leading Chinese scientist where the work I was doing with the Golden Brain of China was headed.' He downed his drink. 'I was shocked. I got out fast.'

Kisley nodded knowingly. They sat in silence for a minute.

'I shall have to talk to Vladimir about your rejection of his offer,' he said. 'Can we meet for breakfast tomorrow?'

'Fine. Just thank the president very much for this offer. Tell him it's nothing personal and I regard his approach as an honour. I am sincere.' He chuckled. 'It is not often that such an offer comes up! But please tell him that my main aim is to develop my leases in my home country; my home state.'

Kisley reflected on the comment, then he smiled and said,

'I shall explain this all to him. He is not used to rejection, you understand.'

'Then we are two of a kind,' Haut said, raising his glass.

***

Kisley, one bodyguard propping him up either side, moved out of the bar, followed by Catherine the Great, who turned and waved to Haut. His expression lit up as he waved back.

The four Russians moved along the canal leading to their hotel. Haut ordered a beer, feeling overly relaxed. The bar began to close up and Haut was asked to leave. He wanted to know the directions to his hotel, which he couldn't recall the name of. Two of the staff took him outside, turned his coat collar up and pointed him towards the canal. Haut thanked them and staggered off, hands thrust into his coat pockets. He zigzagged to the canal, which was not well lit. A fog was moving in.

Haut stumbled on. A ship's foghorn sounded somewhere out to sea. A small boat jugged along the canal and gave him some comfort. He looked back and stopped. Four shapes were following him. He got glimpses of them when they moved under streetlights. Three came close and surrounded him. Haut was pushed to the ground. He tried to fight back but was too drunk and was easily overwhelmed.

Suddenly, Cavalier and Jacinta, both in black tracksuits and sneakers, moved forward, having followed Haut at a distance. They swooped on the three attackers. Cavalier delivered a rabbit-killer chop to the back of the biggest thug's neck who had been about to pummel Haut. He collapsed. Two of the thugs were forced to leave Haut and face Jacinta, who let go a flurry of punches and kicks that felled them.

A fourth thug emerged from the shadows carrying a knife. Cavalier stepped in front of him, pulling a handgun from under his jacket.

'Stay out of it!' he warned.

The fourth thug hesitated. Cavalier aimed at his chest. The fourth took another step. Cavalier fired, hitting the man's wrist. The knife clattered to the cobblestones. The thug fell to his knees, screaming.

Jacinta stood over the fallen thugs, who hardly moved. One groaned but could not get to his feet. Jacinta moved closer and gave him a fearful kick to the behind, sprawling him flat again. Jacinta then moved close to the fourth thug, who was now on his back moaning. She ceremoniously picked up his knife, moved close and bent over him.

'You are right-handed?' she asked.

The fourth thug nodded. He blubbered, wondering what she might do. Jacinta bent to one knee, lifted his left arm over her thigh and pushed down hard. Snap! His arm broke at the elbow. The fourth thug collapsed from the shock and pain.

Jacinta stood and hissed at the barely conscious man,

'Have fun cleaning your arse!'

She and Cavalier turned their attention to Haut, lifted him to his feet and helped him along the canal the few hundred metres to his hotel.

***

The next morning Haut and Kisley walked the coastline littered with shipwrecks and World War II submarine scraps, which formed a breakwater near the Blankenese Lighthouse.

Both men wore sunglasses and heavy overcoats. Kisley had a fur hat. His two bodyguards walked about thirty metres behind. They were on constant vigil along the cold and deserted coastline.

'I do apologise,' Kisley said. 'We should have escorted you to your hotel. Are you okay?'

'Some bruises,' Haut said, 'otherwise I'm fine.'

'Who were they?'

'No idea. Probably just local thugs.'

'Did police save you?' Kisley asked.

'A couple of guardian angels. . .'

'Your bodyguards?

'In a way, yes. But I didn't know they were in Hamburg.'

'Are they the ones who dealt with Conquer's assassins?

Haut smiled mysteriously but said nothing. Kisley removed his dark glasses to reveal puffy cheeks and slits for his green eyes.

Haut blinked in surprise.

'It seems that my hangover-proof vodka does not cater for the next morning's appearance,' Kisley said ruefully. 'I look far worse than you, and you were mugged!'

They walked on, stopping to look at a submarine wreck.

'I spoke to Vladimir last night,' Kisley said. 'He was disappointed. But he would like to ask you a favour.'

Haut nodded.

'He wants you to ask your American friends if they would be agreeable to him removing Conquer from Siberia.'

'I can do that.'

'Thank you. He wants your advice on who should replace them.'

'In return, I'd like to have dinner with Catherine the Great.'

'Who doesn't?' Kisley smiled. 'Very sorry, but she returns to Moscow with me this afternoon.'

***

Cavalier rang Haut and they arranged to meet at the Hamburg Museum. They strolled past the artefacts relating to the city's long history.

'Where's that stunning Asian you had with you last night?'

'Jacinta? She is shopping. She has a nice budget.'

'A nice everything, I'd say from my hazy memory of her intervention. She is amazing! Are you, you know . . . ?'

'We're just good friends.'

'I've already heard from Mr X,' Haut said. 'Putin's request went right up to the White House. Potus said, and I quote Mr X: "Conquer isn't American, is it? Putin can do what he wishes. We won't retaliate." I told Kisley this morning. Conquer will be booted out soon.'

'Another huge blow from you. Will they know you advised Putin?'

'I wouldn't want it public, but . . .' Haut shrugged. They stopped at an enclosed glass case containing a stake through an ancient skull. Next to it was a life-sized waxed figure, labelled Klaus Stortebeker.

'I really relate to this guy, Klaus,' Haut said. 'He was a fourteenth-century German pirate who fought off Danish ships. His team, the Victual Brothers, had a battle-cry: "God's friends and the whole world's enemies."'

As they left the museum, Haut asked, 'How long is Jacinta in Hamburg?'

'As long as you are.'

44

THE SCOOP

Haut walked out of the airport at Washington DC and was ushered to a bulletproof limousine. Inside it was his close friend and backer, William Donnelly. They shook hands as the vehicle moved off.

'Sorry to be so mysterious about where we're headed,' Donnelly said, tipping back his huge Akubra hat, 'but given your current circumstances it's best to keep everything private. We're going to a meeting that is about as high-powered as you can make in this town. Only Potus's attendance would make it stronger. And believe me, he is aware it's going on. I'm making sure your area comes to his attention. He has an interest in it.'

'You're talking about his uncle's writing up of Tesla's notes?'

'I am.'

The limousine pulled up at the impressive European so-called 'Second Empire' designed Eisenhower Executive Office Building.

As they were alighting from the vehicle, Donnelly remarked.

'Just sit back during the meeting. There may be a bun fight.'

'Over what?'

'Your services.' The Texan snapped his fingers and added, 'Before I forget. Your seismic techniques are being used big-time in Texas. The president will be able to announce soon that America is a net producer in oil and gas. We are already the world's number one producer, taking over from Saudi Arabia and Russia. Thanks to you, Al!'

'Think nothing of it, William. I've just added a trillion to the US's wealth!'

'You're right, you know.'

'I was obligated to do it. The head of my church, Chuck Flynn, wanted me to protect Potus, which meant supporting him and his goals. I really had no choice.'

Guards in naval uniform escorted them to an elevator which took them to a third floor and the Diplomatic Reception Room. There were twenty-two people seated or standing around chatting. Donnelly began introducing Haut. He was soon immersed in a lather of names from the navy, the army, the air force, NASA, aerospace companies such as Lockheed Martin and Tielisten Allan, the CIA, the FBI and National Security Agency.

A few minutes later the meeting was chaired by the Commander in Chief of the Navy, Admiral Richard Ingram, a well-built sixty-year-old with the bull-neck of an ex-weightlifter who still worked out. Haut sat in pride of place next to him at the head of the table. Ingram called for comment from the CIA Deputy Director, the lean 44-year-old Melody Smith, the only woman at the table.

'We have been involved with Mr Haut for some time,' she said with a grin of acknowledgement to Haut. 'We believe we should be his continuing case officer, if you will. He is, I believe, comfortable with our people now dealing with him at the Theodore. We have the resource, the skills and the firepower. . .'

The mention of 'firepower' caused Ingram to interrupt her.

'With respect, Miss Smith,' he said, 'we at the navy can call on the power of the entire US military, if we wish. A lot more power than you could muster in a thousand years. And most importantly, we have Potus in support.'

'The president is happier with our agency than he was a year ago,' Smith said.

'He has never lost faith in us,' Ingram said. 'But that aside, if Mr Haut can access that oil in Tasmania, he will represent a most valuable asset in the Pacific. We don't have to hide the elephant in the room. Or should I say, dragon.'

Ingram called for a comment from Donnelly, who was sitting next to a bemused Haut. Donnelly got to his feet and pushed back his hat.

'I'm not going to take sides here, Mr Chairman,' he said, 'but I want to say this. Thanks to Al Haut's seismic technology we are now once more the world's prime producer of energy—oil and gas.'

All heads turned to Haut. There was spontaneous applause.

'But, apart from that, Mr Haut's water-as-fuel technology is going to be important for all engine development. His other inventions are going to be vital for space travel and the military.'

'So you're saying the navy should be involved?' Ingram asked.

'I care about who defends him, of course,' Donnelly said. 'The navy is already guaranteed access to the oil in Tasmania, if Al holds those leases. The other main issue is which institution deals with him and his military products, which of course, the navy will benefit from.'

The CEO of Tielisten Allan, Mark Anderson, caught the chairman's eye.

'That's where we come in, sir,' he said. 'We have already been in touch with him. He wants to work with us . . .'

The Deputy Director of NASA, Bob Cowper, was on his feet appealing to the chair.

'We've also had discussions with Mr Haut,' he said. 'We believe his ultimate aspirations are closest to our future developments. . .'

Admiral Ingram indicated Donnelly should comment.

'William has had more to do with our guest today than anyone,' Ingram said.

'I sure have, Admiral. This man is a serious genius. I pulled him in to plug the biggest oil well blow in history, you all will recall in the gulf two years back. No one, not even Red Adair, had a clue what to do. Al did.'

'Which corporation do you think he should work with?' Ingram asked.

'It's a no-brainer: NASA.'

Bob Cowper beamed. The scorned representative of Tielisten Allan, Mark Anderson, looked grim.

'However,' Donnelly continued, 'I want to add an important caveat in dealing with Mr Haut. He has already set up an American corporation of his own, which I shall be investing in. That way he will be better able to control his products. It will avoid all the fatal pitfalls, no disrespect to any of you here, which have occurred with similar solo inventors in the past.' There was silence. "We owe Mr Haut that much since he has given us the technology to build our energy reserves to our current dominant position in very quick time. He has asked for not a cent for this huge advantage to our nation. His corporation, American Energy, is the pay-off for that extreme generosity.'

There was more applause.

At the close of the meeting, Admiral Ingram leant across to Haut and Donnelly and asked quietly: 'What did you mean by "fatal pitfalls"?'

'Some inventors have been bought off or screwed financially,' Donnelly replied.

'Others have been murdered,' Haut added.

45

PLAN B

Two weeks later, a big front-page story appeared in *The Wall Street Journal* headlined: 'Putin takes control of $80bn Gas Project'.

It was 'by a special correspondent' and began:

Conquer has been forced by the Russian government to hand over its controlling stake in the world's third biggest liquefied gas project. After months of pressure from Moscow, the European giant company has to cut its stake in the $80bn Sakhalin III scheme in the far east of Russia. It is believed that the state-owned Gazprom group has taken it up.

It is also believed that another Western oil producer was invited by Putin to take over the interest. But industry insiders say the offer was rejected because the company concerned was working with the US government on another oil and gas project . . .

'You realise they may work out who was behind the piece?' Haut told Cavalier over the phone.

'I'm prepared for that. They may be many things but they're not stupid.'

'Have you good security at your homes?'

'Melbourne is a fortress. I'm beefing up Chiang Mai.'

'You have firepower?'

'It's my business.'

'I'm picking up stuff on my radar. We must be extra vigilant now.'

'Conquer will react. You have dealt them two big blows now—the fraud over reserves, and now knocking them out of Russia.' Cavalier paused. 'The Australian federal government did an audit of Conquer Australia. They found forty million dollars was missing from the accounts. No one could say why.'

'That indicates Farquar was paid off in cash and Texas land with an oil well.'

'He may have done a deal that he "retired" there to avoid any investigation, whether or not he succeeded in eliminating you.'

'I'm still a target. He may strike again.'

***

James the butler drove his boss Bleulance, and Mawnie Schwartz, his chief of security, in a dark blue Mercedes across his Napoleon V estate past arable fields, horse stables, tennis courts and a dairy barn. Landscaped terraced gardens and flowing fountains, with marble cherubs peeing, were either side of the road.

They turned a corner and pulled up at a miniature chateau, with its tiny turrets and towers, where Bleulance liked to admire his Rembrandts, Picassos of all periods, a couple of huge modern frescoes and some more modest Reynolds and Gainsborough portraits.

James used a remote to unlock a massive double gate and then the chateau front door. Windows were barred, just in case some foolish robbers might want to chance their arm with a burglary in the highly fortified estate.

Bleulance led the way into a red drawing room and spent some time showing around an interested Schwartz, who liked to remind everyone he had a fine arts degree, perhaps to balance his thuggish, flat-nosed appearance, gnarled knuckles, and an eye affliction that didn't help his credibility.

James, in his usual unobtrusive manner, prepared tea using

seventeenth-century French silverware.

Schwartz gave his boss a verbal report on Haut's activity in New York and then Hamburg.

'Do you think his business in Hamburg was connected to Conquer's dismissal from Russia?' Bleulance asked.

'Excuse me, Baron, but is the Pope a Catholic?'

Bleulance took a deep breath. James poured the tea for both.

'He has the backing of the CIA, at least in the States,' Schwartz said.

'Now this kicking of Conquer out of Russia! But how? Why?'

'Not sure. But Haut met Kisley, and Kisley is one of Putin's closest buddies.'

'How do we stop Haut?'

'Too dangerous to eliminate him at the moment. I don't want my team in a gunfight with the CIA. I have the best team in the world, but the CIA can call on the American military, if it wants.'

'What do you suggest?'

Schwartz sipped his tea. In his enthusiasm to respond, he clunked the fine crockery too heavily for Bleulance's liking.

'There are other ways that you can deal with him. Keep up the sabotage and so on. But the next best deterrent to getting rid of him is to hurt . . .' Schwartz paused to make a snapping motion with his hands, 'those closest to him.'

'Family?'

'Yes,' Schwartz said with a pulled face, 'family, but more his loves. A close girlfriend or wife, for instance.'

'He's not married, I don't think.'

'We can check that out. If he has a woman, we can do some damage in a way that no one could ever shoot home the blame to you or Conquer. The CIA can't protect everyone around him.'

'But he'll be damaged?'

'Exactly.'

'I wish you'd stop saying "exactly",' Bleulance said. 'It grates. Find another word, will you?'

'Yes, Baron. Sorry, Baron.'

46

THE NIGHTCLUB

After six months of CIA protection, Haut was told by Mr X that he could base himself outside the US, but was cautioned against returning to Hobart.

'You are most vulnerable there,' Mr X told him, 'especially as we believe there could well be another assassination attempt. It may be that there is still an assignment to eliminate you.'

Haut decided he could risk a move to London, where he could step up his drive for funds to develop his oil leases and cold fusion technology.

***

Haut packed his models of the elements and booked an early morning flight from New York to London. He sat at a window seat and was joined by a lean, moustachioed man, wearing a white, lightly checked jacket. He had a young female companion. The always outgoing and loquacious Haut was pleased when the man reached out a hand and introduced himself as Ryan Gram and the bespectacled woman, his secretary, as Anne Marie Blanchette.

When breakfast was served Haut asked Ryan why he was going to London.

'We're with Tielisten Allan,' Ryan said.

'Special Scientific Development—SSD, by any chance?' Haut asked.

'We are. . .' Gram responded, feigning surprise.

'I've had talks with the director.'

'Doug Ackerley. Really?'

'He's interested in investing in my plasmoid technology. . .'

'Forgive me, Mr Haut,' Gram said, 'but didn't you decide to go with NASA, not us?'

'NASA has been slow in coming forward,' Haut said, 'but you're right. They are the frontrunner for me to deal with in the US.'

Over breakfast and the next three hours, Haut outlined his inventions to the rapt attention of Gram and Blanchette. After exhausting their attention, Haut remarked, 'This meeting is no coincidence,' which startled them both.

'What do you mean?' Blanchette asked.

'It's meant to happen,' Haut replied with certitude. 'It's God's will.'

The others smiled with apparent relief and nodded their agreement.

***

Haut took an apartment in the West End's Jermyn Street, St James, that had strong security, and whose guards were linked with those of the Magic nightclub across the road. This meant that if he ventured out, he need only go a few steps for relief from his apartment confinement.

The club had garish maroon-coloured furniture, and urinals shaped in the form of lipstick-laden huge mouths, which brought lots of laughs from patrons, but did not help their aim. The nightclub was run by a flamboyant nightclub identity, Ernie North. The former flower and grocery salesman at Romford market had bought himself a title on eBay—Lord of the Manor of Cosselley. The underworld figure was a bootlegger who liked to be called 'Lord North'.

Haut began spending time at the club. The guards were former

Russian soldiers hired by North on his many trips to Moscow for his vodka importations and other dealings. Haut liked the club's demi-monde atmosphere and struck up a friendship with North. They had much in common. Both had enemies that had tried to kill them, and they both liked the company of attractive women. Magic and North's adjoining You There! Club had them in abundance; a foreign legion of escorts from Russia, Eastern Europe, France and several other countries.

Haut increased his attachment to North by exchanging fifty thousand pounds worth of VAT receipts he had accumulated over several deals, for cash. It worked for both. Haut had much needed money. North needed the receipts for tax purposes. Haut saw the transaction as yet another 'act of God' to supply him with the means to proceed with his plans, similar to the way he had overcome his twenty-five million dollar debt owed to Australia banks when he claimed God told him to 'tell jokes'. This kind of financial deliverance had been witnessed by many of Haut's friends, family and business partners. He had become the Houdini of the mining world.

Haut further endeared himself to North during a court case when the London Council tried to shut down the club due to noise violations. Haut proved in court, with tapes and pictures, that the noise that had upset locals at night was not from the club but food sellers rattling their carts along the road. The magistrate dismissed the council's claim.

The Magic club was mainly a hangout for Russians and Eastern Europeans: some local suited and seedy types; older women wearing fur coats; and showgirls in red outfits and feather-adorned hats. The young women seemed to make themselves 'available', discretely enough, for men who wished to spend more time with them after hours. Haut was happy not to venture more than fifteen metres from his apartment to be in this haven of exotic and erotic femininity.

He found the women from Russia, Poland, East Germany and elsewhere accommodating. Haut, however, was less enamoured with the free and easy attitude to drugs, particularly cocaine. He observed a covered sugar bowl on the bar counter, topped up with cocaine, which was used by some customers.

North informed Haut, 'Its place at the bar is in case of a police raid, in which it could be claimed that someone, a customer, must have left the drug there.'

Haut would dine there some nights and North would make sure that his cubicle had blinds drawn just in case a hitman or squad could see into the club and carry out a mission.

Every late afternoon Haut would have a coffee liqueur with North at the bar, accompanied sometimes by North's girlfriend Hannah, a former Miss Israel. They were served by a chubby French–Mauritian, Florence. Haut flirted with her. North turned to her one afternoon and said, 'You can sleep wiv him if you want; that's if you can put up wiv him quoting bible verses.'

They all laughed. Haut's access to a mine of quotes from the Old and New Testament made an impression on all he met.

When Florence was out of earshot, North said to Haut, 'I know you like her but I have somefink coming up that will provide opportunities beyond your dreams, mate. You see, I own a modelling agency. Every year I hold a ball.' He winked at Haut. 'Best women in the world compete in a beauty contest.'

One evening North invited Catherine the Great to have drinks with him and Haut.

'I don't believe it!' Haut told North. 'I know her! Well, not actually. But I've seen her in Hamburg! What is she doing here?'

'On a working vacation, she told me when she asked for a job. She wants to improve her English, which is very good anyway.'

When they were introduced, they sat drinking in a cubicle with North. Catherine claimed she could not recall Haut. After several drinks, North suggested she 'look after other guests'. Haut stood to shake hands with her. She was lean of limb, flirtatious of manner and ready to laugh.

When North moved away from the table to greet other patrons at the bar, Catherine returned to the cubicle.

'Has anyone ever told you—' Haut began.

'That I am Marilyn Monroe's double?' Catherine said.

'I was going to say "double Marilyn Monroe".'

Catherine laughed and touched his arm.

'Never heard that before?' Haut asked with a boyish grin.

'Oh, yes, by just about every Westerner over forty years of age!'

'Well, you know it's not a pick-up line then.' Haut smiled. 'But this is. Would you like to have dinner with me?'

Catherine bent her tall frame down and kissed Haut on the cheek, leaving an imprint of red lipstick.

'I thought you'd never ask,' she said, causing them both to laugh.

After dinner at the club, and several glasses of wine each, Catherine, who was wearing a skimpy mini-skirt, revealing top and high heels, challenged Haut to a game of pool. Haut soon learned why she had wanted a game. Catherine was very good and prompted Haut to call her 'Walter', which led to a windy explanation of who Walter Lindrum was. The Monroesque Catherine didn't seem to grasp the explanation, or didn't care. She was concentrating on clearing the table of balls. Haut didn't care either. Her shoes lifted her to more than two hundred centimetres.

They played five games and Catherine won all of them. She enjoyed her dominance and this put her in a most convivial and receptive mood as they helped each other across the road and up to Haut's apartment.

Haut and Catherine quickly became an item and within weeks Haut was talking about getting engaged and married.

***

Three weeks later in Moscow, a special Kremlin meeting of Russian State Security was held, with Putin in attendance. Anatoly Kisley and the chief intelligence officer in Siberia, Yuri Norkov, wondered where they stood with Haut now.

'I think we should monitor him,' Putin said. 'What would you suggest, Yuri?'

'Has he a female partner?' Norkov asked.

'He has a relationship with a beautiful Russian.' Putin smiled. 'Whom he met in London.'

'Yes, Catherine Ferinsky. I am aware of that. She sends us some information but not enough, in my opinion. Haut is not unfavourable towards us. We should learn more about his activity, especially about his falling out with the Chinese over what we assume was for military applications for cold fusion. We should know what he is doing with the CIA and the American Navy.'

'I read that report,' Putin said. 'He is also still seeking finance for his Tasmanian oil project.'

'All the more reason we should have someone close to him to learn his aims and plans,' Kisley said.

Putin pulled an agreeable face.

'Do you have someone in mind for this operation?' he asked. 'She will have to be exceptional, given Ms Ferinsky's proportions.'

That drew a round of smiles from the twelve key Russian security men.

'I do,' Norkov said. 'She is a beauty and, with respect to Catherine, someone better qualified for such a project.'

'Oh? Who?'

'My daughter.'

47

RIGGED

Haut was brightened and excited when North asked him to be a judge of the 'Miss Wintertime Wonderland' contest.

'Dares one girl I reckon is right for you, mate,' North told Haut.

'I'm engaged to Catherine.'

'But not married yet, eh? I suggest you hold your horses until you see this one, all right? She's about the best from the whole European Con-i-nint. But I'll wait and see which one you choose, all right?'

Thirty attractive women, some from the nightclub, North's modelling agency and brothels, paraded themselves in bikinis and smart outfits. Each contestant had to do a special dance, which ranged from rock and waltzes, to the can-can and salsa.

One girl in particular—180-centimetre, fair-haired Natalia Moronova, a 27-year-old from St Petersburg—caught Haut's eye. She happened to be best friends with North's partner Hannah. Natalia performed a gliding, seductive, hip-wiggling salsa, then the hit song, 'Mambo No. 5', which Haut felt was directed at him. He voted her the winner, and persuaded the other four judges that she was the best all-rounder.

'Good choice, my son,' North said. 'I 'ad her ear-marked for you, didn't I?'

'Her English is excellent, to the point of pedantic precision,' Haut noted. 'Her deportment outstanding, and she has ingredient X. I can define this as charisma coupled with a vibrant character.'

'Did you miss 'er tits and bum, den?' North asked with a straight face.

Haut met Natalia and they seemed to hit it off. When he complimented her on her command of the language, she replied in a drawl that would make the British Royals proud, 'I can speak like an upper-class Sloane, if I so desire.'

Haut was impressed by her mimicry, and the humour associated with it. He soon discovered this was the least of her talents. Apart from her native Russian, she spoke French and German, and had basic Mandarin. Haut was enthralled and not a little surprised at the ease at which they became close. He took her out to dinner, with a guard from Magic in tow, and explained that he was engaged to another Russian girl, Catherine.

Natalia showed only mild interest. She appeared neither put-off nor perturbed by his ties to someone else. Their relationship blossomed but not in an intimate sense. Haut asked Natalia to be his personal assistant, an apparently alluring proposition for a young, educated Russian woman loose in Europe for an as-yet unspecified purpose, apart from doing a business degree part-time at the London School of Economics.

Haut wondered how he would disengage from Catherine but was surprised to see that the two women got on when they met at the club. There was not an ounce of enmity between them. After several weeks Catherine dropped out of the picture and Natalia widened her job description to satisfy Haut's amorous interests.

48

THE SET UP

'Dodgy,' Cavalier's senior MI6 contact, Liam Hunter, said when asked about the Magic club. Cavalier was on assignment in the UK and France, and on such occasions he always met with Hunter to chat about everything from cricket to terrorism, or anything else on the intelligence services radar. He was planning to meet up with Haut again.

Cavalier asked, 'In what way is it dodgy?'

'Ernie North has interesting connections. He comes and goes from Russia with great facility, importing his cheap vodka and other items. He employs Russian men and women. He runs brothels and nightclubs. We believe the former subsidises the latter.'

'You're implying a Russian security link?'

On matters of intelligence, Hunter would use conundrums or even riddles. He said, with a smirk, mangling a children's nursery rhyme:

'You shouldn't go out in the woods tonight, the bears are there but the women are quite enchanting, and sometimes "bare".'

'How so?'

'Let's just say that we monitor said nightclub.'

'Agents?'

'Better the devil you know than the one you don't know. It's never used by Russian embassy people.'

Cavalier nodded.

'Illegals,' Hunter added, in reference to foreign spies who work independently of their nation's embassies. 'Magic is a haunt in which they feel comfortable.'

***

Cavalier accepted Haut's invitation to dine at the Magic club, where they were joined by Natalia. She looked out of place in her dark covered-up dress that followed her curves but dropped below the knee. She had some champagne and then disappeared.

'She has a card game tonight with girlfriends,' Haut said, explaining her cameo appearance in their cubicle. 'Well, what did you think of Natalia?'

'I don't think you could do better than her,' Cavalier replied. 'I've been to Russia five times. I met some magnificent women in St Petersburg, but none better than her.'

'Think I'm fighting above my weight?'

'Depends on desires and needs, doesn't it?'

'You didn't notice the age gap?'

'She is very affectionate towards you. Seems genuine.'

'*Seems?*'

'How does one ever know?'

'I plan to marry her.'

'Congratulations!' Cavalier said, shaking hands. He frowned and asked,

'Aren't you engaged to that big Russian you told me about?'

'That sort of petered out. But we're still friends. She's mates with Natalia.'

'That's cosy.'

'You should meet her.'

Cavalier paused to watch every patron in view.

'Looking for someone?' Haut asked.

'Sorry, force of habit.'

'I do it too.'

'Is the heat still on with Conquer?'

'They are causing mayhem in Hobart. So are the Chinese.'

'Are you safe here? Is Big Brother your insurance?'

Haut gestured with his hands at the club.

'This is more my insurance. Ernie North and his men understand my situation. Bleulance won't do anything with them behind me. But I have issues with the Chinese. They seem intent on destroying my business after I refused to work on certain things with them.'

Cavalier waited for an explanation. When it looked like Haut was not going to expound, Cavalier prompted him,

'Go on.'

Haut sighed and looked uncomfortable.

'You know I had to leave China in a hurry, which was *after* a Chinese front company in Hong Kong—VictoryPlus—put five million dollars into my Tasmanian mining operations. That was a sort of quid pro quo arrangement.'

'Pay-off for the secret work you were doing in China?'

'Correct.'

'Very dangerous, Al! So the Chinese front. . .'

'VictoryPlus, in Hong Kong.'

'It wants its money back?'

'It's more complicated. They realise those Tasmanian oil leases are huge so they have bribed one of my company's directors, Bob Lawrie, who has in turned "persuaded" a corrupt mines official in the state government to hand over my licences to him. You'll recall Fat Bastard Ingrid Orangey announced the licences would be rescinded because she claimed there was no oil under Tasmania. Lawrie knows this isn't true. Among many things, he moved a big, expensive drilling rig off my lease era and placed it elsewhere. He sabotaged my operations.'

'Is this because you've left Tasmania? While the cat's away the rats play up?'

'It's worse. The Chinese through VictoryPlus don't give a tinker's cuss for the five million dollars they ploughed into my company. They are very happy to have a foothold in Tasmania and access to such amazing oil discoveries. That way they will have control over huge supplies and they can cut the Americans out of access. The Chinese are now attempting one of their "Belt and Road" deals with the Tasmanian government.'

'Won't the federal government intervene?'

'No. It believes the VictoryPlus front.'

'Not good!'

'My sentiments too. The bastards are also pursuing me in the courts for the five million dollars, which is a red herring. They want to destroy me and my operations along the way.'

'Payback for you refusing to work in China.'

Haut nodded. The conversation was draining him. They watched a club hostess sit in a cubicle with a handsome, lean Englishman in a pin-striped shirt. It broke the tension. She noticed them, smiled and from then on avoided their gaze.

'So you have Conquer *and* the Chinese, and a few corrupt Tasmanians to deal with. Not to mention some sections of the bikies who'd like your guts for garters. A few challenges . . .'

'When the time is right I'll go after Lawrie and VictoryPlus in the courts. His day of reckoning is coming.'

They paused to observe two mature women, both wearing dated fur coats, sit at a nearby table. Haut suddenly brightened and asked,

'Why don't you come to a fashion show this week?'

'What show?'

'Handbags.'

'Oh, Al, I didn't know you were into them.'

Haut smiled.

'Natalie and Catherine will be modelling them. You'll get to meet the giant Marilyn Monroe replica.'

49

HANDBAG OPENING

The show was held in a room at the Chelsea Town Hall on the King's Road a few hundred metres from the arts club at which Cavalier was staying. He arrived minutes before the parade began and was introduced to blue-eyed Catherine, in high heels, who towered over everyone. She was preoccupied with the modelling job at hand, not having done it before. Both she and Natalia were striking, partly because of their height. Catherine wore a black, backless dress, while Natalia was in white with a similar show of her back, but with a slimmer figure.

Eight women of different shapes and sizes walked around the catwalk to show the audience that every woman could own a French-designed, Serenity label bag accoutrement. There was an upmarket female audience of about a hundred, including many French ex-pats. All drooled over the one-off display of handmade, top-drawer bags. They gasped, clapped and cheered the items.

Haut leant across to Cavalier as Catherine floated up near them, stopped and posed for video and still cameras. She had at an outsized navy blue bag.

'I think that suits you,' Haut whispered.

'The woman or the bag?' Cavalier said.

'Both.'

After the show the guests mingled, and became more convivial as the champagne flowed and the tasty finger food of Russian caviar and French cheese were consumed. Cavalier hung back, observing. After a half hour, he made light conversation with Catherine.

'I'd love to have the handbag I displayed,' she said with a mock swoon.

'I did like the design and colour,' Cavalier agreed. 'It was big enough to put manuscripts in too.'

'I adore it. I am told it will be the third prize in the raffle. I am going to buy ten tickets worth! Fifty pounds!'

'How much is it worth? Or should I ask, how much is it being sold for?'

'Fifteen thousand pounds!'

'I'm in the wrong business,' he mumbled.

Catherine laughed. The champagne, her first ever catwalk performance and dreams of possessing the bag, had excited her. Cavalier moved discreetly to the raffle-seller and bought twenty tickets.

The raffle was drawn by the French designer. First prize was an Air France trip to Paris for two with accommodation and expenses included. Much delighted screaming came from women near the winning ticketholder, an elderly woman with a walking stick. The second prize was dinner for four at a top London French restaurant. Cavalier held the ticket, but did not present it. There was a redraw. The winner was a teenage girl who looked as if she might faint from the thrill. The third prize of the navy blue handbag with a brown, circular motif was the one that most women in the room seemed to want. The designer made dramatic play of dipping her hand into a hat and drawing out the raffle ticket.

'H5!' she said into a microphone, holding the ticket high. Everyone scrambled to read their numbers. There were groans. It seemed as if there might be another redraw when Cavalier strolled to the designer and presented the winning ticket. There were cheers and clapping.

'And what might you do with it?' the designer asked, handing him the bag.

'I may use it myself, or give it to a girlfriend,' he said.

That drew laughs. The crowd went back to their champagne and further loud chatter. After a few minutes, Catherine joined Cavalier.

'You have a girlfriend, dollink?' she asked.

'Sort of,' he replied. 'I'd like her to be.'

'Is she here?'

Cavalier looked around the room.

'I think so,' he said.

'Who is she?' Catherine asked.

Cavalier lifted his hand as if to point at someone on the other side of the room but ended up pointing at her.

'Me?' she shrieked, her hand planted between her breasts, 'really, dollink?'

Cavalier handed her the bag and went to kiss her on the cheek, but Catherine lunged at him. She kissed him on the mouth smearing lipstick on his lips, nose and cheeks. Others clapped and whistled. Cavalier used a napkin to wipe his face. More champagne was called for as several women surrounded Catherine, examining the prized possession.

Haut and Natalia came to him.

'Very smart move!' Haut said. 'Catherine will be attracted after that gesture.'

Cavalier sipped his drink but said nothing.

'Do you fancy her?' Natalia asked.

'C'mon, darling,' Haut said, 'any real man would.'

'I am asking Victor,' she said.

His smile was his reply.

The party continued. Another crate of champagne was opened. Cavalier told the others the next day would be big for him and began to leave. Catherine followed him out, clutching the handbag that now contained a bottle of champagne.

'Hey, you!' she called. 'You are leaving without a kiss goodbye?'

She gripped him by the back of the head with her free left hand and kissed him on the mouth again, this time lingering and with plenty of tongue. Cavalier responded, but not with her passion.

'My apartment is very close by, dollink,' she purred. 'Would you like to come up?'

'For coffee?' Cavalier asked.

'No! Champagne and great sex, dollink!'

Cavalier glanced at his watch, smiled and nodded. Catherine put her arm around his shoulder and they took the short walk along King's Road to Kings Court North, a block of apartments opposite the Chelsea fire station and Sydney Road. She led him up one flight of stairs to number eleven. Her rented apartment faced the King's Road, and the sound of traffic gave off a low buzz through the double-glazing. She put on the light in the front room and pulled the curtains.

Catherine looked at her watch. She kicked off her shoes.

'It's approaching midnight,' she said. 'The porn show will start soon.'

'Did you say *porn* show?'

She beckoned him to a bedroom. The curtains were opened. They looked down into a small courtyard. Opposite and below them, a light was on in a ground floor apartment bedroom, which was empty.

'Won't be long now, dollink,' she said. 'Sit and watch. Must leave our light off.'

A bemused Cavalier did as instructed. Catherine returned a minute later with the champagne and two glasses. He opened a window and popped the cork so that it was propelled across the courtyard and hit the glass to the bedroom they were looking at.

Catherine giggled and pushed him on the bed. They looked down to see a fit young man standing naked at the window squinting out. A woman, also naked, was soon next to him.

'They are newlyweds, dollink,' Catherine whispered. 'Every night at this time they begin an acrobatic sexual show for about an hour. I've had dinner parties where everyone has left the table to watch the performance. Each window—from the kitchen, toilet, bathroom, spare bedroom and this one— looks down into the "stage" below. They have not hung curtains in the room. My friends think they are exhibitionists. I think they just can't afford the curtains.' Catherine paused to laugh. 'I see them in the village or coming into the block but

I can't make eye contact. I think I would give myself away by smiling.'

They watched the couple climb onto the bed. The man was erected. He lay on his back. The girl began a slow kissing ritual, starting with his face, neck and ears and sliding down his taut arms and torso.

'Interesting technique, don't you think, dollink?' Catherine said as she poured the champagne.

'She has copied me,' he said in mock indignation.

'Really, dollink?' she said.

They watched as the young woman kissed down to his inner thigh. She began vigorous fellatio.

'I don't think she has had dinner tonight,' Cavalier said.

Catherine laughed. She eased off Cavalier's jacket. He loosened his tie. She slipped out of her dress. He removed his shoes and clothes. Soon they had forgotten about the couple below and were entangled in their own pleasurable and passionate coupling, but without an audience.

50

HONEY-TRAPPED

Cavalier stayed the night and Catherine prepared a breakfast of vegetable omelette, juice, toast and coffee and served it in the front room of the apartment. It was Saturday morning. They were both in robes. The King's Road below was abuzz with activity at the farmers' market opposite them and with weekend shoppers. A steady clip-clop of shoes on the thick glass pavement reverberated up from the street.

'I cook for a man if I like him, dollink.'

'That's what all the Russian girls say, dollink!'

Catherine laughed.

'Why do you mimic my accent, dollink?'

'Most journalists are mimics, admittedly third rate,' Cavalier said, in his Cockney accent. Catherine cocked her head slightly as she sat with him and ate.

'You know,' she said, 'you appear very like that old British actor when you speak like that.'

'Michael Caine perhaps?'

'I don't know his name, but he is the butler in the Batman movies.'

'Michael Caine,' Cavalier said with a rueful nod.

They chatted as they ate. When they had finished the food, Cavalier stood, went to the window and sipped his coffee.

'How long have you known Natalia?' he asked.

'A year or so.'

'Are you best friends?'

'We get on very well. Her best friend is Lord North's partner.'

'You were never upset when she took up with Al?'

'Not too much. I came to know and like her. She is a wonderful woman with a generous soul.'

'What made you come to London?'

'Natalia suggested it.'

'So you knew her before you were engaged to Al?'

Catherine evaded the question.

'She helped me obtain a visa. There is work for me here.'

'This is an upmarket spot in Chelsea. What do you do?'

'I'm an escort.'

'Oh?'

'What we did in bed would normally cost you. But because you gave me the handbag . . .'

'A freebie?'

'Dollink, I must pay the rent; send money to my parents.' She put a disc in a CD player. Adele sang 'Skyfall'. Catherine mumbled along with the words:

'. . .*This is the end,*

Hold your breath and count to ten. . .. . .'

She sauntered over to him, put her hand under his robe and kissed him. 'Besides, I do like you.'

She sang a few more words. . .

'. . .*wherever you go, I go. . .*

Whatever you see, I see. . .'

Catherine threw back her blonde hair and laughed. They embraced. Soon they were indulging in more lovemaking on a sofa. Just as they finished, two fire engines rattled out of the station across the road, sirens blaring.

'Wonder where the fire is, dollink.'

'Silly to use two trucks when they can walk across the road and hose us down,' he said.

'You!' she said with a grin.

Catherine made fresh coffee. They sat on the sofa in silence for a few minutes before he asked,

'Is Natalia in love with Al?'

'You'd have to ask her. Why do you ask, dollink?'

'Just wondered. He is a bit older.'

'Yes, remember, he is rich, dollink. Very rich.'

'Hmm,' Cavalier muttered.

'There is more to it,' Catherine said, 'a mix of business and pleasure.'

'How so? She told Al she wanted to marry the smartest man in the world.'

'That would be Putin, dollink. Or maybe one of the Rothschilds. But they are already spoken for.'

Cavalier waited. She added, dropping her voice to a near whisper as if there were others within earshot,

'She is not what she appears to be.'

'Really?' Cavalier said as if mildly interested.

'She is here on a false passport.'

'How do you know?'

'I have heard her on the phone talking to her father. He calls her "Valeria". I asked her about it. She told me in confidence.'

'But why a false passport?'

'She hides her real name, dollink. I think her father is high up in State Security. Only a guess, mind you, but some things she has said hint at it. I believe he is a billionaire.'

'She is here on *that* sort of business?'

'It is more than intuition, dollink. But I cannot say for sure.' She eyed Cavalier and frowned. 'You must not say a word, dollink.'

'I promise I won't say anything,' he said, leaning across and kissing her again.

'Tell me this. Is she State Security herself?'

'I honesty cannot say, dollink. But her manner is disciplined. She is very fit.'

***

'How did it go with Marilyn Monroe?' Haut asked when they met for a drink at the Magic club that evening.

'She's a lot of fun,' Cavalier said. 'Her personality matches her physique.'

'Will you see her again? Catherine likes you.'

'The feeling is mutual. I owe her another meeting to exorcise her tick.'

'What tick?'

'She says "dollink" in almost every sentence. Nearly as irritating as people inserting "like" into all utterances.'

Florence handed them both a Scotch on the rocks.

'Tell me how you met Natalia,' Cavalier asked. Haut responded with the tale about the beauty contest.

'This place is fun but, let's face it, it's not London's most upmarket establishment,' Cavalier said. 'I'm surprised such an attractive, highly educated young woman as her would bother coming here.'

'She doesn't work here. She was invited to be in the contest.'

'What's her background? Where's she from?'

'She spoke about her father working in Siberia. But she has spent most of her life in St Petersburg.'

Cavalier nodded.

'What are you thinking?'

Cavalier leaned forward and dropped his voice.

'So Natalia—a highly educated, well-groomed and intelligent woman with great looks and charm— comes into a less than savoury nightclub populated by Russian mafia. . .'

'You don't know they are mafia.'

'I have eyes, Al. They are probably mafia. The boss is likeable, I grant you. But in essence he is a small-time criminal who likes a glamorous lifestyle.'

'I told you. Natalia has nothing to do with the club.'

'Don't you think it's a little odd, Al? A woman much younger than you makes an unabashed play for you.' Haut went to protest. 'You said yourself she pursued you. Told you she would marry the smartest man in the world, or something like that.'

Haut frowned.

'What are you driving at?' he asked.

'The Russians are masters at organising honey traps.'

'What?'

'Where a woman is sent to seduce a target.'

'You're saying I'm a Russian target!'

'Not as in Conquer's interest in you, no. Maybe the opposite. Putin wanted you working for him. He knows you are the top oil man on the planet. You are on the threshold of this new technology, which puts you where Oppenheimer was in 1945.'

This frank remark gave Haut pause.

'I just don't believe Natalia would do something like you are insinuating.'

Cavalier smiled.

'The Russians are a little more dedicated to doing things for the state than in Australia and here.'

'Natalia isn't like that.'

'You may be right. But remember men's egos, including mine and yours, are sucked in when a beautiful woman makes a play. Seduction is the oldest profession. She's your bed partner and PA. She's learning every detail of your life. Don't tell me that intelligence on your business operations would not be of interest to Putin, your vodka-drinking buddy Kisley and maybe Natalia's father. They wanted you on the team. Still do.'

Haut frowned and thought back over the run of events that led to the affair with Natalia.

'Just be aware, Al. Find out more about her connections, family and background, if you can.'

'I shall,' Haut said.

'I can cheer you up on one issue. I don't think she is after your assets—I mean financial. But you must wait for her to tell you.'

'Go on,' Haut said.

'A little bird told me that her father is a billionaire; a Putin crony.'

'I had no idea.'

'If so, you can rule out her wanting to marry you for your money.'

Cavalier paused and ordered more drinks.

'I forgot to ask you,' he said, 'what made you choose your apartment across the road?'

Haut thought for a moment and then looked furtive.

'I discussed living in London with plenty of people,' he replied.

'Can you recall who actually suggested Jermyn Street? It's an upmarket London area.'

'I believe it may have been Anatoly Kisley.'

PART SIX

STRIKE AND COUNTER-STRIKE

51

KIDNAP

Mawnie Schwartz drove to the Napoleon V Chateau for another meeting with Bleulance, this time at the estate's winter property, known as Quartz House. The grey, forbidding building blended into the sunless, drizzly months of winter. Hidden at the top of the eight thousand acre manor, it was covered in a quartz skin. Schwartz could see the changing colours of the stone as he drove closer along a path under overhanging trees, weighed down by recent rain, and giving the impression of a tunnel. He stopped his Jaguar at the entrance. Now that he was up close he marvelled at the different colours, which changed with every step he took towards the entrance: purple amethyst, rose quartz, red carnelian, then milky and smoky quartz. Ten metres from the front door, red-brown tiger's eye, orange citrine and mint green prasiolite predominated in and around the door.

He was so enchanted with this bland box-like structure, with its transforming hues, that he did not see Bleulance coming down the steps to greet him.

Bleulance gave him a perfunctory nod and grimace rather than a smile. There was no handshake.

'Sorry, Baron, sir . . .' Schwartz began but was cut off by his paymaster, who pointed to a sculpture in the garden just beyond some trees.

'Come, Schwartz, I want you to be the first to admire my new creation.'

Bleulance strode ahead of him and they had a clear view of the new acquisition. Schwartz stopped when he caught sight.

'What is it?' he asked. 'Skeletons of what?'

'The four horsemen of the Apocalypse, of course,' Bleulance said, with disdain.

'Oh, yeah, I see now,' Schwartz said. 'Chilling.'

'Chilling? That's a Thomas le Hodgarcon. It's genius!'

'I . . . I meant in this setting,' Schwartz said, trying to cover his faux pas. 'It must have cost a fancy Franc.' He put on dark glasses to hide his left eye, which was flapping furiously.

'A very attractive twenty million *euros*,' Bleulance corrected.

'Wow!'

They strolled closer.

'What were you wanting to tell me?' Bleulance asked.

'Um, we've discovered Al Haut has a girlfriend.'

'Lucky him. But he has had quite a few, hasn't he?'

'He's serious about this one.'

'Australian?'

'No, Russian, we believe. He's in love.'

'This is not the one everyone says is a tall Marilyn Monroe?'

'No, another one.'

'You were thinking about dealing with her?'

'We are. She's living in London. Haut won't visit Russia.'

'Because of his deal with the CIA?'

Schwartz nodded. Bleulance had not taken his eyes off the sculpture as they spoke.

'Exquisite, don't you think? The way le Hodgarcon has blended the entire quartz concept in the structure? Each figure is a different, understated quartz colour. If you move, it will change its overall appearance.'

'Marvellous!' Schwartz said, his South African accent evident.

Bleulance lowered his eyes for a split second. 'So you think you should deal with this new woman?'

Schwartz was about to say, 'Exactly', but checked himself after the Baron's admonition at an earlier meeting. Instead he nodded.

'It will hurt him? Otherwise it's not worth doing.'

'Oh, yes. He will be gutted, Baron. He says this is the most wonderful woman he's ever met.'

'Where did they meet?'

'In a downmarket London nightclub.'

'Russian, you say?'

'We think she must be a tart; a hooker. London is flooded with Russian prostitutes.'

'Hmmm. A worthy object for our purposes.'

'We think so.'

'Will you carry it out?'

'No, sir. I have a former senior British policeman on the payroll. He is, shall we say, brutal and efficient.'

'Good idea to delegate.'

'Exactly.'

Bleulance glared.

'Sorry, Baron.'

'This policeman doesn't know of our connection?'

'No way, Baron.'

***

Natalia was on the way home after dining with Russian girlfriends in London's West End. She jumped on a tube at Hyde Park and alighted at Notting Hill Gate just after 10 p.m. She walked along narrow Uxbridge Street towards Campden Hill Road. She became aware of a car behind her. She looked around and could only make out shapes in a black Mercedes sedan. The car roared forward and onto the footpath, blocking her. Two men in suits and hats grabbed Natalia and bundled her into the back seat. The car drove off, turning right in Campden Hill and left towards Notting Hill Gate. Natalia was shocked, but remained calm.

'We are taking you to a safe place,' a solid Englishman the others called Ben said.

'What is this?' Natalia asked, 'a kidnap and ransom. What?'

'Worse than that, I'm afraid.'

The man next to her tied her hands behind her back. Natalia did not resist. She was led into a warehouse in Pembridge Square and pushed to the ground. She was punched in the face and kicked several times in the stomach until she fainted.

Natalia woke the next morning just before dawn. Her stomach and clothes were soaked in blood, some of which had formed a small pool around her. She was in terrible pain. Natalia began trying to make sense of her whereabouts. Her wrists were still strapped together with rope that had lacerated her wrists. No one else was in the warehouse, which had boxes stacked against all walls. A motorbike was parked near a roller door.

Every movement brought more pain. Natalia persevered with wriggling her wrists to a point where she could free one hand and then the other. She was about to pull away the rope when she heard voices. She lay as if still unconscious.

'She's still out to it,' Ben said to the other man. 'Let's work her over again after we've had breakfast.'

They left the warehouse.

Natalia waited a minute and then loosened her hands. She flexed her wrists and tried to stand, but fell over due to the pain in her midriff. She could feel warm blood trickling down her right thigh. With a supreme effort she got to her feet, gripping the nearby boxes until she was upright. She trembled as she dragged herself to the roller door.

She contemplated the motorbike, which had a key in the ignition, but she did not think she could ride it in her condition.

Natalia pushed a button on the wall. The roller door moved up a foot. She rolled through and struggled to her feet again. Clinging onto the wall of the building, she dragged herself past the Mercedes used to kidnap her, which was sitting in the driveway. She had the presence of mind to memorise the number plate.

It was 6 a.m. but there were cars in the dark street. Natalia stumbled through the rain into the path of a vehicle, forcing it to stop.

The female occupant wound down her window.

'Please help!' Natalia said. 'I've been kidnapped!'

'Do you want to go to the police?'

'No, no! Jermyn Street!'

52

ON THE RUN AGAIN

Haut made an instant decision that he and Natalia should depart London without delay.

'My radar is picking up danger at airports,' Haut told Cavalier in a quick phone call. 'I may take a train out.'

'What about Natalia? Shouldn't you take her to hospital?'

'She wants to run for it. They were set to kill her. We'll be tracked. We're packing now.'

'Take the Chunnel Eurostar at St Pancras. There are always doctors on board. The trains run regularly. I'll book her into a good Paris hospital.'

'You know one?'

'I won't say it over the phone, but yes. Had first-hand experience there some time ago.'

Haut piled two suitcases into a taxi and helped Natalia into the back seat. Haut had already sedated her to relieve the pain from the vicious assault. The bleeding from her abdomen had stopped but Haut was very concerned about her condition.

Cavalier arrived at Jermyn Street and they took a cab to St Pancras, arriving just minutes before a train was due to leave. The three of them were stepping aboard when Cavalier noticed a disturbance at the barrier.

British Rail staff were in dispute with four men. Two policemen stepped into the fracas, guns drawn. The four men trying to board the Paris-bound train backed off.

Cavalier and Haut were on full alert as they settled into a first-class carriage, wary that they might be joined by Natalia's attackers at any moment. Even when the train entered the tunnel under the Channel, they were still watchful.

Cavalier found the train's doctor. Screens were erected in the middle of the carriage and Natalia was examined. The French doctor told Haut and Cavalier she needed urgent surgery.

'She is booked into the Val-de-Grâce,' Cavalier said.

'How did you arrange that?' the doctor asked. 'It's an exclusive military hospital used by the armed forces and the French elite.'

'I was in there once for a short stay.'

'For treatment?'

'Severe lead poisoning.'

Natalia slept for the first hour of the 150-minute, 500-kilometre trip. Once the train was hurtling along the track to Paris through rural France, she awoke and insisted she talk to Haut about 'something serious'.

'My name is not Natalia, but Valeria,' she said, tears welling. 'I came into England on a false passport.' She paused to smile faintly and added, 'I prefer my new name. Please continue to call me Natalia.'

Haut let her continue but was concerned as every sentence caused her physical pain, and perhaps mental too. She lowered her voice.

'Please believe me,' she said, her hand squeezing his arm. 'I am in love with you. This is true. But I had to have a false ID because. . . because . . .'

'Take it easy, darling,' Haut said, holding her. 'Rest now. You can tell me in Paris.'

'No,' she said, 'you must know now. My father . . .' Natalia pulled out her phone, excused herself and rang her father in Moscow. She had a tearful chat on the phone for ten minutes. After it, she said,

'My parents will fly to Paris tonight.'

'From Moscow? Can they do that at such short notice?'

'This is what I wanted to tell you. My father, you see, is very high up in the security police.'

'The KGB?'

Natalia nodded.

'Yes, SVR. That is why I had to have a false passport. My identity had to be secret.'

Haut frowned. This prompted her to add,

'My father has many enemies. Enemies of the state.'

Haut had questions. Burning in his mind now was Cavalier's cautioning that he could have been caught in a honey trap. Yet he was still in denial over the possibility.

'There is something else,' Natalia said, struggling to speak. 'My father and mother are very close friends with President Putin.'

Two previous comments from her above all others now took on a different perspective: '*You were very, very hard to catch,*' and '*I wanted to marry the smartest man in the world*'.

Haut could not put his mind on anything else but Natalia's health, but he would later reflect on her comments and 'pray into it' for answers.

'There is one other thing,' she said. 'My father is a very, very wealthy man. I tell you this, so you know I never went after you for money.' She managed a wan smile. 'If anything it should be the other way round.'

Haut held and kissed her.

'I love you more than ever,' he said. 'God and I will get you through this. I promise.'

'I believe you. Remember, my family is Christian.'

Haut gave her a further heavy sedative and she was soon asleep. He bought a sandwich but had trouble eating it, such were his nerves. He and Cavalier drank black coffee to stay vigilant. Every person in the carriage came under scrutiny. They even watched train staff in case Natalia's attackers could be in disguise.

After the pointy-nosed express sped on, Natalia was awake again with much on her mind. Despite a recurring ache in her midriff, she went over how she had managed to escape her captors. She had remained as calm as possible, despite the brutal experience.

'I don't know how you or anyone could do that,' Haut said.

'I have been trained,' Natalia said. 'Every child of State Security has instruction on such possibilities.'

'Trained?'

'Of course. It began at thirteen. I have had fourteen years of being taught how to handle all manner of situations concerning attempted murder or kidnapping.'

Haut shook his head in further amazement. Again, he recalled Cavalier's words on how all Russians, including the young family members of KGB/SVR operatives, were expected to work for the state in whatever manner required. Haut could not help but admire his partner more than ever. Natalia may have been in her late twenties, but she was mature many years beyond her biological age. Her language skills and her apparent broad education in politics and business added up to an impressive character, who just happened to have catwalk good looks.

The train pulled into the vast Gare du Nord at 4 p.m., its platforms and tracks appearing like a giant bowling alley. It was a cool, early autumn day when Cavalier, Haut and Natalia eased from the train. Haut found a trolley for their luggage and pushed it along the platform, while Cavalier found a pre-booked hire car.

'My radar is picking up things again,' Haut said, glancing around.

'Let's take her to the hospital,' Cavalier said as they moved through the traveller throng and out the main entrance.

They loaded a green Citroën wagon.

Cavalier was about to jump in the left-hand driver's seat when he saw a vehicle moving about fifty metres behind them.

'I think we have company,' he said as he got in. He drove the wagon into the car park aisle, heading for the automatic barrier. By the time he reached a boom gate the pursuing vehicle was thirty metres behind. Cavalier slowed up at the barrier, but there was no time to insert the payment card. He put his foot down on the accelerator. The wagon snapped the boom gate and drove on at speed. Their pursuers, in a late model Audi, followed.

Cavalier spun the Citroën down a side street and headed for the hospital on the Boulevard de Port Royal in the fifth arrondissement.

'You told the doctor you were treated for lead poisoning there.'

'In the form of a bullet.' Cavalier glanced in the rear-vision mirror. The Audi had fallen behind but had kept the Citroën in sight. He kept up the speed and ran a red light, causing on-coming cars to hoot and drivers to abuse him. 'The Val-de-Grâce has the best security,' he said. He looked again in his side mirrors. 'Those pricks won't get in.' Cavalier pulled a mobile from his jacket pocket, slowed the car at a red light and made a call. The pursuit vehicle was hemmed in on an inside lane, only twenty metres away. Cavalier craned his neck to read the Audi's registration number.

In French, he said,

'Cavalier here. We have that special patient. But there is a problem. We have armed attackers following us.' He paused. 'Audi, colour dark blue, number six-seven-four-three-five.' He paused again. 'Yes . . . yes. . . that's good. *Merci beaucoup.*'

'We have some useful help.' Cavalier took a risk and swerved out of his lane and powered on, leaving the Audi now about forty metres behind and dodging its way through traffic, trying to keep pace. After another twelve minutes, Cavalier pulled up at the high iron gates to the hospital. The gates slid open. He handed over his ID just as three military guards with sub-machine guns walked close to the rear of the car and stood facing the Boulevard de Port Royal. The Audi appeared.

The gate guards examined Cavalier's card and waved him through. The three military guards cocked their weapons. The Audi pulled up hard, burning rubber. It then sped off past the hospital.

White-coated medicos hurried to the car and escorted Natalia to the entrance. Cavalier removed a handgun from his satchel and placed it under the driver's seat. He and Haut were frisked by security at the Val-de-Grâce front door. While they filled in Natalia's registration particulars, she was taken straight to an examination room, where two female doctors were waiting.

53

THE FORGIVEN

Haut and Cavalier were ushered to a waiting area. Haut told Cavalier more about the incident and the confidences that Natalia had disclosed to him on the train.

'Her father is Yuri Norkov. He is a very senior security man and close mate of Putin's. He and his wife are coming to Paris today. They will want to see her.'

Cavalier nodded, and began dialling on his phone again. He spoke in French to his DGSE contact, Jacques Gilmond, who was its assistant deputy director. He told him of the tail from the train station, and the probable arrival of a Russian heavyweight and his wife.

'We know,' Gilmond said. 'We've already been alerted. They will receive top security clearance and protection.'

'Good.'

'We always show respect, as they do to us in moments of crisis.'

***

Three hours later 58-year-old Siberian-born Yuri Norkov arrived in a bullet-proof limousine with his handsome fifty-year-old wife, along with two rugged bodyguards. The 192-centimetre, strongly built Norkov was nervous as he was introduced to Cavalier for a perfunctory handshake before being led by Haut and doctors in to see Natalia.

Cavalier was left with the two bodyguards in the waiting room. He wished he had his handgun, not because of his tough-looking company but because he was half-expecting the Audi occupants to burst in and finish the job they had started. Military personnel, some armed, were walking in and out of wards. Three sat in the waiting area for half an hour, their sub-machine guns resting in their laps.

The room was silent. Not even the two Russian guards spoke to each other. Hospitals were sober places, but there was an uneasy mix of Russian security operatives and French soldiers, who sat and waited for other people and doctors to come out of wards.

The doctors in Natalia's room told her father that his sleeping daughter would survive but would need surgery. The sad news was that the mutilation she received might make it difficult for her to have children. Her mother began to cry. Haut was upset. Norkov was distressed but in control enough to take Haut aside for a 'chat'. Haut was expecting to be blamed for the attack because of his work. To his surprise, Norkov was sympathetic.

'Don't blame yourself,' he said, rubbing his bulbous nose and wiping his narrow, sweeping Asiatic eyes. 'She is lucky to be alive.' He glanced at his wife, who sat at Natalia's bedside holding her hand. 'I wish to tell you something in confidence. We are aware of your strong relationship. You had plans to marry, no?'

'Yes,' Haut said.

'Has Valeria—er . . . Natalia—told you of my position?'

'Yes, on the train here.'

'Good, good.' He dropped his voice to a hoarse whisper and added, 'You see, my role was to defeat the mafia, which had gained strongholds through Russia in the early 1990s.' He sighed. 'It has taken many years to clean up the gangs, but we are on top of it now thanks to President Putin. When Natalia was thirteen, we were in Siberia where the mafia was attempting to move in and take control. Our family was staying at an apartment block. We were in apartment six. Across the hall was apartment nine. The number on the door had slipped. The nine became a six. I watched through a window as the mafia—five of them—burst in and killed the poor occupants—a family of three. We were the target, but because of the nine looking like six, we were spared.'

Norkov ran a hand through his longish hair. He chortled harshly. 'After that we obtained greater security in a block we thought was secure enough.' He paused and stared at Haut. 'You see, Al, by all rights Natalia should have been murdered then. Today's experience is very bad. Could not be much worse if she cannot have children. But, you see, I have a different perspective. She is alive.'

Haut nodded. He was relieved and surprised at this reaction, but claimed later to Cavalier that a 'download' had prepared him for a positive reaction from her parents.

Doctors suggested everyone leave the hospital as Natalia would not be operated on for several hours, maybe the next morning, depending on her response to medication. The doctors said they would be in touch to say when they could see her again.

The Norkovs departed under escort from their two bodyguards. Cavalier retrieved his handgun from the Citroën, which they decided to leave at the hospital until the next morning. He and Haut were led by a security guard through a secret tunnel out of the hospital that led them into a narrow laneway leading into Rue Claude Bernard and then up the steep and busy, narrow Rue Mouffetard.

'My favourite street in Paris,' Cavalier said, gesturing at cafes and queues at cheese and bread shops. 'A bit clichéd and privileged. A slice of the city that retarded time. It was like this when I first came half a century ago.'

Ever watchful, they walked through Contrescarpe Square to the high-walled old-fashioned Hotel des Grandes Ecoles on Rue de Cardinal Lemoine, still in the fashionable fifth arrondissement. Cavalier had stayed there many times and felt comfortable in the cosy atmosphere. The walls and gates were five metres high.

They settled into their rooms and met in the hotel foyer at 10 p.m.

'Let's go and see the sights,' Cavalier said, and then laughed at Haut's surprised reaction. 'I'm kidding. Pity we can't walk around.

This is a nice location. The Pantheon and the Sorbonne are near. St Germain on the Seine is a ten-minute stride down the hill.'

'I think we can risk a meal out, can't we?' Haut said. 'I haven't eaten all day. Didn't even feel like a sandwich on the train.'

'Okay, let's go. I know a couple of spots on Rue Mouffetard.'

They left through the big double gates. Just up the road at number seventy-four, Cavalier pointed to a plaque indicating American writer Ernest Hemingway had lived there.

'You a fan of his?' an edgy Haut asked, eyeing anyone who came close.

'Used to be.'

Haut cocked an eyebrow.

'He set a standard and style that many writers, particularly Americans, aped. Sentences and descriptions that never ended. He seemed devoid of humour and his obsession with bull-fighting has carbon-dated him. But he was a different kind of war-reporter and a trendsetter from the 1930s to the 1950s.'

They both felt uncomfortable as they walked back through Contrescarpe Square and passed an abandoned cafe, Delmas.

They headed back down Mouffetard. The street was blocked off, allowing a promenade for diners, shoppers and strollers, which gave Haut and Cavalier marginal comfort. Cars could not get through. They stood briefly outside several cafes and restaurants while Haut's invisible 'radar' adjusted. He hesitated and squinted at cafe L'assiette aux Fromages. Cavalier followed him as he stepped back to La Crete.

'C'mon, Al,' Cavalier said, 'you're making me nervous now.'

Haut settled on Bistro Italian. They sat out of sight at the rear and ordered food and wine.

Haut outlined the surprising encounter with Norkov and how the Russian had not held him accountable for the attack on Natalia. Cavalier listened without interrupting. Haut finished with,

'I suppose you will say "I told you so"?'

Cavalier shrugged.

'My guess is that Norkov was not angry because they sent Natalia to seduce you.'

Haut nodded his reluctant agreement.

'It is most likely that she fell for you in the process. After all, marrying you would link you to Russia. Have you seen the old Bond movie, *From Russia with Love?*' Cavalier asked.

Haut nodded.

'It's not a perfect analogy,' Cavalier said, 'but the seduction principle is similar to your case. Except for one salient point. The movie is fiction. You're living this.'

Haut picked at his food, while his eyes flicked often to the cafe entrance. He was reflective, going over the whirlwind series of events and people he'd dealt with in the last year.

'It's Bleulance,' he muttered. 'He would be behind what happened to Natalia.'

Cavalier waited.

Haut added, 'It's clear to me. He and Conquer know there will be dire consequences if they are stupid enough to kill me. So they strike at someone close to me. Their big mistake, that not even I knew, was that Natalia is the daughter of a high State Security person, who is close to Putin.'

'I believe that's all most likely.'

'They mutilated her,' Haut said, tears welling. 'They tried to stop us having a family.'

'I think you're right.'

'It's the way the devil works. Kill the unborn or the young. Remember Moses? In Jesus' case also, Herod killed all the newborns in an attempt to get rid of the son of God.'

Cavalier didn't respond. He preferred to listen to such utterances rather than comment. Haut's words often brought back memories from when he was eight or nine at Sunday School.

'Conquer has made itself a very powerful, unwanted enemy in Russia's president,' Cavalier said. 'Now the CIA and its Russian counterpart are its enemies. You can't get bigger than that.'

'I could,' Haut said.

'What?'

'Nothing.'

'You said Natalia got the registration number for the kidnap vehicle.'

'Yeah,' Haut said, picking up his phone. He found the number and Cavalier wrote it down on a notepad.

'I'll run it past my MI6 contact. We may be able to trace its owner.'

They were alerted as three men hurried past, glancing inside the cafe without noticing them at the rear.

'Jesus!' Cavalier muttered.

He called over a waiter, and gave him fifty euros for their food and wine. He asked in French if there was a rear exit.

'We have some unwanted drunken friends looking for us,' Cavalier said calmly.

The waiter led them through the kitchen to a rear gate and showed them out.

'We shouldn't go back to the hotel,' Haut suggested.

'They won't know we're there,' Cavalier said. 'I booked it over the phone.'

He led Haut through streets down to Rue Monge and then back up to the hotel at 75 Cardinal Lemoine. They walked past it, waited a minute and then doubled back. Cavalier used an electronic key and ushered Haut in. They strolled up the path to the entrance but did not go in immediately. Two couples were sipping wine in the forecourt. Cavalier spoke to the woman in reception and asked casually if anyone had been in to see them.

'Non, Monsieur,' the receptionist said with a pout and shake of her head. The two men made their way to their adjacent rooms and barricaded themselves in for the night. Cavalier slept with his gun within easy reach on a bedside table.

54

REVENGE SERVED HOT

Cavalier had the registered owner's name the next day.

'The name is Peter Black,' he told Haut. 'But get this. Black is a former senior British police commander. Even has an OBE from the Queen.'

'Wooo!' Haut mouthed.

'There's more. I have it on good authority that the man has gone on to do dirty work with standover tactics in the debt collection business, among other things. He has half-a-dozen known criminals working for him. Business is good, I'm told.'

'Wonder if Ernie North knows him.'

***

A fortnight later, Haut returned to London, leaving Natalia in her parents' care. He met North at the club and they spoke in a corner of the bar. North had been furious at the way Natalia had been handled. The news about Peter Black angered him more.

'Peter flamin' Black! What an arsehole! What an idiot! I'm gunna get even, believe me. To do dat to such a vewy special young lady! She's like a daughter to me; a daughter, I tell you. She's my girl's best friend.' North leaned close and dropped his voice to a husky whisper.

'You know about 'er farver?' Haut looked around and nodded. 'The Russians are gunna be very, very unhappy abart this. We gotta do something.'

'I'll help,' Haut said, 'anyway you like.'

'Nar, nar, my son,' North said. 'Leave this to professionals. Don't you worry, I'll look after it.'

***

Two nights later, Haut was lying in his Jermyn Street apartment bed at 1 a.m., praying as he almost always did. Over and above the steady thump of a bass guitar, the clang of food trolleys and the odd voice in Jermyn Street, he thought he heard muffled screams and howls, like ghosts in a haunted house. They were muted and just discernible but went on for so long that Haut was compelled to leave his bed, pull on clothes and wander down to the street. There was a heavy guard at the entrance to the Magic club.

He listened hard. He could hear nothing, so he returned to his bed. He heard a couple more low screams at about 2 a.m. and, after that, nothing. Haut prayed again and drifted off to sleep.

The next day, he met North for their usual special liqueur coffee in the bar at 4.30 p.m. North had just showered but had not managed to clear away his puffed-up eyes.

'Late night?' Haut asked.

'Late morning,' North grumbled. He indicated to Florence that he wanted more liqueur in his drink, saying, 'Air on the dog, innit.'

'Last night, in the early hours, I thought I heard screaming; shrieks of pain. Quite blood-curdling,' Haut said.

'Nightmare, perhaps?'

'No.'

'The basements are sometimes linked around dis area,' North observed. 'You know, tunnels, vents, secret passageways. Da noise may have come up to your apartment, from anywhere. I dunno.'

'Interesting.'

'Yeah. I'm told that there's even a secret passage from da Palace to a nightclub in Piccadilly.'

'Tell me more.'

'Yeah, da Duke of Edinburgh apparently makes use of it from time to time. Or 'e did when 'e was a bit younger.'

Florence added more liqueur to both their drinks. They sat in silence, idly watching her as she busied herself behind the counter. North seemed in no mood to make conversation. But after a minute or two he had a mumbled phone call, in which he turned away from Haut. Then he leaned close to Haut and said,

'Al, Natalia's butchers 'ave been dealt wiv; good and proper.'

Haut scrutinised him, prompting North to add, 'Day won't be butchering anyone, ever again. And you, my God-fearing son, will not have to ask your God to get back at 'em. It's done.'

'I never pray for revenge, I pray for God's judgement. But he does act if anyone steps in the way of his prophet's missions.'

'Yeah, whatever,' North said with a dismissive wave of the hand. 'Well, I just done God's work. Didn't I?'

There was another long pause. They watched Florence fix a drink for a suited man at the other end of the bar.

North leaned close to Haut's face and added, 'And you know what, Your Grace? I feel very, very good about what 'appened. Does that make me a devilish bastard too?'

'Revenge doesn't have to be bitter or, indeed, a sin.'

'I knew two of da four cunts that got it. Could not have happened to a more wervy couple. One of them once worked for me. Standover stuff.' North downed the last of the liqueur coffee and called for another. 'As for ex-commander Black, well 'e was given the most graphic warning of his illustrious life. 'E knows exactly what will happen to him if 'e ever repeats his kidnap exercise or something like it, at least in dealing wiv my mates. If he was stewpid enough to interfere again, he'd be another kind of OBE.'

'Meaning?'

'Obliterated By Ernie.'

55

A WIN FOR BLEULANCE

'They're still trying to get to me by targeting my close friends,' Haut told Cavalier over the phone. 'Our SAS mate Ken Pringle is dead.'

Cavalier was stunned.

'How?'

'No one knows. His son found him in bed. He had not been well, but no one thought he was near death. There had been a raid of some sort the night before. His van had been broken into. All the weapons—the Uzi and the Glocks—had been taken from inside the panels.'

'What did the police say?'

'They searched his home when his son alerted them.'

'Is it possible he died of natural causes?'

'I doubt it. My downloads say he was murdered.'

'The rifle and Uzi won't have our prints on them. Nor will the Glocks.' Cavalier thought for a moment. 'What will happen to Ken's property? His vacant allotment where our three friends reside?'

'Don't worry, he was building a house. The cement has already been laid.' Haut paused and added, 'It's Bleulance, moving on my friends, again.'

'You can't be sure about that, Al.'

'Yes, I can.'

'How's Natalia?' Cavalier asked, deflecting the conversation.

'Not good. I think she may go back to Russia. She's still in Paris. Her mother is looking after her.'

'No fault of yours, Al, but it is tough on her.'

'I've already prayed into it.'

Cavalier knew this to mean that Haut was asking God to judge the actions of those who had transgressed against him.

'Any response?'

'It has been dealt with.'

'Let me guess what you have told Natalia,' Cavalier said. 'The relationship will remain as it is.'

'That's what I told her.'

'So, if I can guess that, knowing your approach to life, then so can your main enemy.'

Haut sighed. 'Meaning?'

'I don't know much about Bleulance after just one interview. But it did instruct me on his cunning and his capacity for deceit. The attempt to assassinate you, and all the other niceties he has visited on you, show how his mind works. He will stop at nothing to destroy you. First it was to snare your leases by foul means, and well, just foul means. Now he realises you have CIA backing, and may have been behind Conquer being kicked out of Russia, he is vengeful. He could, of course, attempt to "destroy" you in the literal sense with another go at assassination. But that would bring reprisals from your supporters. That leaves him with an alternative.'

'Which is?'

'Attack those around you.'

'Like Ken Pringle?'

'The closest person to you is Natalia.' Cavalier paused. 'He has hurt her to hurt you.'

'He won't break me. It's impossible while I'm on God's mission; while I fulfil the vision.'

'I am witness to that, for sure. But just be prepared for anything.'

***

'I cannot have my name and my family exposed this way,' Natalia told Haut when she returned to London after a month's convalescence. They met in Hyde Park. 'The media here in England would crucify us if they learned that my father was close to Putin and so senior in the security service.'

'We could return to Australia,' Haut said, knowing that such a move would be high risk because of Conquer.

'That won't solve it. Bleulance will pursue you and me to the ends of the Earth, which is where Australia is!'

Haut was crestfallen. He knew what was coming. Natalia held and kissed him.

'I must return home.'

Haut sat holding her hand in his for several moments. She began crying. His eyes welled.

'You are the one true love of my life,' he said, wiping away tears.

'I love you so much too, Al. But the situation leaves me no choice.'

They stood and held each other for several moments. She kissed him on both cheeks and walked away. Every instinct in Haut told him to run and beg her to stay. But he knew this would be useless and prolong the agony.

'Watching her walk away,' he told Cavalier, 'was the saddest moment of my life.'

Without informing him, Natalia took a flight to Moscow the next day, leaving Haut devastated. He tried phoning her but could not get through.

Bleulance had succeeded in taking from him his most precious relationship.

56

A STUMBLE IN GRACE

Conquer's interference in Haut's business also succeeded. All his funds had dried up. The value of his company had plummeted and the shares were down to a tenth of a cent each. The Tasmanian government had finished the paperwork in the sale of his leases to a Chinese-controlled Tasmanian, Bob Lawrie. Haut had no cash to play with.

'God informed me that I had to be stripped down to owning no worldly goods at all,' he told Cavalier on a cold early October day in London when they met for breakfast at a cafe near Notting Hill Gate tube station. 'Then I would be most valuable to him.'

'God must be a Scot then?'

'How so?'

'He wants you in a frugal state.'

'In this position, I have no distractions. I can more easily follow the vision; the mission he sent me.'

'You couldn't go to the pokies and win a modest amount?' Cavalier asked. 'Your old lecturer mate Harold Burnside told me how you won at an electronic poker machine when you needed five thousand for staff wages.'

'I can do it, sure. The machines are metal. I can command metal; influence the numbers to go my way. But I won't do it. It takes a lot out of me, and besides it is an abuse of my powers. It draws down on my credit with the Holy Spirit.'

'C'mon, mate,' Cavalier goaded, 'I'd love to see you do it, even for a hundred quid. I'm a member of the Sportsman's Club. We can go—'

Haut cut him off mid-sentence, chuckled and said,

'Get thee behind me, Satan. I can tell you a funny story about that. I was once at the casino in Hobart on a Friday night and I was out to dinner there with half-a-dozen others. The bill for a big night of eating and drinking ran to well north of a thousand dollars. The night was meant to be on me. Harold Burnside was there and quietly asked me how I was going to pay. He said I should use my credit card. "No money in it," I said. He urged me, as you are now, to gamble for it. I prayed hard—it's exhausting—and won the amount needed playing roulette.' Haut laughed throatily again. 'The irony was that on the floor below me the delightful Madam Ingrid Orangey was working her way through ten thousand in chips that the House gave her to play with every Friday night!'

***

They took a Hansom cab back to Jermyn Street.

'Want to see my new sleeping arrangements?' Haut said, as he unlocked the front door to the Magic club. Cavalier looked back at the smart block where Haut had had an expensive, big apartment.

'You're not living there?'

'How the mighty have fallen,' Haut said with a careless laugh. He led Cavalier down to the basement. It was dank. A thin partition separated his bedsit arrangement from a storage room. The glass squares above reverberated with footsteps.

'It's freezing here!' Cavalier said, pulling up his coat collar.

'Tell me about it! But North has been kind enough to put me up here for no rent. All I have to do is let the backpackers in at all hours. There's a hostel on the floor above. I often close the place up.'

Haut showed Cavalier up to the front entrance. Smart-suited businessmen were walking past, half of them with a cell phone to an ear. A garbage truck trundled by noisily upturning bins and blocking traffic. It stank.

'The dusty dirty city . . .' Cavalier began, screwing up his nose.

'*Clancy of the Overflow*.' Haut broke in with the line:

'"The round eternal of the cash book and the journal."

Banjo Paterson got that right, didn't he?'

'He'd only have to change the lines a bit today,' Cavalier said, looking skyward for inspiration. 'Perhaps . . . "The internet infernal of the e-book and the *electronic* journal" . . . or words to that effect.'

'I march with them every day to the oil industry's offices in the Strand, not far from Australia House,' Haut said. 'I dress very well. Starched collar, polished shoes, straightened tie. Have to keep up appearances for the industry, like poor old Clancy.'

'Never mind,' Cavalier said, 'all for a good cause.'

They shook hands. Just then an ashen-faced Florence came up to Haut and took him aside.

'Ernie's dead,' she whispered. She broke down, crying.

'How? When?'

'Last night at his Willesden mansion. His girlfriend found him when she got home. He'd been stabbed.'

'Who did it?'

'Don't know.'

Haut held her as she sobbed. She broke free and disappeared into the club.

'Natalia, Ken, now Ernie!'

'You should leave London,' Cavalier said, handing him an envelope before he hurried inside the club.

***

'He was stabbed in the heart,' Haut told Cavalier in a phone call later in the day. 'I insisted on seeing the body. This was Satan's work!'

'Is there a suspect?'

'His son, who's a drug addict.'

'Then it was coincidence that this happened about the time of Ken's death.'

'You don't understand,' Haut said, saddened rather than exasperated. 'It's spiritual. It's demonic. They're getting at *me*.'

Cavalier wanted to debate this but stopped himself. Every now and again, Haut would speak about the spiritual that no one else, including close friends and associates, understood.

'My radar is warning me to go,' Haut said.

'As long as you have your phone and a computer, you can run things from anywhere, at least until you market the technology.'

'William Donnelly told me of a place on the remote east side of the Thai island Koh Samui. It's a set of villas formerly owned by a US merchant bank. After the 2008 crash they sold them off. A few are vacant. They're on the top of a mountain with good security. The mountain is so steep that cars can't even reach within three hundred metres of it.'

'That puts you two hours away from me by plane. I'll be back in Chiang Mai soon.'

'I have no money to get there.'

'Did you look in the envelope I gave you?'

Haut pulled it out of the jacket pocket.

'I had forgotten about it in the rush to see Ernie,' he said, opening it.

Inside it was two thousand pounds in twenty-pound notes. Haut uttered one of his hackneyed phrases: 'Various acts of God.'

57

AS YOU WERE

Bleulance, in top hat and tails, kept his binoculars on the horses in the Grand Prix de Paris at Longchamp, in the Bois de Boulogne, Paris. His horse, Antoinette, had led most of the way on the scenic racecourse, France's most famous.

Mawnie Schwartz, similarly dressed, stood a few feet away in the members' enclosure. He was also watching the race and waiting for the chance to speak to his boss. Bleulance hardly reacted as Antoinette streaked across the line first, much to the delight of the big crowd, who roared their approval of the short-odds favourite. His concession to excitement was to wave a hand at the seventy thousand spectators and say,

'That should keep the punters happy.'

He turned to Schwartz, gave a jerk of his head and wandered to a quiet corner of the enclosure.

'I want you to go back to the plan to eliminate Haut,' Bleulance said. 'There are rumours that he will begin marketing his water-for-fuel invention later this year. Enough is enough!'

'Baron, we're concerned about retaliation from the CIA. We've been, er, active in handling those close to Haut.'

'Circumstances have changed. Our information is that the CIA is not looking after him unless he stays at the Theodore in New York. I think you should finish what you set out to do originally.'

'Use Farquar again?'

'Tell him he must organise it or he'll have to sell the Texas property and refund the proceeds to us.'

***

Haut, who was beginning to accept his fate as a new-age nomad, took only a few days to settle in to his latest home atop a mountain. Koh Samui was known as an idyllic holiday location for foreigners, and Haut was appreciating all the benefits that thousands of others enjoyed on their short visits, except for one factor: he was on the remote, unfashionable east side of the island. Haut found one good restaurant, Mud, on a beach within ten minutes by taxi, and thirty minutes by foot. The nearest village was twice as far away.

He always proclaimed he was okay being alone as it allowed him to be closer to his God. But, underneath that, he was a gregarious human being. He needed company.

Haut was pleased to receive a call from Ryan Gram. They had been chatting and exchanging emails since they'd first met on the plane trip from New York to London. Gram had expressed his disappointment that Haut was likely to take his technology to NASA, as suggested by Donnelly, rather than Gram's corporation, Tielisten Allan.

'I have to take my advice from William,' Haut told Gram during a phone discussion. 'He knows the business side of things with my stuff better than anyone.'

'And he is backing you big time?'

'That too.'

'I have been giving my situation a lot of thought since we first met,' Gram said. 'How would you like it if I came to Koh Samui to work with you?'

'But your job with Tielisten Allan?'

'I'm willing to give it up. Your inventions are so important to the future of the planet.'

'I can't pay you . . .'

'Just some modest investment in your new corporation would

suffice.'

'We can work something out.'

'I have invested well,' Gram said, 'enough to live cheaply. You said Thailand was inexpensive.'

Haut was delighted. Gram was a high-tech engineer who would be more than useful to him in creating his designs.

**

A month later, Haut was excited in a phone call to Cavalier. He began with his often used,

'You won't believe this . . .'

'I never do,' Cavalier responded lightly.

'You remember I sent you pics of the beautiful Mon?'

'Vaguely. She was a Burmese theoretical physicist you met in a Chiang Mai?'

'She wants to come and live with me.'

'What? Can you arrange it? You said she didn't even have a passport.'

'She has one now. Mon went to Bangkok under the auspice of a Christian church group. They must have arranged it. Anyway, she has become Christian. She'll be in Koh Samui within a few weeks.'

'Al, she is a lovely woman. But you said she has a career as a physicist. Is she going to give that up? Don't you think it's a bit.....'

'Don't say it,' Haut interrupted. 'I've told you many times, Vic. There are no coincidences.'

'I think you may be right, in this case.'

'All cases. It's God's will.'

**

Haut readied his villa, and one next door, for the arrival of his two guests. Both villas were spacious with three bedrooms. They featured patios and open spas. There were grand views of the ocean and a secluded beach at the base of the cliff, which was reached by two hundred steps. Haut likened it to his wonderful Sandy Bay home, with his access to the stars and mountaintop views of vast expanses of water.

Gram arrived just seven weeks after he announced his desire to work with Haut. He was on foot, lugging two suitcases. He wore a baseball cap and a white jacket, despite the heat.

'You should have rung,' Haut said shaking hands with the sweating Gram.

'I took a taxi to the checkpoint. The driver wouldn't go any further because it was too steep. The guards knew who I was. They laughed and pointed up the goddamn mountain. So I walked.'

Haut allowed Gram a few hours to rest and then took him to his villa's basement, which was built into the mountain and naturally cool. He showed Gram the doughnut-shaped models of the elements and an engine he was working on. Gram helped him.

'How did you explain to Tielisten Allan that you were leaving to work with me?' Haut asked as he tightened the bolts on the combustion chamber.

'I didn't. I just resigned.'

'You didn't say anything to your companion, Anne Marie?'

'No, not really, although my departure from the corporation shocked her and precipitated our split.'

'I'm sorry to hear that.'

'Don't be. We were on the way to a break-up anyway.'

Haut added water to the engine, and a small amount of oil to fire it up. It spluttered and stopped. He examined some parts and tried again. This time it kicked to a steady hum and was running.

'My God!' Gram said. 'It's what I came for!'

'Seeing is believing, eh?' Haut said with a wide grin. 'There is much refinement to be done. I need more effective and better equipment. But it's a start.'

Later, after a swim on the beach, Gram asked about security.

'You saw how hard it is to get up from the road,' Haut replied. 'The guards are armed and aware of my need for protection.'

Gram looked up the steep steps to the villas.

'But if someone was coming up from the beach here . . .?' he said.

'Don't worry,' Haut said with a secretive grin. 'I have certain things up there.'

'What?'

'A rifle and handgun.'

'But the engine and your models are in the basement.'

'It has a good lock. They'd have to smash the windows. We'd hear them.' Haut paused and added, 'The main guard is down there too.'

'Huh? A guard lives there too?'

'Remember, I am a Prophet of Nature. This island has a spirit. I am in touch with it.'

Gram appeared uncomfortable.

'It lives in the basement,' Haut said without a flicker of mirth, 'and it's big.'

***

Mon arrived three weeks later.

'I love this woman for going to so much trouble to get here,' Haut told Cavalier. 'We're going to marry. We have already decided on several children.'

'If all that happens,' Cavalier said, 'your life will have equilibrium at last. I wish you the best with it.'

'It's not a matter of "if". It's going to happen. You'll have to come and stay; we have two spare rooms. And you should meet Ryan Gram too.'

'Is he being helpful to the project?'

'Oh, yeah. He had twenty years' experience at Tielisten Allan as an aeronautics engineer.' Haut chuckled. 'But, in reality, he's learning a new science; *my* science and engineering. The model of the elements is a starting point.'

***

A fortnight after Mon's arrival, she, Haut, Gram and a local Thai woman, Ning, who Gram had met in a Koh Samui massage parlour, were at a dinner in Haut's villa. Ning prepared phat Thai for the four of them.

At one point, just as the meal began, Gram seemed startled.

'Mon,' he said, 'you've got Al's plate. I asked Ning to give him more.'

'That's okay,' she said, 'in Thailand we share. If he wants more, he can have some of mine.'

They all had white wine and, after a convivial evening, Gram stood.

'Let's go, Ning,' he said with a lascivious look, 'I want that special massage you promised.'

'Not on full stomach,' Ning said, admonishing him.

'Full or empty,' Gram said, 'as long as it's special!'

He and Ning left for his villa.

Mon complained of a headache and said she wasn't feeling well. Haut gave her two Panadol and they went to bed.

At 6 a.m. Mon began to get out of bed, but couldn't move her left side. She fell back and groaned. Haut tried to help her up. He massaged her left arm and leg. Mon remained in pain and was dizzy. She moaned and was in and out of consciousness.

'You seem to have some kind of paralysis,' Haut said, trying to remain calm. He was soon in his hire car, taking her to hospital.

***

An hour after Mon was admitted, two doctors, one Thai and one English, took Haut aside.

'She's had a stroke,' the English doctor told him.

'What? She's just twenty-six!'

'That's her best advantage. She has a strong body and heart. If she rests, she should make a full recovery.'

'Should?' Haut said.

'We can't say at this moment. We'll assess her further in a few hours and decide on medication.'

Haut left in a quandary and went over in his mind everything that had happened to Mon in the past few weeks. He had taken her to Bangkok for dental work, but the doctors who examined her said this was unlikely to be the cause of the stroke. He knew Mon had been under stress over an illness her mother had endured in the last few days.

Two weeks later, Mon was back in Haut's villa. She was still weak, but insistent that she return to Mandalay in Myanmar to see her mother, whose illness had worsened. The doctors told him it was a risk for her to travel but agreed that more stress over her mother might make her condition deteriorate. They let Haut make the decision.

He had just put her to bed in the villa one night when he received a phone call from New York. It was Christine Donnelly, William's wife. She was nervous.

'William died suddenly this morning,' she said, her voice tearful.

'Oh, God no! What was it?'

'Doctors say a brain tumour.'

'I'll get to New York as soon as possible.'

'Oh, really, Al, you don't have to.'

'He always said that if anything happened to him, he would want me to give the eulogy.'

Haut decided to fly Mon to Mandalay, return to Bangkok and then fly the seventeen hours to New York.

Just before boarding the plane to Mandalay, Mon closed her phone and burst into tears. Her mother was in a coma.

'I don't care about the money,' Mon said, 'I just want her to be well.'

Haut comforted her as they sat in the plane.

'I can pray into it,' he said, 'if you give me details—her full name, age and what the doctors say about her condition.'

'That's a problem,' Mon said, wiping her eyes, 'nurses are looking after her, not doctors. I'm not sure if she is even receiving food.'

Haut waited until they were airborne before he asked,

'What did you mean when you said you didn't care about the money? What money? Who is giving you money?'

Mon turned away and sobbed.

***

'We were wondering if you could follow up on something in New York?' Wombat said in a phone call to Cavalier.

'Haut's on his way there.'

'We know. He's cut up about his best mate dying. Sounds a little unhinged. He claims to be in touch with Donnelly in the spiritual. Thinks he was murdered.'

'By whom? How?'

'He has had "poison" coming on his radar.'

'But who did it?'

'Al doesn't know. But he mentioned "Occam's razor", the most obvious and simplest reason being the most likely.'

'And what's that?'

'Well, Donnelly was going to put a billion dollars into backing Al. Now that will be in doubt. So whoever benefits from thwarting Al's inventions is on his list.'

'Bleulance and Conquer, yes . . .'

'And Tielisten Allan. On the point of thwarting our friend, we are receiving data which may indicate related activity. It seems that some-one may be going to pick up where that sad trio left off at Sandy Bay.'

Cavalier was silent for several seconds.

'You there, Vic?'

'How solid is it? Is Farquar involved?'

'He seems to be active again, judging from his dark web, social media and email traffic. It's all in code of course. But we can decipher bits of it, enough to deduce certain things. He is having the target monitored for some sort of action.'

'Will the target need protection? What about Big Brother?'

'They can protect him while he stays in the Theodore. But not when he leaves the building.' Wombat paused and added, 'We'd pay all expenses.'

'Wombat, you know that's not necessary.'

'Just a suggestion. We know you agree with us that the target is worth preserving.'

'If I do anything, I don't want any assistance.'

'Not even from our lovely Melody who keeps asking after you?'

'You know the answer to that.'

58

THE FOURTH MAN

Cavalier would love to have contacted his step-daughter Far in New York but was aware that his visit might be correlated later with any action he might need to take. He checked in at the Algonquin Hotel, Times Square, where he had stayed before, again using a false English passport. He was surprised to be given a diplomatic courier pouch at the front desk. He settled into his suite and then opened the pouch. There was a note from Anthony Jones.

Dear VC,

We—Wombat and I—thought hard about what to send you on your New York visit. We settled on using a diplomatic pouch which by law can't be opened by anyone except embassy officials or the intended recipient. Keep the lining inside the packaging. It will allow you to travel with the handgun in planes, but best to stow it with your main luggage.

We chose another Glock. We know you favour them. If you lost it or left it anywhere, it would be just another American agent's gun. Most US law enforcement agencies have at least some of them in use. This modified version has a new-style in-built silencer, which is a minor step up on the one you took to Tasmania. Your comment on it would be appreciated.

I've added a couple of new multi-purpose keys. One is an electronic card, which should open most modern hotel doors. The other will open any old-style lock. Also find some new design slippers [gloves]. You can wash these more easily than ever before.

Very good luck. And a word of advice: be careful how often you play with your Glock. I am told you can go blind with overuse!

Cheers,

AJ

Cavalier removed the outer layer to reveal a black, plastic-like inner packet. He unzipped it. The contents included the gun, a new lightweight shoulder-strap holster, fifty bullets and the all-purpose keys. Cavalier examined the packet's lining, which was made up of a fabric he had not seen before. He ran his hands over the weapon and strapped on the holster, which fitted on his side and under his left armpit. The cold weather ensured he would wear a zip-fronted jacket that concealed the weapon. There was no bulge. Even when his jacket swung open, the holster could not be seen.

Not even Mr X, who had liaised with Haut, was aware of Cavalier's presence in New York. Cavalier sent Haut a text, suggesting they meet outside the Theodore.

Haut replied in twenty minutes.

Meeting Donnelly's brothers at The Freemasons' Arms pub over the billion he promised to invest. Let's meet there after at 8 p.m.

***

Haut sat facing the door to the pub. Prim Texan Shelley Northam, Donnelly's 45-year-old former secretary, walked in and sat with Haut. Northam, her blonde hair coiffured and fingernails painted a bright pink, smiled unconvincingly and apologised for the fact the brothers were not turning up. She quickly changed the subject.

'Your eulogy was so beautiful,' she purred in a warm Texas drawl, 'I've never heard anything better.'

Haut gave a small smile of thank you and asked,

'Why won't Christine let me see William's body? It's part of my ministry to pray over it.'

'Sorry, Al,' Shelley said, 'you'll have to ask her.'

'She won't answer my calls. Nor will the brothers.'

Shelley blinked, smiled nervously and shook her head.

'I don't really know, Al.' She brightened and added, 'But everyone just loved your eulogy!'

'I know we've not met until this week,' Haut said, 'but I've spoken to you many times during the five years I've been dealing with William. What's going on?'

'I can't answer that.'

'Can't or won't?'

'Now that William has gone,' she said, her voice shaky, 'God rest his soul, the brothers have other agendas. They are going to invest in other things.'

'William's soul is not resting,' Haut said, 'not now.'

Shelley looked startled.

'I'm in touch with him,' Haut said, 'he has not gone over yet.'

Shelley stood and said,

'I really must be going.'

'Can you send my models of the elements to me? They're in William's office.'

'Those doughnut-shaped things William called the holy grail of science?'

'That's them,' Haut said, standing.

'They're cute, but I never understood what they stood for.'

'The models unify everything: the elements, sound, colour, positive and negative charges, valency, paramagnetism, biomagnetism. . .'

Shelley's eyes glazed over.

'I'll see what I can do,' she said, walking towards the front door. 'But all his property is owned by Mrs Donnelly and his brothers.'

'Not those models!' Haut said. 'Send them to me at the Theodore.'

Haut glanced around and noticed a bald man in a grey suit and bland tie. He was a few metres from him. Their eyes met. The man's pupils were dead. Haut, from long experience, recognised the look. This grim-looking fellow was there to assassinate him.

He walked up to the bar to buy another drink and noticed the man circling closer. He could sense he was a few metres behind him. The barman took Haut's order. He moved in front of a mirror behind the bar and could see his stalker. Haut pretended to gather the drink, but left it on the counter as he noticed his phone flashing a message. It was from Cavalier. Haut phoned him and, keeping his voice calm, while smiling, told him of his predicament.

'Leave there fast,' Cavalier said. 'Head for the Flatiron building at Fifth Avenue and Broadway on Twenty-third Street.'

'Why there?'

'It has plenty of security guards.'

Haut dashed for the door. Something told him to run left—*left*! He lifted his knees high as he dashed along 23rd Street for several blocks. He looked back. The stalker was less than forty metres behind. Haut dashed for the triangular-shaped Flatiron building. He scurried inside and startled five security guards who were taking up a night shift from five others.

'I'm being chased by a killer!' Haut said. He turned and pointed. The man was already pushing his way through the revolving doors. 'That's him!' The stalker was holding a handgun. He was confronted by all ten guards, who drew their weapons.

'Drop it!' one of the guards yelled. 'Now!'

'That guy,' the man said, pointing his gun at Haut, 'raped my wife, just now.'

'Drop the weapon!' another guard called, and moved close.

'I have to avenge my wife!' the man yelled.

'That's a lie,' Haut said. 'He wants to assassinate me!'

At the third call to drop the weapon, the stalker did as ordered. A guard swooped on the gun. The stalker glared at Haut and gabbled on about his wife. Two guards tackled the stalker to the ground. Haut ex-plained he was a businessman from Australia doing oil deals and capital raising.

'I've never seen this character before,' he said.

'Sir, why don't you leave?' a security guard said. 'We'll handle this.'

'Thank you,' Haut said, taking a wallet out of his pocket and handing the guard a business card. 'Give that to the police.'

The guards lifted the stalker to his feet and frog-marched him out of the Flatiron. Haut hurried out and walked briskly back towards the Freemason's Arms. His phone rang. It was Cavalier. Haut, breathless but relieved, explained what had happened.

'Where were they taking the him?' Cavalier asked.

'Don't know. They moved towards Broadway. Where are you?'

'I'm in a cab heading your way. Did he have a weapon?'

'Yeah. He had it drawn when he entered the Flatiron. The guards took it off him.'

'I'll call you later,' Cavalier said and rang off.

***

Cavalier directed the cab down Broadway. He caught sight of several men circling one man in the street opposite. Cavalier asked the cabbie, an Indian with whom he had been talking cricket, to stop. Cavalier waited. The stalker seemed to be trying to move back the way they had come. The guards were pushing him in the chest and indicating he should go the other way. The guards moved a few metres away and looked back. The stalker seemed to be doing as instructed. The guards had a quick conference. They moved to the stalker and began leading him away again.

Cavalier felt a twinge of memory in the way the man loped, Neanderthal-style, his long arms dangling. A tingle went up his spine. Could it be Gerard Dubois, the fourth man in the Mekong killing squad; the one who shot and nearly killed him in Laos?

Cavalier paid the fare, alighted from the cab and moved along Broadway on the opposite side. The guards edged and pointed the stalker to the 23rd Street subway. They escorted him down into the bowels of the underground network, watched him buy a metro-card and then move onto the platform for the uptown train.

Cavalier pulled his collar up and his fedora down. He adjusted his special infra-red glasses that he had used when he killed the three assassins in Hobart. Then he descended the steps along with a rush of people venturing home after work. Cavalier bought a metro-card and eased down the platform to within twenty metres of the stalker.

Cavalier stole a glance at the man, and felt it could be Dubois. The stalker did not know it, but he had become the stalked.

The uptown train nosed into the station. The stalker jumped in. Cavalier stepped in at the other end of the carriage. It was full but Cavalier could see his target's bald head over the sea of commuters. The train thinned a little over the next twenty or so minutes which it took to reach 79th Street West. The stalker alighted there with a dozen other people, including Cavalier.

Cavalier followed the man up into the street and along 79th Street. The location gave Cavalier a weird feeling. He'd had an apartment on this street in 1980 while based in New York during the presidential election, which he was covering as a journalist. Forty-year-old memories of the area flooded back.

The stalker's head jerked left as people moved over the road. Cavalier stayed fifty metres behind.

The stalker stopped at Central Park West. He looked at his watch. Cavalier did the same. It was just after 8 p.m. The stalker moved two blocks west. Cavalier followed in the shadows and was thankful for the number of New Yorkers strolling in both directions.

The stalker stopped outside 81st Street where Cavalier's favourite cafe, Museum Cafe, had once been. It was a fast-food burger place now, Shake Shack. Cavalier was momentarily confused and wondered if his memory had played tricks on him. He pulled his jacket collar over his neck, adjusted a scarf and crossed Central Park West to the American Museum of Natural History.

He could see the stalker just inside Shake Shack in discussion with a waiter. It seemed the cafe was full. The stalker walked out, looked both ways and then proceeded up 81st Street on the left side. Cavalier strode up the right side and pretended to be on the phone. The stalker entered an apartment block at number thirty-five. Cavalier, still with his phone to his ear and fumbling for a skeleton key, entered the twelve-storey building behind two other people.

Cavalier noted that one of the two elevators was stopped at the fourth floor. He sat on a sofa in the lobby, with its impressive marble floor, and continued his fake, soft phone chat. There were no doormen or desk receptionists. The couple who had entered with him close behind pressed the button for the elevator and a minute later disappeared into it.

Cavalier silenced his phone and waited until the elevator was moving before he walked up the stairs to the fourth floor. He had no idea where the stalker's room was. He walked to a small access area where bins were stored and was out of view of anyone coming from the apartments.

He waited, his heart pounding. He began yoga breathing to calm himself.

59

DEATH ON 81ST STREET WEST

After ten minutes, he heard a lock being turned. He glanced from behind the alcove wall. The stalker was coming out of number forty-four. Cavalier remained out of sight until he heard the elevator reaching the ground floor. He moved to number forty-four. It had an electronic lock. Cavalier slipped on the gloves sent by Anthony Jones and used the electronic key card. It didn't work. Cavalier tried several times. The lock flashed green. He was in.

He became aware of the offensive aftershave that he had noticed on Gerard Dubois on the Mekong. Could his nose be playing tricks on him? He wondered if he could be *wishing* it were Dubois. Cavalier switched on the light and began checking the stalker's luggage. He found two handguns, which he emptied of bullets and stuffed under the double-bed mattress. There was also a map of the area around the Theodore Hotel. There were several photographs of Haut. On one, a pencil mark encircled his hair and noted: 'dyed black'.

There was a manila envelope inside a suitcase. Cavalier opened it. Enclosed was a passport in the name 'Juan Lopez' and print-out pages of bank account details. A savings account with Bank of America in the Lopez name had a balance of $1,500,580 dollars, with the latest entry being for $1.5 million from a bank in the Bahamas.

Cavalier scrutinised the passport photo. Could it really be Gerard

Dubois? The hair had been thick and long. Now it was sheared off. The eyebrows that once almost joined had been cut back. The eyes were blue in the photo. Dubois's had been brown. The nose had been gnarled with a knob in the middle. Now it was trim and smaller. Had he had cosmetic surgery? Cavalier stared at the eyes. It was the hollow dead look that was familiar. He thought, and hoped, it was Dubois.

Cavalier noted the time as 8.23 p.m. and calculated that if the stalker had booked a seat at the cafe, he would be back at around 9.15 p.m. He recalled Dubois gobbling down more food than anyone on the Mekong tour and anticipated his wait being another fifty minutes.

Cavalier cleared a leather chair beside the door, removed his gun and rested it on his lap. He was comforted by the probability that the stalker did not have a weapon on him. He had lost a gun to the security guards at the Flatiron. Cavalier had hidden two more. He had learned never to assume anything, but even if the stalker had more concealed weapons, Cavalier expected to have the upper hand.

At 9.27 p.m. he heard the elevator whirr to the fourth floor. Seconds later, the electronic lock sounded. The stalker entered the room. He switched on the light.

'Good evening, Monsieur Dubois,' Cavalier said, his gun pointing at him. The stalker jumped. His dead eyes flashed shock and fear, expressions never seen on the Mekong or in Luang Prabang, even when he shot Cavalier. His long arms dangled. His hands flexed to fists.

'Sit,' Cavalier said, waving his gun at a chair against the opposite wall. 'Any stupid move by you and you're dead.'

The man hovered.

'Sit!'

He backed to the chair and almost fell into it.

'Nice to be remembered,' Cavalier said, 'especially when you shot me.'

'I had to . . .' the man said, his voice shaky.

'I survived,' Cavalier said. 'You won't if you don't answer my questions.'

Dubois's eyes flicked to his luggage.

'Don't even think about it. I found your other weapons.' Cavalier lifted his gun, pushed it forward in his right hand and took out a tiny recorder with his left. He started it.

'I want you to tell me who sent you. Was it Farquar?'

'I . . . I just receive messages.'

'You have five seconds. Five, four, three . . .'

'Yes, yes, it was Farquar.'

'How much is the down payment for the Haut kill?'

'Nothing . . .'

'One more lie will demonstrate you are wasting my time. In that case, I shall kill you.' Cavalier pointed at Dubois's hands. There was a tremor in the left.

'Terrible, isn't it, when someone has control over you?' Cavalier held up his left hand. 'You see? My hands are steady.' He smiled. 'I repeat: how much down payment did you receive for the Haut kill?'

'One million, five hundred thousand.'

'You know that Hollos, Leni and Castro received ten million up front *before* being sent to assassinate Haut? You were short-changed by Farquar, who's now trying to sell his San Antonio ranch, for guess what?'

Dubois's eyes flicked this way and that, but he did not reply.

'Fifteen million,' Cavalier said. 'You're getting a small percentage of the amount he is, and you have to do his dirty work! He's taken the rest that was due to you.'

Cavalier could sense the dials of Dubois's mind whirring. Could he talk his way out of this? Could he jump Cavalier? Apart from the hand tremor, which could have been permanent, his manner was cool, ever-testing, searching for a weakness, a loophole, a chance, a *tell*.

'I can offer you half,' Dubois said. 'I can write a cheque for you right now. Right away!'

Cavalier pretended to consider the offer. He nodded. Dubois eased a wallet, biro and a new Bank of America chequebook from his jacket pocket.

'How quaint, a chequebook,' Cavalier remarked. 'To avoid electronic surveillance no doubt?'

Dubois did not respond.

'Make it one and a half million,' Cavalier said. 'Very slowly now.'

Dubois's jaw dropped; not in shock, but anger.

'You want all of it? You want to rob me of everything?'

'Look at it another way. What's your life worth?'

Cavalier aimed the gun at Dubois's head and said,

'Make it out to Sally Deere.'

Dubois looked up. Cavalier spelt her name.

'That's the wife of the Australian agent you murdered,' Cavalier said with a hard stare. 'Sign it Juan Lopez.'

Dubois wrote out the cheque and signed it as directed, still buying time, even a split-second.

'Put it on the table, without standing.'

Dubois obeyed. Cavalier stood and glanced at the cheque.

'One of your many pseudonyms?'

Dubois stared. Then he lunged. Cavalier fired. The gun made a *zip* sound, no louder than the popping of a champagne cork. Dubois clutched his side below the heart. The force of the bullet pitched him sideways and back into the chair. Cavalier hovered over him. Dubois was groaning. His breathing was laboured.

'Hurts there, doesn't it?' Cavalier said.

Dubois went pale. He continued to clutch his side. Blood began to trickle through his fingers. His jaw sank and he looked up at Cavalier, as if to say, 'Won't you help me?'

'I had to fly to Chiang Mai like that,' Cavalier said. Dubois's face was now drained of blood from the trauma. He kicked up a leg. Cavalier pulled the trigger again, this time catching the quarry in the other side. The victim's eyes bulged as blood began to seep from the other side of his body. He seemed to pass out. Taking no chances, Cavalier fired a third time, hitting him in the forehead.

Cavalier turned off his tape, picked up the cheque, pocketed them and the two phones and moved to the bathroom where he grabbed towels. He packed them around the slumped Dubois's torso and head, which stopped the blood from flooding the floor. The bitter, sickly sweet smell Cavalier knew so well made him feel bilious.

'I'm getting a bit old for this caper,' he mumbled to himself.

Cavalier carefully emptied the dead man's pockets and removed any reference to Dubois/Lopez, including the passport, bank details, his phone, wallet, chequebook and other items such as car keys and a second phone. He placed them all in the manila envelope. Cavalier examined the wallet, and removed eleven hundred dollars in cash. He placed this in a small envelope from the hotel room desk, and printed on it:

To the Manager.
Please see advance payment for ten days. Do not clean the room. I have valuable private papers in there. Please accept one hundred dollars as a tip for your services.
Sincerely,
Juan Lopez

Cavalier locked the room and walked down the stairs. The lobby clock said 10.03 p.m. He pushed the envelope containing the rent money into a post box marked 'Manager' and left the building without encountering anyone. He removed his gloves and placed them in the manila envelope under his arm.

Cavalier walked a few blocks and hailed a cab that took him close to the Theodore. New York was alive with traffic jams, honking horns, bright flashing lights and huge, blinking video screens. He began breathing easier.

'You stayin' at a hotel?' the West Indian driver asked.

'Maybe under a bridge tonight,' Cavalier said.

The driver laughed.

Cavalier checked his phone. There had been eight calls from Haut. Cavalier rang him.

'Let's not say names,' Cavalier said.

'Good to hear from you,' Haut said, with palpable relief. 'I didn't want to leave town until I heard from you.'

'You don't have to leave.'

'What?'

'You don't have to worry about the stalker anymore.'

'You've . . . ?'

'You know the old saying "dead men tell no tales"?'

'Jesus!'

'Not an exclamation I expect from you, Your Grace!'

'Get thee behind me, Satan!'

'In this case, get thee in front of me, Satan,' Cavalier said.

'Why don't we meet for a drink?' Haut said. 'I need one and I reckon you might too.'

60

A GRAM OF DECEIT

Cavalier and Haut met at the Botanica Bar, East Houston Street, in Lower Manhattan.

'I've been in touch with Wombat,' Haut said. 'He's on his way to New York.'

'The cavalry is coming! A bit late for the real combat, but that's fine.'

Cavalier's eyes roamed over the other patrons.

'I'm in the mood for an exotic drink,' he said, looking around the packed bar where women out-numbered the men two to one.

'Let me buy you a Ginger Yum Yum,' Haut said. 'It has rosemary-infused vodka and ginger.'

'Is that a drink or a red-headed woman?' Cavalier said.

When the cocktails arrived, Cavalier downed his quickly and ordered another.

'I always need alcohol and chocolate after adrenaline-pumping moments,' he said. 'Helps me come down to earth.'

'Can you say anything about—'

'Best you don't know anything, Your Grace.' Cavalier grinned and added, 'As for my condition and handling the aftermath of "events", it's a bit different from the late, great Don Bradman. After belting a triple hundred, he'd hide in a room and listen to Chopin's second sonata for up to four hours. He'd come down from the heavens of one of his magnificent performances with Chopin, another genius! Wouldn't drink with the other team members.'

Cavalier looked around the bar again. 'Look at that!' He nodded towards a tall, well-dressed African-American woman. 'Looks like one of New York's finest!'

'I don't know how you can do anything,' Haut said. 'After the events at my Hobart home, I was a nervous wreck for months. I still have nightmares. Now . . .'

'A double malt scotch, the only way out.'

'What about tomorrow's headache?'

'A hangover? Sure. But guilt, conscience, fear, remorse, depression—never. Life is too short.'

'The devils you have liquidated have deserved their fate.'

'Your Grace, you are edging close to the way I think and what motivates me.' Cavalier raised his glass. 'Or did. I want to settle down with a good woman, or even a not-so-good one, and live the hedonist lifestyle I have always aspired to and never attained.'

'That sounds like an impossible combination—hedonism and a good woman.'

'Not at all. The trick is to find a partner with a similar sense of living—for pleasure.'

'I've never known one.'

'I have. A one-night stand with a Bangkok Thai physio. I will try to find her one day soon.'

'What about that amazing Thai female who kicked the arses of those thugs in Hamburg?'

'I told you. She's one of my closest friends,' Cavalier said with a grin. 'And that is the way she shall remain.'

'I'm thinking about Mon,' Haut said in a maudlin tone. 'I think now you may be right about her. Things are coming back. She may have been in a conspiracy against me.'

'What?'

'I just learned today that Gram broke into my Koh Samui villa and stole all my computers, and Mon's.'

'Shit!'

'The manager of the villas told me. Someone witnessed the break-in.'

Cavalier sipped his drink, smiled at the tall African-American woman and said,

'You're confirming something that has bothered me since you said Mon had turned up soon after Gram.' He waved a hand at the barman, indicating he wanted a third Ginger Yum Yum, and a second for Haut.

'Let me run this past you,' he said. '*Just suppose*, for argument's sake, Gram is still on Tielisten Allan's payroll, and that he has been sent to spy on you; steal your technology ...'

Haut shook his head.

'Just hear me out,' Cavalier said. 'Tielisten Allan realised that they would lose the contract for your services to NASA so they sent Gram to you. Now here's the bit you'll hate and be in denial over. Suppose, just suppose, Gram knows about Mon. He tracks her down at the Spotlight club on Koh Samui and offers her, say, twenty grand to carry out the scam on you ...'

Haut looked away and nodded to a redhead as if he were more interested in her than what Cavalier was saying.

'Your Grace, forget your human Ginger Yum Yum and please hear my narrative.'

'That's all it is, a bloody *narrative*.'

'Okay, hear out the possible "story" then. Mon spins you a cock-and-bull tale about turning Christian because she's in love with you and wants to live with you.'

Haut became more attentive. He inclined his head and grimaced.

'She did say to me she "didn't want the money", without explaining what she meant.'

'Did you notice anything about her and Gram on Koh Samui?'

Haut sipped his drink and then said,

'I thought at one stage he was coming on to her. I'd come out of the water after a long swim and they were on the beach, sitting close and in discussion.'

'Food for thought, Your Grace.' Cavalier clinked glasses with Haut and said, 'I can say this frankly, as one Aussie to another, you are an inventive uber-genius, regardless of your spiritual affiliations, but you are also bloody naïve!' He paused, smiled again at the African-American woman, and added, 'This naivety is, in its own way, endearing.'

**

They chatted with the women at the bar. Two hours later, when they were leaving the bar, Haut dropped his voice and said,

'Been thinking.'

'A dangerous thing in this superficial world of tweets and twits, Your Grace.'

'The evening Mon had her stroke,' Haut said as Cavalier hailed a cab, 'we had a little dinner party in my villa. There was me, Mon, Gram and a girl he'd picked up, named Ning. Ning did the cooking. Gram looked shocked that the bigger meal meant for me ended up with Mon.'

'Now you are *really* cogitating,' Cavalier said. 'Suppose Gram added something to your intended meal; something like a coagulant that would kill a sixty-year-old.'

A cab pulled up at the curb.

'Yeah, something that a fit young person might survive, with a stroke.'

'Exactly, Your Grace.'

Cavalier got into the cab next to Haut and said,

'I'm escorting you right into the Theodore lobby. Even with the cavalry on the way, you need serious security right now.'

61

POISON PACKAGE

Shelley Northam, carrying a package, bustled in through the revolving door of the Theodore. She was met by several pairs of eyes as she placed a package on the reception desk.

'This is for Mr Al Haut,' she said.

The receptionist pushed a form in front of her, which Shelley had to sign. She looked around to see two suited men wearing dark glasses standing behind her. One had a hand in an inside jacket pocket. The other had both hands in front of his genitals as if in a human wall defending a soccer goal.

'Do you have ID?' the receptionist asked, pleasantly enough.

Shelley, both nervous and irritated, took a driver's licence from her handbag. She leant forward on the counter.

'You know this man Haut is insane?' she said to the receptionist.

The receptionist did not meet her eyes or respond.

'He ... he's a drug addict,' Shelley added. 'A dangerous drug addict ...'

The receptionist made a note of her ID.

'Did you hear me?' Shelley asked. 'He is a crazy drug addict, and ... dangerous. Yes, dangerous!'

'Thank you,' the receptionist said, losing eye contact. She placed the package on the floor below the counter. Shelley hesitated. Then she turned on her heel and walked out of the hotel.

***

The two men brought the package to Haut in his third-floor apartment.

'Oh, thank you, guys,' Haut said, reading the package markings. 'I know what this is: my models of the elements. It's okay.'

The two men nodded and left. Haut opened the package. The models were wrapped in several layers of plastic. He noticed an unfamiliar smell. The inside of the package and the models were smeared with slimy, white crystals. Haut touched the crystals. He used his phone to photo the crystals and sent the photos to Cavalier and Wombat, and added a text:

'Crystals all over my models and the package. Any idea what it could be?'

Haut used toilet paper and a sponge to wipe the models clean. He washed them in a sink. Then he put them in the apartment washing machine. He tried to wash his hands of the crystals but found them difficult to scrub off. Haut finally took a shower and used a nail brush over his skin in the hope of removing any remnants of the strange substance.

He dressed and prepared to go down to the Theodore restaurant for breakfast. Then he collapsed.

***

Haut awoke in the ward of a small private hospital two blocks from the Theodore.

Cavalier and Wombat were standing at his bedside. Two hospital guards were outside the ward.

'Bloody hell, Al,' Wombat said, 'about time! You've been out to it for nearly two days.'

'Not quite.' Haut looked at his watch by the bed. 'I woke up last night, had a meal and then slept again until this morning.' He sat up. 'Can you tell me what happened?'

'You tell us, mate,' Wombat said. 'A maid at the Theodore found you on your hotel room floor. You had vomited. Big Brother's people rushed you here. Their doctors examined you.'

'And?'

'The crystals you sent pictures of were crystal meth,' Cavalier said. 'It has been analysed. We suspect it had a poison mixed in it. Any idea who might have done it, Al?'

'Bleulance,' Haut said, sipping water and sitting up.

'Bleulance would most likely have been behind Dubois. But the poisoning too?'

'We were talking about this the other night. Tielisten Allan's man Ryan Gram could have poisoned Mon on Koh Samui, when he meant to kill me. The crystal meth and poisonous substance on the models could have been a second attempt.'

'Especially when the woman who delivered it, Shelley Northam, told the receptionist a couple of times that you were a crazy drug addict,' Wombat said. 'It sounds like a set-up. A "Mad scientist drug addict dies of overdose" scenario.'

'Shelley would not have been involved with the poison or packaging the models,' Haut said. 'She's just the messenger. She would have been forced to say that.'

'The question then would be by whom?' Cavalier said. 'Who did the packaging? Who added the crystal meth and poison?'

'I can tell you the CIA is mystified,' Wombat said. 'They have their agents at the Theodore. Melody Smith even suggested a faction at the FBI—which is in an internecine war with the CIA at the moment—is connected to Tielisten Allan.'

'I believe William was poisoned too,' Haut said. 'Why wouldn't the family let me see his body?'

'But really, Al, we can't think who'd want to bump you off,' Wombat said with a cynical smile.

Haut looked glum.

'A month ago several things happened,' he said. 'William died, probably murdered; Mon had a stroke; her mother is in hospital, close to death. Then an assassin is sent to kill me; and when that fails, I'm poisoned. Bleulance is behind it. He wants to stop me and my inventions. He won't.'

After a thoughtful silence, Wombat said,

'The upshot is we—the AFP—are escorting you back to Australia. Just as soon as the doctors say you are well enough.'

'The Feds?' Haut said confused. 'The Federal Police?'

'The *Australian* Feds,' Wombat said.

'Not to Tasmania!' Haut said, trying to sit up.

'No,' Wombat said, easing him down on a pillow. 'We agree you would be in danger there.'

'We've found investors who are interested in your engine invention,' Cavalier said.

Haut beamed.

'Oh, and another thing,' Cavalier said, 'did you see the President's State of the Union address?'

'No, I was out to it.'

'He just happened to mention that the US is now a net-exporter of oil and gas, and the world's biggest energy supplier. It stunned everyone, including his supporters.'

Haut smiled.

'Thought that would please you,' Cavalier said. 'And, you know, no analyst has asked how the US was able to makes such strides so fast.'

'I wish my best mate William was here to see it,' Haut said. 'But he already knows.'

62

ENGINEER OF DELIVERANCE

Two months later, Haut, who'd managed a partial recovery from the poisoning, directed a group of Australian engineers to rebuild a prototype of his engine at Hastings, fifty kilometres south-east of Melbourne.

Cavalier drove to Hastings in blistering heat to view the invention's progress. He was met by a seventy-year-old burly engineer, Reg Monical, at a coffee shop, and later followed him to a country property and a large warehouse. It contained a variety of vehicles from motorbikes and sports cars, to speed boats and mobile homes. A familiar whiff of oil and petrol greeted him.

Cavalier was given a display of the bigger engine in question, which featured circular spheres. Water was inserted into it. Cavalier was given eye-glasses to view the activity of Haut's beloved plasmoids—the working elements of his invention—inside it.

Monical flicked an ignition switch and, within seconds, the engine vibrated to life. There was no shake or rattle like the one that accompanied earlier versions. Small amounts of vapour emitted and then it ran smoothly. Cavalier was able to view the 'action' as the plasmoids operated. Sparks were seen. Little lights flashed as moving 'dots' collided.

After the demonstration, Cavalier asked,

'When do you think it will be refined enough to market?'

'It will take another year with patents and everything,' Haut said.

'The smaller one is for cars, and motorbikes—anything with a combustion engine can be upgraded to use water. But this big one?'

'Will be for ships, spaceships, power plants, nuclear power plants; everything that needs a bigger scale of energy.'

Cavalier moved away from the others to take a call from Wombat.

'Vic. Just wanted to let you know that a certain Mrs Sally Deere recently had about two million Australian dollars cleared into her electronic bank account.'

'Very pleased to hear that.'

'She wondered who the benefactor was.'

'Better not tell her, eh?'

'No, I guess not.' Wombat paused. 'I've been in touch with Big Brother. There will be no investigation into how Dubois's nearly *ill-gotten* gains ended in an Australian woman's bank account. They are just happy that the killer of our man Deere, who had worked for them more than I realised, had been dealt with.'

'I hoped you would caress that through with your usual finesse.'

'Melody phoned me. She wondered if you may have been involved in what happened to Dubois. I just said the end result was the important thing, and didn't confirm anything. I can tell you she is more than keen for you to work with her again.'

'Not on.'

'The way she gushed, I think you could name your own price for a special assignment in Southeast Asia.'

'I can only guess which target that might be. It would mean a Big Brother team working overtime. Forget it.'

'I had a chat to Al an hour ago. He is over the moon about the bigger engine version.'

'That's where it might end up.'

'Try Mars and every other planet. Since his return to Australia, he has created his second, bigger engine for boats, spaceships, power grids, and so on. Think of that!'

'I've just viewed the engine in action.'

'He has to finance and market it first. That will be a challenge. . .'

'So will staying alive.'

'You mean Bleulance will pursue him?'

'Yes, and the Chinese, led by Richard Ni, who is connected to Lawrie, the bloke who double-crossed Al over his Tasmanian oil leases. They will want to kill him or bring him back to China. They feel invested in him because he and the Golden Brain worked closely together on cold fusion.'

'Why worry about Lawrie? He is such small fry in the list of Al's antagonists.'

'Al wants justice. It's part of his DNA. He will pursue him through the courts over fraud and theft. We're monitoring Lawrie. We expect him to try to do a runner soon.'

'And Farquar? I suppose he is the assignment Melody and Big Brother would like me involved in?'

'Very intuitive, Vic. He has abandoned his Mekong River cruise business and sold his Texas property. We believe he is hiding out somewhere in Indonesia. We and Big Brother would like to find him, not to mention Bleulance and Conquer. He has taken the money and failed in the plan to eliminate Al.' Wombat paused. 'He did commission Dubois to murder Deere, too. . .'

'Don't even suggest it, Wombat.'

'Not even if you were to act alone?'

'I don't have the stomach for it anymore.'

'Okay, I understand,' Wombat said. 'You've gone well beyond what was expected.'

POSTSCRIPT

The black BMW skidded its way towards the slopping road where Al Haut was on an electric bike riding downhill. Haut heard the crunch of wheels on gravel. He turned his head to see the car and managed to just push forward of it before any collision. He sped off the road and onto a footpath, pursued by the vehicle. Haut wheeled off down a bike track. The car skidded to a stop. The four Chinese in the car alighted but Al was out of sight down the twisting, narrow path.

He attempted to mount another footpath but crashed to the ground, breaking his shoulder. Fearful the Chinese would come after him, he struggled onto the bike, left arm dangling, and rushed back via side streets to his hideaway on Queensland's Gold Coast.

**

Cavalier had just returned to his Chiang Mai apartment when Wombat informed him of this further attack on Haut.

'I'd better get there,' Cavalier said.

'Don't bother. It happened a few days ago He's already on a flight to Chiang Mai for protection from a certain person. He'll be in touch. One of his best mates, a Brisbane doctor, patched him up, shoved a painkiller into him and helped him on his way.'

'Do they know who tried this time?'

'Al said the BMW had blacked-out windows except for the front windscreen. He was certain the occupants were Chinese.'

'Richard Ni's boys?'

'We suspect them, yes.'

'What will Al do in Chiang Mai?'

'We've given him a false passport and name, Duncan McPherson. He'll receive an untraceable phone and new computers. He'll have a completely new identity.'

'That won't stop him following through on his technology; the financing and marketing. He believes the carbon problem is more pressing than ever because we are now in a solar minimum—only a few or no sun spots—that will last into the next century.'

'Meaning?'

'Meaning the sun is giving off fewer flares of ultra-violet light, which normally disperses carbon monoxide. The result of reduced UV light is a build-up of CO circling the globe.'

'Isn't that good—less UV light, less skin cancer?'

'That's a very small part of the importance of it. If you don't have UV light from sun spots, spores and fungus are not destroyed. Instead they release viruses and bacteria into the air.'

'Hence, China's coronavirus?'

'That's what Al believes. I think he is right. He said in January there would be 170 million corona infections worldwide.'

'So the build-up of carbon combined with less sun spots, means massive problems for the world?'

'Al looks at history; it repeats and repeats. He believes that civilisations and nations rise and fall in parallel with the solar minimum periods. He points to things like the Great Plague of Europe, the Spanish Flu, locust plagues, and so on. Crops also die without UV light, which means a drop in food production.'

'His technology is more vital than ever right now.'

'Everything is set up for him in Thailand,' Wombat said. 'He'll be meeting another billionaire investor similar to William Donnelly who wants to be involved. Financiers are ready to provide funds.'

***

'I guess this almost world lockdown over the coronavirus has meant you are much safer now,' Cavalier said in a phone call to Haut, who had settled into his Chiang Mai hideaway. 'It would be more difficult to set something up for a kill. No one can cross borders.'

'Maybe. You more than anyone know how easy it is.'

'What are you going to do here?'

'I'll keep instructing my Melbourne team on the various engine developments, from generators to cars. We have bought a Ford Fairlane that will be running on water—plasmoids—very soon.' Haut paused. 'I'm ready for my final big invention.'

'Surely you should follow through on this carbon eradication and then worry about other issues!'

'Vic, remember I have five brain orbits. I can multi-task like no one else.'

'Okay, what's the new task?' Cavalier asked.

'I'm following through on a Tesla design: to produce endless free energy for the entire world.'

'Pray tell, how?'

'By transmitting massive amounts of electrical energy from the ionosphere, above the Earth's surface.'

'Sounds like harnessing of plasmoids via lightning?'

'Yes, but with infinitely more energy downloads.'

'That will thrill Conquer and all energy companies! Makes me wonder if you are on a death wish. How do you plan this latest venture?'

'I'm going to produce a magnetic field conductor in Iceland. That will rush the energy down to capacitors on Earth.' He paused and added,

'I want free energy for every person on Earth, which was what Tesla proposed more than a century ago.'

ACKNOWLEDGEMENTS

Many thanks to the Shaman himself who gave so much of his precious and highly contested time over seven years from the beginning of 2017. Several others, including the character on whom I have based Wombat, along with the engineers who worked on the car run on water, were also generous with their time in showing me both the generator and Ford Falcon Futura in action. Thanks also to Dean Golja and Jordan Collin for taking a video recording of the inventions. Leon Levin deserves gratitude for his interviews over the book as does Emma Ruhlmann-Bleicher for the edit of this new edition.

Roland Perry
October 2024